THE SIXTH WIFE

ALSO BY JEAN PLAIDY

FROM THREE RIVERS PRESS

THE WIVES OF HENRY VIII
The Rose Without a Thorn
The Lady in the Tower
Katharine of Aragon

THE TUDOR PRINCESSES
The Thistle and the Rose
Mary, Queen of France

THE TUDOR QUEENS
In the Shadow of the Crown
Queen of This Realm
The Royal Road to Fotheringhay

THE NORMAN TRILOGY
The Passionate Enemies
The Lion of Justice
The Bastard King

THE PLANTAGENET SAGA
Plantagenet Prelude
The Heart of the Lion
The Battle of the Queens
Edward Longshanks
The Vow on the Heron
The Star of Lancaster
Red Rose of Anjou
The Revolt of the Eaglets
The Prince of Darkness
The Queen from Provence

The Follies of the King
Passage to Pontefract
Epitaph for Three Women
The Sun in Splendor

THE TUDOR NOVELS
Uneasy Lies the Head
Katharine, the Virgin Widow
The Shadow of the Pomegranate
The King's Secret Matter
Murder Most Royal
St. Thomas' Eve
The Sixth Wife
The Spanish Bridegroom
Gay Lord Robert

THE STUART SAGA
The Captive Queen of Scots
The Murder in the Tower
The Wandering Prince
The Three Crowns
The Haunted Sisters
The Queen's Favorites

THE GEORGIAN SAGA
The Princess of Celle
Queen in Waiting
Caroline the Queen
The Prince and the Quakeress
The Third George
Perdita's Prince
Sweet Lass of Richmond Hill
Indiscretions of the Queen
The Regent's Daughter
Goddess of the Green Room
Victoria in the Wings

THE SIXTH WIFE

JEAN PLAIDY

A NOVEL

DOUBLEDAY LARGE PRINT
HOME LIBRARY EDITION

THREE RIVERS PRESS · NEW YORK

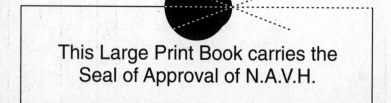

This Large Print Book carries the Seal of Approval of N.A.V.H.

AUTHOR'S NOTE

The life-story of Katharine Parr, from the time she became Henry VIII's sixth Queen until her death, reads, in many respects, more like a tale of fiction than of fact. I feel therefore that I should say to those readers who are not fully acquainted with the events of this time, that although some of the extraordinary happenings related herein may seem incredible, I have founded my story on the basic facts recorded by historians of the period. As an example: Strickland, Tytler, Speed and Fox all record as historical fact the fortuitous dropping of the all-important document and the discovery of this by Katharine's faithful servant; yet this incident might appear to be manufactured melodrama; and indeed, but for this event, Katharine's story would undoubtedly have had a different ending, and Henry might have been known as the husband of seven instead of six wives.

Historians, while agreeing in the main as to events, disagree widely in their estimation of character. Froude, for instance, would have us believe that Henry was a hero; yet Tytler says of him: "It may be doubted whether in the wide range of English history, there is to be found any monarch whose moral features, upon minute examination, become more harsh and repulsive than Henry VIII. Vain, capricious, profligate and tyrannical, he seems, even in the generous season of youth, to have exhibited but few indications of a better mind."

In view of the wide differences of opinion, I feel that my estimation of character is likely to be as near the truth as others.

I wish gratefully to acknowledge the help I have had in writing this book from the following:

The National and Domestic History of England. William Hickman Smith Aubrey.
The Lives of the Queens of England. Agnes Strickland.
Henry VIII. A. F. Pollard, M.A., Litt.D.

The Political History of England (1485-1587). H. A. L. Fisher, M.A.

The Private Character of Henry VIII. Frederick Chamberlain, LL.B., F.R.Hist.S., F.R.G.S., F.R.Ast.S., F.S.A., M.R.I. of Gt. Brit.

The Wives of Henry VIII. Martin Hume.

Foxe's Book of Martyrs. Ed. by Dr. A. Clarke, M.A.

British History. John Wade.

A History of Everyday Things in England. Marjorie and C. H. B. Quennell.

Henry the Eighth. Francis Hackett.

England in Tudor Times. L. F. Salzman, M.A., F.S.A.

History of England: Henry VIII. James Anthony Froude.

—J. P.

THE SIXTH WIFE

Spring had come to England. There were marsh marigolds along the banks of the river, and in the royal park the saxifrage showed gold and green on the damp sweet-smelling earth; the buds were bursting open in the hedgerows; and the songs of the thrush and the blackbird filled the air.

In his royal palace of Greenwich, his "Manor of Pleazaunce," the best-loved of all his palaces because it was his birthplace, the King was aware of the coming of spring. He was melancholy and he knew the reason for his melancholy. It was little more than a year since his fascinating but unfaithful wife had, at his command, lost her head. A whole year! It was a long time to be without a wife.

The small eyes seemed to sink into the puffy face, the mouth grew prim, as he thought of all he had suffered at the hands of his wives. The first and second had deceived him; he had divorced one and beheaded the other; the third had died giving him his son; the fourth he had not loved at all and had lost no time in divorcing her; and the fifth—that faithless wanton, Catharine Howard—whom for the last year he had been unable to banish from his thoughts, had walked out to Tower Green on a February day of last year and laid her head on the block.

This was an unnatural deprivation for a man to suffer; and, he reminded himself, if I am a King, I am also a man.

And the remedy for his melancholy? A wife.

The King must look for a sixth wife.

Blustering March winds buffeted the walls of a mansion close to the Charterhouse Priory in the City of London. On one of the window seats, her tapestry in her hands—although she was paying little attention to the design she was working—sat a woman. She was small and her hair, which was fair and abundant, showed beneath her hood of black velvet; her gown of the same material was richly embroidered, but in dark colors; and the skirt was open in the front to display her silk petticoat, which was a somber shade of purple; the long veil flowing from the back of her headdress proclaimed her a widow. Her face was charming, but the charm came from its expression rather than a regularity of features; at the moment it seemed to wear a borrowed beauty; her cheeks were flushed, her eyes bright, and it was as though this beauty had snatched away ten years of her thirty and made her a young woman of twenty again.

She was in love; and the eager glances which she cast down at the courtyard suggested that she was waiting for her lover.

Why should she not have a lover? She had married twice to please her family. Why should she not marry this time to please herself?

Soon he would come riding into the courtyard. He would look up and she would wave her hand, for there was no subterfuge in her nature, and she would not hide her feelings. He was quite sure that she loved him and that he had only to ask her to become Lady Seymour and she would most readily agree.

He was the handsomest man in the King's court. It was not only her love that told her this. Others said the same; even his enemies—and he had many—granted him that. He was the brother-in-law of the King; and he was a favorite of the King, for all knew that the latter liked to have about him those who were gay, young and handsome. Some thought that Thomas Seymour had become too ambitious since his sister Jane had married the King; others said that favors won through a female relative and not as a reward for a man's prowess, were built on flimsy foundations. Thomas, they said, lacked the ability of his elder brother, Edward, Lord Hertford. Edward had crafty diplomacy to set against Thomas's charm. Edward was cautious; Thomas was reckless.

It mattered not, Katharine, the widow, assured herself. He was the most charming, the most delightful of companions. He was the only man she would ever love, and he loved her too. He was going to ask her to marry him and she—widow of a few months though she was—was going to marry him.

Contemplating her third marriage must naturally make her think of the other two. They had been no real marriages. She smiled now, a little tenderly, thinking of the poor frightened child whom they had married to Lord Borough of Gainsborough, an elderly widower, with children who had seemed to Katharine quite old. Her mother had arranged that match, and she and her sister and brother had always obeyed their mother without question. Katharine could not remember her father, for Sir Thomas Parr had died when she was only four; and in the capable hands of his wife, Maud, he had left the care of his children.

Lady Parr had been a stern mother, continually scheming for the advancement of her children; and when young Katharine had been told she was to marry the rich Lord Borough, it had not occurred to her to protest.

And perhaps, Katharine told herself, as she threaded her needle with crimson silk, she had not been so unfortunate, for my Lord Borough had proved to be a kindly man, gentle and tender, and not so demanding as a young man might have been. She had been sorry when at the age of fifteen she had found herself to be a rich widow.

The first widowhood had been allowed to last only two or three years when another wealthy widower had been found for her. John Neville, Lord Latimer, was an excellent match, so said her family; and recognizing in him the same kindly tolerance which had made her first marriage less frightening than it might so easily have been, and finding friendship with his grown-up children, Katharine had allowed herself to be married a second time—indeed, she had had little say in the matter—and had taken up residence in the beautiful mansion of Snape Hall, or sometimes in another of his houses in Worcester, or, when they visited London, here in the mansion near the Charterhouse.

With Lord Latimer she had attended court and had become acquainted with the Princess Mary, who was of an age similar to her own; they had interests in common and had found pleasure in each other's company.

She had been a good wife to Lord Latimer; she had nursed him in sickness and she had astonished him with her wisdom, since but for her he might have come to a tragic end. He had taken an active part in the "Pilgrimage of Grace," that insurrection against the reforms of the King and Cromwell, and it was only by great good fortune that he had escaped the King's wrath; and this was due to his listening to Katharine's entreaties that he should not join in the second rising.

Katharine could shudder now remembering those times, but they were behind her since she was widowed for the second time. She was still young—only in her thirty-first year—and she was rich, possessing several stately mansions and the fortunes inherited from two husbands. She was also in love.

Sir Thomas Seymour was quite different from either Lord Borough or Lord Latimer. The flashing eyes, the chestnut beard, the curling hair, the great stature, the booming voice, the air of jaunty recklessness, the sailor's oaths which rose to his lips at the least provocation, set him apart; he was a man in a thousand. Perhaps she was rather foolish, she a widow of thirty, to love the most charming man at court. She would certainly have been had she not been sure that her affection was returned.

As she stitched she thought of their meetings in this mansion. Lord Latimer had been a Catholic, but she even during his lifetime had been attracted by the New Religion. She had friends who were interested in it; and how she had enjoyed their conversations, the books which had to be smuggled to her apartments because they were forbidden reading. She had never talked to Lord Latimer of her feelings for the New Religion. How could she when he was a staunch Catholic and supported Rome with such fervor that he was ready to disobey the King and risk his life to do so? She had been taught that it was a wife's duty to follow her husband in all things. But when Lord Latimer had died there seemed no longer any reason why she should not admit to herself that she had these Protestant leanings.

She had first become interested through her conversations with a friend named Anne Askew, the daughter of a squire of Lincoln. Anne was fervent in her beliefs and Katharine felt that she herself could never be so pious. Her intentions were noble, but worldly matters came between her and her piety. She smiled as she paused in her work to smooth the folds of her velvet gown; she enjoyed wearing beautiful garments and rich ornaments.

It was at a religious gathering which she had arranged should take place in this house that she had first become aware of Thomas. He had looked incongruous at the gathering; he had not seemed in the least devout; his extravagant clothes and gay manners set him apart. Did he come for religious reasons? She doubted it. He came because the meetings were anti-Catholic and antagonistic to those—such as the Duke of Norfolk, Gardiner, Bishop of Winchester and Sir Thomas Wriothesley—who wished to wrest the King's favor from himself and his family.

Katharine was not interested in his reasons for coming; she only cared that he came; and from the moment he had selected her for his attention, she had to admit that the religious purpose of the gatherings seemed to lose its importance.

At that moment her woman, Nan, came into the room.

Nan was younger than Katharine by a year or two; dark-haired and pretty, she had

been with Katharine since her marriage with
Lord Latimer; she was a very loving servant.

There was a cloud in Nan's eyes today
because she knew the reason for her mistress's elation, and it disturbed her. Nan felt
that Katharine judged all men by the two
she had married, and innocently thought
that Sir Thomas Seymour was a younger,
more handsome and more charming ver-
sion of Lord Latimer.

"Well, Nan," said Katharine, "how do you
think the pattern goes?"

Nan came and surveyed it.

"Very well, my lady."

"It is cold today. But the spring will soon
be here. There are signs of it everywhere."

"They are saying, my lady, that the King
feels the effects of spring."

"The King?"

"Yes, my lady. And it is rumored that he
looks for a new wife."

"Oh, yes." Katharine glanced down at her
embroidery. Her mood had become solemn.
There was not a lady at court who did not
become solemn at the thought of the King's
last marriage, which had ended so tragically
just over a year ago.

"It seems such a short while ago that we

had a Queen," went on Nan. "We thought the King was happy at last. And then quite suddenly . . ." She paused and shivered. "She was so pretty," she went on. "I do not think I ever saw anyone quite so pretty. Queen Anne Boleyn was more striking to look at—more fascinating too, they say—but I do not think I ever saw one so dainty, so sweet to look upon as Queen Catharine Howard."

"Don't speak of it, Nan. It is . . . upsetting."

But Nan went on: "I remember how she ran screaming down the gallery at Hampton Court when the King was at chapel. I can't forget the sound of her voice."

"It is best forgotten, Nan."

"But I shall never forget. I was there at the end. I should not have gone, but I could not help it. I had to go. And I saw her walk out and lay her pretty head on the block . . . like a child who had learned her lesson. They say she practiced how she should do it while she was waiting in her cell. And now, my lady, the King looks for a sixth wife."

"A sixth wife!" said Katharine. "How I pity her . . . whoever she shall be. But what are we saying? This is no affair of ours. The

King grows older—although doubtless it is treason to say so. Let us hope he is putting all thought of another marriage from him. And, if he should marry, now that he is older, there is less likelihood of his fancy's straying."

"It did not stray from Catharine Howard, my lady."

"Let us not speak of it. Do I hear the sound of horses' hooves in the courtyard?"

She looked out of the window, smiling, for riding into the courtyard was Thomas Seymour.

The King was becoming more and more occupied with thoughts of a wife. He was no longer young on that March day in the year 1543. Fifty-two. There were times when that seemed a great age for a man to be, particularly when in his teens and his twenties he had been one of the most vigorous of men, over six feet tall, of great girth, delighting in all sports and pastimes—and more than any in the sport of love.

In his thirties he had been a giant among men, unmistakably a king. It had been his delight to go among his subjects feebly disguised and to play a pleasant little game of make-believe which all saw through. "Who is this man?" people were expected to ask. "Why, he has the bearing of a king!" And when they had speculated and marveled, he would throw off his disguise and say: "Cudgel your pates no more, my friends. I am your King!" That was just one of the games he had delighted to play. But a man of fifty is not to be compared with a man of twenty or even thirty, and now he was no longer able to win games with skill, and he would not play except to win. There were days when he could but hobble about his palaces, and then he must have the aid of a stick and the arm of a courtier to lean on. His leg—his accursed leg—grew worse instead of better; he had tried he could not remember how many remedies. He had promised a fortune to the man who could heal it; he had threatened to lop off the heads of those who failed. All to no avail. The leg might seem better for a while; then the ulcer would make itself felt again and the pain could at times be so agonizing that he would cry out with it and hit out at any who irritated him.

Last year had been a trying one for him. He had made fresh claim to the throne of

Scotland, had attacked the Scots and given them a trouncing at Solway Moss. But the battle was not decisive. State affairs were pressing and he needed escape from them at times. For, as he often said to his friends, a king is a man for all he is a king. And he had suffered—as a man, as a husband— great sorrow.

Now, with the trees budding and the birds disturbing the royal slumbers in the early morning, so that he would awaken in his lonely bed (or if it was not lonely, it was oc- cupied by one whose presence there dis- turbed his conscience), he felt that he, like the trees and flowers and grasses, was re- newing his strength. As a husband, Fate had treated him cruelly. But did that mean he would never know good fortune in mar- riage?

The plain fact was (and, thought Henry, I am a plain man to whom facts should be plain) the King was in need of a wife.

So on this March day, when the winds seemed to penetrate the Palace of Green- wich, the King stumped up and down his Privy Chamber, while outside in the audi- ence room several of his courtiers awaited his summons; none dared approach without it. They feared his anger. And he wanted none of them; he wished to be alone with his thoughts. Yet, because he needed a new wife, he could not shut out of his mind memories of his other wives.

Five of them! It was a good tally. François Premier, across the water, had had only two; but his mistresses were legion.

There, thought the King of England, we differ—the King of France and I. His little mouth grew prim; his little eyes were complacent. It was a habit of his to compare himself with the lecher, François. They were of an age; and love was the ruling influence in the life of the French King. Henry liked to think that kingship occupied that place in his. All knew that Madame d'Étampes ruled at the French court as once Madame de Chateaubriand had ruled.

Using his healthy leg, Henry kicked a stool out of his way. The veins stood out on his temples. The very thought of the dark, sardonic face of his enemy infuriated him at all times.

"He has no conscience," he muttered. "And I . . . I am all conscience. Oh God, Thou knowest what a man of conscience I am." The King often addressed God, addressed Him as an equal; for as the King saw himself to be always right, always obeying his conscience, he felt sure, as a man of God, of the constant approval of the Almighty.

Two wives of his had died at his command, young women both of them; and some called them martyrs. Not that any dared say such things in public . . . if they had any respect for their tongues, for tongues could be cut out for saying such words; and ears could be lopped off for listening to them. Henry insisted (and God must know this too, for Henry continually explained to God) that he had been reluctant to order the death of those two wives of his; but he was a good man, a man of God; he had a conscience which would not allow him to find happiness in an irregular union. It was better that a woman should die than that the King should be forced to illicit pleasure.

God understood that he was right, because the King and God saw through the same eyes. Henry was sure of that. Anne Boleyn haunted his dreams now and then, with her mocking black eyes and her clever tongue; but God had given him a sign that in the case of Anne Boleyn he had acted with wisdom and righteousness. Had not Jane Seymour, Anne's successor, produced a son? Little Edward was now safely past his fifth year; he was the heir for whom, through the barren years with Spanish Katharine and the fiery ones with Anne Boleyn, he had longed. And Jane had given him that son. Meek little Jane. He had forgotten how quickly he had tired of her; he liked to say now: "Ah, God, if only Jane had lived, how different my life would have been!" Then he would smile and add that God doubtless had had His reasons for taking Jane. The King did not question the Almighty's reasons, as doubtless the Almighty did not question his.

The King laughed suddenly. He had thought how angry those brothers of Jane's must have been with her for dying when she did.

Edward Seymour was a clever fellow, taking good advantage of the fact that he was young Edward's uncle. Full of craft . . . diplomatic . . . a good servant. As for Thomas, the King could not help liking the fellow. In Thomas he saw something of the man he himself had been—a pale shadow, of course, a very pale shadow. But that breezy air, the great oaths, and his way with the ladies! Yes, it was big, hearty men like Thomas Seymour that the King liked to have about him.

He had heard rumors of Master Thomas's ambitions, and that he did not like so well. It was necessary to be watchful of those who were too ambitious. There was that scoundrel Norfolk and his son, Surrey—they had to be watched. They were too near the throne for comfort, and the Tudor tree was not as firmly rooted as Henry would like to see it.

That was why he needed more sons to grow up with his little Edward . . . sons, sons . . . Tudor sons to live after him and keep the throne for his house.

Marriage! That was the answer. Marriage was in the air because it was springtime. Young Seymour wanted to marry, so it was said, and he had cast his insolent eyes on the King's own daughter, on the young Elizabeth—Anne Boleyn's bastard. For all that she was her mother's daughter, he could not help having a certain feeling for her. He detected some fire within her, something she had inherited from him. He pretended to doubt that she was really his daughter. He had tried to believe she was like his old friend, poor Norris, who had gone to the block with Anne. He could feel the hot jealousy swelling in his head now when he thought of that May day when Anne had sat beside him in the tiltyard and Norris had ridden there. Although that was seven years ago he could remember it vividly. Seven years since the executioner's sword, specially procured from Calais, had slashed Anne's lovely head from her graceful body, yet whenever he saw the girl Elizabeth he remembered. She lacked her mother's beauty and inimitable charm, but there was something of Anne in Elizabeth—something of Anne and something of himself. And now that rake Seymour had cast his eyes upon her.

The King had learned from his spies that if Thomas could not get the lady Elizabeth he would take the Lady Jane Grey, granddaughter of Henry's sister Mary, whom—so long ago now—he had sent to France to marry old Louis, and who, after leading that poor old monarch such a dance that in a few months he died, had secretly married Charles Brandon before returning to England. The fruit of that marriage had been Frances Brandon, who had borne Jane.

"Elizabeth for preference then," said young Seymour. "But if I can't get the King's daughter, I'll have his kinswoman."

Henry considered them as he could not help considering all women. Elizabeth would be the more suitable. She was ten years old; Jane was only five.

But did it matter what plans Seymour made, since they would come to nothing unless the King willed otherwise? The important factor was the King's marriage.

Whom should he choose? Who could be compared with the dainty Catharine Howard? The lady must have all that fair wanton's charm and none of her wickedness.

He was aware that the ladies of the court were not eager for the honor he would bestow on one of them. That was a little disturbing. He could force the woman of his choice to marry him; but he could not force her delight in doing so. When Catharine Howard had died, he had made it a capital offense for any woman to marry a King of England if she were not a virgin. Surely there were some virtuous women in his court. Yet if any caught his eye upon her, she would seem overcome by embarrassment, and when he looked for her again he would find her absent; should he inquire of her, he would doubtless be told that she had fallen sick and was keeping to her apartments.

He shook his head sadly.

It was said—though he pretended not to know this—that no unmarried woman would care to risk marriage with him because she knew that when he was tired of her he could trump up a charge against her virtue. He preferred not to know of such talk. There was his giant conscience to be appeased. The King must always be right; his motives must always be of the highest. The conscience demanded that it should be so, and the conscience, if necessary, was monster enough to stamp out the truth.

Could they say that Catharine Howard was not a slut, not a wanton? Could they say that he had trumped up charges against her? Surely those charges had been proved.

But Anne Boleyn: only young Smeaton had "confessed" to adultery with her, and that under dire torture.

But he was tormenting himself. The past

was done with. Forget it he must, and remember the need of the present. He
needed a wife. Yet he could not think of one
he would care to honor. He wanted a
Queen. He was growing tired of the hunt—
both in the forest and the women's apartments at the palace. He wanted comfort
now; he wanted a peaceful old age. He
wanted a woman—not too young and frivolous, not the sort who might hanker after
younger men. She need not be a beauty if
she were comely enough. He called to mind
the five he had had: Katharine from Aragon,
Anne Boleyn, Jane Seymour, Anne from
Cleves and Catharine Howard. How unsat-
isfactory they had all been in their different
ways! And yet what he wanted now was a
woman who would embody all their virtues
and none of their faults: the piety, poise and
nobility of the first Katharine; the great fascination of Anne; the meekness of Jane; the
good sense of the second Anne (for that
woman from Cleves had been sensible and
had regarded herself as lucky to get away
with a pension and her head on her shoulders to enable her to enjoy it); and the
sweet, complacent beauty of little Catharine
Howard. Yes, she must have all those qual-

ities and she must be a good and faithful wife, a consort of whom one could be proud, a gentle, serene lady to soothe him when necessary, to enchant him, to make him feel young again, to be a stepmother to the children he had, and a mother to those he might yet have. Edward was sickly (what a perpetual anxiety the health of that boy was!), and there was always the need to get more sons.

That reminded him of the pretensions of his brother-in-law. He shouted to his attendants, and a page came fearfully into his presence.

"Find my brother, Sir Thomas Seymour, and bring him hither," ordered the King.

The page bowed low, assuring his gracious Majesty that his will should with all speed be done, and set off in search of Sir Thomas.

Seymour was preparing himself for a trip on the river that he might call on Lady Latimer. His short gown, girdled at the waist, reached his knees and was of rich blue satin. His dalmatica was adorned with the widest sleeves; his hose were of white satin and his cap sparkled with sapphires and diamonds.

He was pleased with his appearance; he was pleased with himself. It was good to be young, handsome and full of vigor, to have ambitions which, because he was by nature optimistic, he was certain would very soon be fulfilled.

Sir Thomas Seymour, the great sailor, was not yet the Admiral he intended to become. But that should come about very soon, he promised himself. The young Prince Edward idolized him; Uncle Thomas was his favorite uncle, and such as Uncle Thomas did not forget that one day little Edward would be King of England, and little Edward was not the sort to forget his favorite uncle. What a good thing it had been for the House of Seymour when the King's roving and most amorous eyes had alighted on his little sister Jane.

Dear Jane! So obedient. She had done just what her brothers had told her to. He was not sure that, in dying when she had, she had not done a good thing too; for the King would soon have tired of her, and who could say what might have happened if Jane had not made a perpetual shrine for herself in the King's heart by promptly departing after the birth of her son? It was so easy for a sentimental, conscience-stricken King to sigh and tell himself and his courtiers that Jane had been the only wife for whom he had cared, the only woman worthy to have been his wife. So, because accommodating Jane had died at the right moment, she was now safely buried, with her head on her shoulders, and all was set fair for the Seymour brothers.

There was one minor irritation in the life of Thomas Seymour at that moment. The Lady Latimer, in mourning for her husband, was not at court; and he must make the long journey to her house if he would see her.

Katharine. Fair Katharine. And rich Katharine. He was very fond of her. She was perhaps not so beautiful as some other women he knew, but she had other qualities. For one thing, she adored him so obviously. What a refreshing change she must find him after those gouty old widowers of hers. She had never really lived, poor soul. She had been a nurse, not a wife. How different she would find life if she were the wife of Thomas Seymour.

He thought of those mansions which were hers; he thought of her fortune; he also thought of her charming person. He would have proposed marriage to her immediately after my Lord Latimer had died but for one thing.

He was well aware that the Princess Elizabeth was only nine years old. But he could wait . . . six or seven years. And who knew what was going to happen in the course of seven years. The King had lived for fifty-two years, and those fifty-two years had been somewhat rashly spent. The kingly body was none too healthy. It was said that the hideous leg was the outward sign of inner evils. The King of France suffered from similar abscesses, and all knew of the life he had lived. Fifty-two were not a great many years, but so much depended on how those years had been spent. And then, when Henry died, there was Edward. Poor Edward! Poor, sickly, learned little boy! His uncles would control him, and England would be ruled by her Protectors; and who should they be but the boy's uncles? And if the boy should die—he certainly had not the appearance of one who would make old bones—and one of those Protectors was married to the King's daughter. . . . It was not difficult to see the possibilities in that situation. Moreover, that red-headed little

girl was not displeasing to him; and he fancied—for there was something of her
mother in her—that he was not altogether
displeasing to her, young child that she was.

"By God's precious soul!" he murmured.
"I see great days ahead for the Seymours—
and in particular for you, my dear Sir
Thomas."

One of his gentlemen came in to tell him
that the King's page had brought a message
for him. He was to go at once to the King's
presence, and it seemed from the King's
mood that it would not be wise to delay.

Cursing softly, Seymour went to the
King's apartment, where he knelt in reverence.

"H'm!" snorted the King, noting the rich
blue satin and the sparkling sapphires and
how they made the sailor's eyes look bluer
and more vivid in his sun-tanned face.
There should be a law, thought the King,
forbidding a King's servant to deck himself
in finery rivaling his King's.

"I had word that Your Majesty desired my
presence and I came with all speed."

"You were wise there, brother," said the
King. "Wiser than you have been in some
other matters."

Seymour opened wide his blue eyes and looked at the King with astonishment. He was ready with his tongue too, the King noted.

"My Gracious Lord, if my unwisdom has offended Your Grace, pray let me know in what cause, that I may hasten to be wise."

"Methinks," said Henry, "that when I honor a subject with a small favor, that subject is apt to look for bigger ones."

"It is such an honor to serve Your Grace, and Your Grace's smiles are treasured. You must forgive your loving subjects if, having received one of your royal smiles, they crave for more."

"Smiles! It is not smiles some look for. Some enjoy lands and treasures which not so long ago belonged to others."

Seymour bowed his head. It was true that, as Jane Seymour's brother, he had received lands and riches from the despoliation of the monasteries; he had grown from a humble country gentleman into a rich courtier. Was the King planning to take away that which he had given? Seymour thought uneasily of another Thomas—Cardinal Wolsey—who had at one time been the richest man, next to the King, in all England; yet he had lost everything, even his life.

"But it is not of lands that we would speak," went on Henry. "We have been hearing rumors of your conduct, Seymour, and we do not like what we hear."

"I am deeply grieved, Your Grace."

"Then that is well. And, hark ye, we shall look to you to mend your ways. We have heard rumors of your gallantry, Seymour. You know what store I set on virtue. . . ."

Seymour bowed his head even lower. It would not do for his master to see the smile which played about his mouth, and, try as he might, Thomas Seymour could not prevent its appearing there. This model of virtue! he thought. This husband of five wives—this lover of how many women! Yet in his own eyes the King remained a figure of virtue. After all, he had always put away one wife before the official ceremony of taking another, even if it meant cutting off her head.

"I know, Your Grace," said Seymour craftily; "and if I have offended, I crave your pardon and Your Majesty's clemency. I would remind Your Majesty that it is not

easy for a humble subject to follow the example of his King."

Henry looked sharply at the man. Insolence? Was that it? He softened in spite of
himself. Liking the fellow, he could not help
it. Yes, he had a liking for Tom Seymour as
he had had for others. Thomas Wyatt, for instance, who was reputed to have been the
lover of Anne Boleyn; Thomas Wolsey was
another who had had his regard. Dear
Thomas Wolsey! A good servant. Henry had
long persuaded his conscience that Wolsey's decline and death lay at the door of
Anne Boleyn, as did the execution of that
other favorite, Thomas More. There was yet
another Thomas who was beloved of the
King—Thomas Cranmer. How different was
pious Cranmer—rather sly, sensitive Cranmer—from this handsome braggart who
now stood before him. Perhaps he liked
Cranmer for his very cunning, for his clever
way of extricating his King from troubles;
and he liked Tom Seymour because he was
amusing, because he seemed a pale
shadow of a youthful Henry.

"There has been too much gallantry, my
lord," went on Henry. "It extends, we hear,

from the lowest to the highest. Take care, brother."

"I know not what tales have been brought to Your Gracious Majesty, but whoever uttered them . . ."

"Lied in his throat, I don't doubt you will tell me. Let us hope that you are right."

"I can assure Your Gracious Majesty that it is so."

"And," went on the King, "that you, my lord, have never raised those handsome eyes to the Princess Elizabeth, our daughter?"

"My Gracious Lord . . ."

"Ah, you would have need of our gracious leniency if we found you guilty of such folly."

"I beg Your Grace to listen to my side of the story."

"We are listening."

"I would not presume to raise my eyes to one so near Your Grace."

"That is well. Eyes raised to the sun become dazzled, brother; and dazzled eyes see not clearly the dangers that lie ahead. Do not allow yourself to be blinded. Neither the Princess Elizabeth nor the Lady Jane Grey is for you, brother."

"Indeed not, Your Majesty. If I seemed to

admire these two, it was as charming children and . . ."

"Then all is well. You may leave us, brother."

Seymour bowed, retired and went from the palace to his waiting barge.

He was sweating a little under his fine garments, particularly about the neck. Necks were so sensitive. How many times did the gentlemen about the King fancy they felt the touch of the ax there? One day a man was in high favor, his ambitions promising fulfillment; the next day he was being rowed to the Tower and taken through the Traitors' Gate. It had happened to so many whom he had known.

That interview meant that, at present, he must curb his hopes. The red-headed Princess was not for him . . . at present. He must forget the little Lady Jane. But there was still the rich widow waiting in her late husband's mansion; and very rich she was, and comely too. He had developed an insatiable taste for riches since his sister's elevation. A rich wife today was a more exciting prize than a royal one in seven years' time. Much could happen in a day, an hour. How much more could happen in seven years!

The King had stumped to his window and watched the progress of the gallant young man as he made his way toward the river.

Whither was he going? wondered Henry. It was to meet a woman, doubtless. Henry smiled slyly. *Not* the Princess Elizabeth, for certain. He had not been unaware of the fear he had planted in Seymour. The gallant sailor would be a little less gallant in that direction and keep his eyes from straying too high.

The King was so curious that he had one of Sir Thomas's gentlemen brought to him.

"Whither goes your master this day?" he asked.

"To London, Your Majesty."

"And why to London?"

"On business, as far as I know, Your Majesty."

"What business? Out with it, knave. You know his errand and you would be wise to tell it."

"My Lord King, if it pleases you, he has gone to call on Lady Latimer."

The King smiled. "You may go. It is our wish that you tell not your master that we were interested in his journey. It will go ill with you if you do."

Lady Latimer, mused the King, when the man had left. He knew her well. Kate Parr, he called her, for he remembered her as Parr's girl. He had noticed her when she came to court, and he had liked her. She had been a good wife, first to Borough and then to Latimer. A sedate and virtuous lady. The kind of woman he liked to see about the court. And why was it he had not seen her at court? Ah, mourning Latimer, he sup-posed.

So Seymour was visiting her. To what end? Wealthy widow. Very wealthy widow. Those Seymours were the most avaricious men in the kingdom.

The King laughed. He believed that Sey-mour, knowing now that the Princess Eliza-beth and the Lady Jane Grey were out of reach, was turning to the more mature charms of the widow.

Seymour could always make the King laugh; perhaps that was why the latter liked him. But even as Henry laughed, he grew solemn. She was a charming woman, this Katharine Parr. A good, virtuous and not un-comely woman, the sort the King liked to see at his court. A good influence on others. She had been friendly with the Princess Mary, and that meant that she was a sober, religious lady, having similar interests to those of his twenty-seven-year-old daughter.

Kate Parr and Tom Seymour. Incongruous!

Later, when he was closeted with his Primate, Thomas Cranmer, discussing State affairs, the King said suddenly: "The morals of the court distress me. I would like to see it influenced by our virtuous matrons. There is one . . . Katharine Parr . . . recently widowed. Latimer, was it not? He died a short while ago. She is a good woman and she would be an influence for good with our young maidens. I do not see her at court as often as I should like."

Cranmer lowered his eyes. He was like a frightened stag, always on the alert for the chase to begin. He had seen Thomas Cromwell fall, and he could not forget it.

Latimer! he thought now. The noble lord had been involved in the Pilgrimage of Grace, as had Katharine Parr's relatives, the Throckmortons. They were staunch Catholics, and Cranmer must be continually on

guard against the influence of Catholic
thought on the King. Yet of late Latimer's
widow had been turning toward the new
faith, which was dear to Cranmer. A Protestant lady's influence on the King would
make Cranmer happy, while it would certainly discomfit his enemies—Norfolk, Gardiner and Wriothesley.

Cranmer said: "Your Grace, we should
command this lady to come to court."

The King nodded.

"Let it be done," he said. "Let it be done."

In the oak-paneled room of the Latimer
mansion, Thomas Seymour was bowing
over the hand of Katharine Parr.

"I have waited for this moment for . . .
for . . ." Seymour lifted his handsome eyes
to Katharine's face. It was a trick of the gallant gentleman, who was rarely lost for
words, to feign a nervousness which made
him tongue-tied. It was a trick which never
failed to please the lady he was trying to impress.

"For?" prompted Katharine.

"Since I last saw you." He smiled and
boldly drew her to the window-seat, keeping her hand in his.

"Do you find it pleasant to be in London, fair lady, after the monotony of Yorkshire?"

"I had too much to do in Yorkshire to find life monotonous there."

"But did you not, when you so nobly nursed your husband, long for court life?"

"No. I was happy. Except . . ."

"Except?"

"I thought of that time when I knew great fear. Not a day would pass when I would not be startled out of my wits by a knock on a door or a sight of a rider in the courtyard. I would look through a window and say to myself: 'Can it be a messenger from the King?'"

"And, your lord husband, did he tremble with you?"

"He did not. He seemed insensible to danger. He was a brave man."

"Too sick, I'll wager, too concerned with fighting death to fear the King's anger."

"And then . . ." she said, "the King pardoned him."

"The King's pardon!" Seymour laughed. "The King's smiles are like April sunshine, Kate."

"I hear he is moody and depressed these days."

"The King! Aye. And looking for a wife."

"May God preserve the poor, unfortunate lady on whom his choice falls."

Seymour raised his eyebrows in mock horror. "Treason, Kate!" he said.

"I know I should be careful. I speak too rashly."

"Rashness? That is a fault I share with you. But 'tis truth you speak. What woman would be eager to share the King's throne since poor little Howard's head rolled in the straw?"

"Poor child. So young. So beautiful . . . and to die thus!"

"Caution!" Seymour took the opportunity to put his face close to hers on a pretext of whispering. "Master Wriothesley hath his spies everywhere, they say. I will tell you something: All through the court people are whispering, asking each other on whom the King's choice will fall. Age creeps on the royal body. Once he was a raging lion; now he is a sick one. The same desires, the same mighty bulk, but a sick lion who stays at home to lick his poor, wounded limbs when once he would have led the chase. Such a state of affairs has not been beneficial to the royal temper."

"'Tis you who are incautious now."

"I ever was, and 'tis true I am more so now. Do you know why? It is because you are sitting near me. You are as beautiful as the sun on the sea, Kate. Oh, I beg of you keep clear of His Majesty's roaming eye."

She laughed. "You are mocking me. I have been a wife twice already."

"Nay! You have never been a wife. You have been twice a nurse. My lord Latimer was old enough to have been your grand-sire."

"He was good to me."

"Good to his nurse! Oh, Kate, you know not how fair you are. Again I say, strive not to catch the King's eye."

"I am thirty years old."

"And look but twenty. But why talk of the King and his marriages? The marriages of others might make better talk."

Katharine looked at him earnestly. It was difficult to believe what she so longed to be-lieve. He was too charming, too handsome; and she, as she had pointed out to him, was thirty years old, and twice widowed. No, it was to some fresh and beautiful young girl that he would turn.

"Which . . . which marriage had you in mind?" she asked.

He put his arm about her then and kissed her heartily on the mouth. "My own!" he cried.

"Yours?" She made an attempt to struggle, but she could put no heart into it because this was where she longed to be, with him beside her, his arms about her, listening to words which she longed to hear more than any in the world. "Since . . . when did you contemplate marriage?"

"From the moment I set eyes on you," was his prompt reply. "That was when I began to think of marriage."

"You forget I am so lately a widow."

"Nay, sweet Kate—scarce a widow since you were never a wife. Sick-nurse! That was you, Kate."

"But . . . should I think of marriage with my husband scarce cold in his grave?"

"Bah! He is lucky to be there, Kate. The King never forgives those who work against him. Better, when one is a sick old man, to die in bed than rot in chains as Constable did. He was a fool, that husband of yours."

Katharine would not allow even the man she loved to speak against the man she had married. "He did what he believed to be right," she said warmly. "The cause of Rome was very near his heart and he supported it."

"A man's a fool who'll support the Pope's cause against the King's when he lives within reach of the King's wrath and out of reach of the Pope's succor."

"We are not all as ambitious, mayhap, as Sir Thomas Seymour."

"Ambitious? I?"

Katharine drew herself away from him and said with a touch of coldness in her voice: "I have heard it whispered that you are very ambitious indeed, and that you have aspired to make an advantageous marriage."

" 'Tis true," he said, "that I seek an advantageous marriage. I seek the advantages that a happy marriage could bring me. I seek the advantage of marriage with the woman I love."

"And who might that be? The Princess Elizabeth?"

"The Princess Elizabeth!" Seymour's expression was a masterpiece of astonishment. "I . . . marry a Princess! Come, Kate, you're dreaming."

"So the reason you have remained a bachelor so long is not because you wait for one whom you would marry to reach a marriageable age?"

"The reason I have remained a bachelor for so long is that the woman I wish to marry is only now free to marry me."

"I wish I knew that it was true!" she sighed.

He laughed and held her closer to him.

"Kate! Kate!" he chided. "You are mad to speak thus. Could you be jealous of a child?"

She smiled contentedly. "It is said that those who study the ways of ambition learn patience," she reminded him.

"Patience! It was never a virtue of mine. That is why I'll not wait a moment longer before I kiss those lips."

How pleasant it was there in the room with its windows overlooking the courtyard, and with him beside her promising such joy as she had never known.

They talked of the future which would be theirs.

"But we must wait awhile," insisted Katharine. "I dare not marry yet. It is too soon."

Seymour feigned impatience, but he was not sorry that there must be a time of waiting. He could not get the picture of the red-headed Princess out of his mind. She had such a white skin and a coquettish air, he fancied, when she looked his way. Not yet ten years old and a coquette already, and not insensible to the outstanding attractions of a man old enough to be her father.

He was not averse to waiting, for, in this age of surprises, events came thick and fast, and one could never be sure what would happen next.

"I warn you," said Seymour, "I shall not wait too long."

"Nor should I wish to, for now I know your mind I could not bear to."

They talked once more of the life they would share. They would escape into the country as often as possible, for there were great joys, she would show him, to be found in the simple life.

When at length he left her, she stood at her window watching him for as long as was possible. It seemed to her that her happiness was almost too great. Perhaps she felt thus because she had waited so long for it.

Yet thirty was not so old. He did not think
so.

She tried to work at her embroidery, to
read a little from her book of devotions, to
write; but it was impossible; she could think
of nothing but the happy promise of the
future. The marriages which had been
arranged for her, and which had brought
friendship and riches, were over; and now
she could make the romantic marriage
which would bring her that perfect contentment of which she had often dreamed.

It was later that day when a messenger
arrived from the court. The King missed the
company of Lady Latimer, and he had discovered that he desired it. Lady Latimer
would therefore present herself at court
without delay.

There was speculation among the courtiers.

Lady Latimer had arrived with a few attendants, and the King had noticeably singled her out for his special attention. On
every possible occasion he extolled the
piety of those women who, in their kindness
and sympathy, nursed their husbands
through sickness. The King's ideal of wom-
anhood was now Lady Latimer. There

seemed to be only one person at court who did not grasp the situation, and this was Katharine herself. It was due to modesty, for she could not believe that the King would really regard her as a possible Queen. She was sure that she lacked all the gay, spirited fascination of Anne Boleyn, all the young beauty of Catharine Howard. Even Jane Seymour had had a pale beauty of her own. And I, Katharine told herself, am no more handsome than the Lady of Cleves; and the King would have none of her. It was true that Anne of Cleves had had strange, rough manners and awkward speech and that her skin was pitted from smallpox; but at least she had been the sister of the Duke of Cleves and of importance in European politics. But what had Katharine Parr to offer a man who had always demanded outstanding physical attraction or political assets in his wives?

What she heard concerning this matter must be merely court gossip, and Katharine would not allow herself to be disturbed by it. She was not going to relinquish her dreams as readily as that. She was going to marry Thomas Seymour; she loved him and he loved her.

Nan, who had accompanied her to court, was looking very mournful. Poor Nan! She was a pessimist by nature. Other ladies also threw her compassionate glances. Naturally, the whole court was concerned as to the King's potential wife, merely because he lacked a wife. They did not realize that when men grew old they thought more often of their comforts than of erotic excitement. Katharine knew. She had had two old husbands.

She therefore persisted in her dreams of marriage with Thomas and refused to admit to herself that he had seemed to grow aloof, that he was often absent from court, and that when the King was present he scarcely looked her way. It was agreed between them that they must wait for marriage; she had been the one who had insisted on that. Naturally, they must wait for a reasonable time to elapse after the death of Lord Latimer; and until they could announce a date for their marriage it was better to keep silent about it and let none guess that they contemplated it.

So Katharine went on blithely dreaming.

Thomas Cranmer watched the progress of events. He was cautious by nature; a man must be cautious in the service of such a master. Lady Latimer was a pleasant woman; she would serve the King well if she could do what most of his wives had failed to do: provide him with sons. Cranmer wished to play the safe game. He would not further the marriage of his master with Katharine Parr; nor would he thwart it. Many men had fallen after taking a hand in the King's matrimonial affairs. Anne Boleyn had caused the downfall of Wolsey; Anne of Cleves that of Cromwell; and because of the frailty of Catharine Howard, Norfolk and his family were in decline. A statesman must play for safety when the King contemplated marriage.

Cranmer's thoughts went back to a long-ago marriage in which he had been bridegroom to Margaret Anne Osiander. Very charming she had been—the daughter of a Reformer with whom he had conferred when he was in Germany on the King's business. But that marriage had been declared void, for Cranmer had had to choose between the King and Margaret Anne. Often he despised himself—the coward who longed to be brave, the priest devoted to his religion, yet longing for a wife and family . . . longing to be a martyr to his beliefs, yet fearing the martyr's flaming crown.

So Cranmer would keep as aloof as possible from the King's affair with Lady Latimer; but he hoped that the marriage would take place, because the lady leaned toward the Protestant faith, and a Protestant Queen was what Cranmer—a Reformer at heart—would have advocated for his King.

Thus, while keeping aloof, Cranmer prayed for the success of the King with Lady Latimer.

Stephen Gardiner, the celebrated statesman and Bishop of Winchester, saw how matters stood and, as he was unaware of the lady's religious leanings and remembered the service her late husband, Lord Latimer, had paid to the Catholic cause, he was not against the match. He was an ambitious man, this Gardiner, this statesman and priest. He wished to rule the country, as Secretary of State, through the King; and as a churchman he wished to stamp out those he deemed heretics. There was only one religion for him; and if he accepted the King as head of the Church of England, that was for expediency's sake; for the rest he wished to support the religion of his youth, which had its roots in Rome.

And Lady Latimer herself? She was a good woman, not likely to cause trouble to the King's ministers. Could she give the King a son? He doubted it. The King, it seemed, could not have healthy sons. Not one of his Queens, except Anne Boleyn, had been able to give him a really healthy child. Anne's other pregnancies had come to nothing, just as had those of Katharine of Aragon. Jane Seymour had had at least one miscarriage. His natural son, whom he had created Duke of Richmond, had died in his teens; Edward, the heir to the throne, caused much anxiety on account of his health. Princess Mary was a sickly woman who suffered frequently. Only the young Princess Elizabeth was a healthy child. Therefore it seemed unlikely that the King would achieve in his declining years what he had failed to accomplish in his youth. Then would the old familiar pattern begin to form? Would he, tiring of yet another partner, desire a new wife and look to his ministers—his long-suffering ministers—to find a way of ridding him of a woman who had become an obstruction?

If all the young ladies at court dreaded the King's attentions for fear of the consequences to themselves when they ceased to amuse him, the King's ministers, remembering the disasters which had befallen their predecessors, also had their fears.

But the King was ageing; perhaps his sixth marriage would content him; and as Lord Latimer had been a good Catholic, so, reasoned Gardiner, would his widow be also. If the King wished to marry the lady and if—as surely he must—he no longer expected children, Gardiner would welcome the match.

He said to Wriothesley when he obtained a private interview with that man: "What think you of this matter of the King and Lady Latimer?"

Sir Thomas Wriothesley, as zealous a Catholic as Gardiner himself and longing for promotion to the Chancellorship, was ready to agree with such an influential Catholic as Gardiner.

"The lady's husband, recently dead, was a good Catholic," said Wriothesley. "The lady was a dutiful wife to Latimer, and would be so to His Majesty, I doubt not."

Gardiner came nearer. He liked Wriothesley as well as he liked any man; he liked him a good deal, for his liking depended on a man's usefulness to himself.

"With a good Catholic Queen," murmured Gardiner, "there would be one near him to whisper wisdom in the King's ear."

"And he needs such whispering," said Wriothesley, "with the Seymours ever about him, paving the way for themselves with young Edward."

Gardiner nodded and laid a hand on Wriothesley's shoulders. "Audley looked sick today; I thought."

They exchanged nods and smiles of understanding.

Wriothesley knew that if Audley became too sick for the post of Lord Chancellor, it would not be Gardiner's fault if Sir Thomas Wriothesley did not receive the Great Seal.

Edward Seymour, Thomas's elder brother, who was now Lord Hertford, being one of the chief Reformers, was aware of Katharine's leaning toward the Party; so he, also, was not averse to the King's marriage with Lady Latimer.

There was only one notable gentleman of the court who was against it. That was Sir Thomas Seymour himself. It seemed to him that the more Katharine became out of reach, the more desirable she became.

He thought longingly of her sweet comeliness, of her gentleness, her unspoiled nature—and her considerable possessions.

Sir Thomas Seymour was a very sad man as that blustering March of 1543 gave way to softer April.

The young Prince Edward was entertaining his two sisters in his apartments.

He was not quite five years old, a pale-faced, puny child, whose health was a source of great anxiety to all those who were responsible for him. It was their constant fear that he would die and that the King would punish them for his death.

His tutors feared either that he might over-tax his brain or that he might not please his father with his learning. Those in charge of his physical training suffered even more acutely. They were apprehensive every time the little boy mounted a pony or played a game of tennis. But these things he must do, for the King wanted Edward to be another such as Bluff King Hal had been. At five, Henry had been a lusty boy, "pink and gold," they had said of him, taller than his brother Arthur, outshining him in everything he did. He had been a Prince who looked a Prince, and that was the sort of Prince Edward must be.

Little Edward knew what was expected of him, for he was knowledgeable beyond his years. Sports tired him, but book-learning did not, and therefore he loved books. He could write Latin and read it fluently. He already knew that one day he must be the King, and a Tudor King. Wishing fervently to please his father and do all that was expected of him, he rigorously performed all his duties; but his greatest pleasure was in being with the younger members of his family, and in particular with his half-sister Elizabeth and her whom he called his cousin—little Jane Grey. He was sure that he loved Jane best of all. There were several reasons for this; Jane was nearer his age than the others, being barely a year older than he was. His sister Elizabeth, who was nine years old, was clever, but not in quite the same way as Jane was. Jane and he were of a kind; but Jane was beautiful and not made breathless by small exertions, as he was; her legs were fine and firm and could support her with the greatest ease;

she had no pains in her head and there were no outbreaks of rashes on her delicate skin.

He was glad this was so. Jane was his dearest.

But he was greatly excited by the presence of his sister Elizabeth—perhaps more excited by her than by anyone else. Her sharp eyes were everywhere; she knew all the court gossip and would tell it, throwing back her mane of red hair and playing the parts of all the people who figured in the stories she told.

She looked for admiration while she talked, and nothing pleased her more than a compliment. Edward never forgot to admire her gown. She had asked him whether he thought Jane prettier than she was, and Edward found it very difficult to give a truthful answer to that, for a reply in the affirmative would have infuriated her; so he told her that as Jane was just a child and merely Lady Jane Grey, and she herself was grown up and a Princess, there could be no comparison.

Then Elizabeth had kissed him in her quick way and burst out laughing. She knew that he deceived her, but she did not mind that. She told him he was a clever little boy.

He was not so pleased to see his sister Mary, for she always saddened him. When she came into a room she seemed to bring sorrow with her. She was often ill, as he feared he was. Mary had been so ill a little while ago that it had been feared she would die. The King had not greatly cared what befell his elder daughter, but when his son was sick there were doctors all about the boy. His father, sparkling with jewels, looking bigger than anyone else in the world, would stump up and down the chamber, haranguing the doctors, threatening them—almost threatening Edward himself—if the Prince should die.

I dare not die! Edward often said to himself. I must not complain of this pain in my head. I must be a King, and a Tudor King. I am my father's only male heir.

It was a great responsibility for such a small boy and such a frail one. No wonder he liked to sit in an alcove with Jane and talk to her of what he had read or what he had learned.

Yet it was pleasant to gaze at Elizabeth, with the color flaming under her pale skin, the freckles across her nose. Such a diplomatic Prince did not mention the freckles—

although they pleased him—for Elizabeth's women prepared lotions to make them disappear, as the vain creature imagined that they spoiled her lovely skin.

When she kissed him and told him he was her dearest brother, he could not be quite sure whether she was not remembering all the time that one day he would be the King and very important, and that she would need him to be kind to a Princess of uncertain birth.

Today she was excited. She had news.

She came in haughtily, as she did when the mood took her; and he fancied that she played a game of make-believe in which she was a Queen and he her subject. With her came Mistress Ashley, her governess, whose life the Princess plagued, though the woman adored her.

Elizabeth was dressed in a new gown of which she was very proud, yet she was angry because she lacked jewels. She had told him that she wished for emeralds, because emeralds suited the color of her hair. He wished that he had emeralds that he might give her. When he was a King he would do so; but he hoped that would not be for a long time; he dreaded that day when he would have to be the King.

Now here was his sister, taking his hand and kissing it. "Nan Bullen's girl," he had heard her called; that was when people were angry with her. "Who is she?" they said then. "Who but Nan Bullen's bastard."

He knew of Nan Bullen, who, some said, had been a witch, a sorceress, and who had died that his father might marry his mother, the one pure Queen whom his father had loved.

Elizabeth, in her haughtiest manner, dismissed all attendants.

"That is what you wish, is it not?" she demanded, almost menacingly of the little boy.

"Yes," he answered. "That is what I wish."

Then Elizabeth looked from him to little Jane and back to him, and said: "Have you heard the gossip, brother?"

"What gossip?"

"The gossip that is all over the court. Our father has chosen his new wife."

"A new wife!" cried Jane.

"A new stepmother for us!" said the boy with a perplexed look.

"But you like your stepmothers. You liked the last one."

"Queen Catharine was so pretty," said Edward wistfully.

"But she died." Jane's gentle eyes filled with tears. It was obvious that she knew in what manner Queen Catharine had died.

None of the children ever mentioned the way in which the Queen had died. The beheading of Queens was a sore subject with Elizabeth. If any lightly mentioned her own mother, her face would grow dark with anger. Edward knew that it was because Mistress Ashley had married a kinsman of Queen Anne Boleyn that Elizabeth kept the woman with her, loved her dearly, and would suffer none other to command and scold her as Mistress Ashley did.

"Who . . . is the new one?" asked Edward.

"Can you not guess?" demanded Elizabeth. "You know her. She has paid you many a visit. You will love her as much as you loved Queen Catharine Howard."

"Please tell me quickly who it is," said the small boy imperiously, for he could be imperious when kept in suspense.

"Lady Latimer."

"Oh!" The two younger children exchanged smiles. They knew her well. She was a delightful lady. A short while ago when Edward had been recovering from a sickness, and there had been one of those dreaded scenes at his bedside, with the King cajoling and threatening all those in attendance, Lady Latimer had come to see him. He had thought her sweet and gentle, as a mother ought to be.

"You are not then displeased by this news?" said Elizabeth.

"Nay. It delights me. She will be Queen Katharine and our stepmother."

"I too am pleased," said the Princess. "I love her well."

Mistress Ashley came into the apartment to tell them that the Lady Mary was on her way and would be with them in a few moments.

"She has heard the news, I'll warrant," said Elizabeth. "It will please her also."

"She will be always at court," said Edward, "when she is our stepmother."

Elizabeth looked momentarily serious. She was old enough to remember a good deal more than Jane and Edward could. She remembered a dark-eyed, very beautiful woman who laughed and cried, who embraced her warmly and called her "Daughter," and who loved her more than anyone in the world had ever loved her. Then quite suddenly Elizabeth had understood that she no longer had a mother; but it was not until some years after her loss that she knew the reason.

Cruel things had been said about her mother; and what was said about her mother must reflect on Elizabeth. Some had said she was not the King's daughter at all, but the daughter of a man named Norris, who was supposed to have been the Queen's lover and had died with her. Some said a thing even more horrible: that she was the daughter of Anne Boleyn's own brother, Lord Rochford. But the King did not believe this. Indeed, how could he? He had but to look at her to know that she was his own daughter. And although there were times when he seemed to care not whether she had a rag to her back or a crust to eat— while if aught befell the precious body of young Edward all the great doctors of the realm must congregate at his bedside—still Elizabeth felt that the King had as warm a feeling for her as for any of his children.

The Lady Mary came into the room and Elizabeth at once went to her, knelt and kissed her hand.

How sick she looks! thought Elizabeth. She is old—old. The idea of being twenty-six—nearer twenty-seven—and without a husband!

So many great men had been promised to Mary and yet not one of them had married her. No wonder she was sick and sad and bore resentment against the world.

How healthy she is! thought Mary. How full of vitality! She cares nothing that they call her "bastard." If I had been the daughter of Anne Boleyn, I would have died of shame ere this.

Mary paid homage to the little boy. She never forgot the relative positions of them all. Edward was the prospective King and the most important member of the family. She and her sister had both been called bastards; they had both been made much of by the King and both scorned by him when he had decided to discard their mothers.

Mary would have envied Elizabeth if she had not believed it was a sin to envy anyone and not to accept that lot which a Greater Power had ordained must be borne. She, Mary, had been the petted darling of the court when she had been a little girl. Her mother, who had adored her, had made great plans for her and longed to see her Queen of Spain. There had been a time when Mary had thought she would be Queen of France. And here she was, a Princess whom her father refused to recognize as his legitimate daughter; for if he did so it would mean that he had been wrong to set aside her mother. The King could do no wrong. That was the order of the day. So from great honor Mary had been cast down—not only to obscurity, but to actual danger, for the King had at one time threatened her life.

She, who had been brought up under her mother's eyes, felt this deeply. She was steeped in tradition. She was the daughter of a Princess, the daughter of a King, and she possessed all that love of solemnity and ritual which came from her Spanish ancestry. There could not be two sisters more unlike than Mary and Elizabeth.

Elizabeth's manner had changed at the entry of her sister as rapidly as Elizabeth's moods could change. She had become demure.

"We were speaking of the news, sister," she said. "You have heard it?"

"You mean that our father thinks to marry again?"

"Yes," answered Elizabeth, watching her sister.

"It is Lady Latimer," said Edward. "Jane and I are very fond of Lady Latimer."

Jane smiled at him. She was awed by the two Princesses. They alarmed her slightly, each in a different way. With Elizabeth she could never be entirely at ease; and Mary seemed so old, dignified and solemn.

"She is a very virtuous lady," said Mary, "and one who should bring great happiness to our father."

Elizabeth looked at her slyly. Did she not know then that Lady Latimer was interesting herself in the reformed faith? Apparently she did not, for Mary would never esteem virtuous anyone who was not a good Catholic.

Mary did not know as much of what was going on at court as did Elizabeth. Mary spent so much time on her knees asking for guidance and courage to endure her lot. Elizabeth kept her eyes open, her ears trained, and had developed the trick of worming secrets out of her women. As for her courage, she was not sure of that, but she hoped that her wits would prevent its ever being put to the test.

"Another stepmother," she said. "I am glad, sister, that the King has chosen one who is such a great friend of yours."

"It will be a pleasure to welcome her," said Mary, thinking: Perhaps she will ask our father to have us reinstated at court.

They had been fortunate in their stepmothers; there was not one of them who had been unkind, except perhaps Anne Boleyn, and she had tried to become reconciled to Mary before her death. Mary refused to see that Anne Boleyn had had no alternative but to ignore and debase her, since any honor done to Mary must minimize that paid to her own daughter, Elizabeth. Mary never saw any point of view but that dictated by her own rigorously observed religion. Jane Seymour had been kind to the Princesses; so had Anne of Cleves and Catharine Howard. But Mary, as did Elizabeth and Edward, believed that their new stepmother would be the one whom they would love best of all.

Mary dismissed the subject; her father had not yet announced his decision to marry Lady Latimer and, until he had done so, it was neither wise nor tactful to discuss it. She must curb that vulgar curiosity of Elizabeth's, inherited from her low-born mother; she must not allow her to chatter of court gossip to the little Prince.

So Mary looked at his books and talked earnestly with him for a while; and Elizabeth, joining in the conversation, immediately became a prim little maiden of nine years, learned for her age—for she too had been made to work hard under her tutors, and as she was avid for all knowledge she, like her brother, had been a praiseworthy pupil.

The Lady Mary at length left the children together, and as soon as she was gone Elizabeth took charge and the atmosphere changed. It was small wonder that Edward was fascinated by this sister of his. It was not only her rude health which so amazed him, but her ability, it seemed, to change her character that she might interest and attract different people.

This was indeed a happy day for the Prince for on it his Uncle Thomas called upon him.

If he had not been a little boy so determined to do what was right, he would have loved his Uncle Thomas Seymour more than his father. How different were those two men! They were both possessed of dazzling personality; yet the King inspired his son with fear and Thomas Seymour filled him with affection. When Uncle Thomas came into a room he would seem to bring the sea breezes with him. He was a great sailor, Edward delighted to recall, an important man in the kingdom, yet not too important to have time to spare for his small nephew.

On those rare occasions when they were alone together, Uncle Thomas became more exciting than ever. He would lift the boy high above his head and make him squeal with delight; he had actually succeeded in making him forget that he was heir to the throne, a King-to-be, and a Tudor King at that! Uncle Thomas had the rare gift of making himself so young that, in his presence, children felt that they were as grown-up as he was.

Edward was not the only one who felt this. As soon as Uncle Thomas appeared, a change took place in the apartment.

Jane grew quieter before that magnificent presence. Elizabeth seemed a more haughty Princess than ever, but a very gay and excited one. As for Edward, he felt that he was a man, as gay and swaggering as Uncle Thomas, discarding all the heavy responsibilities which must rest on the shoulders of a boy of five who was being trained as a King.

"A good day to you all!" cried the gay Sir Thomas, and his bright twinkling eyes surveyed them all. "Your Princely Grace." He kissed Edward's hand, but mockingly, so that Edward knew he had no need to receive the greeting ceremoniously. "My dearest Princess." The Princess's eyes glittered, for the sailor surely had accentuated the adjective. "And my sweet Lady Jane." His voice had grown tender as he kissed the hand of the quiet little girl who had risen to receive his greeting. "And how conspiratorial we all look today! What's afoot?"

They all began to laugh, like small children in a nursery . . . any children . . . happy children who need not be constantly on the alert to do what was expected of them.

"Secrets, eh? Secrets! Secrets that should be kept from Uncle Tom?"

"No, indeed, dear Uncle," said Edward.

"There are no secrets we would keep from you."

"You deceive me." The blue eyes flashed and Sir Thomas stroked his beard and scowled wickedly from one to the other. He began to growl through his teeth. "Methinks I must make myself aware of this grim secret."

He considered them. Poor Edward, just for a few moments a little boy! His great head was so packed with learning that his puny body seemed to protest against carrying it. Little Lady Jane, lifting her solemn eyes to his face, divorced from her habitual gravity, was at this moment, like Edward, a child just because the magic youthfulness of Sir Thomas Seymour could cast a spell upon her. And Elizabeth . . . ? Ah, Elizabeth! She was no child. She was standing before him, against the hangings, those which had the greenish pattern upon them that would set off her flaming hair so beautifully. Her eyes were downcast, but her mouth was sly. Elizabeth was refusing to play the child; she wished to play the woman. And . . . she was enjoying the banter more than any of them.

"By God's precious soul!" cried Seymour. "I shall discover this plot against me. I shall tear this secret from you. Who shall tell me? You, my lord?"

He had taken Edward in his arms and lifted him high above his head. Edward laughed aloud, as he rarely did.

"Will Your Grace tell this dread secret?"

Edward's hand which had only just lost the pudginess of babyhood, grasped the beautiful brown locks of Sir Thomas.

"Put me down, Uncle Thomas. Put me down, I say. I will pull your hair if you do not."

"I tremble. I am in fear. So Your Grace refuses to tell me his secret?"

"There is no secret."

Sir Thomas lowered the Prince and gave him two hearty kisses; and Edward put his arms about his uncle's neck. Oh why, thought Edward, are not all men like my Uncle Thomas?

Sir Thomas set him on the floor and went to Lady Jane Grey.

"And you, my lady, will you tell me the secret?"

"There is no secret, Sir Thomas."

"I would force it from you," he cried, "were you not so beautiful that I could not bear to hurt you."

He let his fingers caress the soft golden curls of the beautiful child, contemplatively, sadly; for she was small and so young and it would be long before she was a woman.

"I must prise the secret from one of you, that is certain . . . and since it cannot be from you, my Prince, or you, my Lady Jane, it must be from the Lady Elizabeth."

She was waiting for him, seeming cool yet inviting, her light lashes lowered over her eyes which might have betrayed too much. He noted the softness of her delicate skin, the provocative powdering of freckles.

She lacked the beauty of Jane, but, by God, thought Sir Thomas, she is the one for me.

He laid his hands on her shoulders.

Haughtily she glanced first at one hand then at the other. "You will take your hands from me, sir." She was very proud, very much the daughter of the King.

He took her chin in his hand and jerked her face up to his. Now he could see her eyes; he could see the curve of her lips which betrayed her excitement, her pleasure in this badinage, which he knew and she knew was not the play between a grown person and a child, but an encounter between a man and a woman.

Nine years old, he reflected. Is it possible?

His hand touched her throat. She was as yet too inexperienced to hide her feelings. She was delighted to have his attention. She had known that his tricks with Edward and Jane had been the preliminaries that should lead to this encounter between them.

He brought his face close to hers. "Will the Lady Elizabeth tell me the secret?"

"How would that be possible, sir, when there is no secret?"

"Are you sure that you hide nothing from me?"

"If I wished to hide matters from you, Sir Thomas, I should do so."

How exciting she was! A nine-year-old girl, a Princess as ambitious as himself. Was her glance telling him now: "Who are you to dare look at me in that way? Do you forget I am the King's daughter?" And his eyes answered: "I do not forget. It but adds to your charm. And I beg of you, do not forget that the King calls you his bastard daughter, and that I am the uncle of the King-to-be. Anne

Boleyn's daughter and Jane Seymour's brother—what a delightful partnership! How the ghosts of Anne and Jane must be laughing—if ghosts can laugh!"

"What shall I do?" he asked. "Prize the secret from you?"

"Do not disturb yourself," she answered. "I think that to which you refer is no secret. My father is to marry again, we have heard. Is that the matter which you call a secret?"

Did she know of his ambitions? He could swear that she mocked him when she continued: "It is on my Lady Latimer that the King's choice has fallen."

He dropped his hands then; he could not meet her eye. She must have heard rumors regarding himself and Lady Latimer. The saucy young coquette was reproaching him with that, as though he were indeed her lover.

"We are all well pleased," said Edward. "For we know her and like her well."

"She is a good lady," said Sir Thomas; and he felt depressed suddenly, but only momentarily; he had complete faith in his destiny. But he had been so fond of Kate. He had visualized such a pleasant life with her.

The Prince then demanded that his favorite uncle should sit beside him and tell
him a stirring story of the sea, and this Sir
Thomas was pleased to do. Very soon all
three children were listening to him, under
the spell of his charm, and at that moment
it seemed that they were all children, even
Elizabeth, excited by his stories of adventures at sea. They watched his face as he
talked; he was their hero. There was not one
of them who could be in his presence and
remain untouched by his charm.

Before he left he drew Edward aside and
whispered to him: "And what is the state of
Your Grace's purse?"

"Very low, I fear, Uncle."

"It is a shame to keep you so poor. You
know that the purse of your favorite uncle is
at your disposal."

"Uncle Thomas, you are the best man in
the world."

"It is good enough for me that I am your
favorite uncle. And would you care to dip
your royal hands into my willing purse?"

Edward hesitated. "Well, there are one or
two items . . ."

"I knew! I knew it."

"I will tell you," whispered the boy. "I wish to buy green ribands."

"Green ribands? Why have you need of green ribands, my Prince?"

"For Elizabeth's hair. She longs for green ribands to adorn it. They become it so. And she, like me, is kept very poor."

"Poor little Princess! Between us, nephew, we will give her green ribands to adorn her hair."

It was not the first time that Sir Thomas had given his nephew money. It was money well spent, decided Sir Thomas. Edward was grateful by nature; and when he was King of England he would be very kind to his favorite uncle.

When he took leave of them all, he whispered to Elizabeth: "I would like to see green emeralds adorning that head. But in place of green emeralds, green ribands might serve."

Now she would know, when she received the ribands, from her brother, who had supplied the money with which to buy them. The sly creature knew of most things that went on at court and would know, of course, that his uncle supplied the Prince with money now and then.

He was thoughtful as he went back to his apartments. He saw himself as the favored of the gods. He had been endowed with all the graces and it was so easy for him to win the love of his nephew. He was indeed fond of children. Ambitious as he was, ready to be unscrupulous, he could yet find great pleasure in the society of the young. He loved them all, Jane, Edward and Elizabeth . . . Elizabeth most of all. He was in love with Elizabeth. He was in love with Katharine. He was fond of the Prince and Jane. When he spoke honeyed words to Kate he meant them; when his eyes shone with silent admiration of Elizabeth he sincerely felt that admiration. When he curried favor with the boy who would one day be King, he was sharing amusement, delighting himself as well as the boy.

It seemed to him that he was the darling of the gods and that they intended him for greatness. He was certain of ultimate success with the Princess Elizabeth; he felt sure she would one day be Queen of England and he saw no reason why the man who married her should not be the King.

Stranger things had happened. Look how

Fate had pointed a finger at his shy sister Jane and made a Queen of her!

Fortune was undoubtedly smiling on the Seymours. If it had denied him the warm and cozy comfort he might have found with Kate, perhaps that was merely because it was saving for him a more exciting life to be shared with the Princess.

While Seymour pondered thus, Elizabeth's thoughts were of Seymour.

The King felt sleepily content. He had dined well on good roast beef, venison, and pies of various sorts; he had drunk deeply; he had listened to music and felt temporarily at peace.

His leg pained him less on this day and he was ready to believe that the new remedies would prove efficacious, although common sense reminded him that he had been trying new remedies for years without avail. There were times when the pain in his leg was so acute that his face became purple, then gray, and he could not suppress his cries of agony.

But now the bandages seemed less irksome and consequently he was less exhausted. He had hobbled into the music-room to hear some verses of Surrey's, and he was determined not to like them even before that arrogant young man had opened his mouth to recite them. He did not care for anything Surrey wrote, for Surrey himself was a source of anxiety to him.

By God, he mused, as he watched him now, a little more of the fellow's arrogance and I'll have him clapped into the Tower. What airs! What manners! And some would doubtless say: What beauty! Have I not suffered enough from these Howards? Anne was connected with them; that witch, that sorceress who deceived me into believing she could give me a son—and deceived me with others too! Then . . . young Catharine . . .

But he could not bear to think of Catharine. That affair was too recent and he had not had time to grow out of love with her. But nevertheless she also was a Howard. She had belonged to that accursed line.

He must not get overheated. His doctors had told him that. If he did, it would be necessary to apply the leeches again. No! He must think of pleasanter things than the Howards. There was Lady Latimer, looking fair enough, but sitting too far away from him.

He roared: "Bring Lady Latimer's chair closer to mine. I would talk with her."

She came slowly behind the men who had carried her chair. She drew it slightly back before she said: "Have I Your Majesty's permission to sit?"

"You have it," he answered, reaching for the chair and bringing it closer. "You must not be over-awed, Lady Latimer, because we like to talk to you."

"No, Your Grace."

"We understand your feelings. We applaud them. We like modesty in our ladies."

His face was close to hers and he noted the fine texture of her skin, the delicate bloom of health; he decided that none would guess she was thirty.

I like this woman! he told himself. I like her serenity. I like the respect she shows for her King. She's no giddy girl. She's no Anne Boleyn; no Catharine Howard. She may lack their beauty, but she's a good woman; she's a modest woman. She's the sort of woman I like to see about my court.

"Believe us, Lady Latimer," he said. "We feel the utmost kindness toward you."

"Your Majesty is gracious."

"We are indeed to those who please us.

Now, Surrey, let us hear these verses of
which you prate."

Surrey stepped boldly forward, displaying
both grace and nonchalance. He was very
elaborately dressed, almost as elaborately
as the King himself. His blue velvet cap was
ornamented with gold, his doublet striped
with blue and white satin, his hose of the
same becoming shade of blue, and his person a-glitter with diamonds and sapphires.
The young poet bore himself like a king;
there were some who said that it was Surrey's boast that his house had more claim to
the throne of England than had the Tudors.
If his folly could be proved, ruminated the
King, that handsome head would not long
sprout so gracefully from those arrogant
shoulders.

"It is a small poem," the young nobleman
was announcing, "on the means to attain a
happy life, an it please Your Grace."

"Let us hear these words of wisdom. We
would fain hear of the means to attain a
happy life." Henry caught Katharine's eye,
and his intimate smile made her shiver.
"Methinks you are over-young, my lord Earl,
to have gleaned already so much knowledge."

Gardiner, who was seated near the King, said: "It is the young, Your Majesty, who consider themselves to be wise men. When they grow older wisdom seems less sure."

Henry grunted and winced with pain as he moved his leg. "Come, come," he said impatiently. "Let us hear the verses and have done with it."

Surrey stood elegantly, the scroll in one hand while the other was laid negligently on the jeweled doublet. Arrogant young fool! thought the King; and he hated him for no more reason at that moment than that he was one of the most handsome young men at court. Henry had reason to hate all handsome men on this occasion, for now, with so many about him, he felt his age and infirmity keenly. These were so hard to accept when one had been the handsomest Prince in Christendom and had excelled at all manly pastimes and had been a King— not, he reminded himself scowling at Surrey, a would-be-King.

Surrey had begun to read:

"Martial, the things that do attain
The happy life be these, I find:

The richesse left, not got with pain;
The fruitful ground, the quiet mind;

"The equal friend; no grudge, no strife;
No charge of rule, nor governance;
Without disease, the healthful life;
The household of continuance;

"The mean diet, no delicate fare;
True wisdom joined with simpleness;
The night dischargèd of all care,
Where wine the wit may not oppress.

"The faithful wife, without debate;
Such sleeps as may beguile the night:
Contented with thine own estate
Ne wish for death, ne fear his might."

While the poet was reading, the King fidgeted in his chair, and all those present marveled at the rashness of Surrey, for it should have been perfectly clear to the poet that those sentiments must arouse unpleasant memories for the King. That talk of health and sleep and, above all, faithful wives! Surrey was a fool. It was almost as though he teased a dangerous bull, deliberately inviting attack.

There was a short silence. No one spoke before the King expressed an opinion, for it was unwise to differ from His Majesty in the appraisal of verses.

"Bravo!" growled the King eventually. "Your meter's good, Surrey."

Surrey bowed low. "My greatest delight in my simple verses must be the pleasure they afford my most Gracious Sovereign."

"Not so simple!" cried Henry. "Not so simple, eh?" He glared about him. "What did you think, eh, Gardiner? A Bishop should appreciate good verses. And you, Master Wriothesley. You've heard enough verses to judge, I'll swear."

Gardiner could always be relied upon to say what was expected of him. "We have heard your Grace's own verses, Sire."

And Wriothesley, always eager for promotion and knowing the surest way to the King's heart, added: "When your Gracious Majesty sets such a high standard . . ."

The Catholic faction must not be allowed to supply all the required compliments. Sir Thomas Seymour interrupted Wriothesley. "The verses seemed to me good enough, but I am a rough sailor, and know little of these matters. I have a fondness for Your Majesty's own rhymes, it is true . . ."

Henry interrupted: "We deemed the verses good." He was impatient with them all, except the woman beside him. He had been too long without a wife. He was wasting time. "Lady Latimer," he said in a gentler voice, "what thought you of the verses?"

Katharine answered nervously: "I thought them good, Your Majesty. Very good."

"You did, did you? And are you a judge of verses, Lady Latimer?"

"I fear not, Sire. I am only . . ."

"Ah!" cried Henry. "You are a lady of much modesty, and 'tis my belief you know more of the value of verses than these men who talk so readily of them. Methinks you should have an opportunity of judging your Sovereign's."

"Sire, my judgment would be of little worth."

Surrey said ironically: "You would doubtless discover, Lady Latimer, that His Grace the King, as well as being the ruler of this land, is also its greatest poet."

Henry shot a suspicious glance at the insolent youth, but he was too intent on Katharine to be drawn at this moment. He leaned forward and patted Katharine's arm. "Such praise," he said, "is to be prized since it comes from Surrey—as good a poet as any to be found in the realm, so some men say."

"I trust Your Grace has never heard my verses compared with your own," said Surrey; and if Henry did not recognize the subtle note of mockery in his voice, others fancied they did.

"Nay!" said the King. "Much sweet praise has been poured in our ears, and though we have heard your verses commended, yet never have we heard them set side by side with our own."

Surrey gave what might have been a sigh of relief. "Your Grace has doubtless heard them compared with Wyatt's?"

"Aye, that we have! And to Wyatt's disadvantage."

"A great poet . . . poor Thomas Wyatt!" said Surrey.

Henry was suddenly aware that Lady Latimer's gaze was fixed on Seymour. The blood seemed to rush through his veins as though it would burst them.

"Seymour," he cried, "you are silent, man."

"I am out of my depth, Sire."

Henry snorted. "He should learn the gentle art of rhyming, should he not, my friends? He would find it of use in his gallant adventures." Everyone tittered, and Seymour smiled charmingly. The King turned away with a gesture of impatience. "Ah yes," he went on. "Wyatt was a good poet and a handsome fellow."

Of Surrey's intentions that afternoon none could be sure. He seemed to be inviting the King's displeasure. Perhaps he was thinking of those royal arms which had been given to his family five hundred years before; perhaps, as he spoke again, he was thinking that he was more royal than the heavy, diseased man who sat in the ornamented chair.

"I like nothing of Wyatt's so well as that which ran thus: 'And wilt thou leave me thus. . . .' Marry! I forget how it goes. Oh, this was it. Your Grace will remember.

"'And wilt thou leave me thus!
That hath loved thee so long
In wealth and woe among:
And is thy heart so strong
As for to leave me thus?'"

Henry's face was contorted, whether with rage against Surrey or the pain of his leg none could be sure.

"You liked those verses, did you?" he roared. "Methinks there is a cheapness in the sentiment."

There was complete silence as the Earl and the King looked at each other. Every member of the gathering was aware that Surrey had quoted the words which Wyatt had written to Anne Boleyn. It seemed to Katharine, sitting fearfully beside the King, longing for the privacy of her home in Yorkshire, that Surrey was like a gorgeous dragonfly determined to tease an already angry bull.

"Cheapness, Your Grace?" said Surrey. "In Wyatt's appeal to an unkind mistress? Poor Wyatt!"

Henry looked almost defiantly at those about him, as though he was determined to show them that Surrey's careless words had not reminded him of Anne Boleyn. "I liked that fellow, Wyatt . . . fool that he oft-times was. I mourned his death. Marry, it is a year ago! But what subject is this for a lady's ears? Death? No! We will not speak of it. I would have speech with Lady Latimer . . . and I would have speech alone."

Even as he said those words he remembered the old days, when, wishing to play the lover, he had grasped his opportunities. He had not then found it necessary to dismiss his courtiers so pointedly. But he would do what he wished . . . now and for ever. He was their King and they should remember it.

They were bowing as they left the chamber. It seemed to him that Seymour hesitated, and Seymour had never looked quite so handsome as he did at that moment.

"Why do you linger, brother?" demanded the King.

Seymour said: "I am sorry if I have offended Your Grace."

"The sight of you offends us when we have dismissed you. Go, I say."

They were alone. Katharine could hear the heavy hammering of her own heart. She had never really been so frightened in the whole of her life as she was at this moment, and when Henry leaned toward her she had difficulty in suppressing a cry of dismay.

Henry was laughing and his voice was

gentle. "What thought you of the verses, eh? Come. The truth."

"They were well enough, I thought," stammered Katharine. "But I, being a woman, could give no judgment that would interest Your Majesty."

"And you, being a woman, must have such soft feeling for the poet's handsome person that you have little thought to bestow upon his verses, eh?"

"My Lord King, I have been twice widowed. I am not a young girl to harbor such soft thoughts of a poet."

Henry patted his thigh—that one which was sound and not affected by the ulcers which were creeping up from his leg. "Are you sure of that, Kate?" he asked slyly. "For 'tis hard to believe you have been twice widowed, and did I not know that you had been to bed first with my Lord Borough and afterward with my Lord Latimer, I'd not believe it."

Katharine smiled nervously. "Your Majesty knows that I am an old woman . . . well past my thirtieth year."

"Old, Kate! Nay. Not so. Not so. For if you are old, what of us? Would you call your

King an old man? Treason, my Lady Latimer. Treason, Kate!"

"My Lord King," began Katharine breathlessly, "I assure Your Highness . . ."

The King gripped her knee. "Rest easy, girl! I feel no anger. 'Twas a joke. Nay, you're as fresh as a young girl, and if you are thirty years old, well then, thirty is as good an age as any."

"But it is old, Your Majesty . . . for a woman. I vow it is."

"I forbid you to say it," said Henry playfully. "You are not old, Kate, and your King forbids you to say you are."

"Your Grace is too kind to me."

His next words filled her with horror. "Aye!" He squeezed her knee. "And ready to be kinder. Ready to be kinder."

Katharine now began to understand all those significant glances which had been cast in her direction during the past weeks. Others had been aware of what she had failed to notice. Yet she could not believe the truth even now. Frantically she sought in her mind for some means of escape.

"I am unworthy . . ." she faltered.

Henry looked momentarily stern. "A King is the best judge of a subject's worthiness."

She was really frightened. He who was accustomed to speaking with the ministers of his own government and the ambassadors of others knew how to imbue his words with deep meaning. He was telling her that it was not for her to say whether or not she would have him. He was the best judge, and he it would be who made the choice.

"We have been lenient with you and yours, have we not?" he said on a softer note.

"Your Majesty is a great and good King to all his subjects."

He nodded, smiling. "That is so. But to some subjects he is known to be over-merciful at times."

"I am but a foolish woman, Sire."

"You're a very pretty one, Kate—which is all your King asks you to be."

She could only repeat nervously: "Your Grace is too kind to me."

"And, did I not tell thee, ready to be kinder? Latimer was a traitor to his King."

"Oh, no, Sire . . . never that."

The King lifted his stick and rapped the floor with it. Katharine drew away from him, flinching.

"We like not contradictions," he growled.

"Your husband was a traitor. Why did I not have him in chains? Do you know?" He laughed and she detected the return of that indulgence which disturbed her more than his anger. "No, you do not know, Kate. You're too modest a woman to know the reason for that. Latimer deserved to go to the block, and I pardoned him. And why, think you?" He slapped his healthy thigh. "Because I liked his wife. That's the answer. By God, that's the answer. I said to myself, 'Latimer's wife . . . she's a good wife to Latimer. Would to God there were more like her in our kingdom!' That's what I said, Kate. Here. Come nearer. Look at me. Don't be afraid of me. Look at your King."

She obeyed him and looked into his face, noting the cruel little mouth, the pouchy cheeks that had once been ruddy and were now purple; she saw the knotted veins at his temples, and those eyes which suggested shrewdness and a certain refusal to face the truth. She read there, mingling sensuality and primness; she saw the hypocrisy, the refusal to see himself except as he wished to be. There, in his face, were the marks of those characteristics which were at the very root of his nature and which had made him the man he was, the man who had sent thousands to their death, the murderer who saw himself as a saint. And she was terrified because she knew that he was inviting her to take that place from which it was an easy step to the block. Inviting her? If only that were true! He was commanding her.

"There!" he continued. "Now you see we speak sincerely. Don't be afraid, Kate. Don't hold back. 'Would to God,' I said, 'that there were more like her in our kingdom. Would to God I was blessed with a wife like Latimer's.' Oh, Kate, you were another man's wife." His voice had dropped to a whisper; the little mouth seemed to grow smaller, tighter, more prim. "And though I be a King of this realm, to pluck where I will, I said to myself, 'A man's wife is his wife.'" His mouth slackened; the shrewd eyes traveled slowly from the neck of her velvet gown to her feet. The sensualist had taken the place of the moralist. "Well, Kate, Latimer's dead now."

"Your Grace, he is so lately dead."

"Long enough for a wench like you to lay aside her mourning. You are too fair to spend your time in mourning. Time won't wait, Kate. How are you going to give your husband all those fine sons he will ask of you if you spend your nights crying for a husband who is dead and gone?"

Oh God, help me, she prayed silently. Now he talks of sons. Thus must he have talked to the first Queen Katharine, to Anne Boleyn, to Jane Seymour. And then those continuous disasters. Two girls and one sickly boy was all he had in spite of his endeavors. Here was a tragic pattern starting again. A son! A son! I want a son. And if you cannot provide one, there is always the ax or the sword to remove you, to make place for another who will give me sons.

"You are overcome," she heard the King say gently. "The honor is too great for you. You are too modest, Kate."

"My Lord . . . my Lord . . ." she began desperately. "I understand not. . . ."

"Over-humble, that is what you are, sweetheart. You have been the wife of those two old men—men of some position it is true, but they have made you humble."

She thought longingly of them now. Kindly Lord Borough; gentle Lord Latimer. They had been old, but they had not looked at her as the King was now looking; they

had not disgusted her, nauseated her. She
had dreamed of a third marriage—to the
man she loved. She dared not think of him
now; she was afraid that if she did she
would be compelled to cry out: "I love
Thomas Seymour."

He could be so malignant, this man, so
cruel. If she spoke those words, not only
she, but Thomas, would be sent to the
Tower. It was so easy, for a woman whom
the King had chosen for his wife, to commit
treason.

"Too humble," he was murmuring, "so
that you dare not consider the prize which is
held out to you. Do not be affrighted, Kate.
Listen to what your lord the King tells you. I
am no longer in the first sweet flush of
youth. Ah, youth! Do you know, Kate, when
I was a young man I would hunt all day, tire
out six horses and be as fresh as when I
started? Then I had that accursed accident,
and my leg broke out in ulcers . . . and none
of the cures in Christendom have been able
to take them away. I was a King among men
then, Kate. Had God not chosen me to rule
this realm, then would men have pointed at
me and said, 'There goes a King!' "

"I doubt it not, my Lord."

"You doubt it not! You doubt it not! That is good, Kate. Ah, did you but know what your sovereign has suffered, you would long to comfort him."

"I would not dare presume . . ."

"We give our permission for the presumption. Think of your King's poor sick leg, Kate, and weep for him."

"Weep for Your Majesty, who is both great and glorious!"

"Tush! You think of matters of state. A king is a man as well as a king. You know I married my brother's widow. Twenty years, Kate—twenty years of marriage that was no marriage. For twenty years I lived in sin . . . with my own brother's widow. Unintentional sin, though. I was tricked. I was cheated. And England all but robbed of an heir! You know our story, Kate."

"I know of Your Majesty's sorrows."

Henry nodded. He was passing into that mood of sentimentality and self-pity which contemplation of the past brought with it. He took a lace kerchief and wiped a tear from his eye. He could always weep for the injustices that had come to him through his marriages. "To some men it would have been simple," he said. "I was happily married. I had one daughter. Suffice it that I had given England a future Queen, though a son had been denied me. Then, Kate, I understood. It was my conscience, my most scrupulous conscience that told me I could no longer risk England's security by continuing with a marriage that was no marriage. No marriage, Kate! Can you realize what that meant? The King of England was living in sin with his brother's widow. Small wonder that God did not grant us a son! So I wrestled with myself, and my conscience told me that I must end that marriage. I must take a new wife."

Henry had stood up; he now seemed unaware of the shrinking woman, who immediately rose, as she must not be seated while the King stood. Katharine realized that it was not to her that he was talking now. He began to shout and his fist was clenched.

"I took to wife a black-browed witch! I was cajoled by sorcery. She would have poisoned my daughter, the lady Mary. My son, Richmond, died soon after she laid her wicked head on the block . . . died slowly, lingeringly. That was the result of the spells she laid upon him. The devil had made her beautiful. I was entrapped by sorcery. She should have burned at the stake." He began to speak more softly. "But I was ever merciful to those that pleased me . . . and she pleased me . . . once."

There was silence in the chamber but for the rustling of the silken curtains as they moved in the draft. The King's face was gray, and his eyes went to the curtains as though he looked for someone there.

He turned suddenly and saw Katharine standing beside him. He seemed startled to find her there.

"Ah, yes," he sighed. "Kate . . . Kate. . . . Sit down, Kate."

"Your Grace," she said, "was most unhappy in his marriages."

"Aye!" He spoke softly now, and all the self-pity was back in his voice. "Most unhappy. And then came Jane . . . poor gentle Jane, Jane whom I loved truly. She gave me my son and then she died. The most cruel blow of all!"

Katharine began to pray again silently and fervently. Oh God, save me. Save me from this man. Save me from the King.

She knew more of him than he realized. In her country house she had heard how he had received the news of Jane Seymour's death. Bluntly he had told his ministers that the death of his wife meant little to him beside the great joy he had in his newborn son.

"Had Jane but lived!" he was saying. "Ah, had Jane but lived!" He turned to Katharine and she felt the hot hand on her knee, caressing her thigh. She longed to beg him to desist, but she dared not.

"You are cold, Kate," he said. "You tremble. 'Tis all this talk of my miseries. Sometimes I wonder if I have paid for my most glorious reign with my most miserable domestic life. If that be so, Kate, I must be content. A king oft-times must forget he is a man. A king is the slave of his country as is never the humblest citizen. You know the rest of my sad story?"

"I do, my lord."

"I am young enough to enjoy a wife, Kate."

"Your Grace has many happy years before him, I trust and pray."

"Well spoken. Come nearer, Kate."

She hesitated, but he had had enough of reluctance.

"Hurry! Now! Here, help me up. This accursed leg gives me much pain." He stood beside her, towering above her. She felt his hot, sour breath on her cheek. "Do you like me, Kate?"

How to escape him she did not know. She fell on her knees.

"I am the most obedient of your subjects, Sire."

"Yes, yes, yes," said Henry testily. "But enough of kneeling. Get up. Be done with maiden modesty. You have been twice a wife. It becomes you not to play the reluctant virgin."

"I am overwhelmed," said Katharine, rising.

"Then you need no longer be. I like you, Kate, and you shall be my Queen."

"No, no, Sire. I am too unworthy. I could not . . ."

"It is for us to say who is or who is not worthy to share our throne." He was losing patience. Now was the time for kissing and fondling, for that excitement which should chase away the ghosts he had conjured up.

"I know it, my lord King, but . . ."

"Know this also, Kate. I choose you for wife. I am tired of the celibate state. I was never meant to bear it. Come, Kate, give me that which I found but once and held so short a while before death intervened. Give me married happiness. Give me your love. Give me sons."

Katharine cried: "I am too unworthy, Your Majesty. I am no longer in my prime. . . ."

Henry stopped the words with a loud kiss on her mouth. "Speak up!" he cried. "Speak up. What's all this you are saying?"

Katharine cried in desperation: "If you love me then . . . then you must needs love me. But 'twould be better to be your mistress than your wife, an it please Your Grace."

He was overcome with horror. The little mouth was tight with outraged modesty. "It pleases me not!" he shouted. "It pleases me not at all to hear such wanton talk. You are shameless."

"Yes, Sire, indeed yes, and unworthy to be your wife."

"You said you would be our mistress and not our wife. Explain yourself. Explain yourself."

Katharine covered her face with her hands. She thought of two women who had knelt on Tower Green, who had laid their heads on the block at the command of this man. They had been his wives. Already she seemed to sense the executioner beside her, his ax in his hand, the blade turned toward her.

Henry had taken her by the shoulder and was shaking her.

"Speak up, I said. Speak up." His voice had softened. He was seeing himself now as he wished to see himself—the mighty, omnipotent King, whom no woman could resist, just as they had been unable to resist him in the days of his youth when he had had beauty, wealth, kingship and all that a woman could desire.

"It is on account of mine own unworthiness," faltered Katharine.

He forced her hands from her face and put an arm about her. He kissed her with violence. Then, releasing her, he began to roar: "Here, page! Here, man! Call Gardiner. Call Wriothesley . . . Surrey . . . Seymour . . . call them all. I have news I wish to impart to their lordships."

He smiled at Katharine.

"You must not be afraid of this great honor," he said. "Know you this: I can take you up and lift you to the greatest eminence . . . and I will do it."

She was trembling, thinking: Yes, and you

can cast me down. You can marry me; and
marriage with the King, it is said with truth,
may be the first step toward the Tower and
the block.

The courtiers came hurrying back to the
chamber. The King stood smiling at them.

He looked at them slyly, all those gentlemen who, a short time before, he had dismissed that he might be alone with
Katharine.

"Come forward!" he cried. "Come and
pay your respects to the new Queen of England."

Katharine was in her own apartments. With
dry, tragic eyes she stared before her; she
was trying to look into a future which she
knew would be filled with danger.

There was no escape; she knew that now.

Nan, her faithful woman, had wept openly
when she had heard the news. Katharine's
own sister, Anne Herbert, had come quickly
to court. They did not speak of their com-
passion, but they showed it in their ges-
tures, in the very intonations of their voices.
They loved her, those two; they prayed for
her and they wept for her; but they did not
let her hear their prayers, nor see their tears.

It was the day after the King had announced his intention to marry her that Seymour came secretly to her apartments.

Nan let him in. Nan was terrified. She had been so happy serving Lady Latimer. Life, she realized now, had been so simple in the country mansions of Yorkshire and Worcester. Why had they not returned to the country immediately after the death of Lord Latimer? Why had they stayed that the King's amorous and fickle eyes might alight on her lady?

There was danger all around, and Sir Thomas made that danger more acute by coming to her apartment. Nan remembered the stories she had heard of another Thomas—Culpepper—who had visited the apartments of another Catharine; and remembering that bitter and tragic story she wondered if the story of Katharine Parr would be marred by similar events. Was she destined for the same bitter end?

"I must see Lady Latimer," said Sir Thomas. "It is imperative."

And so he was conducted to her chamber.

He took her hands in his and kissed them fervently.

"Kate . . . Kate . . . how could this happen to us?"

"Thomas," she answered, "I wish that I were dead."

"Nay, sweetheart. Do not wish that. There is always hope."

"There is no hope for me."

He put his arms about her and held her close to him. He whispered: "He cannot live for ever."

"I cannot endure it, Thomas."

"You must endure it. We must both endure it. He is the King. Forget not that."

"I tried," she said. "I tried. . . . And, Thomas, if he knew that you were here . . ."

He nodded, and his eyes sparkled with the knowledge of his danger.

"Thus do I love you," he told her. "Enough to risk my life for you."

"I would not have you do that. Oh, Thomas, that will be the most difficult thing that faces me. I shall see you . . . you whom I love. I must compare you. You . . . you who are all that I admire . . . all that I love. He . . . he is so different."

"He is the King, my love. I am the subject. And you will not be burdened with my presence. I have my orders."

"Thomas! No . . . not . . . the Tower?"

"Nay! He does not consider me such a serious rival as that. I depart at sunrise for Flanders."

"So . . . I am to lose you, then?"

"'Twere safer for us, sweetheart, not to meet for a while. So thinks the King. That is why he is sending me with Dr. Wotton on an embassy to Flanders."

"How long will you be away?"

"Methinks the King will find good reason to keep me there . . . or out of England . . . for a little while."

"I cannot bear it. I know I cannot."

He took her face in his hands. "My heart, like yours, is broken, sweetheart. But we must bear this pain. It will pass. I swear it will pass. And our hearts will mend, for one day we shall be together."

"Thomas, can you believe that?"

"I believe in my destiny, Kate. You and I shall be together. I know it."

"Thomas, if the King were to discover that you had been here . . ."

"Ah, perhaps he would give me this hour, since he is to have you for the rest of his life."

"For the rest of my life, you mean!" she said bitterly.

"Nay. He is an old man. His fancy will not stray to others as once it did. One year . . . two years . . . who knows? Cheer up, my Kate. Today we are broken-hearted, but tomorrow the future is ours."

"You must not stay here. I feel there are spies, watching my every movement."

He kissed her and caressed her afresh; and after a time he took his leave, and on the next tide sailed for Flanders.

In the Queen's closet at Hampton Court, Gardiner performed the ceremony. This was not hurried and secret as in the case of Anne Boleyn; this was a royal wedding.

The Princesses Mary and Elizabeth stood behind the King and his bride, and with them the King's niece, the Lady Margaret Douglas. Lady Herbert, the Queen's sister, and other great ladies and gentlemen were present.

The King was in excellent humor on this his marriage morning. The jewels flashed on his dalmatica; the shrewd eyes sparkled and the royal tongue licked the tight lips, for she was a comely creature, this bride of his, and he was a man who needed a wife. He felt, as he had said that morning to his brother-in-law, Lord Hertford, that this marriage would be the best he had ever made.

The July sun was hot and the bride felt as though she would faint with the oppressive atmosphere in the room and the fear within her.

A nightmare had sprung into life. She was here in Hampton Court being married to the King, here in a palace surrounded by gardens which Henry had planned with Anne Boleyn, on whose walls were the entwined initials, the H. and A. which had had to be changed hastily to H. and J. Along the gallery which led to the chapel, the youthful Catharine Howard had run one day, screaming for mercy. It was said that both Anne and Catharine haunted this place. And here, in the palace of hideous memories, she, Katharine Parr, was now being married to Henry the Eighth.

There was no longer hope of escape. The King was close. His breath scorched her. The nuptial ring was being put on her finger.

No. No longer hope. The King in that tragic moment had made Katharine Parr his sixth wife.

CHAPTER

11

The King was not displeased with his new wife. She had the gentlest hands that had ever wrapped a bandage about his poor suffering leg, and in the first few weeks of his marriage he discovered that he had not only got himself a comely wife, but the best of nurses. Nervous and timid she was during those first weeks, as though feeling herself unworthy to receive the great honors which were being showered upon her.

"Why, bless your modest heart, Kate," he told her, "you have no need to fear us. We like you. We like your shapely person and your gentle hands. We know that you have been raised to a great position in this land, but let that not disturb you, for you are worthy, Kate. *We* find you worthy."

She wore the jewels—those priceless

gems—which had been worn by her predecessors.

"Look at these rubies, Kate." He would lean heavily on her and bite her ear in a moment of playfulness. Why had she thought that elderly men were less interested in fleshly pleasures than the younger ones? She realized that the experience afforded her by Lords Borough and Latimer had taught her little. "You'll look a Queen in these! And don't forget you wear them through the King's grace. Don't forget that, my Kate."

And she herself, because she was by nature kindly and gentle and looked for that good in others which was such an integral part of her own character, was more quickly resigned to this marriage than others might have been.

Yet there were nights when she lay awake in the royal bed, that mountain of diseased flesh beside her, thinking of her new life as Queen of England. Of the King she knew a good deal, for the affairs of kings are watched closely by those about them, and this man was a supreme ruler whose slightest action could send reverberations through the kingdom.

What sort of man was he whom she had married? First, because she had been the victim of this quality, she must think of him as the sensualist. Indeed, his sensuality was so great that it colored every characteristic he possessed. But he was far more than a man who delighted in pandering to his senses with fair women, good food and the best of wine; he was a King, and for all his self-indulgence, he was a King determined to rule. When he had been a young man, his delight in his healthy body had proved so great that he had preferred to leave the government of state affairs to his able Wolsey. But he had changed. He was the ruler now. And through that selfishness, that love of indulgence, that terrifying cruelty, there could be seen the strong man, the man who knew how to govern in a turbulent age, a man to whom the greatness of his country was of the utmost importance because he, Henry the Eighth, was synonymous with England. But for his monster conscience and a surprising primness in the sensualist, he would have resembled any lusty man of the times. But he was apart. He must be right in all things; he must placate his conscience; and it was those acts, demanded of him by the conscience, which made him the most cruel tyrant of his age.

What would happen to her in the months to come? wondered Katharine, staring at the ornate tester, although there was not enough light to show her its magnificent workmanship. And what of Thomas Seymour, temporarily banished from his country because he had been known to cast covetous eyes on the woman the King had decided to make his wife! How was he bearing the banishment?

What are this King's subjects, Katharine asked herself, but figures to be moved about at his pleasure? Some please him for a while, and he lifts them up and keeps them close beside him until he sees others who please him more; then those who delighted him a week before are discarded; and if that prim quality within him suggests that the favorite of yesterday be removed by death, the conscience demands that this should be done. For the King must always be able to answer his conscience, no matter how much blood must be spilled to bring about this state of concord between a self-willed sensualist and his conscience.

So Katharine prayed in the silences of the

nights for the courage of which she knew she would have great need. Often she thought of a friend with whom she had been on terms of affection before she came to court. This was the Reformer, Anne Askew, herself the victim of an undesired marriage; she thought of Anne's courage and determination and she longed to emulate her.

But I am a coward, thought Katharine. I cannot bear to think of the cell, and the sound of tolling bells, bringing to me a message of destruction. I cannot bear to think of leaving that cell for Tower Green and the executioner's ax.

Her prayer for courage, it seemed, did not go unanswered, for as the days passed her fears diminished and she felt that a new sense was developing within her which would make her aware of encroaching danger and give her the calm she would need to face it.

Some might have loathed the task which was thrust upon them. Each day it was her duty now to bathe the leg, to listen to his cries of rage when he was in pain; but oddly enough, instead of nauseating her, this filled her with pity for him. To see this man—this all-powerful King—such a prey to his hideous infirmity, was a sorry sight. Once when he looked at her he had seen her eyes filled with tears. He had softened immediately.

"Tears, Kate? Tears?"

"You suffer so."

Then those little eyes, which could be so cruel, also filled with tears, and the fat hand which was heavy with flashing jewels came down to pat her shoulders.

"You're a good woman, Kate," he said. "Methinks I made a good choice when I took you to wife."

She had asked that her sister Anne, Lady Herbert, might be a lady of her bedchamber, and that Margaret Neville, the only daughter of Lord Latimer, be one of her maids of honor.

"Do as you will, Kate," said the King when she had made the request. "You're a good woman and a wise one, and you'll surround yourself with others of your kind."

Yes, the King was pleased. This marriage had not begun with one of those burning infatuations such as he had felt for Anne Boleyn and Catharine Howard. That was all to the good. This, he assured himself, was a wise choice, a choice made while the judgment was cool and sober.

Then there were the children. He had made it clear to her that he wished her to take a stepmotherly interest in them, and for this she was grateful. It had been one of her deepest regrets that she had no children of her own, and that her strong maternal nature had always to be placated with stepchildren. Well, it had been so before, and never had she found anything but joy in mothering the children of those other women.

The royal children were as responsive as had been those of her other marriages. How happy she was to be so obviously welcome in their apartments! Poor children, they had known so many different stepmothers and they were accustomed to such changes.

When, as their stepmother, she paid them her first visit, they were all ceremoniously assembled to greet her.

Little Edward looked so puny that she wanted to take him in her arms and weep over him. Yet while he moved her with pity, he filled her with dread. This was the only male heir, and the King wished for others.

He put his hand in hers and, on sudden

impulse, dispensing with that ceremony due to the heir to the throne, she knelt and kissed him, and, following her lead, he put his arms about her neck.

"Welcome, dear Mother," he said; and in his voice was all the yearning of a little boy who has never known a mother and always longed for one, and whose childish pleasures had been overlaid by the great duties demanded of an heir to the throne.

"We are going to love each other," she said.

"I am glad you are to be our stepmother," he answered.

The Lady Mary knelt before her. Poor Mary, who was almost as unhealthy as Edward. She never dispensed with what she considered the right formalities, and this was a solemn occasion for Mary—the greeting of the new Queen of England. Previously it had been Lady Latimer who must kneel to the Lady Mary; now the position was reversed, and although there had been warm friendship between them, Mary never forgot the demands of etiquette.

"Rise, dear Mary," said Katharine; and she kissed the slightly younger woman.

"Welcome, dear Mother," said Mary. "I am glad to welcome you."

And then Elizabeth came forward, dropping a pretty curtsy and lifting her sparkling eyes to her stepmother's face.

"I, too, am pleased," she said; and when she had received her stepmother's kiss, as though on sudden impulse, she followed her brother's example and, putting her arms about Katharine's neck, kissed her.

Little Jane Grey, who was waiting with her sister Katharine to welcome the Queen, thought that Elizabeth seemed more pleased than any of them. Little Jane noted a good deal more than people guessed, for she never spoke, even to her beloved Edward, of all that she saw. She did not believe that Elizabeth was really half as pleased as Edward or Mary, although she was not displeased. (Who could be to welcome such a gentle and charming lady as the new Queen?) It was merely that Elizabeth could show great pleasure or great sorrow as she wished, and the more easily than others because she did not feel these emotions deeply and could remain in control of herself.

Now Elizabeth stood back that the Queen

might greet the little Greys, and while Jane knelt before the Queen and was kissed by her, she was thinking that Elizabeth was not really so pleased because the King had married a *good* lady, but because this lady would be easy to persuade; and Elizabeth would know how to persuade her to ask the King to give her what she most needed; and what Elizabeth needed was that position which she considered hers by right. She wished to be received at court, not as the Lady Elizabeth, the bastard, but as a Princess; and she wished to have an income that she might buy beautiful clothes; she wished to have jewels with which to adorn her person. Jane felt sure that that was what Elizabeth was thinking as she greeted Katharine Parr.

And yet, when they had dispensed with ceremony as far as Mary would allow them, and were all gay and happy together, Jane noticed that it was Elizabeth's gay chatter which most charmed the Queen.

Edward kept close to Jane, and now and then held her hand and looked at her with fresh tenderness. He was thinking that his father must be very happy to have this new stepmother for a wife, and that a wife could be a great help to a King.

Then he felt suddenly happy because of Jane, who was quiet and gentle and very clever—she was not unlike the new stepmother in these things—for Edward knew that Queen Katharine was quiet, gentle and learned.

While Elizabeth was talking to their stepmother, Edward said to Jane: "It is a good thing to have a wife, Jane. If a king loves her dearly and she is good and kind and clever, that is a very good thing. You are kind, Jane, *and* good *and* clever. You are beautiful too."

Then he and Jane smiled at each other, because there was such accord between them that they did not always have to put their thoughts into words, and Jane knew that Edward meant that he wished he might have her for his Queen when he grew up.

The King too visited his son's apartment on that day, for he wished to see how his wife was faring with his children.

His approach was heralded as he came slowly to those apartments.

"The King comes this way!"

Waiting women and ushers, guards and gentlemen-at-arms were alert, terrified that he might glance their way and find some fault, hoping that he would give them a nod of approval.

And into the room he hobbled, beside him one of his gentlemen on whom he might lean. His doublet was of crimson velvet, striped and slashed with white satin. About his neck was a gold collar from which hung a magnificent and very large pearl. His cloak was of purple velvet; and on his left leg he wore the Garter. He glittered with jewels; they adorned his cap, his doublet and his cloak; they sparkled on the pouch of cloth of gold which hung at his side and which hid from view the dagger with the jeweled hilt. The color of his face almost matched that of his cloak, so purple was it with the exertion of walking; but at the moment its expression was one of beaming kindliness. It pleased him to see his new wife and his children together.

As he entered the room all fell to their knees.

He surveyed them with contentment, until he examined more closely the face of his little son. The boy was wan and there were dark shadows under his eyes. That tutor of his was letting him work too hard; he would have a word with the fellow.

"Rise," he commanded; and they rose and stood before him in awe and fearful admiration.

He limped to the Prince. The boy tried not to shrink, but found it difficult, for in the presence of his dazzling father he felt himself to be more insignificant than usual. It always seemed to Edward that he shrank to a smaller size under that scrutiny; his headaches seemed worse, and his palpitations returned with violence; he was aware of the new rash which had broken out on his right cheek. The King would notice it and blame someone for it—perhaps dear Mrs. Penn, his beloved nurse. Edward was always terrified that Mrs. Penn might be taken from him.

From the boy the King turned his gaze on Mary. He felt an almost active dislike toward her, for she was a continual reproach to him. She ought to have been married, but what royal Prince wanted a bastard for his wife, even if she was a King's bastard? And how could he declare her legitimate and still insist that he was right to put her mother away? No wonder the sight of her depressed him.

Then Elizabeth. She grows more like me every day, he was thinking. That hair is as mine was; once I had such a fair and glowing skin. Perhaps you didn't make a cuckold of me with Norris after all, Anne.

He wanted to dislike Elizabeth, but he found that impossible, since to do so would be tantamount to disliking himself.

"Well . . . fostering friendship?" he asked.

Katharine spoke. "We were friends already, Your Majesty."

"It pleases me to hear that." He smiled, reminding his conscience that he was above all things a benign parent who had chosen a wife, not for carnal pleasures, but because he wished to benefit his children. He gazed at her and was pleased with what he saw. Her bodice of cloth of gold was a pleasant change after her widow's black. The bodice fitted tightly, showing her neat but womanly figure, and at her throat glowed the great ruby which he had given her.

A comely Queen! he reflected. A good stepmother into the bargain. Not too old to have sons of her own. She was a healthy woman, small but sturdy. She would have sons. And he would be looking to her to provide him with one very soon.

He signed for his chair, and one of the attendants hurried to place it for him. He made his son come to him and he questioned the boy as to his studies. He placed his great hand on the small head.

"You must be healthy," he said. "When I was your age I was twice your size."

"I crave Your Majesty's pardon for my size," said the boy. "I ride every day, as did Your Majesty at my age, and I jump and run."

"You're a good boy," said Henry. "But I should like to see you grow somewhat faster."

He would like to hear the boy read to him in French and Latin, he said; and books were brought; but while the Prince stood at his father's knee and read aloud, the King was watching the others, who stood, without speaking, in his presence.

This boy is all I have, he reflected sorrowfully. Oh Jane, why did you not live to give me more? And healthy ones too. His breathing's bad, and he's too thin. I'll see his cook this very day. He shall be made to eat. He shall be made to grow strong and lusty.

This boy and two girls . . . a pretty state of affairs! He remembered his son, Richmond, and the delight he had felt when that boy had been born, proclaiming his father's manhood to the world; for he had feared, before the birth of Richmond, that he could not beget a son. Then Richmond had died that horrible, lingering death.

Henry was afraid that the small child at his knee might go the way of Richmond. Mary had managed to cling to life, but he felt that that had been something like a miracle. Elizabeth alone seemed capable of living to the normal span. He wished there was some magician at his court who could change the sex of the girl. Ha! What an achievement that would be. If Elizabeth could be changed to a boy he would make her heir to the throne, by God he would!

But there was no one who could perform such a miracle, and he felt that it was cruel that it must be Anne's girl who should claim his attention, whom he should long to make his successor. He had always believed that Anne might have the power to mock him from the grave.

Then he contemplated his Queen again. He had a good wife. She was small and dainty and he would like her better when her body broadened with his child. Well, it was early yet, but perhaps this time next year there would be another Tudor Prince to delight his heart.

"Have done," he said to Edward. "Have done. Your reading's good. I'll compliment your tutor instead of berating him. And how do you like your new mother, eh?"

"Sire, I love her dearly."

"That is well." He touched the boy's cheek with his sparkling forefinger. "More spots, eh?"

"They came only today," explained the Prince apologetically. "I feel in very good health, Sire."

"That is well."

He rose painfully and Katharine came forward to help him. "Good Kate. I rejoice to see you here. Now help me back to my apartment."

He took her arm and leaned alternately on her and on his stick.

When they were in the royal apartments he said: "The Prince looks poorly. My only son. I would I had a dozen more to follow him." He pinched her cheek. "We'll get ourselves a son, eh? We'll get ourselves a son, Kate, my little pig."

This, she brooded, is the height of royal favor. The King calls me his "pig" and asks for sons. If I provide them I shall continue to be his pig. If not . . . ?

Why should she not have a child? She longed for a child. Some of the wise women said that those who longed for children most easily conceived them. And yet how those unfortunate Queens must have longed for sons!

She refused to be depressed. She had her friends about her—her dearest sister Anne and her beloved stepdaughter, Margaret Neville. She had her dear Nan with her, and Nan would serve her faithfully as long as they lived. And she had her new stepchildren, who had received her with warmth; and at the moment she was the King's little pig.

"My lord," she said, "I have a favor to ask of you."

He surveyed her benignly. He wished her to know that, being pleased with her, he was in the mood to grant favors.

"Well, Kate, speak up. What is this favor?"

"It concerns your daughters. It is one of

my dearest wishes to see them reinstated at court. My lord, I cannot help but feel that it is wrong that they should not be recognized as royal Princesses."

He narrowed his eyes. "You know what I suffered through their mothers. Mary's a bastard. You know that. And so is Elizabeth."

"But were you not married to the Lady Elizabeth's mother?"

"Nay. You meddle in things you do not understand. I never liked meddling women, Kate." He caught her cheek between his thumb and finger and pinched it. "Mind you, Kate, I know your motives. You meddle for them and not for your own gain. I like you for it. The form of marriage I went through with Elizabeth's mother was no true marriage. She was precontracted to Northumberland. That made our marriage void, and her girl a bastard. They're both bastards, I tell you."

"Yet they are your daughters. And how like you is the Lady Elizabeth! My lord, could you not have them brought back to the position they enjoyed when you believed yourself to be married to their mothers?"

He pretended to consider, pretended to

be faintly displeased. This was one of the games of make-believe which he so liked to play. He was not considering; he was not displeased. He knew that the people thought it wrong that his daughters should live in penury; providing all agreed that they were bastards—which they must do if his conscience was to be satisfied—he would not be unwilling to give them a position at court. And how pleasant it was to do this thing which he wished to do and still make it a favor to Kate, his new wife, his sweetheart, his little pig.

"Methinks I find it hard to deny you aught, sweetheart, for now you ask this favor I am inclined to grant it."

"I thank you. I thank you most heartily. Your Majesty is indeed good to me."

"And you in turn shall be good to me." She knew what he meant. It seemed to her as though the bells in the chapel had begun to toll. "Sons. Sons," they seemed to say. "Give me sons."

"But first," he said, with the air of one who offered yet another honor to a subject already overloaded with them, "you shall dress my leg. The walking has shifted the bandage and it plagues me."

->-<-

There were two men who were not pleased with the King's felicity. One of these was Thomas Wriothesley and the other Gardiner, Bishop of Winchester.

It was Wriothesley, the sly and cunning, who discovered through his spies that, in the privacy of her chamber, the Queen read forbidden books, and he hastened to his friend Gardiner to acquaint him with the discovery.

The court was at Windsor, and Gardiner, greatly disturbed by the news that he had helped to put on the throne a Queen who leaned toward Protestantism, suggested that Wriothesley and he should walk together in the Great Park to discuss this matter which he would prefer not to mention within castle walls.

When the two men had put some distance between themselves and the castle, Gardiner said: "This is indeed disturbing news, my friend. I would have sworn that the Queen was a good Catholic."

"A sly woman, my lord Bishop, I fear. While she was Latimer's wife, she allowed it to be understood that she was as good a Catholic as you or I. As soon as he dies and she marries His Grace, we find her playing the heretic."

"A foolish woman, friend Wriothesley. Playing the heretic when she was Latimer's wife would have been a mild matter. Playing the same as the wife of our Sovereign Lord is another affair. But we waste time *tattling* of the follies of such a woman. We must *act*."

Wriothesley nodded. This was what he expected of Gardiner. He would be ready to strike a blow for Catholicism and strike it in the right direction. Gardiner was a strong man; he had served under Wolsey; his tact and enthusiasm in the affair of the King's first divorce had placed him in high favor. When Wolsey had fallen, Gardiner became Secretary of State. The Archdeaconry of Leicester and the Bishopric of Winchester had speedily fallen to him. And if the King did not care for him as he had cared for some of his ministers, if Gardiner's origins were obscure, these facts merely meant that his rise to power was the more spectacular, and if he did not win the King's love, he had his respect.

"Tell me what you have discovered of the Queen," went on Gardiner.

"She surrounds herself with those who are interested in the new religion. There are her sister Lady Hertford, the stepdaughter Margaret Neville, the Duchess of Suffolk, Lady Hoby and others. They are secret 'Reformers' . . . as they call themselves. Remember, my lord Bishop, she has some charge of the education of the Prince and Princess. Prince Edward and Princess Elizabeth are but children; their minds could be easily perverted. The Lady Mary is a staunch Catholic and safe from any contamination. But not only has the woman charge of the young Prince and Princess, but of the two Grey girls, and they are near enough to the throne for that fact to be disquietening."

"You have no need to warn me on that score. We cannot have heretics sharing the throne with the King."

"Could we not take this matter to the King and lay it before him?"

Gardiner smiled ruefully. He let his gaze rest on the two towers of the castle which were approached by the drawbridge. He was standing on a mound and could see the straggling street with its gabled houses, black and white, which formed the town of

Windsor. He could see the winding river, silver under the summer sky, cutting its way through meadows gold with buttercups. But Gardiner had not a thought to spare for the beauties of Nature. Instead he thought of other Queens whom ministers had planned to destroy. He knew that any minister would be a fool to approach an amorous King with tales against the woman he had married as recently as two weeks before.

Cranmer had brought Catharine Howard to the block, but that had been some time after the marriage; yet the King had undoubtedly been infatuated with the woman. But what tales Cranmer had had to set before the King—such tales and such proof that poor nervous Cranmer had dared deprive Henry of a wife with whom he had been in love. And what Protestant Cranmer could do to Catharine Howard, Catholic Gardiner could do to Katharine Parr.

But not yet. Timing was all-important in such matters.

"This needs much thought," he said slowly. "To strike at the Queen now would be to invite disaster. The King is pleased with her. Two weeks of marriage have increased rather than diminished his pleasure in her. I can assure you, Wriothesley, that she delights him more now with her nursing and her gentle ways than she did before the marriage. The time is not yet."

"I am sure that you are right, my lord Bishop, but might not delay prove dangerous? It is while the King sets such store by her that she will have the best opportunity of whispering her heresies into his ears."

The Bishop patted Wriothesley's arm. "Yet we must wait. Later we shall no doubt have Seymour back at court. Then, mayhap, it may be possible to bring a case against those two. Such a case would be sure of success . . . if proved, and there are usually ways of proving these matters." The Bishop's lips formed into a smile, which disappeared as he looked toward the Castle walls. But they were far-distant and there was no one but his companion to hear this dangerous conversation.

"Ah, Seymour!" said Wriothesley. "If we could but prove something against those two! His Majesty would be mad with fury and we should bring down two groups of enemies at the same time. The Queen and her heretic friends . . . and the Seymours. What could be better?"

"We must remember if Seymour returns that it may not be as simple as you assume. Seymour is a very ambitious man. I doubt that he would allow his feeling for any woman to interfere with his ambitions. The King, moreover, is fond of the fellow."

"Still, the Queen was enamored of him before her marriage with the King. He wished to marry her. And the King must have felt some uneasiness to have dispatched him to Flanders. It may well be that the King will keep him there. Oh yes, his jealousy is aroused—if only slightly—by the fascinating sailor."

"That's so; but his love for the Queen is not the white-hot passion it was in the cases of Anne Boleyn and Catharine Howard. We might attack through Seymour, I do not doubt; but Seymour is not here. That may come later. In the meantime, we might strike, not at the Queen, but at her friends."

"Her friends? You mean her sister and the ladies? . . ."

"Nay, nay. You have something to learn, Wriothesley. We strike first at little deer and wait for the head deer. There are Reformers in most towns, and it is my belief that if we looked we might find them here in this town of Windsor. There is a priest I know of, a certain Anthony Pearson. The people flock to hear his sermons, and the good honest Catholic lawyer, Simons of this town, has already conveyed to me his suspicions of this man. Simons declares him to be a Reformer. There are others. A little inquiry into the life of this man Pearson would doubtless disclose their identities and give us what we desire. We could strike at the Queen through them and, while we await the opportunity to implicate Her Majesty, doubtless these men would help add a little fuel to a Smithfield fire."

"I applaud your wisdom, my lord."

The Bishop slipped his arm through that of Wriothesley. "Keep close to me. I will have you informed of the progress of this affair. Let us strike at the little deer before we bend our bows to bring down those at the head of the herd. We will return to the Castle, and I will seek an early opportunity of an audience with the King; and when it is over I will let you know how I have progressed. Watch me, my friend, and you will see how I intend to deal with this delicate affair, and I promise you that in a matter of months—

though it may be a year or two—you will see
Her Majesty following in the footsteps of
other foolish Queens."

"It would be the block."

Gardiner nodded. "His Majesty has had
two divorces. He does not like them. He
prefers . . . the other method."

"I doubt not," said Wriothesley, "that it will
be the . . . 'other method' . . . for Katharine
Parr."

In St. George's Hall the King had seated
himself in that chair of state above which
was the ornate canopy of Edward the Third.
It was at the head of the banqueting table,
and on his right hand sat his Queen. The
Lady Mary was present in a place of high
honor, and as Gardiner said grace he
reflected that his task might not be a
difficult one, for Queen Katharine Parr must
be a foolish woman so to raise such a
staunch Catholic as the Princess Mary to
work against her.

Before the King knelt one of his gentlemen with a ewer, another with a basin, yet
another with a napkin. The great table
seemed as though it must collapse under
the weight of heavy flasks of wine and the

enormous gilded and silver dishes. Venison, chickens, peacocks, cygnets, salmon, mullet and pies of all sorts were laid out. Gardiner watched the King's eyes gleam as they studied the food. The King's love of women was, it was said, being surpassed by his interest in food. The Bishop must speak to the King after the meal and he must make sure of doing so before his blood became overheated and his digestive organs complained of the great amount of work their royal master would give them to do.

The minstrels began to play and a humble chorister from the town of Windsor to sing one of the King's songs. The King's eyes were glazed with pleasure; next to his love of food, wine and women came his love of music; and there was no music that delighted him as much as his own.

This was a state occasion and the hall was thronged with men at arms, yeomen and halberdiers. Thus, thought Gardiner, must feast Henry the Eighth by the Grace of God King of England, France and Ireland, Defender of the Faith and Sovereign of the Most Noble Order of the Garter.

Defender of the Faith! His ministers, decided the Bishop, must needs keep him to that defense.

When the music was over and before the feasting began, the King sent for John Marbeck to come before him.

The man, deeply conscious of the honor done him, knelt in a reverence which was far from displeasing to Henry. He had always been eager to win the approbation of his humble subjects.

"Your name?" said Henry.

"John Marbeck, Your Most Gracious Majesty."

"We liked your singing. You shall sing to us again. I said to the Queen that rarely have I heard my song sung so well."

"I shall treasure the memory of those words for the rest of my life, Your Grace."

The Queen gave Marbeck one of her smiles, and the man looked at her with a devotion which equaled that he gave to the King, for in those circles in which he moved he had heard of the Queen's sympathies with that religion which he, Marbeck, was convinced was the true one.

The King gave orders that Marbeck should be given good food and wine, and the banquet began.

"I liked that fellow," said the King to Katharine. "Methinks I know an honest face when I see it."

"Your Majesty must have him to sing more of your songs," said Katharine.

"That I will. And it shall be while we are here at Windsor. I hear he works with Priest Pearson and is a good churchman."

When the King was heavy with much food and wine, Gardiner craved private audience, saying that he had matters of great importance which he wished to set before His Majesty.

Henry nodded, and before retiring to his bedchamber received the Bishop in his private closet.

"What now, Bishop?" he asked.

"It has come to my ears, Your Grace, that there are a number of heretics in the realm, men who doubt the word of Your Majesty and plan to work against those laws which you have set down."

"What's this?" cried Henry.

"Books are being circulated, books which Your Majesty has forbidden his subjects to read. They are being compiled against Your Majesty's orders. There are men who seek, by sly and secret means, to work against you. They disagree with the Six Articles. They would defy Your Grace and teach a false religion."

"Oh, these meddlers!" groaned Henry. "They torment and plague me. Why cannot they accept the religion which their King has given them?"

"They are wayward subjects, Your Grace. It is the books which are at the root of the evil. I ask Your Majesty's permission to make a search of every dwelling in this town. Give me this permission, and I will have the ringleaders in a week."

Henry was silent and Gardiner went on: "These heretics, Your Grace, they creep into every corner of the court. Even about Your Majesty they gather."

He stopped, noting his master's frown. Henry did not wish to be disturbed with these matters now. He had eaten well; he had drunk well; and he wanted his pleasant little Queen to sit beside him. They had been married for two weeks, and the more he saw of her, the more he liked her, so he wished that nothing should interfere with his post-marital courtship.

Clever Gardiner was a good servant, the sort he needed about him, but there were times when the fellow irritated him. He knew whither Gardiner wished to lead him. His Queen had been betraying her thoughts. She was not a foolish, frivolous woman, and she spent much time with her books. Some of these books, Henry guessed, would not have given great pleasure to his Catholic Bishop. Let the Queen read what she would; he wanted no fool for a wife, and as long as she did not imagine herself to be too clever, he was pleased that she should display a certain good sense. Most of the clever people at his court had a desire to examine new ideas; it was natural.

Regarding his wife, Henry was in a benevolent mood. He was happier than he had been since they had brought him the news of Catharine Howard's infidelities. The fact was he had needed a wife, and now he had one. She was a good little woman who gave him much pleasure. He wished, therefore, to be left alone with his pleasure; and if Master Gardiner had the good sense he imagined himself to have, he should realize this.

"Your permission, Sire, to search the houses of Windsor, and I will bring you proof."

"Oh . . . very well, Sir Bishop. Go to your searching."

"Every room in Windsor, Sire, shall be ransacked in the service of Your Grace."

The King narrowed his eyes. "You'll not search the Castle apartments, my lord. You'll keep your fingers out of them, Sir Bishop."

Gardiner bowed, well pleased. So the King already knew of the Queen's sympathies, and he did not wish to be disturbed with the knowledge. This could mean only one thing: the present Queen was in such high favor that her religious opinions were of little moment. They were to be ignored . . . for the time being.

Certainly the Bishop was not displeased. Once the King had tired of his little pig, he would be only too eager to listen to an account of her heresies. And, cogitated the Bishop, if and when that came about, and Master Thomas Seymour returned to court . . . the stage would be set.

The Bishop's first action after that interview with the King was to send for a certain Dr. London, whom he knew to be in the town of Windsor.

Gardiner had a special reason for sending for this man. He had watched the career of the Doctor of Divinity and knew him for a man of great resource and cunning. Dr. London had worked under Thomas Cromwell in the dissolution of the monasteries and he had been the perfect tool of his master. Cromwell had said: "Bring me evidence of the infamies which persist in such and such an abbey." And Dr. London had never failed to bring what was required of him; he was an indefatigable exposer of foulness; he was a reviver of old scandals; and if he could find no scandal foul enough to please his master, well then, he was a man of ready wit and it was not beyond his power to invent them.

Moreover, Dr. London was a man who needed to show the Bishop his loyalty. As he had once been Cromwell's man, he could not easily become Gardiner's. In these dangerous times a man must take sides; and Dr. London had shown the Bishop that he wished to establish himself as a good Catholic.

The man had wisdom. He looked into the future. The present King was ailing; his son was weak; and there was Catholic Mary waiting to take the throne. Dr. London—like Gardiner—saw a return to Rome not far distant. He had no wish to feed the flames of Smithfield.

Such a man, the Bishop was sure, would work with zeal.

"Dr. London, I have work for you. You have shown me that you wish for preferment. You have sworn loyalty to me and the true religion. Now is the time to prove it."

"I am at your service, my lord Bishop."

"The task to which I am appointing you, good Dr. London, is the smelling-out of heretics in Windsor."

"Ah. They abound in this town, sir. They abound."

"Alas, 'tis true. I have the King's order to bring them to justice. Whom do you suspect of heresy?"

"There is a priest, Anthony Pearson. I have made notes of his sermons, your lordship. He has said enough to send him to the stake."

"Mayhap examination of his house will lead you to others."

"I doubt it not."

"Go to it, good Doctor. I doubt not that you will find evidence against these rogues."

"My lord Bishop, it is said that these people are given aid by some at court."

The Bishop nodded. "For the time, Doctor, let us keep to the herd. We will shoot at the head deer later."

The Doctor's eyes gleamed. He understood. Great things lay ahead of him. This was but a beginning. He would perform the task required of him, and another and greater would come his way. That was what the good Bishop, the mighty Bishop, was telling him.

"How many heretics would my lord Bishop require?"

"Not too many. We might say . . . four. They should be humble men. The court is to be left alone. Start with this priest Pearson and see whither that leads."

The Doctor bowed himself out of the Bishop's presence and at once went to his task.

As he left the Castle of Windsor, John Marbeck was singing softly. It had been a successful evening, a wonderful evening indeed when the King had singled him out to express his pleasure.

John Marbeck was a simple man, a

deeply religious man, a man of ideals. His greatest desire was not that he might win fame and fortune at court, but that he might help to give the Bible to the people of England.

He had many friends in Windsor, men with ideals similar to his own; he met them in the course of his duties at church and he sometimes joined gatherings at their homes and, on occasions, they visited his. During these meetings there was one subject which they discussed with passion: religion.

Each of these men wished to do some work which would aid others to reach the great Truth which they believed they had discovered.

Pearson did it by his preaching, as did Henry Filmer, a friar, who, being turned from his monastery, had become interested in the new learning and was now a vicar in Windsor.

Marbeck's friend Robert Testwood, a fine musician and the head of the choir to which Marbeck belonged, had introduced him to these men; and how happy Marbeck had been to show them the great work which he was doing!

"I shall go on working at my Concordance," he told them, "until I have made possible a greater understanding of the Bible."

"Then keep it secret," Pearson had warned him.

It was strange, thought Marbeck, looking back at the gray walls of the castle, how simple men such as himself and his friends, knowing the risks they ran, should continue to run them.

Robert Testwood had said: "This is more than a religious issue, my friends. We do these things because within us we feel that a man should have freedom to *think* as he wishes."

Marbeck was not sure of that. The religious issue, to him, was all-important. And on this night he wished merely to be happy. The King had complimented him on his voice; the Queen had smiled graciously upon him—the Queen, who, some said, was one of them.

He smiled, thinking of the future. Perhaps he would dedicate his Concordance to that gracious lady.

He was singing the song he had sung before the King, as he let himself into his house.

He stood at the door listening. He heard noises within. Strangers were in his house.

His heart was beating fast as he opened the door and went into that room in which he did his work. There stood two men; he noticed that his cupboard had been turned out, as had the drawers of his table. In the hands of one were several sheets of his Concordance. These men had forced the lock; they had discovered his secret.

"What . . . what do you here?" he stammered.

"John Marbeck," said one of the men, "we come on the King's business. You are our prisoner. There will be questions for you to answer."

"Questions . . . questions? I beg of you, give me those papers. . . . They are mine. . . ."

"Not so," said the man. "These papers are our prisoners also. Come, master chorister. There is no time to waste."

"Whither do you take me?"

"To London. To the Marshalsea."

Marbeck was trembling, remembering tales he had heard and had bravely not heeded. Now they were close to him and he would have to heed them. He thought of torture and death; and as he left Windsor for

London in the company of his captors he thought of the smell of crackling wood and burning flesh; he thought of the martyr's death.

Anne, Lady Herbert, came to the Queen and begged a secret audience with her. Katharine forthwith dismissed all her attendants.

"What ails you, sister?" asked the Queen. "I declare you look as if you have seen a ghost."

Ah! thought Anne Herbert. Mayhap I have. The ghosts of Anne Boleyn and Catharine Howard warn me.

"Gardiner is moving against you. He, with his friend Wriothesley, has ordered a search of the houses in this town."

"A search!"

"There have already been arrests."

"Whom have they arrested?"

"Four men of Windsor. Two priests and two musicians. Pearson is one of them, Marbeck another."

"God help us!" cried the Queen. "I know why these men have been taken."

"It is a blow at you, dearest sister. They dare not attack you now because you have the King's favor. But this is a warning. As soon as they consider they have a chance to work against you, they will do so. Dearest Majesty, you must give up your reading, give up those little gatherings of our friends. It was unsafe when you were Lady Latimer; but now that you are the Queen it is desperately dangerous."

"Anne, what will happen to these men?"

"I know not. Dr. London is preparing a case against them."

"Dr. London! That rogue. He was Cromwell's man. That is he, is it not? He roamed the countryside and turned the monks from their monasteries while he took their treasure."

"He took those treasures for his master, Kate. He is a man without principles. Then he worked against the Catholic monks; now he works for Catholic Gardiner and the King's Secretary, Wriothesley. He is wily; he is clever and he is unscrupulous. What is to become of these men, I do not know. They say they have found Marbeck's notes on the Bible. That will ensure a fiery death for him."

"But, Anne, the King has a fondness for Marbeck. He complimented him on his singing."

"Gardiner has no fondness for Marbeck's religious views."

"The King is all-powerful."

"But, Kate, Gardiner will show that Marbeck has disobeyed the King's orders. I am afraid . . . desperately afraid. Not only for these men . . . but for you."

"We must help them, Anne. We cannot let them die."

"Let well alone. Listen to me, dearest Kate. Remember those who went before you. You have the King's favor now. Keep it. Do everything you can to keep it, and stay away from trouble."

"But I must do everything I can for these men, Anne."

"You tempt Fate."

"No, Anne. I must prove my courage in this. I have to acquire courage. Something within me tells me this. If I fail now I should fail later."

"Later?" said Anne Herbert fearfully.

"Anne, there may come a time when I shall have to be very brave indeed." Katharine put her arm about her sister. "Speak what is in your mind, dearest. You talk of four men of Windsor, and you think of two Queens. Remember, I have an advantage over them. I know what happened to them; though they, poor souls, had no indications of what they would come to. All will be well, I promise you. The King is fond of me and he grows fonder."

"Dearest sister," said Anne, "I would that you were merely my sister and not my Queen."

In the darkness of the royal bedchamber the Queen whispered to the King: "My Lord, you are pleased with me?"

The King's laugh was a deep, satisfied rumble.

"Your Grace has been good to me."

"Well, sweetheart, that is what I would wish to be to one who pleases me as you do."

"In my happiness I think of others less happy."

"That's like you, Kate. You're a kind woman."

"I trust my ways do not displease you."

"And what is all this talk of pleasing and displeasing? It seems that women talk in this way when they would ask a favor."

"You are clever. You follow the workings of my mind."

"I am well versed, Kate, in the ways of women."

"It is of those men of Windsor so recently arrested that I think. They have been condemned to the flames."

The King grunted. This was no time to talk of state matters. He wished Kate would ask for something for herself, some ornament, some fancy velvets to make a gown. Now, first, she must ask that his daughters might be reinstated; then she must ask for money for them. He had given way to her there. Now she was going to plead for these heretics who were condemned to die.

"Poor Marbeck!" she said.

"Aye!" said the King. "Poor Marbeck." The man had an enchanting voice. A plague on Gardiner for arresting him. Why should he interfere with the King's pleasure? For Marbeck, with his pleasant singing, had brought pleasure to his King. "It would be well if Marbeck's accusers spent their time in no worse way than he does," growled Henry.

Katharine felt exultant. "Your Majesty will pardon this man?"

Henry himself had been thinking of doing that; but he was not going to say that he would immediately. Katharine was going to ask a pardon for all four, and he did not wish to pardon them all. He was not going to allow men to act with impunity against himself; and these men, in acting against laws which he had approved, were acting against him.

Blood must flow, he reasoned. If any lift the mildest voice against the King's command, blood must flow . . . or, as in this case, flesh must burn.

He could not therefore pardon all the offenders; but he liked Marbeck. What if he gave Marbeck to Katharine? But the other three would have to go to Gardiner.

"Kate," he said, "this man has been condemned. Books have been found in his house."

He felt the Queen's shiver, and he knew that, had he allowed those men to search her apartments, they would have found similar books there. Well well, let her read her books for the time being; it was pleasant to discourse with a woman of good sense.

"Pardon them, my dearest lord," pleaded Katharine. "Show your clemency."

"Only fools show clemency, Kate. If I let those men go free, what would happen, think you? Others would proclaim themselves heretics without more ado."

"Only those who do so in secret already would do that."

"When men practice in secret what they fear to do in the open, that is not a good thing, Kate. Perhaps we should find more of these rogues."

"No, my lord, I beg of you."

"There, sweetheart. You are a woman and soft. You plead for these men because it is in your nature to be soft with all. You are our Queen—our well-loved Queen. We will do something to show you our regard."

"Thank you. Thank you, Your Majesty."

"I give you Marbeck."

"A thousand thanks, Your Grace. And Pearson. . . . Testwood and Filmer?"

"You're greedy, Kate. No. Take Marbeck, and be grateful. I cannot interfere further with justice, even for your sake."

"My lord . . ."

"The matter is closed, sweetheart."

She was silent, and the King smiled smugly in the darkness. He felt loving and benign. He had granted his Queen's request, and he had saved his friend Marbeck, which, after all, he had long made up his mind to do.

Gardiner was pleased with the Windsor episode. As he explained to Wriothesley, the Queen had Marbeck, but they had kept the other three for the flames which had now consumed them. This was no true victory for the Queen, as the King himself had not wished Marbeck to die and would doubtless have saved him even if the Queen had not asked for his life.

"The woman is soft and a fool," said Gardiner. "She should have asked for one of the others and left Marbeck to rely on the King's favor. Well, she is new to her position and I prophesy that she will not long hold it. And this is not an end to the matter. I have set the good Dr. London to pursue his inquiries, and ere long he will have more men and women to bring up for examination. And this time, Master Secretary, I think he might look a little higher. Oh, not so high as I intend him to go, but creeping up, creeping upward."

"The Queen will protect her friends."

"She has no chance against us. Remember there is the Act to suppress what is called the New Learning. Has not the King himself said that the ignorant people have contaminated and perverted the Scriptures by their translations, and that these translations are not in accordance with the Catholic Church of which he is head? Tyndale's translation has been condemned as crafty and false. It is an offense to be in possession of such books. As for those who add to their sins by further translating and writing, they deserve the flames. If these people are allowed to proceed, the Latin tongue will become a dead one. The three men of Windsor have been rightly burned under the Act of the Six Articles. Rest assured that more arrests will follow. And very soon we may be in a position to take our aim at the main target, eh, Wriothesley, my friend?"

Gardiner was smiling as he spoke. Soon he hoped to see Cranmer fall with Katharine Parr, as Wolsey had with Anne Boleyn, Cromwell with Anne of Cleves. And after Cranmer it would be the turn of those men who had become the greatest enemies of all—the Seymour brothers, Lord Hertford and Sir Thomas. As brothers-in-law of the King, they had enjoyed special favor since

Henry's marriage with their sister; but as uncles of Edward they would be more dangerous still. Gardiner believed that Edward would still be a boy at the time of his accession and, if he were, he could easily be the tool of his uncles. Lord Hertford was constantly with the boy, molding him, dominating him. Hertford was not only an ambitious man; he was also a strong one. He would aim to be nominally the Protector of England and in actuality England's ruler. Sir Thomas Seymour was even more to be suspected, for while the boy Edward feared his elder uncle he doted on the younger. It would, therefore, be a masterstroke to have the two brothers in their graves before the accession of their nephew. And why not? Powerful as they were, they leaned toward Protestantism, and that created a flaw in their armor. Moreover, Thomas had cast his eyes in the Queen's direction.

These were ambitious schemes, in which Gardiner would need the help of the entire Catholic Party; they were not, however, impossible of achievement, if crafty patience were employed; and employed it should be.

He could visualize a future with the Lady Mary on the throne—Queen Mary, that true and loyal supporter of the Catholic cause. It might well happen in his lifetime, and he doubted not that if it did he would be one of those whom she would raise to a lofty eminence. He must be beside the Queen; he must teach her what should be done with heretics. When he contemplated his good Catholic Queen Mary on the throne he could almost smell the fires of Smithfield.

"Have no fear, my dear Wriothesley," he said now. "Our good friend Dr. London will smell out our enemies. I think you will be surprised when he has done his work. We can rely on that man's help."

In a way Gardiner was right. When Dr. London contemplated the future he saw a similar picture to that conjured up by Gardiner: Queen Mary on the throne and the Catholics triumphant.

He was very anxious to show himself a good Catholic, and how could he do this better than by pleasing the Catholic Bishop of Winchester and the King's Catholic Secretary?

They had brought down the little game; now they looked higher.

"But not too high, good Doctor." Those were the very words.

As usual he selected his victims, and his choice fell on the learned Dr. Haines who had been the Dean of Exeter and was now a Prebendary of Windsor. But he would go even higher than that; he would creep a little closer to that one who he knew was the most important on the list. He would go to the Queen's household and select Sir Philip and Lady Hoby, together with Sir Thomas Carden. He would also take some of the minor gentlemen and ladies. That would suffice.

He outlined his plan to his friend Simons, the lawyer who had been a great help in the affair of the men of Windsor.

"A difficulty presents itself here," said the wily lawyer. "We need evidence, and we have not the King's permission to search the royal apartments."

Dr. London confessed himself to be in a quandary. These people he had selected, he knew, had interested themselves in the New Learning, but how could he prove it?

He was disturbed, but, remembering the methods he and his master Cromwell had used during the dissolution of the monasteries, he decided on a plan of action. After all, had not the Bishop of Winchester something like this in mind when he had selected the experienced Dr. London for this task?

"It would be necessary," said Simons, "for us to find men who would testify against them. That would not be easy."

"We have not been given enough power," said Dr. London. "Did not the three men who have recently been burned at the stake mention the names of these people?"

Simons looked at the Doctor sharply.

"That was not so, Doctor."

"An oversight. Doubtless had we tried to extract these names from them we should have done so."

"But we did not."

"There was written evidence of what these men said during examination, was there not?"

"There was."

"And where are these documents?"

"In the hands of the clerk of the court."

"A man named Ockham. I know him well. He should be easy to handle."

"What do you propose, Doctor?"

"My good man, the evidence is not there

because of an oversight. It is always possible to remedy such oversights."

"Do you mean to . . . forge evidence . . . to insert something those men did not say concerning and implicating these men and women?"

"Hush," said the Doctor. "You speak too freely."

"But that . . . would be criminal."

"My dear lawyer, when the Bishop of Winchester asks for victims, he must have them."

"You wish me to see . . . Ockham?"

"I will see the fellow." The Doctor laid his hand on Simons' shoulder. "Do not tremble, man. This is the task which has been set us. Success is expected of us; never doubt that we shall achieve it."

The Queen sat in her apartment with a few of her ladies. They were working at their tapestry, but the Queen's thoughts were far away.

On a stool beside her sat little Jane Grey. The child attracted Katharine. She was so small and so beautiful. She was only six years old, but she was wise enough for eleven; she was also clever with her needle, and most happy to be beside the Queen.

Little Jane believed that one day she might be a Queen. Edward had whispered to her that he would ask if she might be his, when he was of an age to ask. They wanted to marry him, he believed, to his cousin, young Mary of Scotland, but he was not sure, because such a matter as the choice of his wife would not be mentioned to him just yet. He had heard too that Mary had been promised to the King of France, and that his father was very angry about that. "But I am not, Jane," he had said, "and you know why."

They had smiled and nodded because they understood each other so well.

So Jane, who might one day be a Queen of England, liked to study the ways of the present Queen, and she found that study of great interest to her. She knew when the Queen was frightened as she was today, although she did not know the cause of her fear.

The tapestry was beautiful. In the center was a medallion about which flowers were being worked in gold and scarlet, blue and green silks. At each corner was a dragon with crimson fire coming from its mouth; and it was on one of these dragons that Jane herself was working.

It is a sad thing, I verily believe, to be a Queen, pondered Jane as she stitched at her dragon.

It was also a sad thing to be a King—a little King. It was all very well when you were mighty and all-powerful as was the King himself. It was when you were a little boy who was unsure of himself, as all young people must be, that it was alarming. It was only when they were in the apartments with Mrs. Sybil Penn that they were really unafraid. Mrs. Penn refused to look upon the Prince as the future King; he was her little one, she always said; and she would rock him on her knee and bathe his skin and croon over him; she would mutter threats against his tutors and his riding masters, and tell Jane that they should not long treat her little princeling as they did.

Edward would sit there contentedly in Mrs. Penn's lap and Jane would sit at her feet.

"Jane," the young Prince would say, "now let us play at being children."

Jane intended to look after him when she

grew up; that was why, if she were to be his
Queen, she wished to know all about
queenly duties.

Life was so difficult. It changed so
quickly. The Princesses Mary and Elizabeth
were now often at court and consequently
the children saw less of them. It seemed a
long time since Uncle Thomas Seymour had
sailed away. Edward complained bitterly of
his loss.

"It all changes so quickly, Jane," he had
said, his brow puckered so that Jane knew
that he was thinking that soon the greatest
change of all might come: the day when
Prince Edward would become King Edward.

And now, what was it that was worrying
this dearest of Queens? She was preoccu-
pied; she was not paying attention to what
her ladies said; every now and then she
would glance toward the door as though
she expected to see someone enter, someone whose coming would be very important; as though she longed for it and yet she
dreaded it.

Jane knew that some of the ladies and
gentlemen of the court had disappeared
suddenly. Among them were Sir Philip and
Lady Hoby and Sir Thomas Carden. People

did go away suddenly, and when you asked
for news of them, strange looks appeared
on people's faces.

Jane had often traveled along the river
from Greenwich to Hampton and she had
seen that gloomy fortress of the Tower. She
had heard terrible stories of what went on
behind those gray stone walls; and she
knew also that when people looked as they
looked now when the names of Sir Thomas
Carden and the Hobys were mentioned,
that meant that those of whom one inquired
had gone to the Tower.

Katharine, as she stitched at her tapestry,
was marveling at her own temerity. Her sister Anne had been against what she had
done, had implored her not to interfere.

"Discard these new ideas," Anne had
pleaded. "Shut your mind to them. These
people are beginning to look to you as a
leader. You know what these arrests mean.
They mean that Gardiner and Wriothesley
are working against you. They have marked
you for their victim."

Anne was right. Katharine knew these
things to be true. She was a meek woman,
but she had a mind and she could not shut
it to ideas, however dangerous. If she

thought they were the right ideas she must accept them; she must read, and be true to herself; and because of some urge within her she must accept Gardiner's challenge.

She had said to Anne: "How can these men possibly have found evidence against the Hobys and Carden? I know they are in possession of books, but those books remain in their apartments. The King has not given his permission that the castle shall be searched."

"Someone has informed against them."

"I do not believe it. Who would have done so? None but our friends here at court knows of their connection with the New Faith. And none of our friends has been questioned. We know that." It came to her as an inspiration. After all, she was no fool. Had not the Bishop appointed that rogue Dr. London to work for him, and did not Katharine know in what manner London's evidence against the abbeys had been compiled?

From that inspiration grew another: If he were going to prove that some had spoken against the men and women of the Queen's household, who could be better informants than dead men who could not speak for themselves? At the house of the clerk of the court would be those documents which had been written at the time of the examination of the three martyrs. If those papers could be seized and they could be proved to contain forgeries, not only would Katharine's friends be saved, but her enemies would be exposed.

It was bold, but she felt the need to be bold. The right action—if her suspicions were correct—could save not only her friends now, but perhaps herself in the future.

She had not hesitated. This day, while the court was sitting, she had sent men on whom she could rely to the house of the clerk of the court. They would seize those documents on her authority.

If she had made a false step her position would be an unenviable one, but the King was still very kindly disposed toward her; if she were right, then would she be triumphant indeed.

No wonder she was nervous. No wonder she kept glancing toward the door.

She looked down and saw the wondering eyes fixed upon her. Was it sympathy she saw in those lovely eyes? Katharine stooped and kissed the upturned face.

"Jane, my dear," she said, "you shall come to my chamber. We will find a post for you. Oh, you are over-young to be a maid of honor, but you shall be there to serve me, because it pleases me to have you with me."

Jane kissed the hand of her royal benefactress and expressed her thanks in the solemn manner which was habitual to her.

She wished she knew what ailed the Queen.

The King was furious. The trial of those members of the Queen's household had been proved to be full of trickery. The clerk of the court had been arrested; papers had been found at his home which contained forgery, inserted by him to implicate the arrested men and women. Dr. London and Lawyer Simons, together with the clerk, had been concocting evidence.

He sent for Gardiner and berated him severely.

Gardiner swore he had been deceived by Dr. London and the lawyer.

"Then let them feel our wrath!" cried the King.

His eyes narrowed, and they told Gardiner, although the King spoke not a word of this matter, that he understood these accusations, purporting to be directed against members of the household, were meant to involve his Primate Cranmer and the Queen; and that if more such tricks were played it would be Gardiner himself who felt the weight of the King's displeasure.

Henry reflected: I'd dismiss this fellow now if he, being so sly, were not so useful to me.

As it was he would be content with the punishment of others.

"Let this Dr. London be set in the pillories of Newbury and Reading and Windsor. Let papers be attached to his person, notifying all who can read them that he has committed perjury, so that all may know what the King's will is toward those who would accuse the innocent."

The King raged up and down the apartment, calling God to witness that he was a just King. He shook his fist at Gardiner.

"Remember it, Bishop. Remember it."

Gardiner was trembling when he left the royal presence.

He found Wriothesley and told him that it

would be unwise to take further action against the Queen for the time being. They had underrated her. They had thought her weak, and this she most certainly was not.

"It would seem," said Wriothesley wryly, "that all we have done is to bring to the stake three men of little importance, while much harm has been done to ourselves in the eyes of the King."

"You are impatient, sir," said Gardiner testily. "We have lost the first battle, but it is the last one that proclaims the victor. This would not have happened but for the fact that the King's marriage is as yet young. In a few months . . . in a year . . . he will have ceased to love Madame Katharine. His eyes will have fixed themselves on another lady. We have acted too soon, and London was a fool. Many men are exposed in these matters of policy . . . exposed as fools. There is no place for fools. Let us not accuse each other of folly. We will wait and, ere long, I promise you, Katharine Parr will go the way of the others."

In her apartments Katharine embraced her friends who had returned unharmed from their imprisonment. They fell on their knees and thanked her; she was their savior and they owed their lives to her courage.

"Do not rejoice too soon," warned her sister.

But Katharine kissed Anne tenderly. She felt strong now. She had made up her mind as to how she should act in a future crisis; it would be as her integrity demanded.

"Beware of my lord Bishop," whispered Anne.

And afterward, Katharine often heard those words when the hangings rustled or when the wind howled through the trees.

"Beware . . . Beware . . . Beware of my lord Bishop."

They mingled with those words which seemed to come from the tolling of the bells.

The first year of Katharine's life as Henry the Eighth's sixth Queen was slowly passing.

It was full of alarms as startling and terrifying as those sudden attacks of Gardiner and his Catholics. During the year, Gardiner had seemed to turn his attention from her to Cranmer; and contemplating the manner in which the Catholic Party had plotted for the downfall of the Primate Thomas Cranmer, and noting how on two occasions it was the King himself who had saved Cranmer, Katharine was comforted. The King, it seemed, could feel real affection for some. In the case of Cranmer, the astute monarch, knowing his well-loved Thomas to be in danger, had presented him with a ring which he might show to the Council as a token of the royal regard. None, of course, had dared attack a man who was possessed of such a token. On another occasion when the Catholics had wished to set up a Commission for the examining and discovery of heretics, the King had given his consent to the formation of this Commission but had foiled the purpose of it—which was to ensnare the Archbishop of Canterbury—by setting none other than that Archbishop, Thomas Cranmer, at the head of it.

Yes, the King had his affections and loyalties. But would he feel for Katharine the same regard he had shown to Cranmer?

How often during the passing months had the King demanded of his wife: "No sign of a child?"

Once he had said: "By God, I have, I verily believe, got me another barren wife!"

That had been said after a state banquet when he had been feeling more sprightly than was his habit, for his leg had been in one of its healing phases and he had been listening to the singing of one of the ladies, a very beautiful lady, whose person pleased him as well as her voice had charmed him.

"No sign of a child?" The words were ominous; and the glance which accompanied them had been one of dislike.

But a few days later the leg had started to pain more than ever, and it was Katharine, that gentle nurse, to whom he turned. He was calling her his little pig again; and when the beautiful young lady begged leave to sing His Majesty another song, he said: "Another time. Another time."

How strange, thought Katharine, with that philosophy which had come to her since she had become the Queen, that the King's infirmity, which made him so irritable with others, should be her salvation!

Uneasy weeks flowed past her. There were nights when she would wake up after a dream and put her hands about her neck, laughing a little, half mocking herself, saying with a touch of hysteria in her voice: "So, my dear head, you are still on my shoulders?"

She was a little frightened of that hysteria. It was new to her. She had always been so calm, so serene. But how could one remain calm when one was close to death?

But what a fool she was to brood on death. It seemed far away when she sat with the courtiers, and the King would lift his heavily bandaged leg and lay it across her lap. " 'Tis easier there," he would say. "Why, Kate," he added once in a rush of grateful affection, "there would appear to be some magic in you, for it seems you impart a cooling to the heat, that soothes my sores."

"Good Kate, good Kate," he would say; and sometimes he would caress her cheek or her bare shoulder. "Little pig," he would call her and give her a ruby or a diamond. "Here, Kate, we like to see you wearing our jewels. They become you . . . they become you." They were gifts given in order to soothe his conscience; they indicated that he was planning to replace her by some fresh victim who had caught his eye; then because of infirmity and age he would decide not to make the effort; if his wife could not always charm him, the nurse, when pain returned, had become a necessity.

It was about this time that the King de-

cided he would have a new portrait of himself.

Katharine remembered that occasion for
a long time afterward, and remembered it
with fear. It seemed to her that this matter of
the portrait showed her—and the court—
how dangerous was her position. The King,
when he tired of a woman, could be the cru-
elest of men. He believed he himself was always in the right, and that must mean that
anyone not quite in agreement with him
must be quite wrong.

Katharine's great sin against the King lay
in her barrenness. So, after a year of marriage, the King constantly brooded on the
fact that there was no child . . . no sign of a
child. Why, he would say to himself, with the
others there were pregnancies. Seven, was
it, with the first Katharine? Four with Anne
Boleyn, two with Jane and one with
Catharine Howard. He remembered wryly
that he had given Anne of Cleves no opportunity to become the mother of a child of
his. Katharine Parr had had her opportunities and there was not even a sign.

Did this mean that God did not approve
of his sixth marriage?

When this King imagined that God did not

approve of a wife, it could be assumed that he was looking for another. And he could not more clearly expose to the court his state of mind on this matter than he did over the affair of the portrait.

His health had improved; he had been recently bled and his ulcers were healing, so that he could move about with greater ease than of late. In this false spring he had been struck by the beauty of one of the ladies of the Queen's bedchamber.

His little eyes grew mean as he considered the manner in which he would have his portrait painted. It had occurred to him that Katharine, his wife, was a little too clever with her tongue. He did not like clever women over-much. The thought made him mourn afresh for little Catharine Howard. The ambassadors and emissaries from other countries seemed to find pleasure in the conversation of this present Queen, and this appeared to delight her. He fancied she gave herself airs. She would have to learn that they paid homage to her because she was his Queen and not because of her accomplishments. He wished to show her that though he had raised her up, he could put her down.

There was that fellow Holbein. He was paid thirty pounds a year. Let him earn his money.

He sent for the man. He had a weakness for those who excelled in the arts. He often declared that, had he not been burdened with matters of state, he would have devoted himself to the writing of poetry and the composing of music. But Master Holbein had painted some fine pictures since he had been introduced to the court by Sir Thomas More. There were two allegorical and certainly very beautiful paintings by the man, on the walls of a salon at White Hall; and there were in addition many portraits of the royal household and the nobility.

The King, however, was not altogether pleased with Master Holbein. He remembered how the fellow had deceived him with a portrait of his fourth wife, Anne of Cleves, representing her as a beautiful woman. Whenever the King saw the painter he would be reminded of the shock he had received when he had gone, with a handsome present of sables, to meet the original of the picture. Ah! The horror, when he had looked into that pockmarked face, so different from the Holbein representation!

Moreover the man revived other memories. It was in More's Chelsea house that he had first met him; and so the painter reminded the King of More, the great man— the greatest statesman of his age, he had been called—the family man who loved to joke with his sons and daughters and who had sought to evade the glories of office when he could not accept them with honor. The King would never forget how More's daughter had stolen her father's head from London Bridge, and how the people had quickly called the man a saint. Saint! thought Henry angrily. People were too ready to apply that word to any who lost his head. Had not More been jubilant at the prospect of burning heretics at Smithfield?

Ah yes, the King liked to remember that. More had not been all softness, not all saintliness. True, he had gone to the block for his beliefs, but one did not forget the Smithfield fires. Every time he smelled the smoke, heard the crackle of flames, he could think of Thomas More . . . *Saint* Thomas More.

He was sage enough to know that these thoughts came to him because he was growing old. Being all-powerful here on

Earth, he must yet placate the invisible powers; and sometimes, with the pain on him and the hot blood pounding through his veins, he could fancy his end was not far off; then the fears multiplied, the uncertainties returned; and then it was consoling to remember the faults of other men.

"Now, Master Holbein," he growled, "I pay you well, and I want you to earn your money. We want a picture of ourselves. We want something larger and grander than anything you have done before. Yes, we will have a picture of our family. My son, my daughters, my . . . Queen. You will start tomorrow."

Hans Holbein bowed. Nothing, he declared, would give him greater pleasure, and he would be eager to start on the royal portrait the next day.

And during that day the lady of the bedchamber, who had caught the King's eye, sang a song of his which greatly charmed him. A strong-looking girl, he reflected, with health as well as beauty. A girl molded to bear children.

When he was alone with the Queen that night he said: "It is a marvelous thing that God denies me a son." And the look which accompanied the words was that which Katharine had begun to dread more than any other.

The next day when Hans Holbein came to the King, Henry's resentment had increased. His son and daughters stood before him, and he surveyed his daughters with distaste, his son with apprehension.

In health he felt well; his leg scarcely pained him at all. Before leaving his chamber he had examined himself in his mirror; he had seen a magnificent figure in a gown of gold and scarlet drawn in at the waist with a sash of white satin, its short skirts embroidered in gold; about his neck was a collar of pearls and rubies; his dalmatica was lined with sables and decorated with pearls to match those in his collar. More than usual he glittered with jewels, and if he did not look too closely he could imagine he was young again.

"By God!" he had told his reflection. "I feel I have many years of health left to me. Have I once more saddled myself with a woman who cannot give me sons?"

He looked at her now, at her meek eyes and gentle mouth. He did not want gentle meekness; they were all very well for a sick man; but when a man feels himself to be in good health and hopes to be cured of the accursed humors in his leg, he does not wish to waste his time with a barren nurse. He wants fire and fertility.

The Prince looked pale, and the crimson cap of velvet with its feather and jewels merely accentuated his pallor; the red damask garment did not suit him, and no amount of artful padding could hide the fact that he was thin and puny.

The two girls in their crimson velvet gowns, wearing their pearl and ruby crosses, angered him; the elder because she reminded him of his first Queen (and he did not wish to be reminded of his past and the Spanish woman's reproaches), the younger because she was the most healthy of his children and had failed to be born a boy.

The picture would be of himself, his children and his Queen; but he would not have Katharine in it. This was a family portrait, and had she helped him to add to his family? She had not.

He growled his instructions. "I will sit as though on my throne, and the boy shall stand beside me. Come here, my son. Let my daughters take their stand by the pillars there, and my Queen should be beside me." He glowered maliciously at Katharine. "Methinks though that there should be another beside me on this day, and that is the Queen who gave me my son."

There was silence. Hans Holbein looked uncomfortable. Katharine forced herself not to show the fear that came to her whenever the King talked in this way.

Henry had seated himself. His son and daughters took the places he had assigned to them. Only Edward dared to look compassionately at the Queen.

"I have it!" cried Henry. "You shall paint the boy's mother beside me. Queen Jane must be the Queen in this family group. She is dead, and that fact grieves me sorely, but she was our Queen; she was the mother of our son. I will have you set her beside me, sir painter. You understand?"

"I shall be for ever at Your Gracious Majesty's command."

"She will be painted pale and shadowy . . . almost like a specter . . . as though she has come from her grave to join our family group. So, madam" (he had thrown a malevolent glance at Katharine), "we shall have no need of your presence here."

Katharine bowed and retired.

This was the greatest insult she had received since her marriage, and it filled her with a terrible fear. It could mean only one thing: the King regretted his marriage. When Henry the Eighth started to regret a marriage he was already looking for a new wife.

Everyone at court now knew how the picture was being painted; all had heard of the spectral Queen.

Gardiner and Wriothesley congratulated each other. Now was surely the time to strike.

Cranmer and Hertford were watchful of Gardiner and Wriothesley. Katharine's closest friends were nervous. As for Katharine herself, she thought constantly of her predecessors who had walked out to Tower Green and died there, for she felt her time was near.

The bells rang jubilantly: Sons . . . sons . . . sons. . . .

And all through the court there was tension and a sense of waiting.

→>-<←

Fate, in the guise of War, distracted Henry's attention.

There had for some months been trouble in Scotland. It was Henry's dearest wish that his son should marry Mary, the baby Queen of Scots, and so bring Scotland and England under one crown. This the French King wished to oppose with all his might. François planned to remove the child and bring her up at his court as the future wife of his eldest son. He had sent ships and supplies to Scotland, and the Scots thereupon repudiated the promises they had made to Henry and began to negotiate with France.

Henry's great ideal was a British Empire; he realized that a marriage between Scotland and France would make this impossible. He decided therefore that the only course open to him at this stage was a war on two fronts.

The Emperor Charles had been seeking England as an ally against France, and Henry decided to join forces with the Spaniard. He had sent troops to the north of France under Thomas Seymour and Sir John Wallop; he was sending his brother-in-law the Earl of Hertford to Scotland. Henry decided that he himself would go to France for the attack; he and the Emperor planned to meet triumphantly in Paris when that city fell to them.

Temporarily Henry had ceased to think of a seventh wife.

There must be a Regent in England, and if his wife had ceased to appeal to him as a bedfellow, nevertheless he could trust her to act in his name during his absence. With Cranmer and Hertford to help her, he decided he could safely leave England and cross with his Army to France.

Thus on a July day he set out for Dover and reached Calais in safety.

While deeply aware of the immense responsibility which now rested upon her, and aware also of what reward would be hers if she failed in her duty, Katharine could feel nothing but relief. After all, when one was married to a man who had murdered two wives and terrified and humiliated three others, one must be prepared for alarms; and it was possible, if not to feel contempt for death, to be less unnerved by the contemplation of it.

He had gone; and she was free, if only for a little while. She rejoiced in secret.

He had parted from her with loving assur-

ances of his devotion, but before he had left
he had given her a special charge with regard to Prince Edward.

"We cannot get ourselves another son,"
he had said reproachfully, "so we must
guard well him whom we have."

When he had kissed her fondly she had
known he was thinking: A whole year and
no sign of a son! Doubtless, as he crossed
the Channel under his sails of cloth of gold,
he was telling himself that he was a patient
man and that a year was a very long time to
wait for the sign of a son.

One day when she was with the children,
superintending their studies, word was
brought to her that a lady had presented
herself at court and, stating that she was a
friend of the Queen, asked if an audience
might be granted her.

Katharine bade the messenger say that
as soon as she was free she would see the
lady; and shortly afterward there was
brought to her a young woman, tall and
slender, a pale primrose of a woman, with
golden hair, and deep blue eyes in which
seemed to burn an emotion not of this
world.

"Your dearest Majesty . . ." The young woman knelt before the Queen.

"Why, Anne! It is Anne Askew. Though I suppose I should call you Mistress Kyme now that you have married. Rise, my dear Anne. I would hear your news."

"Pray call me Anne Askew, Your Majesty, as you did in the old days, for that is how I wish to be known from now on."

Katharine, seeing signs of distress in the face of her friend, dismissed her attendants with the exception of little Jane, whom she sent to her needlework in the far corner of the apartment.

"What has happened?" asked Katharine.

"I have left my husband. Or perhaps it would be truer to say that he has sent me from him."

"He has turned you out of his house?"

"I fear so, Your Majesty."

Anne laughed without mirth.

"I am sorry, Anne," said Katharine.

"Do not look so sorrowful, Your Majesty. It is no great sorrow to me. I was married to Mr. Kyme, as you know, because he is the richest man in Lincolnshire. He was to have had my elder sister, but she died before the marriage contract could be completed; and so, my father gave me to him. I had no wish for the marriage . . . nor indeed for any marriage."

"Alas," said Katharine, "such as we are, we have our marriages made for us. Our wishes are not consulted."

She thought of her own three marriages, particularly of the present one.

"And now," she went on, "he has turned you out of his house?"

"Yes, Your Majesty. I was forced to marry him, but I cannot be compelled to abandon my religion."

"So, Anne, he has discovered where your sympathies lie?"

"How could I deny them?" She stood before the Queen, her eyes a burning blue, her hands clenched. "Your Majesty, there is one true religion and one only. I have studied much in the last few years. I know that there is only one way to the salvation of England, and that is for her to adopt the true religion, the religion of Martin Luther."

"Hush, Anne! Hush!"

Katharine looked fearfully about her; the little girl in the corner had her head bent low over her needlework.

"There are times when I think I am past caring what becomes of me," said Anne.

"Heads have rolled in the straw because their owners have dared say words such as you have just said," the Queen reminded her severely.

"Your Majesty would betray me?"

"Anne! How can you say such a thing! I am your friend. You have my sympathy. I too love the new learning. But I pray you, have a care what you say. Terrible things happen in the torture chambers of the Tower. Have you ever heard the shrieks of agony at Smithfield stakes? So recently three gentlemen of Windsor were burned to death."

"Such shrieks," said Anne, "are but the triumphant shouts of martyrs."

"Martyrs indeed, poor souls!" said Katharine. "And, methinks, there are some of us who are born to wear the martyrs' crown. But let us not be rash, dear Anne. You have come to me now because you have nowhere else to go, since your husband has turned you out. Is that so?"

"I put myself under Your Grace's protection."

"Rest assured, my dear friend, that I shall do everything in my power to help you. You shall stay here; but Anne, have a care. We are surrounded by enemies here. Your movements will be watched. You will be spied on. Oh, Anne, have a care."

Anne knelt and kissed the Queen's hands.

Katharine was uneasy. This burning love of the new religion in Anne Askew bordered on fanaticism. She guessed that it had been enhanced by her experiences. Anne should never have been forced into marriage with Mr. Kyme nor with anyone. Anne was not meant for marriage; she was without the desire for physical love.

Katharine longed to help Anne. She decided she would give her a place at court and see that she had leisure for her reading and study. And above all she would try to infuse into Anne the need for caution.

Katharine found that the very absence of the King brought fresh fears to her.

The heat was intense that summer. From the noisome pits and sloughs of the highways rose the stench of decaying refuse. In the narrow streets flanked by houses with their high gabled roofs and the stories which projected one above another, the atmosphere was stifling although the sunlight was almost shut out. The hovels in which the poor lived were made of wood and clay and, in them, vermin flourished. The rushes on the floors were added to month by month and not removed until they were halfway up the walls; they abounded with lice; the dogs slept in them; bones and gristle lay rotting beneath the top layer; and it was only when the noses of the inhabitants, long accustomed to the smell of decay and sewage, were nauseated beyond endurance that any attempt was made to "sweeten." The windows were small and not made to open, and the sick lay with the healthy on the malodorous rushes.

And one day a man, walking along the highway which connected the Strand with the village of Charing, collapsed and lay there on the road; when he was discovered it was seen that his face was covered with spots and was of a dark purple color. Some who saw him recognized the symptoms and turned shuddering away. There was nothing to be done for him; he had but a few hours to live.

Later that day one body was discovered by the Church of St. Clement Danes and another in Gray's Inn Lane; more were found on the causeway leading from Aldgate to Whitechapel Church.

The news spread. The plague had once more come to London.

When Katharine heard the news, her first thoughts were for the young Prince. She was terrified. He was so weak that she felt he might be a ready prey for any fever that stalked the town.

She watched him; he seemed listless; and she could see that his headache was more acute than usual.

Should she shut him into his apartments, order that none should approach him, and hope that the pollution would not reach him? Or should she take the risk of riding through the plague-infested streets, far away to some spot as yet unvisited by the plague?

She was uncertain. Haunted by visions of the King's wrath if any harm should come to the all-important heir, she could not help putting her hands about her neck and shivering. She was no martyr. She was no Anne Askew. She wanted to live, even though she must not so much as think of the man she loved, even though she must be on perpetual guard against her enemies.

While the King had been away she had conducted herself with caution. Cranmer and Hertford, without whose advice she would not have dreamed of acting, were pleased with her, admiring her calm judgment. She herself had written regularly to the King, and in a manner which she knew would please him. Hypocritical, some might say those letters were. Always she applauded his greatness, speaking of him as though he were a god rather than a King, stressing her gratitude for the honor he had done her when he raised her to the throne.

What is a woman to do, she asked herself, when any false step might cost her her life? And is it not better to try to believe that I am honored and should be grateful, to make an attempt to see myself as the King sees me, rather than to rail against my fate? It is the presence of Anne Askew that has set me despising myself. Anne would never demean herself with hypocrisy. Anne would tell the truth and nothing but the truth. She would die rather than write or act a lie. But how different we are! Anne cares nothing for life, and I want to live; I want desperately to live.

In her heart she knew why. The King was

not a healthy man; he was many years older than she was . . . older than Sir Thomas Seymour. Thomas had said: "The future is ours." She could not help it if she longed for the future, if, while she tried to do her duty as the wife of the King and to accept the cruel fate which had been thrust upon her, she tried also to put the best face upon it and to give herself courage by believing that it could not last for ever and that she would outlive it.

She did not want to die, and if it were necessary to write those fulsome letters, to flatter the monster who could cut off her head with a stroke of the pen, then she would be a hypocrite. She would at least fight for her life.

During Henry's absence the campaign in Scotland had, mercifully, gone well for the English. Hertford had sacked both Leith and Edinburgh; and Katharine had been able to send this joyful news to the King. Henry himself was full of optimism. François was already putting out inquiries for a secret peace, but Henry had for some time cast longing eyes on Boulogne and did not intend to leave the soil of France until he had captured the town.

Henry was satisfied with the way the regency was being conducted, but if anything were to happen to the little Prince, he would certainly blame the consort who had so far failed to provide him with another boy. Moreover, if the heir to the throne died, it would seem imperative that the King find a wife who could supply an heir.

What can I do? Katharine asked herself. Get him out of London to the country, or stay here? Which would be the greater risk?

Lady Jane Grey was watching her. The child was always watching her.

"What is it, Jane?" asked the Queen, laying her hands on the soft curls.

The little girl said: "Your Majesty is uneasy. I would I could do something to help."

Katharine bent and kissed the pretty head. "You do much to help me with your presence," she told Jane. "You are like my own child. I wish to God you were."

"Is that what ails Your Majesty . . . that you have no children?"

Katharine did not answer. She bent swiftly and kissed the child again.

The wise little creature had struck right at the root of her fears. If she had a child, if she had a son, she would have no need to be continually in fear of losing her life. If Princess Elizabeth had been a boy, it might well have happened that Anne Boleyn would still be alive and on the throne.

Yes, that was the very root of her troubles. It was the old cry of "Sons!"

"Have you seen the Prince today, Jane?"

"Yes, Your Majesty."

"And how was he?"

"He had the pain in his head and he was tired."

Then Katharine made up her mind suddenly.

"Go to the Prince, Jane. Tell him we are leaving for the country. We leave this very day. Go, my dear, quickly. I wish to leave as soon as possible."

Katharine was proved to be right in the action she had taken. The plague had died down with the passing of the hot weather, and the little Prince's health was no worse than it had been before his father left England.

Katharine had been fortunate during those months of the regency. Might it not be that fortune had decided to favor her? She was full of hope.

The King came home not altogether displeased with the way affairs had gone abroad. He had taken Boulogne; but it was not long before he and Charles had fallen out. They had been uneasy allies. The enemy was a common one, but the motives of the two allies were quite different. Henry wished to force the French to abandon Scotland to the might of England; Charles wished François to give up his claim to Milan and his help to the German Princes. The Emperor, convinced that Henry's possession of the town of Boulogne would satisfy him, and that having achieved it he would desert his ally, made a secret peace with the French. Henry was furious. The French and the Spaniards were now allies, and England was their enemy. It was necessary for him to return to England, for there was a possibility that the French might attempt an invasion of his island. This he did, leaving Boulogne heavily fortified. Yet, he was not displeased. He had set out to capture Boulogne and he had captured the town; he swore to keep it, no matter at what cost.

There had been great rejoicing at the capture of Boulogne all through the country, and the King returned, a conquering hero.

The journey across the water had not improved his health. The sores on his leg were spreading; the other leg had become infected; and both were so swollen that it was difficult for him to move about his apartments. A chair on wheels was made for him, and this had to be pushed about by his attendants and carried up staircases.

All this did not improve the royal temper; yet again Katharine realized that his infirmity made her more important to him, and her position seemed less precarious than it had before he left the country. She was once more his sweetheart and his little pig; as he told her, none could dress his legs as she could.

"We missed you on our journeyings," he said. "None but clumsy oafs to bandage me! I said: 'I'll not stray far from my Queen again!' And I meant it, sweetheart. Aye! I meant it."

Then would come those days when he would feel better and could walk with the aid of a stick. It was the well-remembered routine. There would be feasting and music; and the King would grow mellow and glance with appreciation at the more beautiful of the young ladies. He would reiterate those reproaches. Why had he not another son? Why should some of the noblemen in his realm have sons—great stalwart men—while their King could not get himself another to set beside Prince Edward? God had been unjust to him. He had given him power but denied him sons. And why should God be unjust to one who served him as had Henry the Eighth of England? There was only one answer: The fault could not lie with the King. It lay in his partners. He had exposed those wicked women who had cheated him; then he had known why sons had been denied him. When he meditated thus, he would watch his sixth wife with narrowed eyes and think what a comely wench was that young Duchess, or that Countess—or perhaps that simple daughter of a knight.

Something was wrong. Why, why should sons be denied him?

Then again the leg would be so painful that he could think of nothing else. There was Kate, dear Kate, with the gentle hands, who never for a moment showed that she did not regard it as the greatest honor to wait upon him.

Chapuys, the Spanish Ambassador and

spy of his master, wrote home to Spain: "This King has the worst legs in the world."

But those legs were the Queen's salvation; and the worse they grew, the safer she became.

But her life was still in danger. There was never a day when she dared not be on the alert. Royal storms could spring up in a moment, and how could she know what the outcome of those storms would be?

Always it seemed that beside her stalked the shadowy figure of the executioner. It seemed that the bells continually warned her: "Sons, sons, sons!"

And then Sir Thomas Seymour returned to the court.

The Queen was in her apartments, working on the great tapestry which she proposed to use as hangings in the Tower. With her were the ladies whom she loved best: Anne Askew, ethereal, remote from them all, her blue eyes seeming a little strained after so much reading; that other Anne, Lady Herbert, Katharine's sister who had been with her since she had become Queen; Margaret Neville, the stepdaughter whom Katharine loved as though she were her own; Lady Tyrwhit and the Duchess of Suffolk, with young Lady Jane Grey.

Their fingers worked busily while they talked, and their talk was of the New Learning.

Little Jane was interested. When she and Edward were alone they talked of the New Faith. Edward read books she brought to him, which had been given to her, with the Queen's consent, by Anne Askew.

Jane knew that these ladies, who had her love and her sympathy, believed that she might one day be Edward's Queen, and it seemed important to them that she be a Protestant Queen, and Edward a Protestant King. Jane had heard frightening stories of what was happening in Spain under the dreaded Inquisition, and how it was the great wish of the Spaniards that the Inquisition should be set up in all countries.

Little Jane could not bear the thought of violence. The stories she heard of the hideous tortures horrified her. There were occasions when the court was at the palace of Hampton, and she had stood in the gallery which led to the chapel and imagined she heard the terrible screams and saw the ghost of Catharine Howard.

How did it feel, wondered Jane, to know that in a short time you would walk out to the block and lay down your head?

As she listened to the impassioned voice of Anne Askew who read aloud from the forbidden books, she knew that Anne was the only one in this apartment who was unafraid of torture and violent death.

The Queen's sister was apprehensive and uneasy, and chiefly for the sake of the Queen.

It was nearly two years since the King had ordered that a picture be painted of himself and his children with Queen Jane Seymour at his side. Edward had told Jane of it and how unhappy he had been to stand there beside his father, and how he had kept glancing over his shoulder to see if his mother had really returned from the grave.

The Queen had felt that insult deeply, but she had given no sign of what she felt. Jane had seen the King and Queen together, had seen the King lay his foot on the Queen's lap, had seen him rest his jeweled hand on her knee; she had also seen the black looks on his face and heard the menace in his voice.

How did it feel to be afraid . . . afraid that one day you would be sent to the Tower, never to emerge again except for that last walk to the scaffold?

Uncle Thomas Seymour was back at court. Jane had noticed how coldly he looked at the Queen, but his looks were not so cold when they rested on the Princess Elizabeth.

The Queen's thoughts were as busy as her fingers on the tapestry. She was not thinking of the doctrines so ardently preached by Anne Askew. She agreed with Anne; she admired Anne; and she was glad that she had been able to protect her here at court. But Thomas was back, and she could think of nothing else. He had been back many months, and she felt that meeting him every day and having nothing from him but cold looks was more than she could bear.

But she understood. His motive was wise and necessary. She would have him run no risks.

The King had evidently ceased to be jealous of him, for he had made him Lord High Admiral and a gentleman of his Privy Chamber. There were times when he was so cordial toward his brother-in-law and looked at him with such sly speculation, that Katharine wondered whether he was hoping to accuse him with his Queen. All through those months Henry had been alternately doting and menacing, assuring her that she was his dear Kate, his good nurse, and shortly afterward complaining that she was not pregnant.

It was nearly three years since their marriage, and there had not been even one pregnancy. Moreover it was remembered that she had had two husbands and not a child from either of them. Three years of these alarms—three years when she must submit to the King's caresses and the King's anger, and accept all with a meek endurance. Three years that seemed like thirty!

She was tired suddenly and wished to go to her bedchamber and rest. She rose and said that she would retire.

"Jane," she said, "come with me and make me comfortable."

All the ladies rose, and when the Queen had left the apartment with the little nine-year-old Jane in attendance, they dispersed to their own rooms.

Anne Askew felt in turns triumphant and resigned. She had many friends at court; her gentle nature, her complete lack of worldliness, her goodness and purity, had made people look upon her as a saint. Others regarded her as a fool to have left her rich husband, to have come to court as a sort of missionary for the new faith, to have laid herself open to the enmity of such men as Gardiner and his friend who was now Chancellor Wriothesley.

A few days before, Anne had received a warning. She had found a note under her bolster when she retired one night. "Have a care. It is the Queen they want. But they will strike at her through you."

And then again there had been another note. "Leave this court. You are in danger."

Anne would not go. She believed she had a vocation. Since her coming to court many ladies had been reading the books she treasured; there had been many converts to Protestantism and there would be many more. Anne knew that she was placing not only herself in danger, but others also. But to Anne there was nothing to be feared save infidelity to the truth. The religion imposed on the country by the King differed only from the old Roman faith in that, instead of a Pope at its head, it had a King. Anne wanted a complete break with the old faith; she believed the new and simpler religion to be the true one. She wanted all to be able to read the Bible; and how could those humble people, who did not understand the Latin tongue, do so unless they were allowed to

read it in English? It was her desire to dis-
tribute translations all over the country.

She was fanatical; she was sure that she
was in the right; and she believed that no
matter what harm came to any who might
be involved with her, if they had to die for
their faith, they were fortunate indeed, for
theirs would be immediate salvation.

The Princess Elizabeth was interested in
the new faith, though her interest was more
intellectual than devotional. Elizabeth's religion would, Anne guessed, always be the
welfare of Elizabeth. She sought power and
she could never forget the days when she
had been a poor humiliated daughter of a
great King who, when the fancy took him,
chose to call her "bastard." Elizabeth then,
favored the new faith but she would never
be a strong adherent to it. She would always trim her sails according to the wind
that blew.

And the Queen? Ah, the Queen was a
good and earnest woman, but was she
made of the stuff of which martyrs were
made? That would doubtless be proved.
Anne prayed for the Queen—not for her
safety, but that she might show courage
when the time came.

She went to her apartments and as soon as she entered the room she was aware that something had happened to it during her absence.

It was some seconds before she noticed the disorder; and a few more before she saw that in the shadows by the hangings were men-at-arms.

One of them came forward as she entered, and two more took their stand on either side of her.

"Anne Askew," said he who stood before her, holding a scroll in his hand, "I am ordered to arrest you on a charge of heresy. It would be well for you to come quickly and make no resistance."

She saw then that they had found her secret store of books and the writing she had done; but instead of fear, she felt an exhilaration. She had expected this for a long time and she found that she could welcome it.

They took her down the river by barge.

Calmly and silently she watched the play of light on the river. She looked at the great houses with their gardens which ran down to the water's edge, and she wondered, without any great emotion, whether she would ever see them again.

The great gray bastion of the Tower was visible now, strong, invulnerable.

Her eyes were shining as they took her in by way of the Traitors' Gate. She remembered that through this gate they had taken the martyrs, Fisher and More.

She was helped out of the boat; she stepped on to the slippery bank and followed the jailor into the cold building, up a staircase, through dark passages that stank of blood and sweat and the damp of the river.

The jailor jangled his keys and to many the sound might have been like notes of doom; but to Anne Askew it was but the jingling of the keys which would open the doors of Paradise to the martyr.

The elegant and most witty Earl of Surrey was sprawling on a window seat in his apartments at Hampton Court Palace. He was in that reckless mood which was becoming habitual to him. Thirty-one years of age and a poet, he was a member of the greatest and most noble family in the land, and there were times when he felt his ambition to be so strong that he was ready to do the most foolhardy thing to achieve it.

Death! He thought of it often. He had lived so near to it all his life that he felt an intimacy with it. So many of his House had died violently and suddenly. None of them could ever be sure which one of them would be the next to die. His family was guilty of the gravest offense against the King: They had a claim to the throne. The Howards of Norfolk were, some said, more royal than the Tudors. The King could never forget that, and he was constantly on the alert for a sign that the Howards were giving this matter too much consideration.

"Have a care!" said Surrey's cautious father often enough. But, pondered the young poet, idly playing a few notes on his lute, there comes a time in the life of a man when he no longer wishes to take care, but rather to be reckless, to stake everything . . . to win, or pay the price of failure with his head.

Wild plans were forming in his mind. This had begun to happen when the King had told him that he had decided to send Edward Seymour, Lord Hertford, to Calais as Governor in place of himself.

These accursed Seymours! Who were they? Surrey asked himself rhetorically. An upstart family! And because young Jane had married the King, the Seymour brothers were fast becoming the most important pair in the country.

Surrey called one of his men to him and cried: "Go to the apartments of my sister, the Duchess of Richmond, and tell her I would have speech with her. Tell her it is of the utmost importance."

The man went while Surrey sat playing with the strings of his lute.

He was thinking of his sister, Mary; she was beautiful with that striking beauty of the Howards, the mingling of dignity with personal charms. Mary had been married some years ago to the King's illegitimate son, the Duke of Richmond, and she was now a widow, ripe for a second marriage.

The Howard women had always pleased the King, though briefly. Surrey's father, the old Duke of Norfolk, Lord Treasurer of England, was not in favor with the King just now and had not been since the unhappiness caused Henry by Catharine Howard. Surrey smiled. But the King was old now, and his fancy would not stray so easily, and he, Surrey, did not see why a Howard woman should not retrieve the family's fortunes.

He was madly impatient. He played with

the idea of quartering the arms of Edward the Confessor on his escutcheon. Why not? He was entitled to do this by the grant of Richard the Second, because of his descent from Edward the First. Flaunting those arms would proclaim to the court that Surrey and his family considered that they had more right to the throne than the Tudors.

Imagine the royal ire at such daring! And what then? wondered Surrey. "To the Tower, my lord Earl. Off with his head. He has committed the mortal sin. He is more royal than the King!"

Surrey burst into laughter. His maternal grandfather, the Duke of Buckingham, had lost his head in 1521 because he had a claim to the throne.

I believe I will do it, he thought, for I am tired of living at the command of the King, tired of seeking the royal favor, tired of placating the angry frown. Is this how men become when they live perpetually on the edge of danger?

His father would call him a fool. The old Duke had been a doughty warrior, a cautious man. He had been less cautious in his hot youth when he had fallen in love with his wife's laundress and raised Bess Holland to the position she enjoyed as mistress of one of the most important men of the time.

Surrey thought of the endless strife Bess had caused between his parents. Was life worth the trouble it brought? he wondered.

He doubted it.

His sister came into the room and, throwing aside his lute, he rose to greet her.

"You have something to say to me, brother?"

"You grow more beautiful every day. Sit beside me, sister, and I will sing you my latest verses which I have set to music."

Mary Howard, Duchess of Richmond, looked at him with sly amusement. She knew he had not asked her to visit him merely to hear his verses.

"I have a new poem," he said. "Even the King has not heard it yet."

She listened, but she was paying little attention to the words.

She could think of nothing but a certain handsome gentleman who dominated her thoughts and desires. It was long since Richmond had died that lingering death, and she wanted a husband. She had been fond of the young Duke—such a fine, handsome man, and the image of the King—until disease had claimed him. But what was her feeling for the Duke of Richmond compared with this passion which now obsessed her?

Her father had started it. He had said to her: "These Seymours are our enemies. Who are they, these upstart gentlemen? Miserable squires, claiming kinship with the King. Daughter, we cannot fight these mighty rivals, but we could link ourselves with them."

"By marriage?" she had asked.

And then a great excitement had been hers, for there were only two brothers and the elder was married. It was the younger, the swaggering sailor, whom her father had in mind.

Sir Thomas! The merry twinkling eyes, the jaunty beard, the charm of the man! No sooner had her father spoken those words than she could think of nothing but marriage with Sir Thomas, and he had continued to dominate her thoughts.

Surrey dismissed his attendants.

"Well?" she said. "Your news?"

He smiled at her idly. "Sister, you are very beautiful."

"So you have already said. There is no need to repeat it, though a compliment from a brother is to be cherished, as there is often plain speaking in families. What do you want of me?"

"I? Nothing. I have had thoughts."

"And those thoughts?"

"They have taken Anne Askew to the Tower."

"I know. She is a heretic. What has that to do with me?"

"I saw her . . . this very afternoon. She was sitting in the barge, her arms folded across her breast. She looked a veritable martyr, which I doubt not she will be ere long. Sister, what does this mean? Have you thought of that?"

"That another heretic is to pay the price of her folly and her treason to the King."

"She is a great friend of the Queen's, and yet they have dared to take her. Gardiner and the Chancellor are behind this, depend upon it. They would not dare to take the Queen's great friend if they did not think her Majesty was out of favor with the King."

"And what of this? We know what favor she enjoys. If he were his old self he would have had her head off by now, and doubtless that of some other lady who had been unfortunate enough to share his throne after her. But he is sick and she is a good nurse. So he keeps her beside him."

"He is not always so sick. I have seen his eyes grow misty and his voice gruff with desire when a beautiful woman passes before him."

"He is too old for such pleasures."

"He will never believe he is too old. He has indulged in them too freely. There will always be his thoughts, his desires, his belief that his powers are not yet past."

"And what would you say to me? Have you brought me here to tell me what the court knows already and has always known?"

"Nay. The Queen's days are numbered. Poor Katharine Parr! I am sorry for her. She will go the way of others." He smiled. "We should not be saddened. It is the fate that threatens us all. We should look on it stoically, for if it comes not today, then it may come tomorrow. The Queen's place will be taken by another lady. Why not you, my sister?"

She was hot with anger. "You are asking

me to be the seventh? To prepare myself for the ax?"

"Nay. Be not the seventh. Be the honored mistress. Smile on his Grace and do not say, 'Your mistress I cannot be!' as poor deluded fools have said before you. Say this: 'Your mistress I will be.' Thus you will keep alive his desire. You will rule him and bring our house back to the favor it once enjoyed."

"How dare you talk to me in this manner! You shame me. You insult me. And the King . . . my own father-in-law!"

Surrey shrugged his shoulders. "You were the wife of his bastard son. There is no true relationship to him in that. Moreover it will not be necessary to get a dispensation from the Pope, for his Holiness no longer carries weight in this realm. The King would get dispensation from the King, and that should be an easy matter. The royal conscience would no doubt be appeased with the greatest ease, for I doubt not that though the King's conscience is the master of the King's desires, the King's desires are so subtle that they will once more deceive the conscience."

"Brother, you talk with folly. You are proud

and foolish. One of these days your tongue will cut off your head."

"I doubt it not. I doubt it not. And, Mary, dear sister, there are times when I care not. Do not think to ally yourself with low-born Seymour. I would stand against uniting our family with that one."

She cried: "More foolish than ever! To unite ourselves with the King's brother-in-law would be the best thing that could happen to our family."

"And to its daughter—who lusteth for the man?" he taunted.

"You go too far, brother."

"Do I, fair sister? I will tell you this: Seymour looks higher. He looks to the Princess Elizabeth. Who knows—he may get her. Unless the King decides to execute him, for that may be necessary in the process of getting rid of the Queen. Seymour had his eyes on Her Majesty at one time, you remember. Master Thomas Seymour is as near the ax as any of us, even though the King may call him brother. Nay, dear sister, do not long so for one man that you cannot see the advantage of casting your glances at another. Be bold. Be clever. Love Tom Seymour if you must, but do not lose the

opportunity of restoring your family to greatness through the grace of His Majesty. I tell
you he is ripe . . . ripe for seduction. And the
ladies of our family are most accomplished
in that art."

She rose and swept haughtily from the
room.

Surrey watched her, plucked a few notes
from his lute, and was still playing when a
messenger came and told him that his presence was required in the King's music-
room.

The King sat on his ornate chair in that
chamber which was reserved for the playing
of music.

He was surrounded by his courtiers, and
the Queen sat beside him. She looked fair
enough, sitting there in her scarlet hood; the
pearls, which made a becoming edge to it,
suited her complexion. Her skirt was of
cloth of gold and cut away to show a crimson velvet petticoat. Crimson suited Kate,
thought the King. If she would but give me
a son I should not be displeased with her.

But she was meddling with religion; and
he liked not meddling women. He was now
persecuting Lutherans as heretics, and Pa-

pists as traitors. Religious matters in this realm had become complicated; and what annoyed him so, was the fact that this need not be. All he wished men to do was worship in the old way, remembering that their King, instead of the Pope, was head of the Church. It was simple enough.

His most comforting thought at the moment was that François across the water was ageing just as he was. He doubted François had more than a year or two of life left to him; he suffered malignant pain, just as Henry did; and the thought of the French King's pain helped Henry to bear his.

Matters of State had been equally trying to them both of late. Neither of them had gained much by the war they had been waging against each other.

On Henry's return to England, the Scottish campaign had gone against him; the French had launched an attack on Boulogne, which, thanks to Hertford, had withstood the attack. But at the same time French ships had entered the Solent and actually landed at Bembridge and tried to force their way into Portsmouth Harbor. But Lisle had caught the foreign fleet and driven it back; and disease aboard the French ships had been a strong ally of the English.

Henry had ridden this storm like the mighty ruler he could be. Ruthless, he did not hesitate. Taxes, "benevolences," were extorted as they never had been before. His enemies thought that surely his long-suffering people must rise against him. He was a tyrant, a murderer, and many had suffered cruelly at his hands; if there had ever been a moment when he could have been overthrown that was the moment. But the people of England recognized him as their King; he was the strong man; they trusted him to lead them from their trouble. Cheerfully they paid what was asked of them; and during those uneasy months the King had forgotten everything but that he was a King and his country was in danger. He coined his own plate and mortgaged his land; if he did expect his people's untiring effort, he gave his own contribution also. He had always played for popularity with the people; now he reaped the benefit of that popularity. To those who lived close to him he was a murderous tyrant; to the people he was the dazzling King.

And so, England held fast behind Henry.

The French were driven back; a decimated army returned to France. François was as eager as Henry for peace, and they had made a settlement. Henry was to keep Boulogne for eight years, after which time the French might bargain for its return. Trouble continued in Scotland, but there was now a war on one front only.

The King could rest a little from his tribulations and give himself to pleasure.

Now there was Surrey entering the music-room, as elegant as ever and as insolent. Why was it that Surrey aroused the King's anger nowadays? He was a good poet, a fine gentleman, but he was arrogant, and each day his insolence was growing. And with Surrey, there was his sister, Mary—Henry's own daughter-in-law—a comely girl, with the Howard beauty, and the Howard slyness, the King did not doubt.

She knelt before Henry and, as she lifted her eyes, he looked straight at her. She flushed a little as though she read something in his glance which had not been there. She seemed shy and fluttering, dazzled by the radiance from the royal countenance; and Henry felt that sudden pleasure which that look on a woman's face had never failed to give him. It was as though they expected to look into the face of a mighty monarch and had seen there instead a desirable man.

The King's eyes softened and his gaze followed the girl as she stepped back and took her place with the Queen's ladies. Expertly, in his mind's eye, he divested her of her velvet and her jewels. "I'll warrant she's as comely without as with her adornments," he told himself; and the room seemed diffused with a more gentle light, and there was a lifting of his spirits that almost smothered the throbbing of his leg.

Gardiner and Wriothesley were in attendance; they looked smug on this day. Something afoot there, I'll swear, thought the King; and when I've heard this music, I'll have it from them.

There was Seymour, now Lord High Admiral. The King smiled. How that young man reminded him of himself! The ladies liked Seymour and Seymour had once had his eyes on the Queen, the rogue! But he had never let them stray very far from the Princess Elizabeth. She was another on whom the King must keep a watchful eye.

But at the moment he could not keep his eyes from Mary Howard. She outshone all the women, he decided; and he fancied he saw a resemblance in her to little Catharine Howard.

The instrumental piece which the musicians were playing had come to an end. It was charming, and he would reward the fellow who had written it.

"Bravo!" cried the King. "Bravo! There's naught that soothes the troubled mind as certain as sweet music."

"I trust," said the Queen, "that Your Grace's mind is not overtroubled."

"A King, wife, must of necessity have much upon his mind."

Wriothesley, who never lost an opportunity of flattering his royal master, murmured: "It is fortunate for this realm that Your Majesty sits on the throne."

Henry lifted his heavy lids to glare at his Chancellor. Too ready, was this Wriothesley, with his honeyed words; true though they were, the rogue was too ready. Yet, as ever, flattery was sweeter in the King's ears than the sweetest music.

"Good Chancellor," he replied, wincing as he moved painfully in his chair, "it is the

kingly lot to bear the troubles of our subjects. For many years we have sat on the
throne of England, but we cannot hope to
rule this realm for ever."

His eyes flickered angrily on the Queen
who had failed to provide him with sons;
then they went to the charming figure of his
daughter-in-law.

Watching them, Surrey speculated: So
my words have borne fruit. Mary has already given him the glance, the promise.
The seed has been sown. Oh, poor
Katharine Parr, my heart bleeds for you. But
you are as safe as the rest of us, so why
should it bleed for you and not for poor Surrey? My head may not remain on my shoulders any longer than yours. I am a poet, and
so is the King. I am the greater poet, and in
that I offend. I am more royal than His
Majesty, and I have written verses. Two of
the greatest literary men of our age have already laid their heads on the block—More
and Rochford. Tom Wyatt was a fine poet
but he was born lucky. The ax did not catch
him though he had his miraculous escapes.
And the next who dares wield his pen with
more dexterity than the King, shall he die?
And is his name Surrey?

Katharine had grown a shade paler, and the King went on with a trace of malice: "We'll not talk of such matters. They disturb our Queen. Do they not, wife?"

"There are topics which please me more, Your Grace," said Katharine quietly.

"We like not to brood on the days that lie ahead," mused the King, "days when we shall no longer be here to lead this country. There is over-much conflict in this land, and we like it not." He glared at those about him and shouted: "We like it not. We would have peace in our time, and though that be denied us beyond the realm of England, we demand it at home." Gardiner had moved closer to the King. The Queen looked at the Bishop and their eyes met. Something has happened, thought Katharine. There is some fresh plot against me.

She had noticed the King's frequent glances at the Duchess of Richmond. Could it be that Gardiner was offering the King the Duchess as his seventh wife? Had it already been suggested that the sixth wife should go the way of the second and the fifth?

"We pray, as Your Majesty does, for peace," said Gardiner. "And it is in the cause of peace that we will keep our vigilance night and day over those who dare to question your command. Though there are many in this land, my liege, who would see your enemies at large, working for the destruction of all that you, in your great wisdom and understanding, have laid down as our way of life. . . ."

Henry waved his hand, interrupting the Bishop. He was accustomed to Gardiner's harangues. The Bishop was one of those unfortunate men who could not win his affection. He did not dislike Gardiner as he had disliked Cromwell, but the Bishop did not charm him as Wyatt had and as Seymour did. Gardiner, like Cromwell, seemed to him plebeian. He must tolerate them for their wisdom, for his need of them; but he never liked them, and with Gardiner, as with Cromwell, at the first sign of failure he would show no forbearance.

"The state of kingship is an uneasy one, my lord Bishop," he said. "None knows the truth of that better than ourselves."

Wriothesley murmured: "And about Your Grace's throne there are many enemies."

His glance rested as if by chance first on the Queen, then on Seymour.

Katharine shivered. Was there some plot

to implicate herself and Thomas? Not Thomas! she prayed. Anything but that harm should come to him.

Then insolently and ironically Surrey spoke: "Enemies of each other, my lord Chancellor, or enemies of the King, mean you? Enemies, say . . . of the Lord High Admiral, or of my lord Bishop?"

Wriothesley's eyes flashed hatred and his smile was venomous as he said softly: "What enemies could there be, of true and loyal subjects, but enemies of the King?"

"We might well ask," continued the irrepressible Surrey. "It would seem to me that there are men in this realm who seek first their own advancement, and secondly that of England—and the latter only if both are on the same road to the goal."

The King glared at the poet. "You make an accusation, my lord Earl. You tell us that there are those about us who would seek their way even though it did not run side by side with that of England's."

"Alack, Your Grace, I make the suggestion because I fear it to be true."

Henry's eyes had narrowed in that fashion familiar to them all. There was no one present—with the exception of Surrey—whose heart had not begun to beat faster, who wondered whither this mischief of Surrey's would lead.

"If any man among you," continued the King, "knows aught against another, it is the sure and bounden duty of that man to lay his knowledge before the members of our council."

The King tried to rise, but with a sudden angry roar fell back into his chair. Katharine hastened to kneel at his feet.

"Your Grace, the bandage is too tight."

"By God, it is!" cried the King, the sweat on his brow, his face almost black with pain. "Mercy on us, Kate. There's none can dress my wounds as thou, for I declare that when others do it, the rags must either be over-loose or over-tight."

Katharine was glad to find occupation with the bandages. "Have I Your Grace's permission to loosen them now?"

"Indeed you have . . . and quickly . . . quickly, Kate."

There was silence while she worked, and the King lay back for a few seconds with his eyes closed. He was clearly too concerned with his pain to think of any enemy other than that.

But at length he opened his eyes and looked at those gathered about him.

Wriothesley said, as soon as he knew that he had the King's attention: "When the Earl speaks of Your Majesty's enemies, he must be thinking of the last to be discovered—the woman Kyme."

"What of the woman Kyme?" said Seymour quickly.

"She lies in the Tower, as should all the enemies of our lord the King."

The Bishop said very clearly: "So be it."

Katharine was aware of the frightened eyes of three of her ladies—her sister, her stepdaughter and little Jane Grey. These were the three who loved her best, and they knew that an open attack on Anne Askew signified a covert attack on the Queen.

Surrey said: "What is this of Anne Askew? She wishes to be called Askew in place of Kyme, I believe. A comely girl. Dainty of structure, tall and over-sad. Her hair is gold as meadow buttercups, and her skin pale as garden lilies; her eyes are blue as skies in summer time."

"What's this?" roared the King, recovering from his pain.

"Anne Askew, Your Grace," said Surrey.

The King laughed unpleasantly. "Like my lord Earl, I remember her well. Over-bold of tongue. I like it not when women presume to teach us our business." He roared out in sudden pain. "What do you, Kate? Thou art pulling our leg this way and that."

"A thousand pardons, Your Grace," said Katharine. "The bandage slipped from my hands."

"Have a care then."

Surrey could not resist continuing with the dangerous subject of Anne Askew. "She left her husband's house, Your Grace."

Lady Herbert interjected quite heatedly: "It would be more truthful to say that her husband drove her from it, Your Grace."

"What was that?" asked the King.

"Her husband, Your Grace, drove her from his house."

"For a good reason," said Wriothesley, throwing a sly smile at Lady Herbert and the Queen. "He liked not her disobedience to Your Grace's commands."

"Then 'twas rightly done," said the King. "We'll brook no disobedience in this land from man or woman . . . comely though they may be."

"Ah," said Surrey lightly, "it is not always

easy to bend the head to the prevailing wind."

The King gave the Earl a malevolent glance, and as he turned to do so, his leg was jerked out of Katharine's hand and Henry cried out in agony.

"It was, I fear, Your Grace's movement," said Katharine. "'Twill be soothed when I have the bandages in place. I have a new ointment which I am assured will ease the pain."

The King took off his plumed hat and wiped his brow. "I am weary of new ointments," he said peevishly.

"How I long to find the remedy!" said Katharine.

"Right well would I reward the fellow who found it. By my faith, I cannot sleep o' nights from the pain in this leg. We'll try the ointment tonight, Kate. Ah, that's better." The King turned to frown at his courtiers. "It is not for women to teach us our business," he said. "We agree with St. Paul on this matter: 'Let your women keep silent in the churches; for it is not permitted unto them to speak; but they are commanded to be under obedience . . .'"

Henry paused significantly to glance at

the kneeling figure of his wife. He trusted Kate would remember that. She was a good woman and she had the gentlest fingers in the court. For that he loved her. But he did not love women who meddled in matters which should be regulated by the superior intellects of men. Kate was another such as this meddling Anne Askew. The latter had most rightly been lodged in the Tower. He trusted his good nurse Kate would heed a gentle warning.

Gardiner obsequiously finished the quotation: "'. . . as also saith the law.'"

Henry nodded and shook a bejeweled finger at the company and then at his kneeling wife. "This woman, Askew—an I mistake not—was found in possession of forbidden books; she has spoken against the Mass. Keep her in the Tower, my lord. Keep her there until such time as she shall learn good sense."

Gardiner had stepped forward; his head was bowed and his voice had taken on a serious note. "The woman is over-saucy, alack, having friends at court."

"What friends are these, lord Bishop?"

"That, Your Grace," said the Bishop, looking for a few seconds at the kneeling Queen, "is what we have yet to discover."

"My lord Bishop," said Seymour, "it cannot be of any great consequence to His Majesty that this woman has friends."

"I understand you not, brother," said the King.

"She is a foolish woman, Your Grace. Nothing more."

"Foolish in all conscience," growled the King.

"Scarce worthy of such notice," said Seymour.

Katharine, trying to steady her trembling fingers, wanted to implore him to take care. He must not involve himself in this. Did he not see that; that was just what his enemies wished?

"Mayhap she is not," said the King. "But we would teach a lesson to those who dare oppose us."

"The female sex," said Gardiner, "can be as troublesome as the male. I would not excuse her, Seymour, on account of her sex. To my mind, any that work against our lord the King is an enemy to England—be it man or woman."

"Well spoken," said the King. He looked

at Sir Thomas and chuckled. "I follow our gallant Seymour's thoughts. She is a woman; therefore to be treated tenderly. Come, brother, confess."

"Nay, my liege."

"Oh?" said the King. "We know you well, remember."

There was a titter of laughter among the courtiers, and Katharine must lift her eyes to look into the face of the man she loved. But he was not looking her way; he was smiling almost complacently. He was so clever, thought Katharine; he was so wise; he was far more restrained and controlled, for all his seeming jauntiness, than she could ever be. It was foolish of her to wish that he could have looked a little hurt at this estimation of his character.

"I would say," went on the obsequious Wriothesley, "an it please Your Grace, that, like Seymour, I do not think of Anne Askew as a woman. I think of her as a menace, for about her are gathered the enemies of the King."

"You are over-fierce, friend Wriothesley," said Henry.

"Only in the cause of Your Majesty,"

replied the Chancellor, bowing his head in reverence.

"That is well, good Chancellor. And now . . . enough of this woman. I would be entertained by my friends' achievements and not made sad because of my enemies. Master Surrey, you skulk over there. You are our great poet, are you not? Entertain us, man. Come . . . let us hear some of those fine verses on which you pride yourself."

The Earl rose and bowed before the King. The little bloodshot eyes looked into the handsome brown ones.

"I am ever at Your Grace's service," said that most insolent of men. "I will give you my description of the spring."

"Ah!" said the King, reflecting: I'll not brook your insolence much longer, my lord. You . . . with your royalty and your words. I see that sister of yours in your handsome face. She is proud . . . proud as the rest of you. But I like proud women . . . now and then.

And for the sake of the young man's sister, Henry softened toward him.

"We would fain hear your description of the spring. 'Twas ever our favorite season."

"Spring!" said Surrey ecstatically. "It is

the most beautiful of all seasons. Wherein each thing renews, save only the lover."

The King shot a suspicious look at the Earl, but Surrey had already begun to recite:

"The soote season, that bud and
bloom forth brings,
With green hath clad the hill and eke
the vale:
The nightingale with feathers new she
sings;
The turtle to her mate hath told her
tale.
Summer is come, for every spray now
springs:
The hart hath hung his old head on the
pale;
The buck in brake his winter coat he
flings . . ."

Surrey stopped short, for the King had spoken. He was saying to Seymour, who stood near him: "What meant he, brother? 'Wherein each thing renews save only the lover'! The lover methinks breaks out in love as readily as any flowers in spring. Aye! Nor does he need to wait for springtime."

Everyone laughed with great heartiness,

and when the laughter had subsided, Surrey said: "The flowers, Your Grace, bloom with equal freshness each spring, but the coming of another spring finds the lover more jaded than did the previous one."

There was a short silence. What had happened to Surrey? Was it that which had been known to break out in men before? They lived under the shadow of the ax for so long that their fear changed into recklessness. Surrey had been showing this attitude for some time.

Katharine looked at the young man and prayed silently for him: "Oh, Lord God, preserve him. Preserve us all."

She said quickly: "Your Grace, listening to the Earl's verses has set up a longing within me to hear something of your own."

Henry's good humor was miraculously restored. How strange it was, thought Katharine, that this great King, this man whom the French and the Spaniards feared, should be so childish in his vanity. The King's character contained the oddest mingling of qualities; yet the brutality and the sentimentality, the simplicity and the shrewdness, made him the man he was. She should not regret these contrasts; she could watch for those traits in his character, and, as her knowledge of them grew, she might find some means of saving others from his wrath, as well as herself. She had indeed now saved Surrey from his displeasure.

"Since the Queen commands," said Henry graciously, "we must obey."

"Would Your Majesty care to come to my music-room, that my musicians may first play the new melody set to your verses?"

"Aye. That we will. And we will take with us those who most appreciate the pleasure in store."

He scanned the assembled company. "Come . . . you, my Lady Herbert, and you, my Lady of Suffolk. . . ."

The King named those whom he wished to accompany him to the Queen's music-room. Surrey was not among them, and for that Katharine was grateful. Let the young man withdraw to his own apartments and there ponder his recklessness in solitude.

But others noticed that Surrey's sister was one of those who received the King's invitation; and that during the musical hour he found a pretext for keeping her close beside him.

→>-<←

Thomas Seymour, not being among those who had been invited to the Queen's chamber, strolled out of the palace into the gardens.

He was thinking of Surrey's words, which had been deliberately calculated to stab the King. What a fool was Surrey! Thomas Seymour had no intention of being such a fool.

He strolled past the gardens which would soon be ablaze with roses—red and white roses which would suggest, to all who saw them, from what the founding of the Tudor dynasty had spared the country. The Wars of the Roses had ended with the coming of Henry the Seventh; now the red roses of Lancaster and the white roses of York mingled peaceably, enclosed by wooden railings of green and white, the livery colors of a Tudor King; the pillars were decorated with the heraldic signs of the Tudors as an additional reminder.

Looking at these gardens, Seymour thought afresh what a fool Surrey was. What was his motive? To undermine the Tudors? That was ridiculous. The Tudors had come to stay.

Seymour leaned on the green-and-white fence and surveyed the rose trees.

Life was good to the Lord High Admiral of England. Ambition would be realized. He was sure of his destiny. But, sure as he was, he knew that he must be constantly on the alert, ready to snatch every advantage; and one of the greatest assets which a kindly fate had thrown into the hands of Sir Thomas Seymour was his personal charm.

Marriage! What could not be achieved by the right marriage!

Now, it seemed, haughty Norfolk was looking his way; and if Seymour was not mistaken, so was his daughter.

Seymour could not suppress the laugh which came to his lips. Her family would have no difficulty in persuading the Duchess of Richmond to become the wife of Sir Thomas Seymour, he fancied.

How far we have come! he mused. The Seymours of Wolf Hall—humble country gentlemen—and now we are related to the King and fit to ally ourselves with the greatest families in the land.

The question was not whether my lady of Richmond would take Sir Thomas Seymour, but whether Sir Thomas would take her.

He liked her. He liked all beautiful women; but a woman must have more than her beauty to offer an ambitious man. "And, my dear Mary Howard," he murmured, "there are others who have more to offer me than you have."

The spring air was like a glass of wine; he could smell the scents of the earth. Life was good; and would be better.

There were four women now whom he must consider before he took the final step. A duchess, a Queen, the kinswoman of a King, and a King's daughter.

There was no doubt on whom his choice would fall, were it possible for him to make the choice. For the Queen he had a great tenderness; he loved Kate and there would be great happiness with such as she was. But she could not be his wife until she was a Dowager Queen; whereas the Princess might one day be a Queen in her own right.

He could love the woman for her sweet nature, but he longed for the red headed Princess. Ambition and desire could mingle so pleasantly.

He left the rose gardens and strolled toward that new pond garden of his master's. How beautiful it was! How quiet! What perfect peace there was in such a garden, with its lily pond, its statues and terraces. Already it was gay with spring flowers and the blossoming shrubs.

He looked into the future—a future in which the King would be dead, and he and his brother would rule; but his brother was a man who would wish to take first place, and it seemed to Thomas that since Edward lacked his own superior personal charms, people thought he must be the more astute statesman. Edward was sly; Edward was clever; and he had an ambitious wife. Those two would wish to rule without the help of Thomas.

Marriage was, therefore, of the utmost importance to the Admiral; but it must be the right marriage.

A movement in the gardens caught his eyes, and his lips curved into a smile of deep satisfaction as a small figure rose from the grass, a figure in crimson velvet, her red hair just visible under her pearl-trimmed hood.

Seymour lost no time in approaching the Princess Elizabeth.

He bowed and took her hand.

"I was admiring the flowers," he said;

"then I saw that I wasted my admiration on them."

"It rejoices me that you realized the wastage in good time," she said, "for I know you are a man who does not care to waste his talents. It grows chilly."

"Then I must fain give you my cloak. We cannot allow the Lady Elizabeth to be cold."

"My walk back to the Palace will doubt-less warm me."

"I hoped that you would tarry and talk awhile."

"Your hopes, Sir Thomas, I doubt not are always high. Perhaps too high."

"Hopes can never be too high, my lady. If we hope for much, we achieve a little. But to hope for nothing is too achieve nothing. That, you will agree, is folly."

"You are too clever for me, my lord."

"Nay. There are times when it saddens me to think that I am not clever enough."

"You speak in riddles and I must leave you to them. My lord . . ." She curtsied, and would have walked past him; but he had no intention of letting her go.

"Could we not dispense with ceremony now that we are alone?"

"Alone! Who is ever alone at court? Such

as you and I, my lord Admiral, are never alone, for there will always be eyes to watch us when we do not see them, and ears to listen. There will always be those who treasure your simplest utterances—and mine— and mayhap use them against us."

"Elizabeth . . . most beauteous Princess. . . ."

She flushed. Clever as she was, she was susceptible to flattery, even as was her royal father; and she lacked his experience in hiding this fact. Important as she knew herself to be in the affairs of state politics since she had been reinstated at court, and much as she enjoyed her new position, she was more pleased at hearing herself called beautiful than she would have been by any reference to her importance in the realm.

Seymour kept his advantage. "Give me this pleasure . . . give me this pleasure of gazing upon you."

"I have heard the ladies of the court say that it is not wise to take too seriously the compliments of the Lord High Admiral."

"The ladies of the court?" He shrugged his shoulders. "They are apart. You are as different from them as the sun from the moon."

"The moon," she retorted, "is very beautiful, but it hurts the eyes to look at the sun."

"When I look at you I feel myself scorched with the passion within me."

Her laughter rang out clear and loud.

"I hear talk of your marriage, my lord. May I congratulate you?"

"I would welcome congratulations, only if I might announce my coming marriage to one particular lady."

"And can you not make the announcement? I have heard that there is no man at court more likely to sue successfully for a lady's favor."

"She whom I would marry is far above me."

She raised her eyebrows. "Do I hear aright? Is the Lord High Admiral losing his belief in himself?"

"Elizabeth . . . my beautiful Elizabeth. . . ."

She eluded him and ran from him; she paused to look back, artful and alluring, urging him on, yet forbidding him to come.

She was aware of the Palace windows. Much as she would have enjoyed a flirtation with this man, who fascinated her more than any person ever had, she did not wish to endanger her new position at court.

If Seymour had his dreams and ambitions, the Lady Elizabeth had hers no less. Indeed, they soared higher even than those of Seymour; and if they were more glorious, they were more dangerous.

He would have followed her, but she had suddenly become haughty.

"I wish to be alone," she said coldly, and she walked from the garden, forcing herself to conquer her desire to stay with him, to invite his warm glances and perhaps the caresses which he longed to give and she would not have been averse to receiving.

Coquettish as she was, she longed for admiration. Flirtation was an amusing pastime, yet beyond the love of light pleasures was her abiding ambition.

As he watched her, Seymour had no doubt that she was the woman for him.

Nan crept silently out of the Palace of Greenwich. She was covered from head to foot in a dark cloak, under which she wore many thick petticoats which she would not be wearing when, and if, she were fortunate enough to return to the Palace that night.

It was not the first time she had made this journey, carrying food and warm clothing with her, but each time she made it she was filled with fears, for it was a dangerous journey.

Lady Herbert had said to her: "If you should be detained, on no account must it be known who sent you."

"No, my lady."

"And Nan . . . be strong . . . and brave."

They both knew that if she were caught she would be recognized as a lady from the Queen's household. But on no account, Nan assured herself, would she let them know that the Queen had played a part in this mission.

"God help me to be brave" was Nan's continual prayer.

The faint light of a waning moon shone on the river, and in the shadow cast by the bushes she made out the barge which was waiting for her.

The boatman greeted her in that manner which had been arranged. "Hello, there! Come you from my lady?"

"Yes," whispered Nan. "From my lady."

She stepped into the boat which began to slip along only too slowly. Nan listened to the sound of the oars and continued to pray for courage.

The boatman sang softly to himself as he rowed. Not that he felt like singing. He must be almost as nervous as Nan; but he, like her, must wear an air of calm, for it must not be suspected that she came from the Queen, and that she was on her way to visit one who must surely be the most important prisoner in the Tower.

"Are you ready?" whispered the boatman at length.

"I am ready."

She scrambled out on to the slippery bank; it seemed very cold under the shadow of the gray walls which loomed before her.

A man was waiting for her and she followed him without a word. He unlocked a door; Nan shivered as she stepped inside the great fortress of the Tower of London. This man held his lantern high, and she saw the damp walls and the pits at the bottom of which was the muddy water of the river; rats scuttled under her feet. She did not cry out, great as was the temptation to do so.

"Hurry," whispered the man with the lantern. "You must be gone before the guard comes this way."

He unlocked a door, and Nan stepped into the cell.

In spite of the intense cold, the closeness of the atmosphere, the smell of dirt and decay, sickened her. It was some seconds before her eyes grew accustomed to the dimness, for the man with the lantern had shut and locked the door; in a short while he would return; she would hear the key in the lock and he would let her out.

She could vaguely see the shape on the straw.

"Mistress Askew?" she whispered.

"Nan! Is it you?"

"Yes, Mistress. I have brought food and clothes. You are bidden to be of good cheer."

"You are a good and brave woman to come to me thus," said Anne. "Have you a message for me?"

"Only that all that can be done for you will be done."

"Thank you."

Nan could see the emaciated face; it looked ghostly in the dimness of the cell.

"Take a message for me," said Anne. "Tell those who sent you that they should not endanger themselves by sending food and clothing for me. I can face hunger; I can face cold and discomfort."

"It is our delight to help you, to let you know that although you are a prisoner and others are free, they do not forget you."

"I thank them," said Anne, and in spite of her brave words, she fell upon the food which Nan had brought, and ate it ravenously. Nan was taking off the petticoats as she talked, and Anne went on eating as she put them on.

Anne's hands were icy and her teeth chattered. There was hardly any flesh on her bones to keep her warm.

Ah, thought Nan, it is an easy matter to wish to be a martyr; but how eagerly she eats and how grateful she is for a little warmth!

Already the man was unlocking the door.

"Hasten, Mistress," he said. "There must be no delay. I have not seen the guard at his usual post. Hasten, I say. If we are followed, remember, I know nothing of you and how you came here."

"I will remember," said Nan.

Hastily he locked the door of the cell, and Nan picked her way through the dark passages, trying not to brush against the slimy walls, praying that she might not step on the rats.

She felt exhausted when she lay, at length, in the boat, listening to the sound of the oars as she was carried away from the grim fortress of the Tower of London back to Greenwich.

The man with the lantern re-entered the Tower and had scarcely taken three steps inside the building when two men took their stand on either side of him.

"Where go you, sir jailor?" asked one.

"Where go I?" blustered the man, and he felt as though cold water were dripping down his back, although he was sweating with fear. "Where go I? To my post, of course."

"Who was the fair lady to whom you have just bade farewell?" enquired the other man.

"Fair lady . . . ? I . . . ?"

"You conducted her to a certain cell, did you not?"

"You are mistaken."

The lantern was suddenly taken from his hand, and he was pinioned.

"This way," said one of his captors. "We have questions to ask you."

They pushed him roughly along through the gloomy passages. Terror walked with him. A short while ago the Tower had been to him merely the prison of others; now it was his prison.

"I . . . I have done . . . nothing."

"Later, later," said a soft voice in his ear. "You shall speak for yourself later."

They were taking him into unfamiliar by-ways. He could hear the fierce chorus of rats as they fought with their human victims; he could hear the piercing screams for help from those miserable prisoners who were chained to the walls and who, when they heard footsteps coming their way, shouted for help without any hope that it would be given to them. They took him past the pits in which men were chained, the dirty water up to their knees; the lantern showed him their faces, wild-eyed and unkempt, faces that had lost their human aspect, as they fought the hungry pests which could not wait for them to die.

"Whither . . . whither are you taking me?"

"Patience, friend, patience!" said the voice in his ear.

Now he was in a chamber, and although he had never seen it before, he knew what it was. He had heard much of this chamber. The dim light from the lamp which hung from the ceiling confirmed his horrible fear.

He smelled blood and vinegar, and he knew them for the mingling odors of the torture chambers; and when his eyes were able to see through the mist of fear, he picked out a man at a table with writing materials before him. Much as he desired to, he could no longer doubt that he was in the torture chamber.

The man at the table had risen; he came forward as though to greet the jailor in friendship. There was a smile on this man's face, and the jailor guessed from his clothes that he was a personage of some importance. He knew that he himself had been a fool to take a bribe and get himself involved with the kind of people who would be interested in Anne Askew. A jailor was subject to bribery. You took a little here, a little there. But he wished he had never meddled in the case of Anne Askew.

"You know why you are here, my friend," said the personage.

"Yes . . . yes, my lord. But I have done nothing."

"You have nothing to fear. You have only to answer a few questions."

God in Heaven! thought the sweating jailor. That is what they are all told. "You have merely to answer a few questions!"

"Allow me to show you round the chamber," said the jailor's host. "You see here the gauntlets, the thumbscrews, the Spanish collar . . . the Scavenger's Daughter. You, who serve the King as one of his jailors, know the uses to which these toys may be put, I doubt not."

"I do, my lord. But I have done nothing."

"And here is the rack. The most interesting of them all. My friend, a man is a fool who lets his limbs be stretched on that instrument. There is no need for it. No *wise* man need let his limbs be broken on the rack. You look pale. Are you going to faint? They deal well with fainting here. The vinegar is a quick restorative . . . so they tell me."

"What . . . what do you want of me?"

The man gripped his arm.

"Answer my questions and go back to

your work. That is all I ask of you. Give me truth and I'll give you freedom."

"I will tell you anything you want to know."

"That is well. I knew you were a sensible man. Sit here . . . here on this stool. Now . . . have you recovered? Let us be quick; and the quicker the better, say you; for when you have given the simple answers to these questions you will go back to your work and never, I trust, enter this place again."

"Ask me," pleaded the jailor. "Ask me now."

"You are ready?"

"Aye, sir."

"Did you conduct a woman to a prisoner this day?"

"Yes, sir."

"That was not one of your duties, I feel sure."

"No, no. . . ." The words tumbled out. He could not speak quickly enough. "I took a bribe. It was wrong. I repent of it. I should not have done it."

"But it was such a big bribe?"

"Yes, sir."

"From a person of quality, doubtless. And the name of the prisoner whose cell was visited? Do not try to deceive me, because then I should have to use these toys to make you tell the truth."

"I will not. I swear I will not. The prisoner was a Mistress Anne Askew."

"That is good. You are doing well. I can see we shall not have to play with those toys tonight."

"Who was the woman you took to Anne Askew?"

"A lady . . . whose name I know not."

"Whose name you know not? Have a care."

"I swear I know not her name. She came with food and clothes for the prisoner. I know whence she came, though I know not her name. It was never told me."

"So you know whence she came?"

"Yes, I know. She came from the heretic friends of Anne Askew."

"The names of these friends?"

"They told me no names."

"You are not being very helpful. I must have names."

"They are ladies of the court."

"Cannot you give me names . . . even of some of them?" He had signed to two men with evil faces; they came forward. "Not one name?" said the interrogator.

"I do not know who sent them. I was told by a man who brought her . . . I know . . ."

"You know?"

"Yes, my lord. I know the woman who comes is a messenger from the Queen."

"The Queen! Ah, that is good. You have been useful. Let him go. Let him go back to his work. Not a word, my friend, of tonight's adventure, or . . ."

"I swear I'll say nothing. I swear . . ."

"You will be watched. Just go on as before. Take your bribe. Let the lady in. Your little journey to our chamber, your inspection of our toys makes no difference. Go, my good man. You have answered well and faithfully."

The jailor's response was to fall into a faint on the earthen floor.

Wriothesley watched him with a smile. He liked the man. He had given the answer he most wished to hear.

When Nan reached the Palace of Greenwich she went straight to the apartments of Lady Herbert as was her custom. The Queen's sister had spent the time of her absence alternately on her knees praying for Nan's safety, and at the window watching for her return.

"Nan," said Lady Herbert, "how went it?"

"Much as before, my lady."

"Methinks you are returned a little earlier."

"Yes, my lady. I had scarcely time to take off all the clothing I had brought when the jailor urged me to leave the cell."

"Why was that?" demanded Lady Herbert, her face growing pale.

"It was merely, he said, that he had not seen the guard in his usual place."

Lady Herbert's fingers played nervously with the jewels at her throat.

"This cannot go on. They suspect something."

Nan threw herself on to her knees. When she had been in the company of Anne Askew she seemed infected by her fanaticism, her desire for martyrdom.

"My lady, I am ready to die, if need be, in the cause of the Queen and the Queen's faith."

Lady Herbert began to walk up and down the apartment.

"Oh, Nan, if only it were as simple as that! If death were swift and painless, how easy it would be! What else, Nan? How was she?"

"As strong as before in spirit, but very frail in body."

"Nan, you must not go there again."

"If the Queen commands me, I should go. There are times, my lady, when I almost feel a desire to be caught . . . though I know I should all but die of fright. There is something about that place, something that wraps itself about one. It is utter desolation, hopeless . . . and yet there is a kind of welcome."

Lady Herbert took the young woman by her shoulders and gently shook her.

"Nan, Nan, do not talk so. You speak as one who is ready to embrace death."

"Willingly would I do so, if the Queen commanded," said Nan. "If they caught me, none should draw the secret from me. They could put me on the rack . . ."

"Hush, you foolish woman!" cried Lady Herbert almost angrily. "You know not what you say. Stronger than you have been broken in the torture chambers of the Tower."

"They would not torture me . . . a woman. They do not torture women. I should be sent to the stake, and because I am a woman they would strangle me so that I should not feel the scorching of the flesh."

Lady Herbert recognized the signs of hysteria. The strain was too much for any but a fanatic like Anne Askew. They must give up these dangerous visits. She must make the Queen see that they dared not continue with them.

"Go to your room," she said. "I will send you a soothing draught. Drink it and draw your bed-curtains; then . . . sleep . . . sleep until you awake refreshed."

Nan curtsied and went to her room.

And when she awoke from the soothing sleep, the lightheadedness had passed. She was herself once more. She could think of her experience with nothing but horror, and instead of seeing death beautified by martyrdom, she saw it evil and horrible, as the cold unhappy Tower had told her it must be.

In the Queen's closet Lady Herbert shut the door and leaned against it.

"I am afraid," she said.

"Why so?" asked the Queen.

"Our father and mother would never have dreamed that you would one day be Queen of England."

"But the Queen of England must be braver than any lady in the land."

"She must also be wiser. Oh, Kate, Anne Askew looks for martyrdom, but she is armed with her faith and her courage. You know that she has always been different from the rest of us."

"Yes, even as a girl she was different. How remote she was from us! Oh, sister, what will they do to her? They have taken her because they wish, through her, to take me, and . . . we know why."

"Yes, we know. It is you they wish to have in prison. They will try to make her admit that you too are in possession of the forbidden books, and that you have offended against the King's laws."

"And then?"

"And then I know not."

"Do you not?" Katharine laughed bitterly. "Everything depends on His Majesty. If he wishes to see me condemned as a heretic, then condemned I shall be." Her laughter grew wild. "It makes me laugh. I cannot help it. Everything depends on his state of health. If he is sick, I am safe for a while. But if he grows well . . . Oh Anne, is it not comic? I have watched his glances. The

Duchess of Richmond is a comely lady. And so is Her Grace of Suffolk. Different types— and he cannot make up his mind which he prefers: the widow of his son, or the widow of Charles Brandon. Both widows, you see! I believe I have given him a taste for widows. And none but a widow would dare return the King's loving glances. Sister, my life hangs by a thread; and who is holding that thread? His Majesty. And how he jerks it, depends on the Duchesses of Richmond and Suffolk . . . and the state of his health!"

"You must not laugh like this. It frightens me. You must be calm. You must be serene. Your smallest action is of the utmost importance."

"Oh, sister, what will they do to poor Anne Askew?"

"They dare do nothing. They cannot torture a woman . . . a high-born woman. The King would not allow it."

The Queen looked at her sister and broke into fresh laughter, and the Lady Anne Herbert had great difficulty in soothing her.

The Bishop and the Chancellor walked once more in the Great Park.

"What news, my lord Chancellor?" asked Gardiner.

"My lord Bishop, good news. I had the jailor taken as soon as he left the court woman. He admitted in the torture room that the clothes and food which the prisoner has been receiving were sent at the Queen's command."

Gardiner nodded. "That is good."

"Well, is it not enough?"

The Bishop shook his head. "It's that accursed leg. The woman is such a good nurse."

"You think he is so fond of her still that he seeks no other?"

"While the King breathes he will always be ready to seek another wife—providing the current one has shared his bed for a month or more."

"My lord Bishop, it was but a week ago that he said to me: 'Three years of marriage, Wriothesley, and no sign of fruitfulness. I cannot think the fault is mine; therefore must I wonder if my marriage finds favor in the sight of God.'"

"That was good."

"And have you seen the looks he casts at my lady of Suffolk?"

"Not so good. She, like the Queen, inclines to heresy. I would my lady of Richmond did not worry his conscience. The warmer his feelings grow for her the better. Everything depends on the warmth of his feelings."

"But . . . if he should turn to Brandon's widow?"

"We must see that that does not happen. But first we must rid him of Katharine Parr." Gardiner looked grave. "We must practice the utmost caution. Remember Dr. London, who has since died of the humiliations inflicted upon him."

"I do remember him. But the jailor *admitted* the woman came from the Queen."

"The word of a low-born jailor could not be of great account. We must remember this, friend Chancellor: The situation is not a simple one. When Cromwell found evidence against Anne Boleyn, the King was already impatient for marriage with Jane Seymour. Now it is less simple. At one moment the King wishes to be rid of his wife, and at the next he remembers that she is his nurse and necessary to him. To bring the jailor's evidence before the King when he needs his nurse, might bring down Heaven knows what on our defenseless heads. Nay! We must learn by the mistakes and successes of others. Think of the King's love for Catharine Howard. Cranmer was fully aware of that. What did he do? He presented the King with undeniable evidence of his Queen's guilt. That is what we must do. But the word of a low-born jailor is not enough."

"You mean the woman herself—this Anne Askew—must speak against the Queen?"

"That is what I mean."

"But you know her mind. She will say nothing against anyone. 'Kill me,' she will say. 'I'm not afraid of death.' And, by God, you will have but to look at her to know that she speaks truth."

"It is easy for a fanatical woman to say these things, and to die quickly is easy. But to die slowly . . . lingeringly . . . horribly . . . that is not so simple. The bravest men cry out for mercy on the rack."

"But . . . this is a woman."

Gardiner's thin lips smiled faintly. "This, dear Chancellor," he said, "is our enemy."

In her cell in the Tower, Anne Askew daily waited for the doom which she felt must certainly be hers.

She had knelt by the barred window and prayed, and praying lost count of the hours. On the stone walls of this cell which had been occupied by others before her were scratched names, messages of hope and words of despair. She prayed not for herself but for those who had suffered before her. She knew that there was some grace within her, some extra strength, which would enable her to meet with courage whatever was coming to her.

It was midnight when she had knelt, and now the dawn was in the sky. It filtered through the bars of her cell; another day was coming and she was still on her knees.

It was some days since Nan had visited her. She had had little to eat, yet she did not feel the need of food. There were times when her mind wandered a little—back to her childhood in her father's house, back to the days when she and her sister had wandered in the gardens and been happy together.

Anne had always been the serious one, loving books more than play. Her elder sister had laughed at her, and there had been times when Anne had envied her. She was so normal, that elder sister of Anne's; she liked good things to eat, fine clothes to wear. She had said: "Anne, you are strange. Sometimes I think you are a changeling— not the child of our parents. You are like a fairy child, and in your eyes there burns such fervor that I feel your sire must have been a saint."

Sometimes Anne imagined that she was back in the days of her sister's betrothal to Mr. Kyme.

She could hear her sister's light chatter. "He is very rich, Anne. They say he is the richest man in Lincolnshire, and I like him well enough."

"How can you go into marriage lightly?" Anne had asked, shuddering. "How I rejoice that it is not for me. I shall go into a nunnery. That is what I long for . . . quiet . . . peace . . . to learn that of which Martin Luther has written."

Looking back it seemed that she lived again through those tragic days of her sister's death. Death was ever near. It swooped suddenly, and one could never be sure from what source it came.

"Now that your sister is dead," her father had said, "you must take her place with Mr. Kyme."

She could see him clearly—Mr. William Kyme, a young and ardent man in need of a wife. He was very willing to take the younger sister in place of the elder.

In vain she had prayed and pleaded with her father. "A daughter's first duty is obedience; so said the Scriptures," she was told.

So said the Scriptures. And she would not fight her destiny.

Now was the most horrible of all her memories: the warm, eager hands of Mr. Kyme, and herself trembling supine in the marriage bed.

He had been kind at first. "My poor sweet child, you do not understand. You are so young . . . so innocent. You must not be afraid."

She had lain, shuddering, bearing that torture as later she would bear others.

Resignation came to her at length, but Mr. Kyme did not wish for resignation. There were angry scenes. "Unnatural!" That was the word he had flung at her.

"Leave me alone," she had begged. "Divorce me . . . do what you will. But release me from this life which is distasteful to me."

He had not been, she was sure, more brutal, more unkind than any man would have been. "I will not let you go," he had stormed at her. "You are my wife and you shall *be* my wife."

She would awake even now with those words in her ears, so that she was almost glad to be in this cold cell because it at least meant escape from a life which had been too humiliating and distasteful to be borne.

"I will make a normal woman of you yet," he had said; but he had changed his mind when he had discovered her books.

"What is this?" he had demanded. "Are you one of these Reformers?"

"I believe in the teachings of Martin Luther."

"Do you want to make us the King's prisoners?"

"I would as soon be a prisoner of the King as of your sensuality."

"You are mad. I will stop this reading and writing."

He had locked her in her room, destroyed her books.

But she had found him to be vulnerable, and she rejoiced that this was so. The servants were talking of her leanings toward the new faith, and when a man's wife is implicated, how easy it is to cast suspicion on that man!

Mr. Kyme was such a rich man; and it often happened that rich men were considered most worthy prey by those who wished to bring an accusation which might result in the confiscation of lands and goods. He trembled for his possessions; he was ready to give up his wife rather than place his lands and coffers in jeopardy.

"You will leave this house at once," he had said. "I'll dissociate myself from you and your evil teachings."

And the day she left his house was a happy one for her. Now, kneeling in her cell, she was glad of that experience. It had taught her courage; and she knew she would have great need of courage.

Early that morning she heard footsteps in the passage outside her cell; the door opened and two men came in.

"Prepare yourself for a journey, Mistress Askew," one said. "You are to go to the Guildhall this day for questioning."

She stood before her judges. The strong, pure air had made her faint; the sunlight had seemed to blind her; and her limbs would scarcely carry her. But she did not care, for though her body was weak, her spirit was strong.

She looked up at the open timber-work roof and down at the pavings of Purbeck stone. It was warm in the great hall, for the early summer sun was streaming through the windows, picking out the carvings of the Whittington escutcheons.

Her trial was considered of some importance; yet she was not afraid. She knew that she was in the right, and it seemed to her that, with God and his company of angels on her side, she need have no fear of the Lord Mayor of London, of Bonner, Gardiner, Wriothesley and all the nobles of the Catholic faction who were there to discountenance her and hasten her to the stake.

She heard the words of the Lord Mayor:

"You are a heretic and condemned by the law if you stand by your opinion."

Her voice rang out—a strong voice to come from such a frail body. "I am no heretic. Neither do I deserve death by any law of God. But concerning the faith which I have uttered, I will not deny it, because, my lords, I know it to be true."

Wriothesley said: "Do you deny the

sacrament to be Christ's own body and blood?"

"Yes; I do. That which you call God is but a piece of bread. The son of God, born of the Virgin Mary, is now in Heaven. He cannot be a piece of bread that, if left for a few weeks, will grow moldy and turn to nothing that is good. How can that be God?"

"You are not here to ask us questions, madam," said Wriothesley. "You are here to answer those which we put to you."

"I have read," she answered, "that God made man, but that man can make God I have not read. And if you say that God's blood and body is in bread because man has consecrated that bread, then you say that man can make God."

"Do you insist in these heresies?" demanded the Lord Mayor.

"I insist on speaking the truth," she answered.

"You are condemned of your own mouth," she was told.

"I will say nothing but that which I believe to be true."

"Methinks," said Gardiner, "that we should send a priest that you may confess your faults."

"I will confess my faults unto God," she answered proudly. "I am sure He will hear me with favor."

"You leave us no alternative but to condemn you to the flames."

"I have never heard that Christ or His Apostles condemned any to the flames."

Her judges whispered together; they were uncomfortable. It was ever thus with martyrs. They discomfited others while they remained calm themselves. If only she would show some sign of fear. If only it were possible to confound her in argument.

"You are like a parrot!" cried Gardiner angrily. "You repeat . . . repeat . . . repeat that which you have learned."

Wriothesley's eyes were narrowed. He was thinking: I should like to see fear in those eyes; I should like to hear those proud lips cry for mercy.

She spoke in her rich clear voice. "God is a spirit," she said. "He will be worshipped in spirit and in truth."

"Do you plainly deny Christ to be in the sacrament?"

"I do. Jesus said: 'Take heed that no man shall deceive you. For many shall come in My name saying I am Christ; and shall deceive many.' The bread of the sacrament is but bread, and when you say it is the body of Christ, you deceive yourselves. Nebuchadnezzar made an image of gold and worshipped it. That is what you do. Bread is but bread . . ."

"Silence!" roared Gardiner. "You have been brought here, woman, to be tried for your life, not to preach heresy."

The judges conferred together and, finding her guilty, condemned her to death by burning.

They took her back to her dungeon in the Tower.

To die the martyr's death!

Had she the courage to do that? She could picture the flames rising from her feet; she could smell the burning faggots, she could hear their crackle. But how could she estimate the agonizing pain? She saw herself, the flames around her, the cross in her hand. Could she bear it with dignity and fortitude?

"Oh God," she prayed, "give me courage. Help me to bear my hour of pain, remembering how Thy Son, Jesus Christ, did suffer. Help me, God, for Jesus' sake."

She was on her knees throughout the night. Scenes from the past seemed to flit before her eyes. She was in her father's garden, with her sister, feeding the peacocks; she was being married to Mr. Kyme; she was enduring his embraces; she was in the barge which was carrying her to prison; she was facing her judges in the Guildhall.

At last, swooning from exhaustion, she lay on the floor of her cell.

But with the coming of morning she revived. She thought: Previously it was so easy to contemplate death, but that was when I did not know I was to die.

Within the palace they were talking of Anne Askew.

She had deliberately defied her judges. What a fool! What a sublime fool!

"This is but a beginning," it was whispered.

Those who had read the forbidden books and had dabbled with the new learning, were, in their fear, looking for plausible excuses.

"It was just an intellectual exercise, nothing more."

"It was not a heresy . . . not a faith to die for."

The Queen took to her bed; she was physically sick with horror. Anne—delicate Anne—condemned to the flames! This thing must not be allowed to happen. But how could she prevent it? What power had she?

The King had been irritable with her; he had ignored her when the courtiers were assembled. Once he had made up his mind regarding the Duchesses of Suffolk and Richmond he would find some means of disposing of his present Queen.

Her sister came and knelt by her bed. They did not speak, and Lady Herbert's eyes were veiled. She wanted to beg her sister to plead for Anne; yet at the same time she was silently begging the Queen to do nothing.

Little Jane Grey went quietly about the apartment. She knew what was happening. They would burn Mistress Anne Askew at the stake, and no one could do anything to save her.

Imaginative as she was, she felt that this terrible thing which was happening to Anne was happening to herself. She pictured herself in that cold and airless cell; she pictured herself facing her judges at the Guildhall.

That night she dreamed that she stood in the square at Smithfield, and that it was about her own feet that the men were piling faggots.

She was with the Prince when Princess Elizabeth came to see him.

Elizabeth was a young lady now of thirteen years. There were secrets in her eyes; she wore clothes to call attention to the color of her hair, and rings to set off the beauty of her hands. She could never look at a man without—so it seemed to Jane—demanding to know whether he admired her. She was even thus with her tutors. And it was clear that Mistress Katharine Ashley, who thought her the most wonderful person in the world, now found her a difficult charge.

Everyone, even Elizabeth, looked sad because of Anne Askew. Elizabeth liked the new learning as much as Jane did—but differently. Elizabeth appreciated it, but would be ready to abandon it. Jane thought: I would not. I would be like Anne Askew.

"Something *must* be done to save her!" said Jane.

Edward looked expectantly at his sister, for she was the one who was always full of plans. If something could be done, Elizabeth would invariably suggest the means.

But now she shook her head.

"There is nothing to be done. Those with good sense will keep quiet."

"We cannot let them send her to the stake!" insisted Jane.

"It is no affair of ours. We have no say in the matter."

"We could plead, could we not?"

"With whom could we plead?"

"With the King."

"Would you dare? Edward, would you dare?"

"With those *near* the King perhaps?" suggested Edward.

"With Gardiner?" cried the Princess ironically. "With the Chancellor?"

"No, indeed."

"Then with Cranmer? Ha! He is too wise. He does not forget how, recently, he himself came near to disaster. He will say nothing. He will allow this affair to pass away and be forgotten—as we all must."

"But it is Anne—our dearest Mistress Askew!"

"Our *foolish* Mistress Askew. She dared to stand up and say that the holy bread was not the body of Christ."

"But that is what we know to be true."

"*We* know?" Elizabeth opened her eyes very wide. "We *read* of these things, but we do not talk of them."

"But if she believes . . ."

"I tell you she is a fool. There is no place in this court . . . nor in this world, I trow, for fools."

"But you . . . no less than ourselves. . . ."

"You know not what you say."

"Then you are against Anne, against our stepmother? You are with Gardiner?"

"I am with none and against none," answered the Princess. "I am . . . with myself."

"Perhaps Uncle Thomas could put a plea before my father," said Edward. "He is clever with words, and my father is amused by him. Uncle Thomas will know what to do."

"'Tis true," said Elizabeth. "He will know what to do, and he will do what I shall do."

She smiled and her face flushed suddenly; it was clear to Jane that Elizabeth was thinking, not of wretched Anne Askew, but of jaunty Thomas Seymour.

-+->-<-+-

The King was in a merry mood. He sat, with a few of his courtiers about him, while a young musician—a beautiful boy—played his lute and sang with such sweetness that the King's thoughts were carried away from the apartment. The song was of love; so were the King's thoughts.

It should be my lady of Suffolk, he decided. She would bear him sons. He pictured her white body and her hair, touched with the bright yellow powder which so many used to give that pleasant golden touch. She was a fine, buxom woman.

Her glances had told him that she found him attractive. He liked her the better because she was the widow of Charles Brandon. There had always been friendship between himself and Charles. How readily he had forgiven the fellow when he had so hastily married Henry's own sister, Mary Tudor, after old Louis' death. Henry chuckled at the recollection of the old days, and a great longing for them swept over him.

He was not an old man. Fifty-five. Was that so old? He decided angrily that he felt old because he no longer had a wife who pleased him.

Why is it, he pondered, that she cannot give me sons?

He had the answer to that. God was displeased with her. And why should God be displeased with her? She was no harlot—he would admit that—as the others had been. No. But she was a heretic. She was another such as that friend of hers, this Anne Askew. And that woman had been found guilty and condemned to the flames. Henry licked his lips. Was this wife of his any less guilty than the woman they had condemned to die?

I would not wish her to die such a death, he thought. I am a merciful man. But was it right that one woman should die for her sins while another, equally guilty, should go free?

There was an unpleasant rumor that the Duchess of Suffolk was one of those ladies who had dabbled in heresy. He did not want to examine that now. He refused to believe it. It was the sort of thing her enemies would say against her, knowing his interest. No! There was no need to occupy his thoughts with that matter . . . at this time.

She was a fascinating creature—aye, and not a little fascinated by her King. Feeling perhaps just a little afraid of such a mighty lover, seeming at times to long to run away?

Perhaps. But he knew how she longed to stay!

In the old days she would have been his mistress ere this. But when a man grows older, he mused, he does not slip so easily into lovemaking. There is not the same desire for haste. Lovemaking must now be conducted more sedately, by the dim light of say . . . one candle?

His Chancellor was at his side. The King smiled. Wriothesley had comported himself well at the trial of the heretic. He had shown no softness merely because she was a woman.

A woman! A new vision of the Duchess's beauty rose before him. Soon to be tested! he thought with pleasure.

Nay! Anne Askew was scarcely a woman. Lean of body and caring for books rather than the caress of a lover. That was not how a woman should be. No! Anne Askew was no woman.

He caught the phrase and repeated it to his conscience, for he was wily and shrewd and could guess what plans were being formed in the Chancellor's mind.

No woman! No woman! he repeated to his conscience.

She was not alone in her guilt. There must be others. A little questioning, and she might disclose their names. The name of the Duchess of Suffolk came quickly into his mind. No, no. It was not true. He did not believe it. Moreover he had no fools about him. There was not one of them who would dare present him with the name of an *innocent* lady.

But why should Anne Askew not be questioned by his servants of the Tower? Because she was a woman? But she was no woman . . . no true woman.

And if I find heretics in my court, he said to his conscience, they shall not be spared. In the name of the Holy Church of which I am the head, they shall not be spared . . . no matter who . . . no matter who. . . .

He could see the fair Duchess staring dreamily ahead, listening to that song of love. Was she thinking of a lover, a most desirable and royal lover?

He spoke to his conscience again: "I am a King, and many matters weigh heavily on my mind. I am the head of a great State, and I have seen that State grow under my hands. I have shown wisdom in my relations with foreign powers. I have allowed nothing to stand in the way of England. I have played off the Emperor Charles against sly François . . . and I have seen my country grow in importance in the world. I am a King and, because of these state matters, which are ever with me, I have need of the soothing sweetness of love. I have need of a mistress."

The conscience said: "You have a wife."

"A wife who is a heretic?"

"Not yet proven."

The little eyes were prim.

"And if it were proved, I should have no alternative but to put her from me. I cannot tolerate heretics in my kingdom. Whoever they should prove to be, I could not tolerate those who work against God's truth."

"Nay! But it would have to be proved."

"Perhaps it is my duty to prove it. And when I talk of love I think not of my body's needs. When did I ever think of that? Nay! I need sons. I need them now in my declining years more than I ever did. If I put away one wife and take another, it would be solely with the object of getting myself sons, of making my line safe . . . for England's sake."

"That," said the conscience primly, "is a

very good motive for putting away a barren wife."

The conscience was subdued. It had been shown that as usual the sensualist and the moralist walked hand in hand.

And now the Chancellor was at his side.

He murmured: "Your Grace's pardon, but have I Your Grace's permission to question the condemned woman?"

"You suspect you can get the names of others?"

"I do, Your Majesty; and I propose to question her in the service of Your Grace."

"If there be those in this realm who disobey their King, I would know of them. Whoever they be, sir Chancellor, they may expect no mercy from me."

The Chancellor bowed. He was pleased to have won such an easy victory.

The door of Anne's cell was opening.

Two men had come for her.

"Is it to be so soon?" she asked. "Do you take me to Smithfield?"

"Not yet, mistress. You have another journey to make ere you set out on that last one."

"What journey is this?"

"You will see soon enough. Are you ready to come with us?"

"Yes."

She walked between the two men.

"Whither are you taking me?" she asked; but she believed she knew.

"Oh God," she prayed, "help me. Help me now as never before, for I need Your help. I am a woman . . . and weak . . . and I have suffered much. I am faint from hunger, sick from cold; but it is not these things which distress me. I mourn because I am afraid."

She fell against the slimy walls in her sickness; she drew back shuddering as she heard the rats scuttling away, alarmed by the sound of footsteps.

"This way, mistress."

One of the men pushed her forward, and before her dazed eyes appeared a short, spiral staircase, down which they led her.

Now they were in the gloomy dungeons below the great Tower. Foul odors from the river were stronger here.

"Oh God," she prayed, "let me die here. Let me die for the Faith. Willingly I will give my life. Let me not bring disgrace on the Faith. Let me be strong."

Now the sickening stench of stale blood

assailed her nostrils. She had no doubt to what place they were taking her. Misery seemed to haunt it. She fancied she heard the screams of men in agony. Did she really hear them, or were they the ghostly echoes of forgotten men?

She was pushed into the chamber—that dread chamber, the sight of which sickened the hearts of the bravest men.

She fell against a stone pillar from which hung the hideous instruments whose uses she could only guess, except that she knew they were made to torture men.

Two men had come toward her—two of the most brutish-looking men she had ever seen. Their eyes betrayed them—their glittering, cold, excited eyes. Those eyes betrayed too a certain lewdness in their thoughts; it was as though they spoke and said: "Ha! Here we have a woman!" These two men were Chancellor Wriothesley and Solicitor-General Rich, whom she had seen at her trial.

She was aware that this was to be one of the most important cross-examinations which had ever taken place in this room, for not only were the Chancellor and the Solicitor-General present, but there also was Sir

Anthony Knevet, the Lieutenant of the Tower.

She looked at him appealingly, for he had not the cruel, animal look of the other men, and it seemed to her that there was sympathy in his eyes, as though they meant to convey the message to her: "I am not responsible for this. I but obey orders."

The Chancellor spoke first. He had seated himself at the table on which were writing materials.

"You wonder why you are brought here, madam?" he said.

"I know why people are brought here. It is to answer questions."

"You are clever. I can see that we need not waste time with explanations."

The Solicitor-General had turned to her. "You will answer my questions, madam."

"Do not weary yourselves with asking me questions," she said. "I have answered them, and I shall not change those answers. I believe that the body of Christ . . ."

Rich waved a hand. "No, no. That is settled. You are a heretic. We know that. You have been sentenced, and that case is closed."

"It is for another reason that you are

brought here," said Wriothesley. "You were not alone in your heresies. You must know the names of many people who support that erroneous belief for which you are going to die."

"How should I know what goes on in the hearts and minds of others?"

"Madam, you are very clever. You have read too many books . . . far too many books. But do not waste your cleverness on us. We do not want sly answers. We want *names*."

"Names?"

"The names of those who attended your meetings, who read those books with you."

"I cannot give you names."

"Why not, madam?"

"If I could say with certainty that such and such a person believes as I do . . . even so I would not give a name."

"It would be wise not to be saucy. We are less patient here than in the Guildhall."

"That I understand. Many may hear your words in the Guildhall. Here, you may say what you will."

"Madam, you are a lady of gentle birth. I do not think you realize the importance of your visit to this chamber."

"I know, sir, why you have brought me here," she said. "Here you bring men to suffer torture. I did not know that you brought women. I understand now that it is so."

"You are insolent, Madam. Have a care."

Wriothesley signed to the two men, who came forward. They were professional torturers; their faces were blank; they were devoid of all feeling, as all must become who ply such a horrible trade.

They had seized her by the arms, and Wriothesley put his face close to hers.

"I do not think even now that you fully understand what will happen to you if you are obstinate. You have heard of the rack, no doubt, but you have no notion of its action."

"I can imagine that," she answered; she hoped that he did not see her lips moving in prayer, forming that one word which made up her desperate plea: Courage.

"Take her to the rack," said the Solicitor-General. "Mayhap the sight of it will bring her to her senses."

She was dragged across the room and her eyes perceived that instrument which none could look on without a shudder. It was shaped like a trough, at the ends of which were windlasses; in these, slots had been cut in which oars could be placed in order to turn them, and about them were coiled ropes to which the wrists and ankles of the sufferer could be tied and made taut by winding the windlasses. By means of the oars, in the hands of two strong men, the windlasses could be turned so that the victim's legs and arms were slowly pulled out of their sockets. Even the dreaded Scavenger's Daughter was not more feared than the rack.

"You . . . you would put me on the rack . . . in the hope that I would betray the innocent?" asked Anne.

"We would put you there that you might betray the guilty."

She looked at the men about her, and her eyes rested on the anxious face of the Lieutenant of the Tower, but he could not bear to meet her glance. He said: "My lords, I like this not. A lady . . . to be put on the rack!"

"Those are His Majesty's orders," said Wriothesley.

Knevet turned away. "If you are sure, gentlemen, that these are the King's commands, then we must obey them." He turned to Anne. "I appeal to you, madam.

Give us the names that we ask of you, and save yourself from torture."

"I cannot give names merely to save myself from pain. How could I?"

"You are brave," said the Lieutenant. "But be guided by me. Give the names . . . and have done with this miserable affair."

"I am sorry," said Anne steadfastly.

"Then," said Wriothesley, "we have no alternative. Madam, you will take off your robe."

She was made to stand before them in her shift, whereupon they placed her on the rack and attached the ropes to her emaciated wrists and ankles.

"Are you sure," said Wriothesley, "that you wish us to continue?"

"You must do with me as you will."

The Chancellor and Solicitor-General signed to the two men who had taken their stand at each end of the trough.

Slowly the windlasses began to turn; her poor sagging body became taut, and then . . . such agony took possession of it that for one terrible moment she must scream aloud for mercy. But almost immediately she was lost in blessed unconsciousness.

They would not allow her to remain in that happy state. They were splashing vinegar on her face. She opened her eyes, but she did not see the men about her; she was aware only of her sagging body held to the ropes by her dislocated limbs.

Wriothesley said: "The pain is terrible, I know. Endure no more of it. Merely whisper those names."

She tried to turn her face away. Her lips began to move; but as Wriothesley put his ear close to her face, he was disgusted to find that she gave no names; it was but prayers she uttered, prayers for courage and the strength to endure her pains.

Wriothesley cried out in anger: "Again! Again! The woman is a fool. Let her suffer for her folly. That was merely a taste. Now let her have the full fury."

"No . . . no . . ." cried Anne's lips. "This . . . is . . . too . . ."

She had believed, a few seconds before, that she had learned all she could ever know about pain, that she had suffered it in all its malignancy, its fullest and most venomous powers. She was mistaken. Here was woeful agony, excruciating, exquisite torture, the very peaks of pain. "Oh God, let me die . . . let me die. . . ." Those words beat on and on in her brain.

But they would not let her die. They would not let her long enjoy the benefit of unconsciousness. They were there, those evil men, bringing her out of the blessed darkness to suffer more pain.

"Names . . . names . . . names. . . ." The words beat on her ears.

"Oh, God," she prayed, "I had not thought of this. I had not thought I could endure so much and live. I had thought of the quick sharp pain. Death by the flames could not bring such agony as this."

She heard the voice of Wriothesley beating like an iron bar on her shattered nerves:

"I will have those names. I will. I will. Again. Again. Give it to her again. You men are soft. You are too gentle. By God, I'll have those names."

Sir Anthony Knevet intervened: "My lords, I protest against this additional racking. The lady has been put to the test. That is enough."

"And who, sir," demanded the Chancellor, "are you to say what shall and what shall not be done?"

"I am the Lieutenant of this Tower. I am in

sole charge in this Tower. The lady shall not, with my consent, be tortured further."

"And who has placed you in command of this Tower? You forget to whom you owe your honors. This is rank disobedience to His Majesty's orders. I will carry reports of this to the King, and we shall see how much longer you remain Lieutenant of the Tower, sir."

Sir Anthony grew pale. He was afraid of the Chancellor and the Solicitor-General, for the two stood firm against him. But when he looked from them to the half-dead woman on the rack, he boldly said: "I cannot give my consent to the continuation of the racking." He turned to the torturers. "Hold!" he ordered. "Have done."

Wriothesley laughed.

"Then must we do the work ourselves. Come, Rich!" he cried; and he threw off his cloak. "We will work this together. We will show the lady what happens to those who defy us. As for you, sir Lieutenant, you will hear more of this matter. I, personally, shall convey the tale of your disobedience to the King."

Knevet walked out of the chamber.

Rich hesitated; the two professional tor-

turers, who dared not disobey the Lieutenant's orders, stood watching. But
Wriothesley had pushed them aside, was
rolling up his sleeves, and, signing to Rich
to do the same, he took an oar.

And venomously and most cruelly did
those two go to work.

Anne was past prayers, past thought.
There was nothing in the world for her, but
the most exquisite agony ever inflicted on
man or woman; there was nothing for her
but the longing for death.

Sweating with their exertions, Wriothesley
and Rich paused.

"She cannot endure more," said Rich.
"She is on the point of death."

Rich was also thinking: And Knevet will
be in his barge at this moment on his way to
Greenwich. And what will the King say? His
Majesty would not want this woman to die
on the rack; he only wanted her to betray, as
a heretic, the woman of whom he was so
tired that he wished to rid himself of her.

Wriothesley followed his thoughts.

"Remove the ropes," he said. "She has
had enough."

The professional torturers untied the

ropes and laid the broken body of Anne
Askew on the floor.

Knevet sought an audience with the King.

"Your Majesty, I come in great haste. I
come to lay before you my sincere apolo-
gies if I have disobeyed your orders. But I
cannot believe Your Most Clement Majesty
ever gave such orders."

"What orders are these?" asked the King,
his shrewd eyes glinting. He guessed that
the Lieutenant of the Tower had news of
Anne Askew.

"Your Grace, I have come straight from
the racking of Anne Askew."

"The racking of Anne Askew!" The King's
voice was noncommittal. He wished Anne
Askew to betray the Queen's guilt, but he
did not care to have his name connected
with the racking of a woman.

The Lieutenant of the Tower lifted his eyes
hopefully to the King's face.

"It is the woman, Your Grace, who is condemned to the stake."

"The heretic," said Henry. "She is condemned with three men, I understand. She
has offended against our Holy Church and

slandered the Mass. She has been tried and her judges have found her guilty."

"That is so, Your Majesty. The sentence is just. But . . . they are racking her to death. Your Chancellor and Solicitor-General are racking her for information."

"Racking her! Racking a woman!"

Knevet was on his knees, kissing the King's hand.

"I knew that Your Grace in your great mercy would never have given your consent to such treatment of a frail woman. I could not allow myself to be involved in the matter unless I had written orders from Your Majesty. I trust I did right."

The King's lips were prim. To rack a woman! He had never given his consent to that. The rack had not been mentioned in his talk with the Chancellor.

"You did right," said the King.

"Then I have Your Majesty's pardon?"

"There is no need of pardon, my friend." The King laid his hand on Knevet's shoulder. "Go back to your duties with a good conscience."

Fervently Knevet continued to kiss the King's hand.

As he was about to retire, Henry said:

"And the woman . . . did she disclose . . . er . . . anything of interest?"

"No, Your Majesty. She is a brave woman, heretic though she be. I left the Chancellor and Solicitor-General working the rack themselves, and with great severity."

The King frowned. "And . . . on a frail woman!" he said in shocked tones. "It may be that under dire torture she will betray others who are as guilty as she is."

"I doubt it, Your Majesty. She was then too weak to know anything but her agony."

The King turned away as though to hide his distress that such things could happen in his realm. "A woman . . ." he murmured, his voice half sorrowful, half angry. "A frail woman!"

But when the Lieutenant had gone, his eyes, angry points of light, almost disappeared in his bloated face.

"A curse on all martyrs!" he muttered. "A curse on them all!"

Memories of others came to him in that moment. Norris and Derham; Fisher and More.

And it seemed to him that the ghosts of those martyrs were in the room, mocking him.

In that square where so many tragedies had been played out, where medieval duels had been fought, where the sixty-two-year-old Edward III had held a seven-day joust for the entertainment of the young woman with whom he was in love, where Wat Tyler had been bettered by the youthful Richard II—in that square of gay triumphs and cruel deeds, men were now piling the faggots around four stakes.

From all over London the people were coming to Smithfield. Today was a show day, and the crowning event of a day's sightseeing was to be the burning of four martyrs, one of them a woman—the famous Anne Askew. They chattered and laughed and quarreled, and most impatiently they waited for the sight of those who were to suffer.

The hot sun burned down on the walls of the Priory renowned for the fine mulberries that grew in its grounds, picking out the sharp stones and making them glitter. The smell of horses was in the air, although this place was to be used for a purpose other than the marketing of horses on this tragic day.

On a bench outside the Church of St. Bartholomew sat Wriothesley, with important members of his party, among them the old Duke of Norfolk and the Lord Mayor.

Wriothesley was uneasy.

The King had not reproved him in private for the racking of Anne Askew, and he knew that he had done what His Majesty had wished even though he could not be commended for it in public. Still, the torturing had been a failure, for the woman had refused to give the names which were required of her; and it was not wise to forge a false confession, for she was a fearless woman who was quite capable of exposing the fraud when she was at the stake and there would be many to hear her.

Yes, the affair was a failure, for clearly the torturing and burning of a gentlewoman had not in itself been the desire of the King or the Chancellor. The motive had been to implicate the Queen, and that had not been achieved.

On this day a fence had been erected on all sides of the square. It was necessary to keep back the press of people. He was afraid of what they might do, what sympathies they might display toward a woman who had been broken on the rack . . . what-ever her faith. He was afraid of what words Anne Askew might speak while the flames crackled at her feet. Fervently he hoped that if she did speak, the fences would prevent the mass of sightseers from being near enough to hear her. He was, therefore, a most uneasy man.

The victims were now on their way from Newgate, whither Anne had been taken af-ter her torturing, to await the day of her death. Anne came first. She was carried to the stake in her chair, for her limbs were useless. The people shouted when they saw her. The cry of "Heretic! To the stake with the heretics!" was distinctly heard. But so also were the words: "God bless you." And some pressed forward to touch the garment of one who they considered would shortly be a holy martyr.

Her golden hair lay lusterless about her shoulders, but how fiercely her blue eyes burned. No torture could douse the light which burned within her. She was the fanat-ical and triumphant martyr. She knew that she had come successfully through the greater ordeal. Death by the flames would offer a welcome release from pain.

With her were three men—three others who had denied the Mass. None of them was considered of any importance; they were humble people. John Lascelles was the most interesting, because he had been the man who had first spread the rumors concerning Catharine Howard and so sent her to her doom.

Wriothesley thought fleetingly that every man was near to death. He who condemned today, was in his turn condemned tomorrow.

He turned to Norfolk. "A woman to die thus! It seems cruel."

"Aye," said Norfolk, who had seen two female relatives, wives of the King, lose their heads. "But she is nevertheless a heretic."

"I have the King's pardon in my pocket. It is hers if she will recant. I wish to let the people know that pardon awaits her if she will see reason."

"Have it sent to her before the sermon starts."

Anne received the message while, about her body, they were fixing the chain which would hold her to the stake.

"I come not hither," she said, "to deny my Lord and Master."

She saw that the three men who were to die with her received similar messages.

They were brave, but they lacked her spirit. They turned their agonized eyes to her, and she saw how their apprehensive bodies longed to recant, although their spirits would firmly ignore the frailty of the flesh.

She said: "My friends, we have suffered . . . I more than any of you. I am happy now. I long for death. I long to feel the flames. To deny your God now, would mean that you would loathe the life offered you on such terms."

She smiled and looked almost lovingly at the faggots about her maltreated legs.

Then the men smiled with her and tried to emulate her courage.

"They are beginning the sermons," she said. "There is Dr. Shaxton. He will preach to us, he who a short while ago was one of us. Now he has denied his faith. He has chosen life on Earth in place of the life everlasting. Do not envy him, my friends, for very soon now you and I will be in paradise. We are to die, and we die for truth. We die in the Lord. God bless you, my friends. Have no fear; for I have none."

She held the cross in her hands. She lifted her eyes to Heaven, seeming to be unaware of the flickering flames. She heard the shrieks of agony about her; but she was smiling as the flames crept up her tortured body.

Soon there was silence, and a pall of smoke hung above Smithfield Square.

The King was dissatisfied.

The execution had availed him nothing. He was a tired man; he was a King in need of relaxation, and my lady of Suffolk seemed to grow more fair as the days passed.

He was overburdened with matters of state. The cost of garrisoning the town of Boulogne and holding it against the French was a considerable drain on his resources, yet he would not give it up. It was an additional foothold in France which he felt was necessary to England. He affectionately called Boulogne "my daughter"; and it was said that he never squandered so much on any child of his as he did on the bricks and soil of that town.

Indeed he needed relaxation. In the days of his youth he had found great pleasure in the hunt; but he could no longer hunt with pleasure. He had enjoyed dancing, jousting, playing games, amusing and distinguishing himself in the tiltyard. But now that he was no longer a young man those avenues to pleasure were closed. There was still love. He needed love; but because he was a virtuous man—and he was continually worried by the thought that his end might not be far off—it must be legalized love; the sort of love which would not distress his conscience while it delighted his body.

All the kings of his age were egoists; but egoism was the very essence of this King's nature. Everything that happened must be colored by his view of it, garnished and flavored to satisfy his conscience.

After he had fallen from grace, Cardinal Wolsey, who had perhaps known him better than any other person, said of him: "The King is a man of royal courage. He has a princely heart; and rather than he will miss or want part of his appetite he will hazard the loss of one-half of his kingdom."

It was true of Henry. He was as Wolsey had seen him. But he was strong and ruthless in an age when strength and ruthlessness were the qualities a growing country looked for in its King; and under this man a little island had become a great power; he, who had seemed to his enemies on the Continent of Europe but of ducal standing when he ascended the throne, had become a mighty King.

But there was more than one Henry. Just as there was the moralist and the sensualist, so there was the strong and ruthless ruler, determined to make his country great, and that other who must at all cost have his pleasure and who was ready to sacrifice half his kingdom for his appetite. But every phase of Henry's character—the moralist, the sensualist, the great King and the weak King—was dominated by the brutal, callous monster.

Those about him, those sly and subtle ministers, continually watching him, sensed his moods.

They had murdered Anne Askew, but they still had to rid him of his sixth wife and provide him with a seventh. And there came a day shortly after the executions in Smithfield when Gardiner found his opportunity.

Gardiner had been granted an audience with the King when His Majesty was alone with the Queen, and the Bishop sensed at once a certain tension in the atmosphere. The King was irritated and wished to quarrel with the Queen; and the woman would give him no opportunity.

When Gardiner had the King's signature to the papers which he had set before him, he spoke of the execution of Anne Askew, a subject which never failed to upset the Queen so thoroughly that it set her emotions above her common sense.

The King scowled.

"The trouble, Your Grace," said Gardiner, "can be traced to these books which are circulating in your realm. They lead astray those who read them." Gardiner had turned to the Queen, and he added pointedly: "Your Majesty has doubtless seen the books to which I refer?"

"I?" said Katharine, flushing uncomfortably.

"I feel sure that the woman, Anne Askew, must have brought them to Your Grace's notice."

Katharine, who had suffered and was still suffering from the tragedy which had robbed her of a woman whom she had loved and respected, said sharply: "The

books I see and read could be of little interest to you, my lord Bishop."

"Not if they were forbidden books, Your
Majesty."

"Forbidden books!" cried the Queen. "I
was unaware that I must ask my lord
Bishop's advice as to what I might and
might not read."

Henry, who could never like Gardiner,
thought his manner insolent, and growled:
"I, too, was unaware of it."

Gardiner bowed. He was a bold man and
he knew that he was but obeying the will of
the King in what he was doing.

"In truth," he said quietly, "it would be
presumptuous of me to direct Your Highness's reading. I would but express an opinion that it might be unwise for the Queen's
Grace to have in her possession books
given to her by those who, by order of the
King, have been found guilty of heresy and
sentenced to death."

The King's eyes glistened; they almost
disappeared into his face as they did in moments of great pleasure or anger.

"What books are these?" he growled.
"Has our Queen become the friend of those
who work against us?"

Gardiner caught the note of excitement in the King's voice. Was this the moment? Could he, by subtle words, trap the Queen, as he and the Chancellor had been unable to do by applying the torture to Anne Askew?

"Indeed not," said Katharine.

She saw the crafty wickedness in her husband's eyes, and because of what had happened to those who had shared his throne before her, she read his thoughts.

"Not so?" said the King. "We would be sure of that."

"Your Majesty will hear me out?" said Katharine.

The King would not look at her. "I am weary of these conflicts," he said. "I will not have my Queen take part in them . . . or if she does, she will not long remain my Queen."

The threat in his words terrified Katharine. "Courage!" she prayed, as Anne Askew had prayed before her. But she knew that she, who loved life so much, could never face death as Anne had. Anne had longed for death, for martyrdom; and Katharine had never ceased to long for life and Thomas Seymour.

"Conflicts . . . ?" she stammered.

"You heard us," said the King; and the scowl on his brow had deepened. His anger shifted from the Queen to Gardiner. At that moment he disliked them both heartily and he was thinking: I am a King, heavily burdened with matters of state. I need pleasure to soothe me; I need gentle relaxation. Instead I have these two to plague me. Methinks it is time I rid myself of them both. "It would appear," he continued, keeping his eyes on Gardiner, "that there are some among us who, in place of preaching the Word of God, do nothing but rail against one another." His eyes shifted unpleasantly from the Bishop to the Queen and back to the Bishop. "If any know that there are those among us who preach perverse doctrines, he should come and declare it before us or some of our council. Have I not said it before?"

Gardiner murmured: "Your Majesty has indeed, and it shall be done. . . ."

The King waved a hand; he was not going to endure one of Gardiner's speeches. If any should speak now it would be the King.

"We now permit our subjects to read the Holy Scriptures," he said, "and to have the

Word of God in our mother tongue, and I will have it known that it is licensed them so to do only to inform their consciences, their children and their families, and not to dispute and to make scripture a railing and a taunting stock. This I have said to my parliament, and now I say it to you, Bishop, and to you, wife. I am sorry to know how irreverently that precious jewel, the Word of God, is disputed, rhymed, sung and jangled in every alehouse and tavern, contrary to the true meaning and doctrine of the same."

He paused and raised his eyes devoutly to the ceiling, as though he knew that God was watching and applauding.

"My lord King," said Katharine, "when Your Most Gracious Majesty says 'to dispute,' Your Grace cannot mean that it is not lawful to discuss, one with another, the interpretation of the Gospel?"

"I should have thought that we had stated our meaning clearly," said the King with weary menace. "What do you, madam? Would you question the decision of our ministers?"

"Never, my lord, but . . . but . . ."

"But? But?" cried the King threateningly. "You would then question *our* decision?"

"I do no such thing, Your Majesty," said Katharine quickly, "since it would be unseemly on my part. I would only beg Your Grace that you might cease to forbid the use of that translation which you previously licensed."

The King let loose his anger. He flagellated it to greater vehemence. He wanted to find fault with his wife; he was tired of her. Through the haze of his fury he saw the alluring body of the Duchess of Suffolk.

"By my faith!" he cried. "I'll have obedience from my subjects; and hark ye! a wife is not less a subject because she is a wife. Madam, when we say it is forbidden to use a translation, it *is* forbidden."

"My lord," said Katharine, trembling before the storm which she had raised, "your word is law indeed, but this translation did so clearly set forth the truth . . ."

"We would hear no more," roared the King. "Therefore you have our leave to retire from our presence."

She knelt before him, but he waved her away.

"Come," he said, turning to Gardiner, "let us attend to matters of state."

When Katharine had gone, the purple color flamed anew into his face.

"A good hearing it is," he snarled, "when women become such clerks; and much to my comfort to be taught in my old age by my wife!"

Gardiner's eyes were glistening; he wetted his dry lips. "Your Majesty, have I your leave to speak to you on a very serious matter?"

The King's shrewd eyes appraised his Bishop. He knew the nature of this serious matter; it was a matter, above all others, that he wished to discuss.

"You have my leave," he said.

"Your Majesty said that if any offended against your laws, no matter what rank that person should hold . . . it was the bounden duty . . ."

"Yes . . . yes . . ." said the King testily. "I remember my words. There is no need to repeat them."

"There are secret matters, Your Majesty, which I have long sought an opportunity of bringing to your ears . . . but since they concern the opinions of the Queen . . ."

"Well?" cried the King. "Get on, man. Get on."

"Your Majesty excels the princes of this and any other age as well as all the professed doctors of divinity. It is unseemly for any of Your Majesty's subjects to argue and discuss with you as malapertly as the Queen hath done. It is grievous for any of your counselors to hear this done."

"You're right, Bishop. You're right there."

Gardiner lowered his voice. "Your Grace, I could make great discoveries, were I not held back by the Queen's faction."

The King looked fiercely at his Bishop, but his pleasure was obvious; and Gardiner knew that the moment for which he had longed was at hand. He would not have been in his eminent position if he had not been a man to seize his opportunities.

Nan wandered listlessly about the gardens of Hampton Court. It was no use pretending that she was unafraid. Every time a messenger came to the apartment she would find herself shivering.

She had heard of the terrible things which had happened to Anne Askew in the Tower. She had been there, at Smithfield Square, and had seen the poor broken creature they had carried out in her chair. She could not look on that gruesome end to Anne's tragedy; she had knelt on the stones praying while the horrible smoke rose to the sky.

And those wicked men who had destroyed Anne now sought to destroy the Queen.

Nan watched a bee fly past, on the way from the flower garden, laden with pollen. She envied the bee who knew nothing of court intrigues, of fear, and the terrible things which could be done to a good and virtuous woman who had asked nothing but to be allowed to think for herself.

And what next? wondered Nan.

She was in constant dread that she herself would be taken to the Tower. What if they questioned her under torture? It was not the pain that she dreaded so much as the fear that she would not be strong enough to keep silent, and that she might betray the Queen.

What tragedies these gardens must have seen! It seemed to Nan that tension and horror were in the very air of this place. So many had suffered here. So many had walked these gardens waiting for disaster to overtake them.

And now, in the court, people were saying that the days of Katharine Parr were numbered.

The King had turned his eyes elsewhere; and here was the same pattern that had been worked before, with Katharine Parr in place of Anne Boleyn.

I would die for her! thought Nan; for dying would be easy. And oh, how I pray that it may never be my evil lot to betray her.

She must not delay. It was time to attend, with the other ladies, in the Queen's apartment. The Queen's apartment. . . . How long before there would be a new Queen in place of Queen Katharine?

She was about to cross the great courtyard when she saw, hurrying across it, that man who had taken off his mantle that he himself might ferociously work the rack and so inflict greater torture on the suffering body of Anne Askew. Nan drew back and hid herself in an archway.

Sir Thomas Wriothesley, the Lord Chancellor, was smiling, and it occurred to Nan that she had never seen him look so smug.

What could this mean? What fresh evil was he planning?

And as he crossed the courtyard, obviously in great haste, by some chance which could only be called miraculous, a scroll fell from his sleeve and came to rest on the cobbles.

Nan waited for him to pick it up, but he was unaware that it had fallen.

He passed on into the palace.

Quickly, and with madly beating heart, Nan ran out of her hiding place and picked up the documents.

She felt them to be of great importance, but she did not stop to read them; she thrust them into her bodice and ran, as fast as she could, to the Queen's apartment. Intuitively she knew that the self-satisfied smile on the face of the Chancellor had something to do with these documents.

When she was in a small antechamber she took them from her bodice and examined one of them. She saw the seal and the King's signature, and with horror, realized what it was.

Benumbed, she stood looking at it, and never in all her life had she felt such misery.

"What shall I do?" she whispered. "What can I do?"

She closed her eyes and said a short prayer asking for help and guidance that

she might do the right thing. Then she thrust
the documents back into her bodice and
went to find the Queen.

In the privy chamber the Queen sat alone
with her sister. She could not bring herself
to work on the embroidery which lay on the
window-seat.

She had been aware of the atmosphere of
brooding disaster which pervaded the
court. She was conscious of the quick
glances which the King gave her now and
then. All the ladies and gentlemen of the
court were aware of it. They waited, with a
certain fatalism, for past events to be repeated.

Lady Herbert felt the tension as much as
any. Not only did she fear for her sister but
for her husband, Lord Herbert, who was involved in the new learning as deeply as she
was. It was true that the powerful Seymours
were with them, but one felt sure, knowing
the mental agility of the Seymours, that if
there was trouble they would, with a few
twists and turns, extricate themselves and
leave their friends to take the blame.

The tragedy of Anne Askew could not be
forgotten or misunderstood. It was a grim

warning, the shadow cast before approaching disaster.

Katharine spoke of it, for to whom could
she speak her thoughts if not to this
beloved sister?

"I cannot bear to refer to it," she said.
"And yet I cannot bear not to."

"Oh, my sister, when the mind is disturbed, it is well to speak of the worry, since
it is not dismissed by silence."

"How brave she was! Oh, Anne, could
any of us be as brave?"

"I doubt it. It seems she was born to be a
martyr. She longed for martyrdom. She was
different from the rest of us. She embraced
death eagerly; but dearest Kate . . . you and
I . . . there is much on Earth that we long
for."

"You speak truth there, sister."

Anne said: "You think of Seymour still, do
you not?"

"I do."

"Dearest Kate, it is not wise."

"Love is beyond wisdom."

"Sometimes I wonder . . ."

"You wonder whether I am a foolish
woman to love him? You see him about the
court, seeming not to care for me, casting

his eyes on others. But, Anne, what could he do? How could he show his love for me, the King's wife?"

Anne Herbert sighed and turned away. The tragedy of Anne Askew was a safer subject than the love of Thomas Seymour.

"I have scarcely slept since they took Anne Askew to the Tower," she said.

"Nor I. I have dreams, Anne . . . horrible dreams. I dream of her on the rack . . . so frail . . . so delicate. And her bearing it so bravely, refusing to name us. I am glad we made her days in prison as comfortable as we could."

"We acted foolishly in sending Nan with comforts," said Anne. "But I am glad we did so. I, like you, dream dreams . . . of discovery. I dream that Nan . . . little Nan . . . is caught and tortured."

The Queen shuddered. "If she had betrayed us they would have sent me to the Tower."

"Dearest Kate, I think that was what Gardiner wished to do. Face the truth, my sister. It was you whom they wanted . . . not poor Anne Askew."

"How I hate that man . . . and Wriothesley . . . Wriothesley the brute who tortured

Anne with his own hands. How I hate them both!"

"Do not let your hatred grow too hot. You must be cool and calm . . . as they are."

"Anne . . . my dearest sister . . . what can I do?"

Anne Herbert rose and, going to the Queen, put her hands on her shoulders and, drawing her toward her, held her close.

"Kate, face the truth. When the King's nuptial ring was put on your finger, your head was placed directly under the ax."

"I know it, Anne. I would be brave, but I am so frightened. When I think of what happiness might have been mine . . ."

"Hush! You must not speak of Seymour. You must not *think* of him." Anne Herbert's mouth hardened. "You must play *his* game. When he looks at you it would seem he has forgotten that he ever thought to make you his wife."

"He is clever. He thinks of me, but he knows that one careless word would be enough to send us both to the scaffold. Oh, Anne, often I think of those others . . . Anne Boleyn and Catharine Howard."

"But you must not! You must not!"

"How can I help it? What happened to them will happen to me."

"Nay!" Anne was frightened by the signs of hysteria in her sister. "We have the advantage of knowing what happened to them."

Katharine laughed wildly, and it was laughter which aroused fresh fears in her sister. Was this calm Kate, the practical one? They had made fun of Kate in the old days at home. Dear, sensible little Kate! they had called her. How placidly she had received the news that she was to marry Lord Borough; and how quickly she had adjusted herself to life with her husbands. There had never been any sign of hysteria in Kate during those years. But she had been living at the whim of a royal murderer for the last three years, and the strain was too much. It would break through the deep composure.

"Death is a dreary subject," said Anne. "And how do any of us know when it will catch up with us? Come. I want you to see this embroidery of mine."

"It is beautiful," said the Queen. After a short silence she went on: "I often think of life in Yorkshire. Long summer days and the buzz of the bees in the lavender. I would sit

in the garden with my husband and we
would talk of . . . little things; the weeding
that would have to be done; the little affairs
of those who labored for us. How different
life was! I was a Catholic then."

"Catholic or Protestant, none is safe,
Kate."

"You are right. From the fury of the King
none is safe."

There was a knock on the door.

"Who is there?" cried Katharine, and the
color left her face.

Every knock, every sound, is to her like
the death knell! thought Anne.

"Please come in," said the Queen in a
breathless voice.

The door was opened and both ladies felt
an immense relief, because it was only Nan
who stood there.

But what had happened to Nan? Her face
was parchment color and her eyes were
wild; she held her hands across her bodice
as though she feared someone might force
from her what was hidden there.

"Your Majesty . . ." she stammered; and
she did not fall on her knees, but stood still,
looking wildly from the Queen to the
Queen's sister.

"You are distressed, Nan," said the Queen. "What ails you?"

"Your Majesty, I know not what I have done. I thought it for the best. . . ."

"Come here, Nan. Tell us what troubles you."

Nan came forward and, as she did so, took the documents from her bodice.

"It was in the courtyard, Your Majesty. I saw the Chancellor. He was smiling, and he looked . . . so evil, that I greatly feared what was in his mind. And then . . . this dropped from his gown. I picked it up, and instead of running after him, something held me back. And . . . I saw Your Majesty's name . . . so I brought it to you. If I have done aught wrong, it was for love of Your Majesty."

The Queen took the documents. She said: "Nan, you did well to bring this to me. If . . . if it is aught that should be passed on to a member of the court, I will see to its despatch."

"I thank Your Majesty."

Nan had recovered her self-possession. She had done all that she could.

Katharine said: "You may go, Nan." And her sister, watching her, was aware of the great effort she was making to keep her control.

"I . . . I trust I did right, Your Majesty," said Nan dropping to her knees.

"Yes, Nan. Yes."

Nan went out, and Lady Herbert said quickly: "What are these papers?"

"They concern me, Anne. They concern me deeply. Read this! You see . . ."

Anne took the paper, and as she gazed at it, realized that what she had feared above all things had come to pass.

"It is a mandate for my arrest," said Katharine slowly, and the hysterical laughter was in her voice.

"Oh God!" cried Anne. "It has come. It has come then." She kept staring at the paper; she longed to tell herself that her eyes had deceived her, that fear and anger had made her see what was not there. But she knew that her eyes were not deceived. She cried out angrily: "Wriothesley has done this. He . . . and Gardiner. I would it were in my power to kill them!"

"But it is not in your power," said Katharine wildly. "It is they who have the power. It is they who plan to kill me."

"Nan saw this mandate for your arrest.

She has endangered her life by bringing it to you. There are many who love you, Kate. Remember that. Remember it, dearest sister. Wriothesley was on his way to the King. He would have done his best to persuade His Majesty to sign."

Katharine's laughter seemed to fill the apartment. "Did you not see then? Did you not see it, Anne?"

Anne stared at her sister.

"The King!" cried Katharine wildly. "The King *has* signed. See. Here! The King has signed the mandate for the Queen's arrest."

Katharine walked to the window and looked out over the gardens where the red and white roses were lifting their faces to the hot sunshine.

She whispered: "I shall go down to the river. I shall take boat to the Tower. I shall enter by the Traitors' Gate. That which I have dreaded so long is about to take place. Can aught prevent it? Oh, Thomas . . . we could have been happy together, you and I. But 'twas not to be so. I might not be your wife, for I must be a Queen. Often I have wondered about those who went before me, who enjoyed royal favor and who suffered royal displeasure. I have no need to wonder now." She turned to her sister. "Do not weep for me, Anne. The shadow has grown large above me. I have seen it grow. Sweet sister, I am no lighthearted girl to imagine that the way which was so thorny for some would be smooth for me."

"Katharine . . . perchance this is not the end."

The Queen shook her head slowly. "This much I know: You spoke truth when you said that the King put a ring of doom about me when he placed the nuptial ring on my finger. None may share the throne of Henry of England and escape disaster. Mine closes in upon me now."

Anne Herbert watched the Queen with wide and terrified eyes. That calmness would break, she knew; and then what would happen?

"Save her," prayed Anne. "Save her. Death should not come to her so soon. She is young; she is sweet and kind and has never willingly harmed any. Oh God, let her live. Let her have a chance of happiness. She is not meant for death . . . not yet, dear Lord, not yet."

And the Queen stood long at the window, looking out on the white and red roses of

York and Lancaster blooming side by side within the Tudor fence.

The Queen lay on her bed. Her ladies had drawn the curtains, but the sound of her un-restrained sobbing could be heard even in the adjoining apartments.

A familiar sound within these walls—a Queen's sobbing! The gallery was haunted by the sound of another Queen's cries—those of the fifth Queen. How could the sixth Queen hope to evade the fate of the others?

"What means it?" asked the gentlemen of the King's bedchamber when they heard the sound of the Queen's distress.

"What has happened? Something of which we have not yet heard?"

They could guess what was about to hap-pen. Had it not happened to others?

How far would this go? Would this mean the end of others besides the Queen? The Seymours seemed strong, but would the downfall of the Queen mean the downfall of their party? Those with Protestant leanings would have to take care, for if the King had decided to rid himself of the Queen, he must show less favor to her party. The

King's physical needs had always in some measure dictated his state policy. He was a ruthless ruler with voracious appetites.

Speculation was rife. And all through the day the Queen's hysterical sobbing could be heard, and many thought that she was on the point of losing her reason.

Lady Herbert and Nan sat together in the ante-chamber. Between those two was a great bond: their devotion to the Queen.

"I fear she will die," said Anne Herbert.

"A terrible thing has come upon us," said Nan, the tears streaming down her cheeks. "It is like a wild storm that sweeps through the forest. It will blow down the little plants with the big trees."

"I trust not. I trust not, Nan. I will not give up hope."

"It breaks my heart to hear her," said Nan.

"I fear for her reason. I cannot believe that this is Kate, my calm sister Kate."

"It is the nearness of the ax, my lady. It would drive me mad, I fear, to know the ax was so close. Throughout the palace men and women speak in hushed whispers. I dreamed last night that I was walking 'twixt two halberdiers, and one carried an ax whose blade was turned toward me."

"You should not set such store by dreams, Nan."

"I awoke with tears on my face. Oh, my lady, I heard the Duchess of Suffolk spoken of with great respect this day. It seems that many do her honor already."

"I cannot think any envy her, Nan. Would she be the seventh? Would she come to this . . . this near madness, this closeness to the ax?"

"Some would do anything, my lady, anything for one short hour of fame."

"Not after this. And if the King will rid himself of the Queen for what he calls heresy, how can he take my lady of Suffolk who could also be accused of the same?"

"The King would do anything that pleased him."

"You must not speak of the King. Oh God, did you hear that? Poor soul! Poor Kate! What torment!"

"She will be heard in the courtyards. There seems to be a quiet everywhere, as though people wait and listen."

"Ah, my sweet sister!" cried Lady Herbert, herself beginning to weep. "What did she ever do that was not kind? And what cares

that . . . that lecher . . . but to satisfy his desires?"

"Hush, hush, my lady. We know not who
may listen."

"Nan . . . dear good Nan, I will say this:
You may be near death, Katharine Parr, but
in your goodness you have made many love
you."

"My lady, I have heard it said that if
Catharine Howard could have spoken to the
King she would have saved herself."

"But, dear Nan, this is not quite the same.
The pattern changes a little. He was deeply
enamored of Catharine Howard. There was
no lady of Suffolk waiting for him then."

"Oh my lady, I think I hear someone at the
door."

"Go . . . go quickly and see. It may be that
we have been overheard."

Even as she spoke there was a loud rap-
ping on the door.

"Let no one in!" whispered Lady Herbert.
"Say that the Queen is sick to death and
can see no one."

With terrified eyes, Anne Herbert stared at
the door. Nan had opened it and closed it
behind her. From the Queen's bedchamber
came the sound of her sobbing.

Nan came back, shut the door and stood against it. Her eyes were wide with terror.

"Who is it, Nan?"

"Sir Thomas Seymour."

"What does he want?"

"A word with her Grace the Queen."

"Then he has gone mad."

"He says it is most important. He is in great haste. He says, for pity's sake let him in quickly, an you love the Queen."

"Bring him here, Nan. Quickly."

Lady Herbert rose and met Thomas at the door.

"My lord," she cried, "you are mad . . . to come thus to the Queen's chamber."

"None saw me come," said Seymour, shutting the door quickly. "How fares the Queen?"

"Sick . . . sick unto death."

"There is yet a hope. I came to warn her. The King has heard her cries."

"And what of that?"

"He comes this way. He comes to see the Queen."

"Then why do you come here? Go at once, my lord, and for the love of God, be quick. Were you found here . . ."

"He will be some minutes yet. He is himself indisposed. He cannot set foot to ground. He will be wheeled here, and that will take time. Tell the Queen that he comes. Prepare her. Impress upon her that if she will fight with all her might there may be a chance. That chance, which was denied to others may be hers."

"Go. Go at once. I will prepare her."

By force of habit he bowed over her hand.

"Please . . . please," she begged. "No ceremony. I will go to her. I will go at once."

He smiled his reckless smile, but there was a touch of anguish in it. Did he then care for Katharine after all? wondered Anne. He must in some measure, for he had come to her apartments at some peril.

She shut the door and ran to the Queen's chamber.

"Kate . . . Kate . . . rouse yourself, my dearest. Gather your thoughts together, sweet sister. All is not lost."

The Queen sat up, pushing the hair from her hot face. She had changed in the last few days; she was unlike the calm, pleasant-faced woman whom the court knew as Queen Katharine Parr.

"What means this?" she asked listlessly.

"The King comes this way. He has heard of your distress and is coming to see you."

Katharine laughed wildly.

"No, no," cried her sister. "Be calm. Be calm. Everything depends on the next few minutes. Let me braid your hair. Let me wipe the tears from your face. The King comes, I tell you. He is being carried here in his chair, for he cannot walk . . . yet he comes to see you."

Katharine had roused herself, but the deep depression had not left her face. If it had changed at all, it had changed to resignation. It seemed to Anne that the listlessness indicated that if she had done with tears it was because she no longer cared whether she lived or died.

"Did you see his signature, sister? His signature on the mandate? Bold and clear . . . signing me to death?"

"The King's moods are variable as April weather. One day a cloudburst, and within the hour . . . bright sunshine. Rain, hail, storm and sudden heat. You should know, Kate."

While she spoke she was combing the Queen's hair, and in her voice there were trills of laughter. This sudden hope after hopelessness was more than she could bear. She felt that if the King did not soon come she herself would burst into hysterical laughter.

"He was ever a strong man, sister," Katharine was saying, "a man of purpose. And now that purpose is to rid himself of me."

"He is a sick man also."

"She is beautiful, his new love; and he desires her as once he desired Anne Boleyn, Jane Seymour and Catharine Howard."

"This is an ageing man. Deft healing fingers mean more to him in some moods than a pretty face."

"I only wish that I might die now, before I am required to walk out to the Green and see in the crowd the faces of mine enemies come thither to watch my blood flow."

"Kate, Kate, while there is life in the body there is hope in the heart. There must be. Tidy yourself. Look your most beautiful. You are fair enough."

"I care not. I care not, Anne; for what would happen if I escaped this time? How long before the King would be signing another mandate for my arrest?"

"You must save yourself . . . for Thomas's

sake. He will be anxiously awaiting the result of the King's visit."

"Thomas?"

"Hush! Thomas Seymour. I trust he is in safety by now."

"What means this?" cried Katharine. "You think . . . he is to be accused with me?"

"If he were seen leaving your apartment he well might be."

"But . . . that could not be?"

"Could it not! He has been here. He has just left. It was he who warned me of the King's approach. At great risk to himself he came here. 'Tell her,' he said, 'tell her to save herself. . . .'"

"And did he then?" said Katharine softly. And Anne felt a new hope within her, for Katharine was beautiful, even in the wildness of her grief, when she spoke of Seymour.

"He came," elaborated Anne, "risking his life that you might be warned to save yourself. He begged that you should do all in your power to win the favor of the King. You must save yourself, sister, so that one day, if the fates are kind . . ."

Katharine's face had lighted up, and she seemed like a different person from the

poor, fear-dazed creature she had been a
short while before.

"One day," she murmured, "if the fates
are kind to me . . . and to him . . ."

"Listen!" commanded Anne. "I hear a
commotion. The King and his attendants
are coming this way."

The two women were silent, listening;
through the apartment from which, such a
short time ago, had come the sound of the
Queen's terrible sobbing, now echoed the
cry of the heralds:

"Make way for His Most Gracious
Majesty!"

The King was feeling his years.

His leg had pained him so much that it
had been necessary for him to take to his
bed; and since the Queen was in disgrace,
it had been the duty of one of the gentlemen
of the bedchamber to dress his leg.

His temper had been short; he had roared
with pain; he had leaped up to cuff the gentleman, only to sink back, groaning in pain.

At such times he could find little pleasure
in the contemplation of the charms of my
lady of Suffolk. In fact, he wished that his
Queen were not indulging in a little sickness

herself, so that she could be at hand to attend to him. There had been times when he cursed her for her clumsiness, but he realized now how deft were those nimble fingers.

He thought tenderly of them, and the more tender his feelings grew toward her, the more angry he grew with those who had turned him against her.

He had sent for her physician.

"What ails the Queen?" he demanded. "What is that noise I hear? It sounds like a creature in distress."

Dr. Wendy answered: "Your Grace, the Queen is, I fear, in a low state of health. She seems on the point of death through melancholy."

"She is in pain, then?"

"Great mental stress, Sire."

"She disturbs our rest with her cries."

"They cannot be silenced, Your Grace. Her distress is such that there is nothing that can be done."

The King dismissed the man.

He knew what ailed his wife. He had heard screams like that before. Sometimes he heard them in his dreams. Sometimes he fancied he heard them mingling with the singing in the chapel.

Kate must have discovered what was afoot.

She was no wanton. He could be sure of her fidelity. But she gave herself airs. She would teach her husband. She had become a clerk with her cleverness. A woman should have more sense.

Yet, to tell the truth, it distressed *him* to hear *her* distress.

Misguided Kate! he mused.

He had merely given his permission to have her examined, that was all. The next day they would come to take her to the Tower. He had no intention of harming Kate if she could satisfy them that she had not been dabbling in heresy. It was naught to do with him. He was a King, not an examiner of his subjects' opinions. Others did that, and brought the results to him.

If Kate were innocent, she would have nothing to fear.

His little mouth was set in prim lines. There was justice in this land; and he had instituted it. If any of that long procession of headless corpses, which sometimes haunted his dreams, had proved their innocence, they would have retained their heads. That was how his conscience said it was, and that was how it must be.

But heretic or not, Kate was the best nurse he had ever had, and he needed Kate.

He roared to his gentlemen.

"I will go to see the Queen. I will see if I can calm her distress. Here! Get my chair and take me there. I declare I cannot put foot to the ground, yet I will make the journey to her apartment, since she is so sick. I will not trouble her to come here."

Even while he cursed them for their clumsiness, he was smiling at his own benevolence. You see, he said to his conscience, what a clement ruler we are! We never condemn unjustly. Now I shall go to Kate and see what I can do for her. I shall try to soothe her malady, poor Kate!

They wheeled his chair through the great rooms, lifting it up the stairs when necessary. When they neared the Queen's apartments, Seymour joined the party, but the King, so intent on his own thoughts, paid no heed to the sudden reappearance of that gentleman.

When the King entered the Queen's bedchamber, Lady Herbert sank to her knees.

The Queen raised herself at Henry's approach.

"Don't rise . . . don't rise," said Henry. "We know of your sickness."

"Your Majesty is gracious," said Katharine.

For a moment her eyes rested on the most handsome gentleman of the King's bedchamber, but Seymour had looked quickly away.

Lady Herbert said: "Your Majesty, I fear the Queen is very ill."

The King looked at her in mild distaste. "We asked not your opinion, my Lady Herbert. It is for the Queen's physicians to give us news of the Queen's health, and that when we ask it." He looked round at the assembled company. "I would be alone with the Queen," he said. "Push me nearer to the bed that I may see the Queen as I speak with her."

They did this and, bowing low, left Henry and Katharine together.

The King began, not without a note of tenderness in his voice: "How now, Kate? What means this?"

"It is good of Your Grace to visit me thus," said Katharine.

"You sound as pleased to see us as you would to see a ghost."

"If I seem ungracious it is on account of the deep melancholy which besets me, my lord."

The King gazed at her—so small and fragile in the huge and most splendid bed, her hair hanging about her shoulders.

"By my faith," he said in those tones which she knew so well, "you're a pretty wench with your hair thus disordered."

She answered as though repeating a lesson she had at great pains taught herself. "I am glad my looks find favor in Your Majesty's sight."

"Looks?" cried the King. "Ah!" He winced as he moved forward in his chair that he might see her better. "Methinks I am too old to sigh because a woman's hair is black or gold."

"But Your Majesty is as young in spirit as he ever was. That is constantly proved."

"H'm," said the King. "But this poor body, Kate . . . Ah! There's the pity of it. When I was twenty . . . when I was thirty . . . I was indeed a man."

"But wisdom walketh hand in hand with our gray hairs, Your Grace. Which would you . . . youth and its follies, or age with its experience?"

And as she spoke she asked herself: How is it that I can talk thus, as though I cared for his opinion, as though I did not know his thoughts, his plans for me? But I flatter him because I want to live. Thomas came to my apartments at great risk to warn me . . . to let me know that I must live because he is waiting for me.

"There speaks my wise Queen," said the King. "Methinks, Kate, that youth should be the right of kingship. Never to grow old! A king should be young for ever."

"Had your royal father been eternally young, we should never have had his great and clement Majesty King Henry the Eighth upon the throne."

The King shot her a swift glance, and she knew that she had made a mistake. Her nails hurt the palms of her hands. There must be no mistakes.

"Methinks you jest," said Henry coldly. "You were ever fond of a jest . . . over-fond."

"My lord," said Katharine earnestly, "I never was less in the mood for jokes."

Henry sighed. "It is doubtless folly to talk of such matters, for when a man would talk of what he has done, he is indeed an old man. It is when he speaks of what he *will* do that he is in his prime. Doth that not show how we—the most humble among us and the most high—love life?"

"You speak truth, my lord, for love of life is the only love to which men are constant."

"Why speak ye of constancy in such a sad voice, Kate?"

"Was my voice sad?"

"Indeed it was. Come, come, Kate. I like not this sadness in you."

Katharine watched him cautiously. "I did not command it to come, my lord. I would I could command it to go."

"Then *we* command it!" cried the King. "A wife must obey her husband, Kate."

Katharine laughed mirthlessly; she felt the hysteria close.

She reminded herself of Thomas, and remembering him, wished above all things to placate her husband. Between the promise of a happy life with Thomas and the threat of death which Henry personified, she must walk carefully.

The King leaned forward; he was able to reach her hand, and he took it and pressed it.

"You and I," he said musingly, "we suit each other. I am not so young that I must be a gay butterfly, flitting from this flower to that. There is a quiet of evening, Kate, whose coming should bring peace. The peace of God that passeth all understanding; that is what I seek. Oh, I have been a most unhappy man, for those I loved deceived me. I am a simple man, Kate—a man who asks but little from his wife save fidelity . . . love . . . *obedience*. 'Tis not much for a man . . . for a *King* . . . to ask."

Katharine smiled ironically. "Nay, my lord. 'Tis not much. 'Tis what a husband might well ask of his wife."

Henry patted the hand over which he had placed his own. "Then we see through the same eyes, wife." He shook his head slowly. "But oft-times have I sought these qualities in a wife, and when I have put out my hands to grasp them, they have been lost to me."

He sat back, looking at her; and, passing a weary hand across his brow, he went on: "We are wearied with matters of state. Our French possessions are in constant danger. The Emperor Charles strides across Europe. He is after the German Princes now. But what will follow? Will he turn to England?

Oh, I have prayed . . . I have worked for England. England is dear to me, Kate, and England is uneasy. These wars bring the trade of our people to a standstill. State matters, I tell you, weigh heavily upon my mind. And when we are worried, we fret. Burdens fray our temper."

He looked at her appealingly, and this seemed incongruous in one so large, so dazzling and all-powerful. She could have laughed, had she not been afraid of him, contemplating this man who, so recently, had plotted against her life, and was now begging for her approval.

She said quietly, but with an aloofness in her tone: "Your Majesty has much to occupy your mind, I doubt not."

He looked at her slyly. "There you speak truth. Aye, there you speak truth. And when a man is tired—and a King is also a man, Kate—he is apt to seek diversion, where mayhap it is not good for him to seek it. Might it not be that she, who should offer this diversion, hath become a little overbearing, that she hath become her husband's instructor rather than his loving wife?"

Katharine did not meet his eyes; she

looked beyond him, at the window, through which she could see the trees in the gardens.

She answered slowly: "Might it not be that she, who should be a loving wife, seemed an instructress because her husband saw her, not through his usually shrewd eyes, but through those of her enemies?"

"By God, Kate," said the King with a wry smile, "there may be some truth in those words of thine."

"I would hear news of Your Grace's health," she said.

"By St. Mary, I suffer such agony, Kate, that there are times when I think I know the pains of hell."

"Your Majesty needs those who love you, and whose joy it is to attend you, to be at your side by day and night."

She closed her eyes as she spoke, and she thought: I believe I am saving my life. I believe the ax is not turned toward me now. It will be there, near me . . . as long as this man lives, but the blade is now turning slowly from me. And I do this for Thomas . . . for the hope that is in the future.

She wondered ruefully what the King

would do if he could read her thoughts; but there was no need to conjecture; she knew. She would be judged guilty—so guilty that neither clever words nor deft fingers would be able to save her.

The King was saying pathetically: "There's none that can dress my wounds as thou canst, Kate."

"Your Grace honors me by remembering that."

"I' faith I did."

Katharine smiled and lifted her hand which he had released. She smiled at it gratefully. "These are good and capable hands, are they not? They are deft with a bandage. Perhaps there are more beautiful hands. I have often noticed how beautiful are those of my lady of Suffolk."

Henry looked nonchalant. "Have you, then? I cannot swear that I have marked the lady's hands."

"Has Your Grace not done so? I am surprised at that. Methought Your Grace talked often with the lady."

Henry smiled deprecatingly, and Katharine found that she could be faintly amused at his discomfiture. "Why, bless you, Kate," he said, "we are over-eager to help all in our realm. The lady, being lately widowed, is in need of comfort. We did but wish to make her happy. She misses our friend Brandon, I doubt not."

"I noticed Your Grace's kindness to the lady. Methinks it did much to help her forget the so recent loss of her husband."

"Then our purpose was achieved," said Henry with familiar unctuousness. He smiled impishly at the Queen. "We need not, therefore, give too much of our time to the lady in the future. Is that what you think?"

Katharine said, with a dignity which was not lost on him, and did not in his present mood displease him: "Your Majesty can be the only judge of how and where he shall give his time."

Henry chuckled benevolently. "We would please our Queen in this matter. By my faith, we did miss her so much, and we were so concerned for her health, that we thought we must put an end to her melancholy by telling her these things without delay."

"Ah, Your Majesty must have suffered much."

"Those fools!" said the King. "My bandages are ever too loose or too tight when thou dost not fix them."

"There's none can fix a bandage, Sire, like a loving wife."

He nodded; but a sternness had crept into his face, and it set her shivering afresh.

His eyes narrowing, he said: "Dost still think I should give license to that translation of the Scriptures?"

Katharine's heart had begun to beat faster.

The mask of indulgence was removed from the King's face, and the expression of well-remembered cruelty was exposed. She wanted to live, to fulfill those dreams which she had had before the King had made her aware of his intention to make her his sixth wife.

She folded her hands across her breasts and lowered her eyes demurely. "My lord King, 'tis not the task of a woman to discuss such matters. Her place is on the footstool at her husband's feet. I would refer this, and all other matters, to the wisdom of Your Majesty."

The King was not to be easily put off. He was watching her shrewdly. "Not so, by St. Mary! You are become a doctor to instruct us, Kate, as we take it, and not to be instructed or directed by us."

"Nay," said Katharine. "You have mistaken my intentions. I know there have been times when I have been led into discourse with Your Majesty, but such was to pass the time, for well I know the pain that besets your royal body. I took an opposite view but to entertain, for, had I shown immediate agreement, then would the discourse have ended ere it had begun, and Your Majesty would have had no amusement from our talk. My one thought has been to entertain Your Grace, to do my small part in taking your mind, when possible, from your grievous pains and burdens of state. Only for such a purpose would I venture such views—not to contradict my most gracious lord, but to divert him."

Fearfully she threw a glance in his direction. He was stroking his beard and smiling. He was pleased with her answer.

She went on: "It was true that I did hope that, by hearing Your Majesty's most learned discourse, I might perchance receive some profit."

The King was laughing.

"And is it even so?" he said. "Then we are perfect friends again, sweetheart."

He sat there, smiling at her. She had pleased him. He was her friend now; and the friendly smile was soon giving place to the lecher's leer.

"Get up from your bed and come and kiss me, Kate," he commanded.

As she rose, she thought: I am safe for a while. The danger is past . . . for a time. Now the pattern will be formed again—starting from the beginning. Will it have the same ending?

He caught her and pulled her on to his knees. She closed her eyes as she felt his mouth on hers. His lips were no longer tight and prim, but slack and eager.

This, she thought, is the price of postponement.

Next morning he sent for her to sit with him in the walled garden.

He was much better, and able to hobble with the aid of a stick.

She came, her sister and Lady Jane Grey in attendance; but he dismissed those two with a wave of his stick.

"Good morrow to you, Kate. Come sit beside me. There's tonic in this morning air. There, there, you may come close. Don't feign to be a modest virgin . . . for I know better, Kate, eh? I know better."

He was in good spirits.

"The pain's relieved a little. A good nurse and a good bedfellow. Well, who could do better than that? That's good enough for a King, eh, Kate?"

He pinched her cheek.

"It is indeed gratifying to see Your Majesty in such good spirits."

"Oh, Kate, I fear I am a sad old bear when the pains are with me. What say you?" He drew back to watch her face, and it was as though he dared her to agree with him.

"Nay," she said; "there was never a man more patient."

"Ah, Kate, for one who has ever been sprightly, ever active, a leader in the jousts and tourneys, it is hard to stand by and see other men excel."

"Your Grace's skill is well remembered and will, I dare swear, never be forgot."

"There was not a man who could tilt against me and be the victor," said Henry sadly. "Ah well, I am skilled in other matters, am I not, sweetheart?"

"I know it well."

"You know it well, eh, little pig? And it pleases you! It is well that we are blessed with a faithful and obedient wife. We shall never seek to change her, Kate, while she is thus."

"Her desire," said Katharine, "is to please her lord in all things."

"If she would but give me a son, I should have naught to complain of." He sighed.

"Ah, my lord, those matters are with God."

That had been a mistake, for his eyes had narrowed at once. But there must always be such mistakes. It was not possible always to avoid words which could conjure up pictures in his mind, pictures which it was unwise for him to see.

"I cannot understand why God should deny *me* a son," he said; there was the faintest criticism in his voice, for the emphasized word was significant. He would never deny *me* a son, those words implied; although He denies *you* one.

But he was too pleased with her on this bright morning to dwell on that dismal subject; he would shelve it for a more appropriate time.

"I like to hear you say you are an obedient wife, Kate," he said. "Forget it not."

"Nay, my lord," said Katharine with great earnestness. "I'll not forget. If I live to be a hundred, I'll not forget."

"A hundred!" cried Henry boisterously. "Why, bless you, Kate, thou art many a long year from that great age. And, by my faith, I swear you look younger than you did the day I made you my Queen."

He turned to her and kissed her; he fondled her throat and let his hands stray to her breasts and thighs.

"Your . . . Your Majesty is kind to me," stammered Katharine.

"To be kind was ever a fault of ours, Kate."

"A fault? I would not call it that. 'Tis a virtue, and in one so great as your august self, doubly so."

The lecher had now been succeeded by the sentimentalist. He took his hand from her thigh and laid it on her arm. "You speak sound truth, Kate. Yet it has been our kindness . . . our softness, which has led many to deceive us. We have been deceived again and again in our life. By those, mark you, who had the best reason to give us their loving regard. This garden doth remind me of another. . . . It was at Hever Castle. A garden of roses . . . walled thus . . . a pleasant place."

Katharine heard the note of regret and longing, the self-pity which she had heard so many times.

"By God," he cried suddenly, "if any try deceiving tricks on us, they shall pay. They shall pay with their blood."

She drew away from him. His moods followed quickly on one another this morning.

"Who would dare deceive the King?" she soothed. "Who would dare deceive a wise and tender King?"

He mumbled: "That is what we would know." He softened again and put an arm about her shoulders. "Thou art a good woman, Kate. Thy beauty is not of the devil; it is the beauty of meadow flowers, sweet and simple, and not to drive a man to torment." He began to kiss her and his ringed fingers caught at the neck of her gown. "Thou and I have many a merry night before us, Kate. Old age? Who dares speak of it?"

"It is years away from us, my lord."

"And we are here, and the sun doth shine. And you are a fair woman and I love you

well. You are my wife, and we will get ourselves a son, eh?"

"I trust so. Indeed, I trust so. I care not
that the sun doth shine. I care only that my
lord's content doth continue to shine on
me."

"It doth, Kate, and it shall. Thou mayest
rest assured of that. Thou art good to kiss,
and I am man enough to do the kissing."

He had lifted his head from her throat
and, with him, Katharine heard the sound of
soldiers' marching feet.

The King stood up and shouted, but the
sound of his voice was lost in the noise
made by the approaching guard.

Katharine stood beside him; she could
see a company of the King's guard, and at
its head marched Sir Thomas Wriothesley.

"Halt!" cried the King. "Halt there, I say.
What means this? Who dares disturb the
King's peace?"

"Your Majesty . . ." began the Queen.

"Wait there!" commanded Henry; and he
hobbled toward the Chancellor and the forty
members of the Guard who had halted at
his command.

Over the morning air their words came
distinctly to Katharine.

"Wriothesley, you knave, what means this?"

Wriothesley ingratiatingly replied: "My lord King, I have come on your orders with forty halberdiers."

"What means this?" cried the King. "I understand you not." His face was purple with fury. "How darest thou disturb our peace?"

"Sire, Your Majesty's orders. I come with forty men to arrest the Queen, and take her to the Tower. My barge is at the privy stairs."

"Fool! Knave!" cried Henry. "Get you gone, or 'twill be you who are clapped into the Tower."

Wriothesley, pale with confusion, yet persisted: "Can Your Majesty have forgotten? You gave the order. Your Grace signed the mandate. . . . To arrest the Queen at this hour . . . wherever she might be."

"Get you gone from here," screamed the King. "You fool . . . you arrant fool!" He lifted his stick and struck at the Chancellor, who managed, most skillfully, to avoid the blow.

"By God," went on the King, "are you a fool, Chancellor? It would seem my lot to be surrounded by fools and knaves. Get you gone, I say. Get you gone."

Katharine watched the discomfited Chancellor lead his men away.

The King hobbled back to her.

"He . . . he was disobeying Your Majesty's command?" asked Katharine in a trembling voice.

"The man's a fool. The man's a knave. By God, I'll not forget this."

"Mayhap he thought he was obeying Your Majesty's commands. Mayhap he thought he had Your Grace's consent to do what he was about to do."

Henry sat down heavily and signed to her to take her place beside him.

"Let be," he said. "Let be." He watched her covertly.

He does not know, she reflected, that I have seen his signature on the order for my arrest, just as Wriothesley does not know that he has changed his mind. From the bed to the scaffold is such a short step. How should Chancellor Wriothesley know that on the King's whim I have turned about . . . away from the scaffold, back to the bed!

She began again: "Wriothesley . . ."

"Enough," said Henry testily. "I command thee not to speak of that knave."

"Your Majesty will pardon me, but I

thought you regarded him as a good servant. Mayhap Your Majesty will not feel too hard toward him, since he has failed to interpret your wishes on this day."

Henry, being ignorant of her understanding of this matter and not imagining that she could possibly know that he had signed a mandate for her arrest which should be her death warrant, looked at her pityingly.

"Do not defend Wriothesley," he said. "Poor soul, poor Kate, you do not know how little he deserves grace at your hands. Come, Kate, enough of this man. You and I have more pleasant matters with which to occupy ourselves."

His hands were caressing her. She was once more his sweetheart, his little pig.

By a miracle, it seemed, she had been saved from death. But was she saved, or had Death merely receded a pace or two?

CHAPTER

V

During that August and September the King made the progress, from palace to palace, which had been a habit of his. From West-minster the court went in state along the river to Hampton Court; and after a brief stay at that palace they made the journeys to Oatlands, Woking, Guildford, Chobham and Windsor.

But when the court had reached Windsor it was seen that this last journey had greatly taxed Henry's strength; and those whom his death would most affect watched him—and each other—with speculation.

Those who had hitherto behaved with the utmost obsequiousness became arrogant. Lord Hertford and Lord Lisle were back from their duties in France, and they were making preparations to rule through the boy King in whom they had instilled a strong appreciation of the new learning. Sir Thomas Seymour was on the alert; his brother was a great statesman and power in the land, but Thomas was the man whom the King-to-be loved more than any other. Cranmer, beloved of the King, was with these men, and they made a powerful party.

On the Catholic side was the Duke of Norfolk and his son Surrey, together with Gardiner, Wriothesley and their supporters.

Now that the King felt death to be near, he knew great anxiety for the future of his House which would have only a young boy at its head. One look from his bloodshot eyes, one gesture, could still strike terror into those about him. After all, he could still wield a pen; he could still sign a death warrant. Callous and brutal as he was, he had to deal with men who lacked his callous brutality, largely because they lacked his vitality. If he was a sick lion, he was still a lion. He was a ruler of men, even now as he lay in his bed, or sat painfully in his chair of state, or hobbled about on his stick, or was conveyed about the palace in that wheeled contrivance which had had to be made for him.

He made his will. Wisely he decided that

the council of ministers, who should comprise the Protectorate during the little King's minority, should be equally balanced by the two parties. Henry was confident that his wishes would be obeyed; he was enough of a King to rule after death.

The people were with him. They were his strength. They had always been with him from the days when he, as a pink and white boy, had ridden among them and sought their applause. It had been his policy to remove the dangerous influential nobles and placate the mob. The people believed that he had freed them from the tyranny of the Pope. The state had taken precedence over the church, and that appealed to the unemotional English as it was done under a cloak of piety. Terrible suffering had been witnessed in the cities: burnings, hangings, beheadings and the most horrible death accorded to traitors; there had been much bloodshed. But on the Continent of Europe the bloodshed had been more fierce; and bloodshed there must be, it seemed, when a new religion was born.

The King was still King and would remain the master of his subjects after death. His word was law and would remain so.

But those turbulent men about the throne were tensely waiting. Tempers ran high and men were reckless.

One November day, Protestant Lord Lisle, during a Council meeting, struck Gardiner in the face. Lisle was banished from the Council.

To be set against this was the fact that Gardiner had been in disgrace with the King ever since Katharine had come so near to being arrested. The King, characteristically, blamed Gardiner for that affair, for he had convinced himself that he had had no intention of allowing Katharine to be removed, and the whole plot had been devised by the Bishop.

The disgrace of Gardiner and the banishment of Lisle kept that balance of power which Wolsey had taught the King was always desirable. A great Reformer and a great Catholic were both in disgrace.

Gardiner tried to regain his position with an offer of money which could be extorted from the clergy. Henry was pleased to receive the money, but refused to reinstate the Bishop; and so Gardiner continued in disgrace. For, concluded the King, he is a man who tried to poison our mind against the innocent Queen! So Gardiner received nothing but scowls from his master. It was unfortunate for him, but that was what so often happened to those who served the King.

Those were anxious days for all, but with the coming of November, the King's health began to improve a little. There was feasting and revelry at court, and at a certain banquet Henry's eyes alighted on a fair lady of the Queen's household. It seemed to him once more that it was a pitiable thing when a man such as he was—a mighty King, a great ruler—had but one legitimate son to follow him.

Surely there must be some truth in those accusations which some of his ministers had tried to bring. Had Gardiner been so wrong when he had plotted against the Queen? Was the barren Katharine a heretic at heart?

During those weeks of tension, the manners of the Earl of Surrey became insufferable by those whom he chose to consider his enemies; the chief of these was Edward Seymour, Lord Hertford.

Surrey hated the Seymours more than he

hated any, and in particular he hated the elder brother. Reckless Surrey, that elegant poet, was no clever statesman as Hertford had proved himself to be. Surrey had been born to a high place in the realm; Edward Seymour had fought for his place. Surrey was proud and foolish, and Edward Seymour was one of the most astute men in the Kingdom. That was why Henry had removed the Earl of Surrey from his post in the garrisoned French towns, to which his conduct had done no good service, in order to replace him by the clever elder Seymour.

This had seemed to Surrey an insult to himself and his house which he could not endure.

Swaggering about the court, he insulted all those who had risen to high places in the land through their talents. His father warned him, but he would not listen to warnings.

"This kingdom," he declared, not caring who heard him, "has never been well since the King set mean creatures in the government. It would seem that His Majesty delights to rid himself of noble blood and to employ none but low people."

This was a direct insult to the Seymours,

so they watched him and waited for their opportunity.

"Since the King," said Edward Seymour to his younger brother when they walked in the Great Park together, "cannot last long it might be well to lower the pride of these Howards while he yet lives."

Thomas agreed that it would be well. "You will remember that Norfolk once proposed a match between Surrey and the Princess Mary."

"The King would have none of it."

"But if the King were dead and there was a young boy in his place, who knows what Norfolk might try? The Princess Mary is a Catholic, and so is Surrey. The Catholic Party would be strongly in favor of such a match."

The brothers looked at each other cautiously—two scheming men; for the moment they seemed to harbor the same desires. But did they? Hertford wished to see himself Protector of this kingdom with the little Edward his puppet. Thomas visualized marriage with the Princess Elizabeth and, as a corollary, the throne.

Temporarily they stood together against the Howards, but only temporarily.

And while they talked, Hertford thought of the great power which would come to him through his little nephew; and Thomas's dreams of a shared throne were tinged with other dreams, of an erotic nature.

Surrey, from his apartments, watched them and laughed aloud.

"See," he said to one of his attendants, "there go the low-born Seymours. They plot against me and my father, I doubt not. They hate our noble blood as we hate their baseness."

He sought his sister.

She was not a very happy young woman at this time. The King occasionally looked her way, but although his desire for her was at times quite strong, he could not forget the affinity between them, since she was his daughter-in-law, and his desire was not quite strong enough to overcome that drawback.

"Look!" cried Surrey, entering her apartments, and not caring that some of her servants were with her. "See the two great men walking together?"

The Duchess looked, and she found it difficult to draw her eyes away from the younger of the Seymour brothers.

"You are a fool," she whispered. "Brother, you are the most reckless fool at court."

He bowed. He was not displeased with the epithet.

"And," she went on quietly, still looking at the tall man who walked beside his brother in the park, "I will tell you this: If your folly takes you to the Tower—which it may well do—I will do nothing . . . nothing to help you."

Her brother laughed aloud and did not bother to lower his voice. "So you think I have persuaded our father against a match with Seymour, do you? Then you are right. I'll not stand by and see our noble family united with such low-born knaves."

"How dare you speak to me thus?" she demanded.

"Because I am your brother. I will never allow you to marry with Seymour . . . even if he would. Ah, but he never would. He looks higher. Low-born as he is, he yet looks high indeed."

"You speak of the King's brother-in-law," she murmured.

"I speak also of the man you long for, sister."

"Go. . . . Go. Do not come here to brawl."

He bowed ironically. He saw that he had won her hatred. He had insulted her before her servants.

The courtiers continued to watch him with speculative eyes. They were beginning to look at him in the way they regarded those whose days they believed to be numbered.

What is wrong with me? he asked himself. He was getting old, he supposed. He was thirty; he longed for excitement; and he was so reckless that he cared little how he obtained it.

He looked about him for fresh mischief, and his interview with his sister gave him an idea.

Surrey lost no time. He dressed himself with the utmost care. Sparkling with jewels, haughty in the extreme, he called on Lady Hertford.

Hertford's wife, who had been Anne Stanhope, was known throughout the court as one of its proudest and most ambitious women. She shared her husband's ideals and ambitions; she was cold and avaricious. She was waiting with impatience for the day when she should be the first lady in the land. She was determined to gain that status, promising herself that when her husband was Protector of England she would take precedence over every other lady, and if any dared attempt to place themselves before her she would persuade her husband to make arrangements for their removal.

She was greatly surprised to hear that the Earl of Surrey had called to see her.

He bowed low over her hand and looked at her most humbly. She was a very conceited woman, so it gave her great pleasure to see the heir of the most noble house in the country bowing so graciously before her.

"Lady Hertford, I have something of great importance to say to you," said the incorrigible Earl, "and it is for your ears alone."

She dismissed her attendants; and as he watched them go, the Earl smiled insolently.

"Lady Hertford," he said, "you are a fair and gracious woman, and it pleases me to see you occupying such a position in the land."

"Thank you, my lord Earl," she said. "But what is this matter of which you would speak to me?"

"I have long watched you, Lady Hertford."

"You have watched me?"

"With great admiration; and that admiration has grown so strong that I have come to the conclusion that there will be no peace for me until I have revealed it to you."

She began to regard him suspiciously.

He had come toward her, seized her hand, and pressed it to his lips.

"You are so beautiful," he said.

"I think, my lord, that you have drunk too freely. I think it would be wise for you to go home."

"Wise!" replied the poet. "But what is wisdom? It is for the old—a compensation for those whom love has passed by."

"Love! You speak to me of love!"

"Why not? You enchant me. You delight me. So I come to lay my proposals at your feet, to beg you not to deny me, for I am dying of love for you."

"I shall be grateful if you will leave at once."

"I will not until you have heard me."

"These are my apartments . . ."

"I know. I know. Your husband's low-born sister married the King. By my faith! I have often wondered how she seduced him to marriage. Well, she did, and thus were her low-born brothers raised to greatness. The King delights in having those about him who are low-born. Do you know why? It is because he need not fear them. It is the nobles whom he must fear. Look at them: Wolsey, Cromwell, Gardiner and . . . the Seymours. All low-born people."

"How dare you?" cried the enraged lady.

She went toward the door, but he barred the way. He seized her and held her fast, laughing as he did so.

"Do not imagine, my dear Lady Hertford, that my proposal is an honorable one. No, I could not . . . even if I were in a position to offer you marriage, and you in a position to receive such an offer . . . make such an offer. It has been suggested that your brother-in-law should marry my sister. But I would not allow that. Marry a Seymour with a Howard! That could not be. There is too great a gulf between our families. But another kind of liaison between your house and mine might be arranged. . . ."

She had broken free and was about to call her servants when she remembered that she could not easily ask them to remove from her apartments such an important nobleman.

She was by no means a hysterical woman and, as she stood there, uncertain how to get rid of him, she was deciding that he should pay for this insult with his life.

There was nothing she could do but walk with dignity to the door. This she did, leaving him alone in the apartment.

Surrey stood watching her leave. He knew that of all the foolish things he had ever done in his life—and they were legion—this was about the most foolish. And he did not care.

He left the apartment. He knew that Hertford would take revenge. But he did not care. He had lost interest in living. There was one thing he would have liked, though; and that was to hear Lady Hertford's description of the scene which had just taken place when she imparted it to her husband.

It was a cold December day and the King was now in his royal palace of White Hall.

He was feeling a little better than of late. He had suffered great pain through the cauterization of his legs, but he believed the treatment to have been successful and he was looking forward to the Christmas revels. His mind kept reverting to the past, and he was thinking now of other revels at which he had been the leading spirit. Wistfully he longed for a return of his youth.

It was at such times that he thought much of women, but his fancy did not stay long on any in particular. His wife? He was fond of her. She was a gentle nurse; but it was not always a nurse that he wanted. In any case, he was at this time preparing a charge of heresy against her. Soon he would have her questioned. But let her stay beside him for a while. Then, if she were proved to be a heretic, it was his bounden duty to rid himself of her. She would have to die. He had had two divorces and he did not like them. They were dangerous. A divorced woman might get a child, and rumor might have it that it was his. There had been such a rumor concerning Anne of Cleves. No! Death was the better solution. He did not want trouble for little Edward.

He merely wanted a wife—a young and comely woman to take his mind off his longing for the past.

Hertford begged an audience which the King granted.

"Ah, brother," said Henry. "You wear an angry look."

"Your Majesty, I have discovered treason."

"What treason's this?"

"My Lord Surrey, your Grace."

"That braggart? What now?"

"He has foreign friends. Your Grace, we have always known that. There is in his employ an old servant of your enemy, Cardinal Pole. He has tried to persuade his sister, the Duchess of Richmond—Your Grace's own daughter-in-law—to become Your Grace's mistress!"

The King burst out: "The rogue! The knave! How dare he suggest such a thing! He should know how I would look upon such a horrible proposal!"

Hertford bowed. "Your Grace is happily married to a lady we all love and respect."

"Indeed it is so," said Henry. "How dare the young fool presume to provide me with a mistress! As if I were not capable of finding my own . . . should I desire one. But I do not. I have tried to uphold the sanctity of marriage. Always this has been my endeavor."

Henry shot a swift glance at Hertford, but Hertford was looking grave, obsessed by his own anger, his own determination on revenge.

"He conspired, Your Grace, to govern you through his sister."

That brought the hot blood to the King's face. "By God, I'll have him in the Tower for this. The man's a traitor."

Now was the moment to clinch the matter. Hertford was wise enough to understand that.

"My lord, in his arrogance, he has had the leopards of England emblazoned on a panel of one of the rooms at Kenninghall."

"What!" roared Henry.

"It is true, Your Grace. This was discovered by an intimate of his, who, having seen that such amounted to treason, felt that he himself would be considered guilty if he did not report it."

"It is treason!" cried Henry. "What right has he to bear the arms of England?"

"He said, when challenged, that he has a right to those arms, for the blood of Charlemagne and Plantagenet flows in his veins."

"By God!" cried the King, rising and leaning on his stick. "He shall suffer for that!"

"He considers himself more royal than

Your Grace. He and his father are both guilty of treason."

"Norfolk also? What has he done?"

"He has seen the royal escutcheon on that panel at Kenninghall and has not testified against his son."

"Aye," said the King. "Aye."

"And Your Grace will remember that he wished to marry his son to the Princess Mary. They are dangerous, those Howards. They are traitors."

"Traitors!" snapped Henry. "Brother, you speak truth." He was remembering the mocking brown eyes of England's greatest poet; he was hearing the words which flowed so easily from the haughty lips. He pictured also the royal arms on a panel in Surrey's mansion; and he foresaw the trouble that important house might bring to his little son, who was but nine years old.

"To the Tower!" he cried. "To the Tower with these traitors!"

And he brooded: I will not die. I will live yet. I will beget more sons. Edward is too young. I will not die until he has brothers growing up about him.

Hertford left gleefully with the King's command. Henry promised himself that when these affairs were done with, and Norfolk and Surrey had lost their heads, he would, without further delay, have that charge brought against the Queen.

He would have a buxom wife—the seventh and the best; and she should bear him many sons in the years that were left to him.

Sir Thomas Seymore rode out to Hatfield House, where the Princess Elizabeth now lived with her brother Edward.

Thomas knew that the children were to be separated and that the following day Edward would be sent to Hertford Castle and Elizabeth to Enfield. These were the King's orders. It might be that His Majesty believed the young Elizabeth to have too strong an influence on the boy.

Thomas felt pleased as he rode through the countryside. He saw the house in the distance and thought longingly of Elizabeth. He guessed that she might be watching his approach, from a window; but if she were, she would feign surprise at his arrival.

She was sharp for her thirteen years and was no doubt watching events as eagerly as any.

A groom took his horse, and he went into

the house. He was received by the tutors of the royal children, Sir John Cheke, Dr. Cox and Sir Anthony Cooke.

"Greetings, gentlemen!" he cried in his jaunty way. "I hear there is to be a parting between our Prince and Princess; and I have ridden hither to see them both while under the same roof."

"They will welcome your coming, Sir Thomas. The Prince speaks of you often and has been wondering when you will come to see him."

"And the Princess?"

"She has not spoken of you, but I dare swear she will have pleasure at the sight of you."

He went to the apartment where the young Prince and his sister were together. There were traces of tears on the faces of both.

Thomas knelt before the heir to the throne and kissed his hand.

"Uncle Thomas!" cried Edward. "Oh, how glad I am to see you!"

"Your Highness is gracious," said Thomas. He turned to Elizabeth. "And the Lady Elizabeth, is she pleased to see me?"

She gave him her hand and let it linger in his while he fervently kissed it.

"You come, my lord, at a sad time," she said.

"We have been so happy here," said Edward passionately, "but we are to be parted. I am to be sent to Hertford, and my sister to Enfield. Oh why, why?"

"Those are your royal father's commands," said the Admiral. "I doubt not that he hath good reason."

He thought how fair she was, this little girl who, in spite of her slender child's body—she was too restless of mind to put on flesh—had all the ways of a woman.

"I have wept," said Elizabeth, "until I have no tears left."

Thomas smiled. She had not wept so much that the tears had spoiled her prettiness. She would have wept discreetly. It was the poor little Prince who was heartbroken at the prospect of their separation. Elizabeth's tears had been a charming display, an outward sign of the affection she bore to one who soon—surely very soon—must be King of England.

"We have been so happy," persisted the

Prince. "We love Hatfield, do we not, sister?"

"I shall always love Hatfield. I shall remember all the happy days I have spent here, brother."

Hatfield! mused Seymour. A lovely place. A fitting nursery for the royal children. The King had taken a fancy to it and had intimated to the Bishop of Ely, to whom it had belonged, that he should present it to his royal master. It was true that His Majesty had given the Bishop lands in exchange, but one's possessions were not safe when such covetous eyes were laid upon them.

And as she stood there, with the faint winter light on her reddish hair, in spite of the fact that she was a girl and a child, she reminded the Admiral of her father.

But I'll have her, he swore. If I wait for years I'll have her.

And so did he believe in his destiny, that he was sure this thing would come to pass.

The Prince dismissed his attendants, and the Admiral sat on the window seat, the Prince on one side of him, the Princess on the other; and never did he take such pains to exert his charms as he did on that day.

"My dear Prince, my dearest Princess,"

he said, "you are so young to be parted. If I had my way I should let you do exactly as you wished."

"Oh, Uncle Thomas, dearest Uncle Thomas," said the Prince, "if only you had your way! Have you seen Jane? I see her so rarely now."

"She is happy at court with the Queen."

"I know. She would be happy with our dearest mother. But how I wish she could be with me. And now they would take Elizabeth from me."

"It may not be for long," said the Admiral recklessly, yet deliberately indiscreet.

The two children looked at him in astonishment.

"My dears, forget those words," he said. "By God's precious soul, I should never have uttered them. It is tantamount to treason. Would you betray me, Edward?"

"Never! Never! I would rather die than betray you, dearest Uncle."

He put his arm about the boy and, holding him, turned to Elizabeth.

"And you, my lady, would you betray poor Thomas?"

She did not answer for a moment. She lowered her silky lashes so that he could not see her eyes. He put his unengaged arm out to seize her.

He said: "Edward, I'll not let her go until she swears she will not betray me."

To the boy it was horseplay, in which Uncle Thomas Seymour loved to indulge.

Her face close to his, Elizabeth said: "No. No. I do not think I would betray you."

"And why is that?" he asked, putting his lips near hers.

He now held the children tightly. Edward was laughing, loving the man who made him forget the difference in their ages.

"Perhaps," said Elizabeth, "it might be that I like you well enough not to."

"Too well?" said the Admiral.

She lifted her eyes to his and hers were solemn with the faintest hint of adoration.

The Admiral's hopes were soaring as she said: "That might be so."

Then Seymour kissed the boy's cheek and turned to the girl. She was waiting. She received his kiss on her lips, and as he held her she felt his heart beating fast.

He kept his arms about her.

"We three are friends," he said. "We will stand together."

How exciting he is! thought Edward. He

makes everything seem gay and amusing, dangerous though it all is. He makes it seem a wonderful thing to be an heir to a throne. He never says: "You must do this; you must learn that by heart." He never tires you. You feel that merely to be with him is an adventure, the pleasantest, most exciting adventure in the world.

Elizabeth was thinking: To be near him, to listen to him, is the most exciting thing that has ever happened to me.

"If our beloved King should die," said the Admiral gravely, "and he is sick . . . very sick . . . Edward, my dearest nephew, you will be the King. You will not forget your old uncle then, will you?"

Edward took the Admiral's hand and solemnly kissed it.

"I will never forget thee, dearest Uncle."

"There will be many to tell you they are your dearest, when you are the King."

"There is only one that could be that in very truth."

"You will be a King. Your word will be law."

"They will not let that be so," said Edward. "My Uncle Hertford, Cranmer . . . Lisle . . . Wriothesley, Brown, Paget, Russell. . . . My

father has appointed them to govern me. I
must be guided by them, he says, for I am
young yet to take the reins of kingship. I
shall have to do as I am told . . . more then
than now."

"You will always be my dearest nephew,"
said Thomas. "You will always receive me,
will you not, and tell me your troubles?"

"As ever, dear Uncle."

"And if they should keep you short of
money, it shall be into Uncle Thomas's
purse that you will dip your fingers?"

"It shall, dearest Uncle."

This was reckless talk. To speak of the
King's death was treason. But he was safe.
He knew he was safe. He could trust Edward, for Edward was a loyal little boy. And
could he trust Elizabeth? He believed he
could. He had seen that in her eyes which
told him that if there was a weakness in her
nature, there was one person who could
play on it; and that person was Sir Thomas
Seymour.

"And you, my lady?" he said. "What of
you? Doubtless they will find a husband for
you. What shall you say to that?"

His arm had tightened about her. This
was, she well knew, flirtation of a dangerous

nature, though disguised, because the words spoken between them had a hidden significance.

"Rest assured," she said, "that I shall have a say in the choice of my own husband."

He smiled at her and his fingers burned through the stuff of her dress.

"May I . . . rest assured?" he said lightly.

"You may, my lord."

Then she remembered suddenly the dignity that she owed to her rank; she removed herself haughtily from his grasp.

When Sir Thomas left Hatfield House he was sure that the visit had been an important one. He believed that he had made progress in his courtship and that he had taken one step nearer to the throne.

Christmas came and went. Everyone, except the King, knew that he was about to die. Henry refused to accept this dismal fact. Ill as he was, he insisted on meeting his council each day and discussing matters of state. He saw little of Katharine. He did not wish to see her. Since the cauterization of his legs he had not wished any female to come near him; and in any case, he was still contemplating ridding himself of her.

January came, cold and bleak. On the nineteenth of that month, the poet Surrey went out to meet the executioner on Tower Hill.

The young man died as he had lived, reckless and haughty, seeming not to care.

People of the court shivered as they watched the handsome head roll in the straw. What had this young man done except carry royal blood in his veins and boast of it? Well, many had lost their heads for that crime.

That was the end of Surrey; and his father, it was said, was to follow him soon.

The King, in his bedchamber, received news of the execution.

"So die all traitors!" he mumbled.

He was, in these days of his sickness, recalling to mind too vividly those men and women he had sent to the block. But he had an answer to his conscience, whatever name his memory called up.

"I have to think of my boy," he told his conscience. "That is why Surrey has gone. That is why Norfolk shall go. He is too young, my Edward, to be without me and surrounded by those ambitious men who fancy their heads fit a crown."

Surrey then. And after him, proud Norfolk.

Norfolk now lay in the Tower awaiting his trial.

Seymour was beside the King, proffering a cup of wine to his lips. There were times when Henry's hands were so swollen with dropsy that he could not hold a cup.

"Good Thomas!" he murmured.

The handsome head was bent low. "Your Grace," said Seymour, "the Lady Elizabeth was grieved to leave her brother. I thought it would please you to know how much they love each other."

"Would the girl were a boy!" muttered Henry.

"Indeed, Your Grace, that would be well. But alas, she is a girl, and what will become of her? Will she grow, like her sister Mary, into spinsterhood?"

Henry gave the Admiral a sly glance. He knew what thoughts were going on in that handsome head.

"'Twould be a sad thing, Your Grace," persisted the bold Admiral.

"Aye! 'Twould be a bad thing," said the King.

"And yet, Sire, on account of the frailty of her mother, and the fact that she was not married to Your Grace because of that pre-contract with Northumberland, what . . . will become of the Lady Elizabeth?"

The King softened toward Seymour. He liked boldness, for he himself had been bold.

He smiled. "More wine, good Thomas."

"Your Majesty might give her to one of your gentlemen . . . if his rank and wealth were commensurate."

"I might indeed. But she is young yet. There's no knowing . . . no knowing, friend Thomas."

And the King's friend Thomas felt elated with his success.

The old Duke of Norfolk lay in his cell await-ing his death. How many years had he ex-pected this? All through his life there had been these alarms which he was too near the throne to have escaped. But he had been a wise man and had always made the King's cause his own.

But the wisest men could be betrayed, and often by those who were nearest and dearest to them.

Tomorrow he was to die.

In the Palace of White Hall the King lay sick. He will not live long after me, reflected Norfolk.

When a man is going to die he thinks back over his life. He had been a great statesman, this Duke of England's noblest House; he had had his place in the building of England's greatness. He was a proud man and he hated to die thus . . . as traitors die.

Proud young Surrey had betrayed him—not with plots, but with vanity, pride.

Norfolk's thoughts went back to his marriage with Buckingham's daughter—a proud woman, a vain woman. He himself had been Earl of Surrey then and had inherited the title of Duke of Norfolk some years later. The trouble with Bess Holland had started when he was still Earl of Surrey.

Bessie! he brooded, seeing her as she had been then, with the sleeves of her cheap gown rolled up over her elbows showing her buxom arms—a slut, some might say, but bearing that indefinable attraction which even a great nobleman—so conscious of his status—found irresistible.

He had seduced her on their first meet-

ing; yet he almost believed that she had seduced him. It had not ended there. One
went back, and back again, to such as
Bessie.

Naturally his wife had been furious. A
daughter of noble Buckingham to be set
aside for a laundress: But Bessie had had
something more alluring than noble lineage.
Bessie had that way of setting aside all the
barriers of class.

Well, it was a lusty age and, although he
was the most noble man in the realm, under
the King, and one of its keenest statesmen,
he had been unable to give up Bessie.

His Duchess had been a vindictive
woman, determined to make trouble; so between her and Bess he had had enough of
that in his life.

His family . . . his accursed family! First
Anne Boleyn—though not all Howard, being
part low-born Boleyn—and then Catharine
Howard. Both of these Queens had brought
wealth and advancement to the Howards,
and when they fell, the Howard fortunes declined with them.

He remembered now—he who believed
he would soon go to Tower Green—how he
had flayed with his scorn those two

kinswomen of his, those fallen Queens. More fiercely than any, his tongue had condemned them. He had stood by the King and deplored the fact—so tragic for the House of Howard—that it was those two women who had made the King suffer.

And now his own son—his elder son—on whom he had fixed his pride and hope, had lost his head. Gay Surrey, the handsome poet who could not keep his mouth shut— or perhaps did not care to do so.

"My son . . . my son . . ." murmured the Duke. "But what matters it, for tomorrow I shall join you."

And as he lay there, waiting for the dawn, he wished that he had often acted differently during his long life. He could not forget the scornful flashing eyes of Anne Boleyn when he had conducted her to the Tower; he could not shut out of his mind the memory of Catharine Howard's tears.

He waited calmly for the dawn.

The King had not yet signed Norfolk's death warrant. He was too ill to deal with matters of state and kept to his bed that day. His limbs were swollen with dropsy; he felt low and was in great pain; and he was only half aware of the candle-lit room in which he lay.

In a corner waited several gentlemen of the bedchamber. With them were members of his Council—the Seymours, Lord Lisle, Wriothesley, and Sir Anthony Denny among them.

They whispered together.

"He cannot last the night."

"He has never been in this condition before."

"He should be told. He should be prepared."

"Who will dare tell him?"

All were silent; and then the King's voice was heard calling.

"Go," said Hertford to his brother. "You go. He has a liking for you."

Sir Thomas went into the chamber and stood by the King's bed.

"Who is there?" asked Henry, peering before him. "Who is it?"

"Thomas Seymour, my lord. Your humble servant and your friend."

"Friend Thomas . . . friend Thomas. . . . My arms are burning stumps of fire. My legs are furnaces. My body lies in the grip of deadly pain."

"Rest, Sire. Speak not," said Seymour, "for speech doth bring out the sweat beads, big as grapes, upon thy brow."

"An we wish it, we will speak," growled the King. "We will not be told, by a subject, when to speak."

"Your Grace's pardon. I but feared for you."

"How goes the hour?"

"Creeping on to midnight, Sire."

"I hear the bells in my ears, Seymour. I seem to be walking on soft grass. I think I ride in Richmond Park. I think I am up the river in my state barge. I think I sit beside my Queen, watching the jousting in the tilt-yard. But . . . I lie here . . . with furnaces for limbs . . . a-dying in my bed."

Two members of the Council had come into the chamber. They stood by the hangings and whispered together concerning the King's condition.

Henry heard them. He tried to lift his head, but fell back groaning.

"Who whispers in the shadows? 'Tis Surrey . . . 'Tis my lord Earl."

Seymour bent his head and murmured: "Nay, Sire. Your Grace forgets. Surrey laid his head on the block nine days ago."

"Surrey!" muttered the King. "Surrey . . . a poet . . . a handsome boy . . . a proud and foolish boy."

"A conspirator against the Throne, Your Grace."

Henry's voice was more distinct. " 'Twas Surrey who first wrote blank verse. I remember it. He gave us the sonnet. A poet . . . but . . . a proud and foolish boy."

"He plotted against Your Grace. He displayed the royal arms on his own. Your Grace forgets. Surrey thought himself more royal than royalty."

The King had become confused. "Buckingham!" he shouted, but his voice immediately fell to a whisper: "To the Tower with Buckingham. To the block, I say!"

Seymour reflected that it must be thirty years since Buckingham went to the block. Now the King remembered. Was his conscience, so long subdued concerning Buckingham, now rousing itself uneasily? The case of Buckingham had been similar to that of Surrey; both had been noble lords obsessed by their nobility.

The King was muttering again. He had returned to the present. "Seymour . . . are you there? Thomas . . . my friend . . . you spoke of Surrey. He has gone, has he? What was his crime?"

"He would have made his sister your mistress, Your Grace. Your Grace was enraged at such a suggestion."

A leer, which made the bloated face more horrible, now curled the King's lips. "Howard's girl . . . a comely wench . . . and saucy . . ."

Seymour felt nauseated. He turned from the King, thinking with amazement: On his dying bed he contemplates his bedtime pleasures! And Kate . . . my poor Kate . . . she was married to this man; and this is the monster who planned to send her the way he has sent others; who was planning, if rumor be correct, but a few weeks since.

"Thomas . . ." cried the King suddenly. "There are men in our chamber. Our enemies whisper and conspire against us."

"Nay, Sire. They are but your Councillors. They come to inquire of your health."

"Is Norfolk there?"

"Nay, Your Grace, Norfolk lies in the Tower, awaiting your signature to his death warrant."

"We'll give it. We'll give it. To the block with these Howards . . . father and son."

"Your Majesty must preserve his strength."

"There's strength enough. . . . I'll sign it. Surrey . . . a foolish boy. A comely wench, thy sister, Surrey. A drink . . . a drink . . . my throat is scorched by fires. Douse them, Seymour. Douse them, my friend. What whispering goes on about me? Come forth! Come forth! Ah, I see you there, you rogue. What news, eh? Why do you look so smug? Am I going to die? Is that what you would tell me? Come. . . . You there, Denny. What news? What news, I say?"

Denny, braver than the rest and certain now that the King was dying, decided to tell him the truth.

"My lord King, all human aid is vain, your doctors fear. It is therefore meet for Your Majesty to review your past life and seek God's mercy through Christ."

There was a second of terrible silence while understanding showed itself on the King's distorted face. But he was quick to recover his calm, to banish the terror which had laid hold on him. He said sternly: "Tell me, Denny, by what authority you come to pass sentence on me. What judge has sent you here?"

"Your doctors, Sire. I will send them to you. They await an audience."

The King closed his eyes wearily, but when a few seconds later the doctors approached the bed with medicines for him, he opened his eyes and glared at them with the old ferocity. "What's this?" he demanded. "You have passed sentence on me, you judges; and when a judge has passed his sentence on a criminal, he has no longer need to trouble him. Begone! Begone, I say!" As they continued to stand there watching him, he shouted: "Begone! Begone!"

The doctors bowed and turned away.

"Your presence can do no good here," said Wriothesley.

When they had gone, the Chancellor approached the bed.

"Your Majesty, would you wish to see some of your divines?"

"Eh?" said the King. "What's that? Ah . . . so it has come to that. Divines! Nay! I'll see none but Cranmer . . . and him not yet."

Wriothesley turned to one of the gentlemen. "Go you to Cranmer. He is at Croydon. Go with all speed. Tell him the King desires his presence at White Hall without delay."

"Your Majesty," he went on, "Cranmer will come."

"I'll have him when I am ready . . . and not before. Begone! Begone, I said. Leave me. . . ."

His eyes glared at them, although, to him they were like shadows at his bedside. They moved away to a far corner of the chamber, and after a while the King closed his eyes and began to speak again.

"Begone. . . . Begone. . . . I'll have none of ye." He moaned and cried out suddenly in a startled voice: "Anne! Anne! You're there, you witch. I see you." He spoke in a whisper then. "Why lookest thou at me with those great black eyes? Thy neck is small. Thou wilt not feel the sword. Ah! You would have a sword from Calais. That is like you. The ax is for ordinary mortals. Haughty to the end! Anne . . . Anne . . . 'tis for England, sweetheart. An heir for England. A King is the servant of his country. He is not the servant of his passions. Anne, thy black eyes scorn me. I'll not have it. To the block! To the block!"

The King opened his eyes suddenly and stared about him in a startled fashion. The candles were burning low and flickering in their sockets.

"Review your past life and seek God's mercy through Christ," he murmured. "That is what they tell me. That is what they tell me now. A great reign . . . a great and glorious reign. Oh God, always did the eighth Henry work for Thy glory and for the good of England. No thought gave he to his own desires. . . ."

His voice died away; his breathing was heavy; then suddenly it stopped, and those watching in the shadows thought the end had come.

But before they could move toward him, he had begun to speak again.

"Is that you, Cardinal, sitting there? Why do you smile, Cardinal? I like your smile not at all. The Cardinal died of a flux. Many die of a flux . . . be they Cardinal or beggar. You keep good wine, Thomas . . . good food and wine. A subject should not keep such state. Look at me not with those great black eyes, Anne. You witch! Sorceress! Poisoner! The roses are beautiful at Hever. Red roses . . . red . . . the color of blood. Shadows . . . shadows move about me. Shadows in my room. There. *There!* Monks . . . *monks.* . . .

Black cowls that drip red blood. Oh, dear God, they creep toward me. Closer . . . closer they come. Monks . . . monks from all corners. . . ." He tried to lift his hands, but he could not move them; he tried to shout for help, but his voice was a whisper. "The candles are going out and the darkness is coming, and with it . . . monks. . . . To Tyburn with them! To Tyburn! I . . . am not at Tyburn. I lie in bed . . . a-dying . . . a-dying."

The sound of his stertorous breathing filled the chamber.

"A drink!" he gasped. "A drink . . . a cup of wine, for the love of God."

"He is scorched with the death thirst," said Wriothesley.

As the Chancellor approached the bed and poured wine into the cup, the King said: "Kate . . . Kate, is that you . . . good wife?"

"It is your Chancellor, my lord," said Wriothesley. "Here is the wine you crave."

"Good Kate," said the King; and his eyes were closed now. "Good wife."

"There, 'tis refreshing, is it not, my lord?"

"It doth but cool the fires ere they burst to wilder fury. Kate . . . Kate . . . I'll not see the sun rise again."

"Speak not thus, my lord," said Wriothesley.

"Kate . . . I loved thee. I loved thee well. I had not thought of putting you from me that I might take another wife. I would not have married. . . . Jane . . . yes, Jane . . . an my subjects had not urged me to it."

Even the grim heart of the Chancellor was moved to pity, and listening to these last words of the King he wished to soothe the monstrous conscience.

"Your subjects urged Your Grace to the marriage," he said softly.

" 'Twas so. Katharine . . . canst thou see a dark shadow there . . . over there by the arras at the door?"

"There is nothing there, Your Grace."

"Look again," commanded the King.

"Nay, Sire. Your eyes deceive you."

"Come closer, Kate. I would whisper. It doth look to me like a fellow in a black robe. Can you not see a monk standing there?"

"It is but the hangings, my lord."

"You lie!" cried the King. "I'll have your head off your shoulders an you deceive me. Suffolk's wife, ah! She doth please me. Her eyes are dove's eyes and she would be a loving wench, I vow. And not too docile. I never greatly cared for too much docility. Jane, dost remember what happened to thy predecessor? A Flander's mare . . . and Howard's niece the prettiest thing that ever graced a court. Is that you, Chancellor? Monks. . . . Chancellor. They come at me. They come at me. Hold them off. Hold them off from your King, I say!" The King was breathing with difficulty. "What day is this?" he asked.

"The morning has come, for it is two of the clock," said Wriothesley.

"What day? What day?"

"The twenty-eighth day of January, my lord."

"The twenty-eighth day of January. Remember it. It is the day your sovereign lord the King was murdered. There in the hangings. See! Take my sword. Ah, you would have a sword from Calais to sever that proud head. The huntsman's call . . . do you hear it? There . . . look. In the hangings. I swear I saw the curtains move. Monks . . . monks. . . . Hanged, drawn and quartered. So perish all who oppose the King!"

Those who had been standing back from the bedside now drew near.

"He dies, I fear," said Wriothesley. "His hour is come."

The King seemed calmed by the sight of his ministers.

"My lords," he said, "my time approaches fast. What of my son—my boy Edward? His sister Mary must be a mother to him; for look, he is little yet."

"Be comforted, Your Majesty. Edward will be well cared for."

"He is your King. Supreme head of the Church. Defender of the Faith. A little boy . . . but ten years old."

"Your Majesty may safely leave these matters to your ministers, those whom you yourself have appointed to guide the affairs of your realm."

The King chuckled incongruously. "A motley lot. You'll have a noisy time, fighting together. But I'll not be there to see it. . . . I'll not be there. Kate. . . . Where is Kate? I see her not. I command you all to honor her, for she has been a good wife to me. We . . . we never thought to . . . put her from us. 'Twas but for sons . . . for England. Wine, wine. . . . I am a burning furnace."

He had not the strength to drink the wine which was offered.

His eyes rolled piteously.

"All is lost. All is lost," he moaned.

Cranmer came hastening to the chamber. Henry looked at this well-loved minister, but he could no longer speak to him.

The Archbishop knelt by the bed and took his master's hand.

"My lord, my beloved lord, give me a sign. Show me that you hope to receive the saving mercy of Christ."

But Henry's eyes were glazed.

Cranmer had come too late.

In the privy chamber, the King's body lay encased in a massive chest; and in this chamber, for five days, the candles burned, masses were said, and obsequies held with continual services and prayers for the salvation of his soul.

On the sixth day the great chest was laid on the hearse which was adorned with eight tapers, escutcheons, and banners bearing pictures of the saints worked in gold on a background of damask.

Dirges were sung as the funeral cortège began its stately journey to Windsor, where the chapel was being made ready to receive the royal corpse.

And the mourners?

There was his wife, now strangely light of heart. How did one feel when the ax which had been poised above one's head for nearly four years, was suddenly removed? She was a young woman in her mid-thirties, and she had never known that happy marriage which she had thought would be hers before the King had decided to make her his wife. Those four years had seemed liked forty; but she had come through them unscathed. The death of the King had saved her; and as she rode with the procession or took her place in the state barge, she could think of little but Thomas, who was waiting.

In his cell in the Tower of London, the Duke of Norfolk felt a similar lifting of the spirits—for he too had escaped death, and in his case, it was by a few hours. The King had intended that he should die, and instead the King had died; and now, without that master of men, there was no one left who would dare destroy the great Catholic leader. The Catholics were too strong, and there must be much diplomacy if the country was to avoid a bloody civil war. None wanted that. The hideous Wars of the Roses were too close to be forgotten. So, like

Katharine, Norfolk, who had narrowly escaped with his life, could not be expected to mourn sincerely the passing of the King.

Lord and Lady Hertford could scarcely wait to take over control. They had the young King in their keeping and they were the rulers now.

There was the little King himself, frightened by the homage which was now done to him. Men now knelt in his presence and called him Majesty, but he was wise enough to know that he was their captive as he had never been before.

And Mary? One life was now between her and the throne. The King was sickly; and so was she; but she prayed that God would take her brother before her so that she might have the glory of leading the English back to Rome.

There were two other important actors in England's drama at this time—two of the most ambitious people in the kingdom—a Princess of thirteen and a man in his thirties.

Why not? the Lord High Admiral asked himself. I verily believe the King would have given me his daughter, had he lived. But he is dead and Kate is free, and the Council will put obstacles between myself and the Princess.

The Admiral had need of caution, and he was the most reckless man in the kingdom.

And the Princess Elizabeth? She was impatient of her youth, impatient of her inexperience. She longed for the Admiral. She had her mother's love of gaiety and admiration and she yearned for the man who titillated her senses and roused within her that which was delightful and wholly dangerous. And yet . . . she must remember. There were two lives between herself and the throne. She was sure that her brother would never have an heir. And Mary with her ills and complaints—how long would she last? And then . . . ! The glory of it was dazzling. She wanted it so eagerly, so urgently. But she also wanted Seymour. She wanted the man *and* the throne. Yet something told her she could not have them both.

Here was a problem for a girl not yet fourteen years of age to solve. What could she do? She could wait; she could watch; she could remember always to act with caution, the greatest caution she could muster. Those who were very near the throne were in great danger until they reached it. And even then. . . . But not a Tudor. No, once a Tudor was on the throne, he—or she—would know how to stay there.

Such were the dreams of those who had lived near the King, as the funeral procession went its solemn way.

The body was brought to rest for a while in the chapel at Sion House; and while it was there the chest burst open and the King's blood was spilt on the chapel floor.

Horror ran through the land when this became known. The terrible tortures, which had been inflicted on many during this King's lifetime, were remembered; and the names of thousands who had died at his orders were recalled.

What has this King to answer for? it was whispered.

And the people shuddered.

A certain William Greville declared that a dog had appeared and licked the King's blood; and although great efforts had been made to drive the dog away, none had been able to do so.

It was a ghost, said the superstitious—the ghost of one whom he had murdered.

It was then recalled that his fifth wife, Catharine Howard, had rested at Sion

House on her way to the Tower, and this was the anniversary of that day when she had laid her head on the block and departed this life.

Had not Friar Peyto, greatly daring, preached against the King when he had put Queen Katharine of Aragon away from him and married Anne Boleyn? Had not the bold man compared Henry with Ahab, and prophesied that the dogs would, in like manner, lick his blood?

In the church of Windsor, Gardiner stood at the head of the vault, surrounded by the chief officers of the King's household while the corpse was lowered by means of a vice and sixteen of the strongest Yeomen of the Guard. Out of favor with the late King and looking fearfully toward a new reign by a King indoctrinated with the new learning, he turned his eyes to the Princess Mary and prayed God that it might not be long ere she took her place on the throne.

The Lord Chamberlain, the Lord Treasurer and all the company which stood about the grave held their rods and staves in their hands, and when the mold was cast down, each in turn broke his staff upon his head and cast it on to the coffin. *De Profundis* was then said and when the planks were laid over the pit, Garter, standing among the choir, proclaimed the little King's titles.

"Edward the Sixth, by Grace of God King of England, France, and Ireland, Defender of the Faith and Sovereign of the most noble order of the Garter," repeated Garter's officers; and three times they said this while the trumpets rang out.

A new reign had begun. A mighty ruler was laid to rest, and in his place stood a pale-faced boy.

It seemed to many who watched that ceremony that among them were the ghosts of murdered men and women.

CHAPTER

VI

The Princess Elizabeth was deeply perplexed.

There had come to her that day a proposal of marriage. It was her first proposal of this nature, because it was an appeal to her direct. There had, in the course of her thirteen years, been other suggested marriages, but she had never been called to give her opinion on these. When she had been a few months old and high in her father's favor, he had negotiated a marriage for her with the Duke of Angoulême, the third son of King François. That could not be expected to materialize after the King had called her a bastard, and it had long been forgotten. Later she had been promised to the heir of the Scottish Earl of Arran—a poor match for a royal Princess of England—and that, as perhaps had been intended from the first, had also come to nothing. Later there had been a more ambitious plan to unite her with Philip of Spain, son of the Emperor Charles, but that was also doomed to failure.

But this proposal she had now received was different from all others. This was a declaration of love; and it had been made by the man whom Elizabeth could now admit that she herself loved. The Lord High Admiral of England, Sir Thomas Seymour, craved the hand of the Princess Elizabeth in marriage.

She sat at a window of her apartments in White Hall, those apartments which her stepmother had begged the King to give her, and which she used when she was with the court and the court was at this palace.

For a short hour she was giving herself up to romantic dreams; she was allowing herself to think that she could marry whom she pleased.

He was handsome, that man. Handsome? That was inadequate to describe him. There were many handsome men at court, but there was none like Thomas Seymour. He was so gay, so jaunty, and there was about him that air of wickedness which delighted her as it must delight so many more. She loved his boldness, the strength in those arms that seized her, the speculation in the laughing eyes as though he were wondering how far he dared go. There was so much in him that called to the like in her; and while he made discreet love to her with the most indiscreet look in his eyes and the most suggestive tones in his voice, she was always aware of that ambition in him which she understood and applauded because that very same ambition was a part of her own nature.

He would be bold and passionate, and so would she. Her need of him, his need of her, were like a pair of mettlesome horses held in restraint by the reins of ambition. And because they were so checked their progress was the more exciting.

I want him, she decided; but I want so much besides.

She was her father's daughter; she was her mother's child. In her was that streak of levity which had characterized her mother; there was that desire to be admired and, because that desire for admiration was stronger than the sensuality which she had inherited from her father, she wished always

to keep the admiration at fever heat; therefore the pursuit interested her more than
any possible fulfillment. Even now she did
not wish the Admiral to be her husband; she
wished him to remain her suitor.

Yet it was not endurable to continue in a
state of uncertainty.

When she had heard the conditions of her
father's will she had been filled with elation.
Failing other heirs, she was placed third in
the line of succession. She was to be
treated with a respect and consideration almost equal to that which was to be be-
stowed on her sister Mary. Three thousand
pounds a year was to be hers, and that
seemed riches after the penury she had endured; a marriage portion of ten thousand
pounds was to be given at the appropriate
time. But there was a condition: This would
only be hers if she married with the consent
of her brother Edward and his Council. If
she married without such approval, she
would forfeit her dowry and, in all probabil-
ity, her income.

She had turned this matter over and over
in her mind.

She longed for Seymour; yet she longed

also to stay where she was in the succession to the throne.

Queen . . . Queen of England . . . and Queen in her own right—not lifted up, as her mother had been, to be cast down again at the whim of a husband. No! Queen—true Queen of England for the rest of her life!

The chances of success were good. Edward was sickly and it was hardly likely that he would produce an heir. Mary was thirty-one—old to marry and have children; and Mary's health was not of the best. Elizabeth was but thirteen years old. Oh yes, the chances of Elizabeth's becoming Queen of England were good indeed.

And if she married? What then?

The Council, she knew, would never approve of her marriage with Thomas. The King could be persuaded. She laughed to think of the little boy's being persuaded by herself and Thomas. That would be an easy task.

But she immediately called to mind those grim men, the real rulers. Thomas's brother would never agree. And Gardiner, Wriothesley, Cranmer? No! They would refuse consent. And then? Doubtless she and Thomas would find themselves in the Tower if they disobeyed, and all knew what could happen to prisoners in that doom-filled place.

There was so much to think of, so much to consider.

Her governess, Kat Ashley, came into the room and, finding her charge brooding in the window seat, asked if aught ailed her.

"Nothing ails me," said Elizabeth.

"Your Grace looks to have a fever. Your cheeks look hot and your eyes are so bright. I am not sure that you should not retire to your bed."

"Pray do not bother me, Kat. I am well enough."

"Your Grace is bothered concerning the letter you have received?"

"And how did you know there was a letter?"

"In my love for Your Grace I keep my eyes open and my ears alert. Tell me, darling, it is from the Admiral, is it not?"

Elizabeth looked at the woman and burst into sudden laughter. There were moments when she was very like her mother, thought Kat Ashley.

"And what if it should be?" asked Elizabeth.

"He's a darling man, Sir Thomas, and I

could love him myself, but he has no right to send you a letter."

"Lord Sudley now, if you please. You know that the first thing my brother did was to raise his dear uncle. Not Sir Thomas Seymour merely, but my Lord Sudley. My brother, like you, my saucy Kat, loves the darling man dearly!"

"Well, all the Council have been raised, have they not? There is Lord Hertford become the Duke of Somerset, and Sir Thomas Wriothesley, my lord Southampton."

"Yes, but Master Wriothesley is deprived of his Seal, while my brother gives love to Thomas Seymour as well as land and title."

"And does the King's sister love the man as much as her brother does?"

Kat Ashley was a born gossip, a lover of tittle-tattle; she was vitally interested in the affairs of those about her and inquisitive in the extreme, though goodhearted; she was always eager for exciting events about which to marvel or commiserate, and if they did not happen quickly enough she was ready to apply a little gentle prodding. But the welfare of her little Princess meant more to her than anything on Earth. Elizabeth

knew this; and because one of the great desires of her life was to receive the loving admiration of those about her, she was always
as affectionate and considerate as she
could be to Kat Ashley.

"How could she?" answered Elizabeth.
"Would it be wise to love such a man and
yet be unable to enter into a marriage with
him?"

"It would not!" cried Kat. "If you as much
as gave him a hint that you were eager for
him—why then, there would be no holding
him back."

They laughed together.

"The Council would never agree to such a
marriage, would they, Kat?" said Elizabeth
wistfully.

"Nay."

"They have their eyes on me now, Kat. I
must walk warily. Do you not think so?"

"With the utmost wariness, my darling
lady."

"Kat Ashley, do you think I shall ever be
Queen?"

Kat was solemn for a moment; she laid
her hands on the girl's shoulders and studied the pale face, the eyes which could at
some times be earnest and at others frivo-

lous, the mouth that provoked and promised, yet denied.

"Oh, my dearest mistress, my dearest
mistress, I beg of you take care."

"It is you who should take care, Kat. You
gossip whenever you have a chance. You
must restrain yourself now. My poor brother
. . . my poor sister! Kat, just think of them.
They seem so sick at times, and then . . .
then there will be just myself."

Kat sank to her knees and took the hand
of her charge. She kissed it, and lifting her
eyes to Elizabeth's face said: "God save the
Queen!"

Then they laughed together, looking over
their shoulders with furtive enjoyment.

How like her mother she is! thought Kat
again; and she held her fiercely and protec-
tively. "God preserve her," she prayed.
"Take care of her. She is young . . . so very
young."

Nevertheless, she was wise; she was
crafty; it was possible to see the craftiness
in her face at times; later she would be
crafty enough to hide it. But she was young
yet.

"Keep her safe until she is old enough to
keep herself safe," Kat continued her

prayer; and she thought: I am a fine one. I am as reckless as she is.

Elizabeth drew herself away from her governess and was solemn, thinking, as she must when she considered her nearness to the throne, of Thomas whom she could not have as well.

I need not fear for her, reflected Kat Ashley. She'll pass through all the dangers. I never knew one so clever.

Her brother was learned, but the Princess was the cleverer of the two. Lady Jane Grey, who had been tutored with them, was also learned; they were a clever trio. But Jane and Edward loved learning for itself, while Elizabeth loved it for what she hoped it would bring her. It seemed as though she had trained herself from her earliest years for a great destiny. She excelled in all subjects; she was a Latin scholar; she spoke French, Spanish, Flemish and Italian fluently, taking great pains with those languages which she thought might be useful to her. Like young Jane and Edward, and indeed like most cultured children, she wrote verses; but while those children loved their verses and spent much time over them, Elizabeth wrote hers merely to show that she could do anything they could. Her greatest delight was to study the history, not only of her own country, but that of others. She wished to know how kings and governments had acted in the past, and the result of such actions. So the greater part of her time was devoted to the study of history, and she had learned foreign languages with such zest, that she might be able to read history written in those tongues. Always she was preparing herself for greatness. Therefore it seemed strange that a girl who, at such an early age, had so serious a purpose in mind which amounted almost to a dedication, could at the same time be so frivolous.

But she was her father's daughter and he, while occupying his mind with great state policies, had found the inclination toward his pleasures irresistible.

Kat Ashley, while she admired her mistress's uncommon astuteness, trembled for her.

"Kat dear," said Elizabeth suddenly, "leave me. I have a letter to write."

"To . . . the Admiral?"

"It is no concern of yours."

"It is. It is. Have a care, sweetheart."

"I intend to."

"Do not forget. . . ."

"I forget nothing. Go now. Go quickly, I say."

Kat Ashley moved toward the door and, when she reached it, paused to look appealingly at the Princess.

"Oh, Kat," said Elizabeth, "do not forget. Tomorrow we go to Chelsea, to be with my stepmother. We must prepare."

"I had not forgotten. I, too, forget nothing, my lady."

"Get you gone, and leave me to my work," said Elizabeth, with a return of the imperious manner which she employed at times and which was always an indication that she had done with play.

She had made up her mind. Kat's byplay had decided her. When she had knelt, and half in earnest had said, "God save the Queen!" she had brought Elizabeth to the point of decision.

The Princess dared not risk the loss of that for which, above everything, she longed.

I will not think of him, she told herself. I *must* not think of him. I will remember the tales I have heard of him. He is a philanderer; he has had many mistresses. If I were a commoner it would be different.

Then she laughed aloud, for if she were a commoner would Thomas have looked her way? Yes, he would; it was not solely because she was third from the throne that he wanted her. If she had been a low serving girl he would have sought her out, even if only to make love to her.

She took up her pen.

"From the Princess Elizabeth to the Lord High Admiral."

Firmly she wrote, thanking him for his letter.

". . . but," she went on, "I have neither the years nor the inclination for marriage, and I would not have thought that such a matter should have been mentioned to me at a time when I ought to be taken up in weeping for the death of my father, the King. . . ."

And as she wrote those words her mouth was remarkably like her father's.

She stared before her, and she was thinking, not of the dead King, but of the charm of Seymour.

Her mouth softened. A Queen, she reminded herself, would choose her own husband. A Queen would not allow a council of ministers to decide such a matter.

Thomas would still be there. She pictured him, calling as often as he dared, and those little scenes when he made excuses to touch her.

She was thrilled at the thought of him; but even more thrilling was the echo of those words: God save the Queen.

Thomas Seymour, the new Lord Sudley, was angered by that letter from the Princess.

He wanted a wife, and he wanted the Princess, but if she would not have him he would have another. He was a man who could love many women; and a motherly, tender woman, a Queen who had become very rich and was of some importance in the land, was not a bad substitute for a prickly Princess.

He, like Elizabeth, realized that had she accepted his proposals they would have been in great danger. He had been prepared to risk that danger. But since the Princess had refused him, he saw no reason why he should remain a bachelor. The Princess was but thirteen; he might still have her, for who knew what the future held?

In any case, he was piqued by the tone of her letter, and, a few days after the receipt of it, he set out for Chelsea, where the Dowager Queen was in residence. The young Princess, who had been assigned to her care, was now there with her. It was a piquant situation—the two women with whom the Admiral had contemplated marriage, together under one roof—a Queen and a Princess.

But he would call to see the Dowager Queen.

It was not quite a month since the death of the King, and he saw that snowdrops were beginning to appear in the gardens before the cottages which he passed on his way through the villages, and the purple flowers of the butterbur were blooming along by the river.

Katharine was staying in the Dormer Palace of Chelsea (which Henry had built after he had seized the Manor of Chelsea), with its gardens that ran down to the Thames. Thomas approached the palace by the only road through the village, which wound between the meadows. He crossed

Blandels Bridge—very pretty now with the hoar frost on the nearby bushes, but so dangerous at dusk on account of the many robbers who infested the place, and who had so often added murder to their crimes that the bridge had become known as Bloody Bridge.

Lord Sudley's eyes glistened with excitement as they turned from the small turrets to the long narrow windows, while he hoped for a glimpse of a red head.

He wondered if the weather was warm enough to walk in the gardens with Katharine, for those gardens had been made very pleasant with their lawns and miniature fishponds.

Katharine received him rather cautiously, because several of her ladies were in attendance. How fair she looked! She wore her royal widow's hood and barb with its sable pall as though she did so with great relief— as indeed she must. She could not hide her feelings for him, so he was glad when she dismissed her women and they were alone together.

He took her hands. "At last!" he said.

"Thomas! How I have longed to see you! But is it not a little too soon?"

"It is most improper," he replied with a laugh.

He knew she was hoping he would take her into his arms, and how could he refuse? He had never been able to refuse such a thing to a woman.

"Thomas . . . what if we were seen?"

"Ah, my brother Somerset's spies are everywhere. Somerset now, remember. No longer merely Hertford."

"And you are no longer plain Sir Thomas."

He bowed. "Lord Sudley at your service."

"Always Thomas . . . my dearest Thomas."

"Oh, Katharine, how I have trembled for you in these latter years."

"And yet you seemed not to notice me. How you made me suffer!"

"How I should have made us both suffer if I had looked at you and betrayed my thoughts!"

"You were the wise one, Thomas. I was foolish."

"Now you understand how greatly I love you. I can even be wise for your sake."

"You make me so happy."

"And when, Katharine, my sweet Katharine, will you make me happier still?"

He was carried on by his feelings, as he

always was. He owed his successes at sea to this very impetuousness. He believed so firmly in the destiny of Thomas Seymour that he was able to forget that five days ago he had asked Elizabeth to marry him; now it seemed to him that he had always loved Katharine, that during those years of danger he had deliberately forced himself to think of others for her sake.

Elizabeth, that child! It was a pretty joke, a pleasant game. And, oh, what an exciting game! But how could he marry the Princess without the consent of the Council? Besides, she was a child; and here was a warm, loving woman, so earnestly, so faithfully in love with him.

He took her roughly in his arms. He liked to play the buccaneer. It was usually successful, accompanied as it always was, in his dealings with women, by an underlying tenderness. See the strong man who could vanquish an enemy, see how he curbs his strength for fear of harming the one he loves!

She was a Queen; he could not help it if, in calculating her desirable qualities, he had in mind not only her gentle nature, her adoration of himself, her charming little body, not too mature, but so comfortable, so pleasant and delightful; there were also her lands, her endowment, her influence. The King loved his uncle, but without a doubt the boy idealized his stepmother. The two of them together would make a team to guide the King. With her riches, her influence and her charm, she was irresistible.

"My dearest," he said, "when?"

"When?" she cried. "And the King not dead a month!"

"I shall not hesitate this time."

"My love, you must . . . hesitate a little . . . for the sake of decency, for the sake of etiquette."

But he had seized her again. "Do you think I care for these things when love burns in my heart? No, no! I lost you once. Do you think I will allow that to happen again?"

"Nay, my dearest, you must be patient."

"Patience and love, dear Kate, go not hand in hand."

"What would be said of me if . . . my husband not dead a month . . . I took another?"

"I would take my fists to the ears of any who spoke ill of you, Kate . . . from the lowest to the highest. Take off the hood."

"I dare not."

"Then I will." He seized it and flung it from them.

She looked at him and laughed aloud. There was a note of the old hysteria in her voice when she said: "It is the end . . . the end of fear. Oh, Thomas, you cannot guess what it was like. Every time I heard footsteps I wondered whether they came for me."

"My darling Kate, my dearest Kate, none shall harm you now, for Thomas will be at your side . . . as long as we both shall live."

"It is so wonderful, my darling. I think I shall die of happiness."

"Die! Ye shall not! You have done with death. Kate, we shall marry soon . . . this very week."

"Now let us talk seriously."

"I speak with the utmost seriousness. I'll brook no delay."

He lifted her in his arms while she laughingly begged to be put down. "For if we were seen, I know not what would be said or done against us."

He refused to release her. He sat on a stool and held her against him.

"Nothing will be done against us, Kate. None would dare." He was about to outline the advantages of a marriage between them, to explain how the little King would be as butter in their hands; but at such moments it was wiser to talk of love and nothing but love. If he was a reckless statesman, experience had made him a perfect lover; and in any case, love between them was a very pleasant topic.

"I am a most impatient man, Kate."

"I am an impatient woman where you are concerned. But, Thomas, I am as yet unready. I have nightmares still."

"You need me beside you to comfort you."

"I dream . . ."

"Forget those dreams. Let us talk of others . . . when you and I shall be married."

"The earliest would be May."

"May! Three whole months away!"

"We dare not before."

"Who says I dare not when I will?"

"My dearest . . ." But he stopped her protests with kisses while his thoughts were racing on.

"A secret marriage," he murmured in her ear.

She caught her breath. "No. No. It would be dangerous."

"May, for our official ceremony then," he

went on. "But I shall visit you. I shall come by night."

"No, Thomas."

But he insisted: "Yes."

"You will ride out to Chelsea after dark? No, Thomas, I forbid it."

"But I shall forbid you to forbid it when you are in my arms."

"Across the fields . . . over Bloody Bridge?"

"Why not?"

"At night! It is most dangerous."

"So you think *I* could not defend myself?"

"I know you are the bravest, the strongest . . ."

"Yes," he said. "I shall come. For I cannot wait till May."

"No, no."

"But yes!" he cried; he laughed and she could not help but laugh with him.

There had never been happiness like this in the whole of her life. Her widow's hood lay on the floor—a symbol of her freedom. She knew that she would deny him nothing, for there was no happiness for her apart from him.

And when Thomas rode away from the Dormer Palace he was affianced—though as yet in secret—to the widow of a King not four weeks dead.

From one of the windows, the Princess Elizabeth watched him ride away. She tossed back her hair and smiled secretly.

He had called at the Palace in the hope of catching a glimpse of her, she was sure; he was pretending to be piqued because she had not accepted his proposal.

She danced round her room, pausing to admire herself in a mirror. She thought how enchanting she looked and of the months ahead when the Lord High Admiral would continue to woo her.

The spring had come to England. Daisies starred the fields, and the marsh marigolds, with the celandines, made a gold pattern along the banks of the river. Then came April, and the wild violets bloomed beneath the trees in Chelsea village.

Elizabeth was waiting for Thomas to act. There were occasions when she felt that she cared for nothing but to be with him and listen to his wooing.

Kat Ashley watched her.

"It is the coming of the spring, my lady,"

she said. "Guard yourself, for in the spring fancy runs riot."

"Mine never would," declared Elizabeth.

The days were fully occupied. There were regular lessons of many hours' duration. Elizabeth was studying now under the very distinguished and learned William Grindal who confessed himself astonished at her scholarship. Katharine conferred with William Grindal on her stepdaughter's studies; but there was a remoteness about the Dowager Queen which Elizabeth did not understand. She was less important as the King's widow than she had been as his wife; yet never had she looked so contented with life as she did now.

Elizabeth had seen Thomas now and then, although he made no special effort to meet her. It seemed as if he no longer thought of her as anyone but the late King's daughter, and sister to the present one. But she fancied she caught a reminder of the old gleam in his eyes, and she guessed that he still wanted her. He was chagrined by her refusal. Arrogant Thomas! He thought any woman ready to submit to him. He had to learn that a Princess—who might one day be Queen—was no ordinary woman.

Avidly she learned all she could learn of the histories of England, France and Spain; and she imagined herself in a place of high state, governing countries. Two pictures dominated her dreams; one was of herself in the jeweled raiment of a Queen with her ministers about her, accepting her merest word as law; in the other she was lying under a hedge, as a serving woman might, and Thomas was beside her.

So passed the weeks with her step-mother at Chelsea.

Occasionally she went to court and saw her little brother. Edward seemed weighed down by his state duties. Whenever she saw him she thought: Kingship is too much for Edward. That which should adorn his head like a saint's halo is but a weight he is not strong enough to carry.

What did her sister Mary think of all that was happening? Mary too, one step ahead of Elizabeth, must have her dreams. Hers were not of power and glory, of adulation, of wisdom to make her country great; her one thought was of turning England back to Rome. The clever girl who was not yet fourteen felt an inner exultation when she thought of Mary, since to force the people to what they loved not, was no way to rule, no way to keep the scepter in the hands and win the love and adulation of one's subjects. She called to mind her father's rule. His policy had been to destroy the dangerous men at the top and placate the mob. Already she was smiling at the people—the cottagers, the merchants and apprentices— when she went abroad. Already they were returning her smiles, liking her youthful beauty and her friendliness. "God bless the Princess Elizabeth!" they cried when they saw her. She was astute enough to know that this sign of her growing popularity must not show itself too often. It must not be known that already she was wooing the people, the common people who, those foolish ones did not fully understand, ultimately decided whether their monarchs should rule.

It was during the month of May when she made a discovery. She was lying drowsily on her bed in her apartment at the Dormer Palace; it was just on midnight, and through the slight opening where the curtains about her bed had not been pulled together, she caught a glimpse of the moonlight which flooded her room.

Suddenly she heard a sound in the grounds below. It might have been the snapping of twigs or the sound of a foot-fall—she was not sure; but she felt certain that someone was down there creeping stealthily about the gardens.

She remembered gossip she had heard among her women.

"They say he comes at night."

"They say she meets him at the postern gate . . . and lets him into her chamber. . . ."

Elizabeth had taken little notice. It was not unusual for a woman to have a lover, to bring him into the palace at night. She wondered now who the man was. If she discovered, she would tease the woman in the morning. She got out of bed and went to the window, creeping that she might not disturb her attendants who were sleeping in the room beyond, with the connecting door open.

She knelt on the window-seat.

Moonlight lay across the grass, and there . . . coming across it, was a man.

She had not been mistaken then. . . .

She drew back suddenly in delighted terror.

He is coming to me! she told herself. How like him! He will climb the creeper to my room. And what shall I do? He will be seen. There will be scandal. I shall have to make them keep quiet . . . I . . .

She placed her hand on her heart and felt its mad beating under the thin stuff of her nightgown.

He must not come. . . .

Yet she hoped, of course, that he would.

Then, as she watched, she knew that she need not fear his coming. She would not have to deal with a delicate situation, for she had no part in it—except that of looker-on. Another person had appeared. There was the small figure of a woman. She ran to Seymour, and he and the woman seemed to melt into one. The woman's hood fell back exposing the head of the Dowager Queen.

Elizabeth watched their kissing, the hot blood in her face, the sweat in her palms.

"How dare he!" she murmured. "And how dare *she*!"

She watched them, her rage increasing. He had released Katharine now. They stood looking at each other; then he put his arm about the Queen and they turned toward the Palace.

So the Queen was taking Thomas Seymour secretly to her apartments. She was behaving, Elizabeth told herself, like any kitchen slut.

She remained kneeling at the window after they had disappeared, picturing them in the silences of the Queen's chamber.

Her women would know, and they would keep her harlot's secrets. Katharine Parr had always won the regard of those who served her. Doubtless Kat Ashley knew, for did not Kat make it her task to discover everything that went on? And Kat would have kept it from her mistress because she feared such news would wound her pride.

If I were Queen, meditated Elizabeth, if I were Queen of England now!

She gave herself up to thoughts of the torture she would inflict on those two.

But her rage was only temporary, for she loved them both. That was what hurt so badly. Who could help loving Katharine Parr? Ingratitude was not one of Elizabeth's failings; she could not forget how the Dowager Queen had changed the state of the neglected princesses when she had become the King's wife. Elizabeth must love

Katharine for her virtues, while she loved Seymour in spite of his sins.

These two had betrayed her; but the Queen, of course, knew nothing of the betrayal. But he knew. He was laughing at her whose hand he had asked in marriage when he was the lover of Katharine Parr.

Elizabeth went back to her bed and tried, without success, to banish thoughts of those two together. The pictures her mind conjured up for her were so vivid. They embodied all that Elizabeth wanted for herself and dared not take, all that was denied her because of her dream of Queenship.

Her mouth grew prim. This was an insult to her father, the great King Henry. They were traitors, both of them. What if she betrayed them? What would be the fate of those two if the Duke of Somerset, the Lord Protector, knew what his brother was doing with the Dowager Queen?

What if there was a child . . . a son! And what if they declared that son to be the late King's! Elizabeth grew cold at the thought. She knew at that moment that her desire for the crown would always be greater than her desire for Seymour or any man.

They would not dare declare their son the

King's son. If they tried to, she would let nothing stand in her way of humiliating them . . . destroying them.

I could have had him, she reminded herself. Poor Katharine! She is the one who is being cheated.

She could not sleep. She lay, conjuring up more pictures of their lovemaking until the dawn came.

She was at the window, watching his hasty departure.

The Lord High Admiral sought audience with the King at the palace of White Hall. This His Majesty was very willing to grant.

"A good morrow to you, my Lord Sudley," said the King.

The Admiral bent low and kissed the little hand. Then, lifting his face which was turned away from the King's attendants, he slowly closed one eye and almost imperceptibly jerked his head. The little King's face flushed with pleasure. Uncle Thomas meant: Let us be alone together.

There was nothing that would please Edward more.

"I would be alone with my uncle," he said. "Pray leave us."

He looked fearfully at his attendants as though he suspected that they might refuse; but there were no gentlemen of great importance among them at that moment to offer that advice, proffered ingratiatingly and yet in such a manner as to imply that His Majesty—for all his titles—was but a child, and a child who was in duty bound to obey his ministers.

When they had gone, Thomas said: "And how fares the King?"

"He was not feeling well until the Lord High Admiral called to see him. That lifted his spirits mightily."

"My dearest nephew!"

"Uncle Thomas, it is long since I have seen you."

"You are so guarded now, continually surrounded by your counselors. There seems hardly room for poor Uncle Thomas."

"There is always room for Uncle Thomas."

"Tell me, what money does Your Grace need?"

"I will show you. I have written out what I need and what I owe."

"Then let Uncle Thomas take care of that."

"Dear Uncle, it seems so strange. I am a King, and yet I have to do what I am told. I am kept short of money, and I have my tutors who call me 'Majesty' and yet hint at stern punishment if I fail in my duties."

"Be of good cheer. To be a King is a great honor. But more so when the King is no longer a boy. Now if you were a man like myself or like your father . . ."

"How I wish I were! Yes . . . like my father, so that I only had to raise an eyebrow to have everyone trembling. How fares my mother? Have you seen her? It seems long since I have. I often think of the days when she would spend long hours with us . . . my sister Elizabeth and Jane Grey . . . while we were at our lessons. I miss them all sorely."

"They are all well. They miss Your Majesty."

"It seems a sad thing to be a King and not to have those you love about you. Oh yes, I would I were like my father."

"Marry! He was a boy once. Soon your boyhood will be over, dear Edward. You will be a man; you will marry a wife . . . and, if you are like your father, mayhap six."

The little King smiled sadly. "One would suffice for me."

"You are wise, dearest Majesty. I myself would be happy with a wife, I am thinking."

"It surprises me that you have not one. You are no longer young and, from all I have heard, the ladies are fond of you."

"My lord King, if you were to command me to marry a wife, then I should have no excuse for remaining single."

"I? Command you? Dearest Uncle, what do you mean?"

The Admiral's eyes were alert. He loved the boy; indeed he did; and he was enjoying this moment. He had committed a great indiscretion. He had married the Dowager Queen, although her husband had been dead little more than three months. It was, to say the least, a great breach of court etiquette; he was not sure that it would not be regarded as a crime. The Council would be furious at his conduct, and he needed the approval of the King.

"If you were to choose a wife for me, whom would you choose? Think carefully, dearest nephew. When I was your age I used to imagine the people I loved best, married to one another. Just tell me; if you could pick a bride for me, on whom would you decide?"

Edward smiled. Like many whose minds are heavily burdened with learning, his humor was a little childish. He shut his eyes.

"I must think of a lady of your own age," he said. "The lady must be one whom I love as much as I love you. There is only one grown lady whom I love as I love you."

"Then you should command me to marry her, Sire."

"How can I do that, my lord?"

"You are the King. Your Majesty has only to command. Tell me her name, Sire."

"It is my stepmother, the Queen."

"But . . . I love her. How did you know? Your Majesty, you are most astute! If I might choose from all the ladies in this land . . . nay, in all the world, I would choose Queen Katharine. So Your Grace commands me to marry her?"

"Yes," said the King. "I do."

Seymour knelt and kissed his hand.

"And none dare disobey the King's command!" he said with a wink, and they laughed together.

"I shall be glad," said Edward, "when I have a wife."

"I know the very one for you. I know the lady of your choice."

"Who then?"

"The Lady Jane Grey."

"I love her dearly," admitted Edward. "It would be wonderful to have her with me always. I am so lonely sometimes."

"I cannot command Your Majesty to marry, as Your Majesty commands me."

"But if you could, Uncle Thomas, would you command me to marry Jane?"

"I would, dearest nephew. But as I cannot, I will do everything within my power to bring about the match."

"How will you do that?"

"As yet I cannot say. But, by God's precious soul, I will do my utmost. There! You have my oath on it."

They laughed together and the pleasant interview continued until some of the King's ministers demanded an audience.

Seymour left, promising the King to return soon. He was pleased with the results of his little game. He had received the King's consent to his marriage; and it would certainly be in the interests of the Reformed Party, to which, for political reasons the Seymours belonged, to have the King married to Lady Jane Grey, for little Jane had been brought up in the reformed faith, and the Catholic influence must be suppressed.

Seymour's thoughts were merry as he rode to Chelsea to spend the night with his wife.

When the court heard the news of the marriage of the Dowager Queen and Lord Sudley it was deeply shocked.

Both the Admiral and the Queen were in disgrace.

This was the worst breach of royal etiquette since Mary Tudor, Henry's sister, had married Charles Brandon, Duke of Suffolk, in such haste after the death of her husband, the King of France. It was remembered that Henry the Eighth had married Katharine Parr quite as soon after the death of Lord Latimer, but he was a King and all-powerful. Such as the Admiral and Katharine Parr should be taught that they could not take the law into their own hands.

Seymour pleaded that he had the King's consent.

Edward said with dignity that this was so.

He had desired the marriage; and, supported by and supporting the two people he loved so dearly, he took on new dignity and authority. He was the son of his father when he told the Council that he approved of the marriage and that it would be as well for the gentlemen to remember that he was their King.

The most furious person at court—with the exception of Elizabeth, who had taught herself to keep quiet when it was necessary to do so—was Anne Stanhope, Duchess of Somerset, the wife of the elder Seymour brother.

She had hated Katharine Parr ever since the death of the King.

It was ironical, she declared, it was ridiculous that the woman should take precedence of her. *She* was the wife of the Protector, the true governor of England; and because of Katharine Parr's marriage to the late King, she was the first lady in the land. The Duchess recognized that the Princesses Mary and Elizabeth, and the King's divorced wife, Anne of Cleves, must have precedence; that was understood. But that Katharine Parr, who was now but the wife of her husband's younger brother, should do so, was monstrous.

She faced her husband when she heard the news and, though fully acquainted with her turbulent moods, never had Edward Seymour seen her so furious.

"The Dowager Queen!" she cried. "And who is this Dowager Queen? Katharine Parr! King Henry the Eighth married her in his doting days when he had brought himself so low by his cruelty and his lust that no lady of honor would venture near him. And I . . . *I*, my lord, must give place to her! Once she was Latimer's widow; now she is the wife of your brother . . . your *young* brother . . . and yet she is placed above me. Methinks we shall have to ask Master Admiral to teach his wife good manners. And if he will not, then I swear *I* will."

The astute Protector, both calm and cold, ever ready to see an advantage and be on the spot to take it a second or two before a rival could do so, was yet gentle with his Duchess.

"Anne," he pleaded, "be calm. Nothing can be done at this moment. You must accept this state of affairs. She has married

Thomas, and, no matter what we do, we cannot prevent that."

"Do you not see that your brother Thomas has done this that he may become more powerful than you are?"

"I am watchful of him," he answered serenely.

"With the Queen his wife, and the two of them preparing to mold the King, what might they not do?"

"The King is in our care. Thomas may be his uncle, but so am I. And I am the elder."

"You have been sterner with him than Thomas has. Thomas has bribed him with gold, and bemused him with charm. Beware of your brother."

"I am wary, dearest Anne. I am ever watchful. Thomas knows how to charm people, but there his accomplishments end. He is a fool, that brother of mine."

"His charm has brought him much. It has already brought him the Queen."

"I fear neither Thomas nor his Queen. I and my Duchess will be a match for them."

She smiled. They were together in all things, bound by affection and ambition. To her he was not cold and ruthless; to him she was not proud and haughty.

"My dear," he said, "this matter of marriage has set me thinking. What would you say to our daughter Jane's marrying the King? It would not be the first time a Jane Seymour sat upon the throne."

The Duchess flushed with pleasure. "Our daughter . . . Queen of England!"

He kissed her cheek.

"You would like that, eh? And what do you say to the Lady Jane Grey for our son?"

She seized his hand and pressed it. "Our daughter a Queen!" she repeated. "Our son married to one who is not so very far from the throne. My lord husband, there are glorious days ahead for us."

"There, my love, you see we are doing well. Do not let us begrudge Thomas his Queen."

She looked momentarily grave. "He *has* his Queen; he has his influence with the King; and our daughter is not yet Queen of England, our son not betrothed to the Lady Jane Grey. Methinks that Thomas should be shown he cannot flout the Protector's authority."

"How should we show our displeasure?"

"By confiscating all the jewelery which King Henry gave to Katharine Parr. It is not in truth her property now, because it belongs to the crown; and you, as Protector, are responsible for it."

He looked at her slyly. "Much of it would become you, my dear."

"That it would! But I could not wear it—and should your younger brother's wife be adorned with jewels that *I* may not wear?"

He put his arm about her waist. "Why, indeed," he said, "should my brother's wife wear jewels which mine cannot!"

To some it might have seemed difficult to concentrate on lessons; this was not the case with the young Elizabeth. Hurt and humiliated she had been, but there were times when she could completely banish that humiliation from her mind. She could welcome what had happened with Seymour as an experience from which she could learn much; and one thing she had learned was that no amount of study could give a Princess that knowledge of human nature which was perhaps more desirable than any other. A good understanding of the people would be the first requirement of one who planned to rule them.

So, even while she wept, while she gave

herself up to silent rages, she could not be altogether angry with the newly married pair.

She was determined to face the truth. Katharine was in love with Thomas Seymour, and she did not see him as the avaricious philanderer; therefore it would be folly to feel anger against the Queen. As for Thomas, he was still Thomas; and she had never believed him to be a saint.

She must be calm; she must try to understand the motives behind people's actions, she must therefore welcome all experience, however bitter.

Her servants were her friends; she had never to ask them in vain for any special service. Her appealing youthfulness, her dangerous position, that troublous childhood through which she had passed, touched them deeply and bound them to her. Moreover, although she could at times be more imperious than any, she could also show the utmost familiarity. She was loyal to them and defended them always if they were in any trouble. These qualities bound them to her, and if she knew the secret of the bonds, that did not make them less secure.

Her cofferer, Thomas Parry, had not hesitated to betray the Admiral to her. When the news of Thomas's marriage to the Queen was bruited abroad, Parry had looked sly, and Elizabeth, sensing this, demanded to know why.

"My lady Princess," said Parry, "he has married the Queen, but to my mind he was hoping for the Princess."

She could not hide her satisfied smile. "Master Parry, why do you say that?"

"It is because of what happened the day after the King's burial."

"And what was that?"

"My Lord Admiral sought me out and put to me many questions concerning your ladyship."

"Questions! And how dared you discuss me with the Admiral!"

" 'Twas not your ladyship so much as your possessions, and doubtless he thought I would be the person most fitted to inform him in such matters."

"My possessions!"

"Yes, he would know what lands and estates were yours, and methinks he was well pleased with what was coming to you."

The Princess's eyes narrowed and she laughed immoderately.

"The Admiral is a very cautious man, Tom Parry."

"Indeed, yes, my lady. But methinks he has a fondness for your person which equals that for your lands."

"My stepmother's possessions were greater than mine, and her person more charming?"

She waited, and Parry, being so fond of her, could not disappoint her.

"The possessions, yes, my lady; but how could the charms of a middle-aged lady compare with those of a young girl . . . and a young girl who . . ." He paused.

"Who . . . ? What were you about to say, Master Parry?"

"A young girl who is acknowledged to be a beautiful Princess."

She held her head very high. "But you flatter me," she said. "I did not come to you for flattery."

Then she left him, and Parry looked after her, smiling. She could not deceive him. He had seen the heightened color, the flash of her eyes. He judged that if she had refused my Lord Admiral—as Kat Ashley had told him she had—she had been in two minds about him. Seymour was a man who knew how to charm the women.

Parry would lose no time in telling Mistress Ashley of their Princess's words. They were a pair of gossips; and since their little Princess's welfare was so near their hearts, they enjoyed, more than anything, discussing her actions.

"God bless her!" said Parry aloud. "The sly, conceited little Princess. God bless her! May she come to greatness, and I doubt not that she will, with her pretty, cunning ways."

Elizabeth went on, feeling just a little piqued that Seymour had asked such questions concerning her property. She could understand his asking those questions; they were such as she herself would have put; and she, like Seymour, would have been influenced by the answers. Such a Princess, determined on practical behavior, could not, therefore, entirely blame Thomas Seymour for making such inquiries.

She remembered now those occasions when they had met since his marriage. He had kissed her with lingering tenderness and his eyes had shown traces of passion when they rested upon her.

We understand each other, they seemed to imply. We are of a kind, made for each other. What a little fool you were to refuse me! Are you realizing that now?

She did understand him. He was a man who could love two women at the same time, for there was no mistaking his tenderness when his eyes rested on his wife. At the same time he could desire Elizabeth.

She also was capable of two loves. One for Seymour and one for power.

They were alone together, a few weeks after the marriage had been announced. She had been walking near the Dormer Palace, and he came upon her when she had eluded her attendants and had walked near Blandels Bridge.

She believed he had seen her and followed her; it was because of this that she had slipped away from her attendants.

"This is a happy meeting," he said, catching up with her as if by chance near a clump of trees which would provide a screen and protection against prying eyes.

"Happy for whom?" she asked. "For you, my lord, or for me?"

"Dare I hope, for us both? I have seen little of you in these last few months."

" 'Twas two days ago, my lord, that we met."

"I mean alone," he said with that low caressing note in his voice which, in spite of her knowledge of him and herself, could not fail to thrill her.

"Alone?" she said, looking about her as if surprised to find herself unattended.

"How beautiful you are!" he said. "As beautiful as this May morning. The year is in its springtime and so are you."

"My lord, your flatteries fall on deaf ears."

"And what has befallen your royal ears that they are deaf to flattery?"

"Do not mock me, I beg of you."

"It is sometimes easy to hide deep feelings behind mocking words."

She could see the bluebells under the trees bowing in the faint breeze, and she fancied they were the men and women of England bowing to her greatness, reminding her of her royalty. But she could smell the May flowers and see the budding and blossoming of the trees; the sun was warm on her face; she felt reckless because there was spring in the air.

She could not resist dallying with him, luring him on to flirtation, that most pleasant of all pastimes, allowing him to give her those toys for which she most longed—flattery and admiration—showing her that if she had not yet the power for which she longed as a Queen, she had the subtle power of an attractive woman.

"I could not take you seriously when you speak of deep feelings," she said.

He tried to seize her hand.

"My Lord Admiral," she went on, "methinks you forget the respect due to me. You find me here unattended and you forget."

"I forget everything," he said, "but that you and I are here . . . alone together."

"Thus speaks the bridegroom?" she said, lifting her eyes to his, mocking and inviting. "The bridegroom of a few weeks! Or is it longer? Methinks you may have become my stepmother's bridegroom before ever you went through the ceremony of marriage with her."

"You're a saucy wench!" he said with a laugh.

"My lord, how dare you!"

"I would dare much with you, my lady; and methinks you invite me to the daring."

"I would be alone. I give you leave to retire."

"Your eyes invite me to stay, Princess."

"How dare you treat me thus . . . because you find me here alone and unprotected?"

The Admiral laughed. She was as fond of make-believe as her father had been. She wished to play the part of the pursued and reluctant maiden.

"You've a droll little face," he said. "And I have a weakness for red hair."

He held a lock of it in his hands and, bending his head, swiftly kissed it.

She pushed him away; she now wished to play the haughty Princess, for she would not let him think she could easily forget that he had humiliated her deeply.

"What dost think the Queen, my step-mother and your wife, would say if she knew that, scarce had the King been dead a week, you were suggesting marriage with me?"

"Have you not told her, then?"

"You must be very sure of your charms, my lord, since you think that I might have told her that, and she still remain so affectionate toward you that she would consent to become your wife."

"I *am* sure of them," he said; and bending his head swiftly, he kissed her lips.

She gasped, but her flush betrayed her enjoyment.

"Aye," he went on, mocking her, "and not only am I sure that I can charm the Queen . . . but others also."

"I could carry tales of this to the Council," she said threateningly.

"You could, my Princess."

"And you would suffer for it."

"And you would not? They would say: 'And how came the Lady Elizabeth to be alone in such a place with the Lord Admiral, her stepfather?'"

"Why should she not be . . . if her attendants had left her?"

"Certainly she could be . . . if she had eluded her attendants."

"You presume too much, sir."

"I would I might presume more."

Her defenses dropped suddenly; he had that effect upon her. She said in a pathetic voice: "You asked my hand in marriage, and then you must have gone straight to my stepmother and made similar protestations of love."

"You refused me," he reminded her.

"I could not marry without the consent of the Council."

"Nor could the Queen . . . but she did."

"You did not seek to marry for love, My Lord Admiral."

"That is just what I did."

"When you asked me, or my step-mother?"

"When I asked you both."

"You thought I should be the better prize. Was that why I had the honor of the first proposal?"

"Why do you ask? I see in your eyes that you believe yourself to be the greatest prize in the world. You respect me for my wit; therefore you must know that I could not fail to recognize that prize."

"You are a bold man, Admiral."

"You are a bold Princess. Is that why we like each other, do you think?"

"Have a care, my bold Admiral."

"I will, my bold Princess. You must have a care. Even more than I perhaps, you must take care."

She stepped away from him. "I beg of you to cease this unmannerly conduct toward me."

He smiled ironically. "My lady Princess, you may be sure that I will follow your *wishes* in that respect, whatever they may be."

She walked away from him, back through the meadows to the Palace. Her cheeks were flushed and her spirits high.

She was pleased, for she was now rid of the tiresome problem of considering a marriage which would be far beneath her; and at the same time she need not dispense with the handsome gentleman's wooing.

Katharine Parr was angry with her brother-in-law and his wife.

Anne, Duchess of Somerset, had refused point-blank to carry her train. She had said insulting things about her sister-in-law, pointing out that it was unseemly for the wife of the Protector to pay homage to his younger brother's wife.

Lady Herbert called at Seymour Place to see the Queen; she was vaguely worried about the attitude of the haughty Duchess.

Katharine embraced her sister warmly. Anne Herbert studied Katharine and found it difficult to believe that this happy woman was the same one who had almost died of terror less than a year ago.

"There is no need to ask how you are," said Lady Herbert. "It is writ on your face."

"I am well, sister. And you? And my Lord Herbert?"

"Both well, Kate. It is wonderful to see you thus."

"Oh, Anne, I never thought to come to such happiness. It seems now that everything I suffered has been worth while, since I could never have appreciated this to the full had I not known great misery."

"You deserve all the happiness in the world. And my lord, your husband?"

"He is well and as happy as I am."

"May God preserve your happiness," said Anne Herbert; and she said it fervently, for she was not so inclined to believe in the fine qualities of Thomas Seymour as was Katharine. There were too many well-authenticated stories concerning his light behavior, his ambitions, and the schemes he had once laid to bring about a union with the Princess Elizabeth. She wondered whether she should warn her sister, but when she remembered that terrible melancholy which she had previously witnessed, she could not spoil, by one word of warning,

this unsullied happiness which her sister
was now enjoying.

"I think," said Lady Herbert, "you are so
happy that you do not care that there is all
this pother about the royal jewels."

"I do not care for the jewels," said
Katharine. "Marry, I am happier without
them than I ever was with them. But I am
angry that my sister-in-law should give herself such airs. I believe she would like to
wear the jewels herself."

"Indeed she would. She fancies herself a
Queen, I doubt not."

Katharine laughed. "Thomas cares not a
jot for my Lord Protector."

"He should, Kate. The Protector and his
wife are very powerful now. Dearest sister,
you have come through great dangers. For
the love of God, do not court more."

"I court danger! Never, Anne. I do not care
for these jewels. Do I need jewels to make
me happy? When I was the King's wife,
those precious gems were mine. But was I
happy then? Oh, Anne, you know the answer to that."

"Then, Kate, why is there so much noisy
talk about them?"

"Thomas thinks that his brother and his wife humiliate me by holding them back."

"Ah. . . . Thomas!"

Katharine smiled. "He is so angry when any fail, as he says, to respect me. He says I am too gentle . . . with others. He says it is a goodly thing that I have his strong arm to protect me, and his wits to work for me. He is always saying that he will put his fists to the ears of any that harm me."

"Lovers' talk!" said Anne Herbert.

"It is . . . and he means it. He looks so fierce when he says those words that I must coax him back to a merry mood."

"I do not think he would put his fists to the Lord Protector's ears."

"He would try to do it . . . if he thought the need arose. I know my Thomas."

"If he is reckless, Kate, it is for you to be cautious. Why, to marry him when you did . . . and to let him visit you at night! My dear, there were rumors about you two before the marriage was announced."

"I know." Katharine laughed indulgently. "Thomas cares for nothing. He said he lost me once and was not going to lose me again."

"Is it true that you were affianced to him within a week of the King's burial?"

"Oh, Anne, pray do not ask me such questions."

"That was very dangerous. It is said that if you had had a child, it might not have been known whether its father was Thomas or the King."

"You know I should not have allowed that to happen."

"Yet it is what people say."

Katharine shrugged her shoulders. She was too happy to consider any termination of her present state.

"Anne," she said, "how I long for a child! Do you think I am too old?"

"You are thirty-six, Kate."

"I know. But I long to bear Thomas's child."

"You would need to take great care of yourself."

"I should. I pray each night that I may have a child, and I have a feeling that my prayers will be answered."

Anne Herbert put her arms about her sister. She felt almost as fearful for her, now that she was the Admiral's wife, as she had when she had been the King's.

Then, thought Anne, she was prepared for disaster; now she is prepared only for bliss.

"God keep you well, Kate. God keep you happy."

"There are tears in your eyes, Anne."

"Are there, sister? It is because I am moved to see you so happy. Is it possible to suffer as you have and emerge from all that horror with your belief in men still intact? I do not know how you can be so sure, dearest sister. I do not know."

"Ah," cried Katharine embracing her, "but then you do not know my Thomas."

The Princess Mary had spent the months, since her father's death, in her country manors of Wanstead and Norfolk.

This was on the advice of her friends, for her name had been mentioned freely at the time of Surrey's execution. One of the charges against the Earl had been a proposed marriage between himself and the Princess, and some had said that Mary had been a party to what might well have been a conspiracy.

Mary had faced death at her father's hands and had miraculously escaped it; she had no wish to court it again. She was a Catholic and she would remain faithful to Rome till her death; the King and his Council were largely of the Reformed Party. Therefore no good could come of the Princess Mary's residence at court, it was decided by those who wished her well.

She knew that many had their eyes upon her and that, in the event of her brother's death, greatness would be hers; and she would welcome it, not for personal reasons, but for the sake of Rome. She spent long hours at her devotions and she guarded her health that she might not fail if the call came.

It was during the month of June that she received a letter from Thomas Seymour. His marriage with her father's widow seemed to Mary an act of the greatest impropriety and evil taste. She firmly upheld all the traditions of royalty. She had been fond of Katharine Parr, although her affections had declined since she had discovered Katharine's interest in the new learning; now her respect for Katharine had waned still further, for she simply did not understand how any lady could have allowed herself to be persuaded to such an action.

So that when she received Thomas Seymour's letter, she looked at it with suspicion and distaste.

He was asking her to give her blessing and sanction to his marriage with Katharine Parr.

A little late in the day! said Mary to herself. For I know full well that the marriage has already taken place, and that this happened in the month of May if not before.

She sat down and wrote a curt note to the Admiral. She thanked him for asking her sanction to his marriage; "But," she added, "I do not think the Queen can so quickly have forgotten the King as to be ready for a further marriage. As for myself, I am a maid and not cunning in the matters of wooing. You must forgive and respect my innocence."

She smiled as she wrote. If he could be sly, so could she. Did he think she was so cut off from the affairs of the court that she did not know he and the Queen were already married?

Then her thoughts turned to her young sister. What a terrible position for a child, to be living under the same roof with a man and woman who had so little care for the proprieties.

That should be set right.

So Mary wrote to Elizabeth, suggesting that she should come and stay with her, for she was sure that she must be most unhappy living in the house with a lady who had so recently been the wife of her father and was now the wife of another.

"See that the Lady Elizabeth receives this letter with all speed," she said to her messenger. "I think she will welcome it. We will prepare to receive her here at Wanstead."

But when Elizabeth read the letter she was a little perplexed. She did not wish to offend Mary by refusing the offer, yet how could she accept it? How could she shut herself away with pious Mary, spending her days in study and prayers and the working of embroidery, when life at Chelsea, or Seymour Place, or Sudley Castle offered so many delightful possibilities?

On no account could she bear to accept her sister's invitation, and yet on no account must her refusal offend. Mary might yet be Queen and, as heiress to the throne, Elizabeth's position would not be an easy one to hold.

I should accept, she told herself. I dare not take the slightest risk of offending Mary. Yet how can I go when every day there is a possibility of meeting Thomas?

Desire for excitement, on that occasion, triumphed over sober sense. She told herself—and perhaps this was the way in which her royal father would have reasoned—that it would be unwise to offend Thomas Seymour by suggesting she was willing to leave his roof. There was a possibility that he might be Lord Protector one day. A little accident to the elder uncle, and who would be more likely to step into his shoes than the beloved younger uncle?

No! said Elizabeth to her conscience. I must not run the risk of offending the Admiral.

She wrote a carefully worded letter to her sister, in which she said that she must submit with patience to what could not be cured. She deplored this marriage as much as did her greatly honored and well loved sister; yet she felt that to offer any objection—which her abrupt departure from her present home might appear to offer—would only make matters worse. They must not forget—her beloved sister and herself—how defenseless they were and always had been; they must remember against what a powerful party such behavior would set them. No, the only thing which they could do was to suppress their pain at the disrespect which had been shown to their royal father's memory; and, deeply as she regretted her inability to join her sister and share the felicity of her roof, she feared that her place was here with the Queen whom her royal father had appointed as her guardian.

She smiled as she sealed the letter. She was well pleased with life. She was beginning to understand herself. She was glad Seymour had married. Unmarried, he was a menace to her prospects of power; as a bachelor he put temptation in her way, while as a married man it was quite impossible for him to tempt her to the indiscretion of marriage.

There was still left to her the pleasures of flirtation, the dangerous interlude which never quite reached the climax which he desired, and which she believed would mean little to her. She wished to travel indefinitely along erotic byways, and the only way in which she could do this was by never reaching the end of the journey.

⇥⭜⭠

There were happy days at Sudley Castle—
that ancient and noble building which had
come to Seymour with his title.

The surrounding parklands were enchanting, and during the summer months the
bride and bridegroom dallied there. It was
to be a honeymoon, so the Princess Elizabeth had not accompanied them.

Seymour was glad that she was not with
them. It enabled him to give his full attention
to Katharine.

They explored the castle, the park and
the beautiful countryside of Gloucestershire
which surrounded it.

"Did you ever dream you would be so
happy in a marriage?" he asked his bride.

"Perhaps I dreamed," she answered, "but
I never knew till now that dreams came true.
Thomas, I was always afraid that you would
find the waiting too long . . . and marry
someone else."

"I would have waited ten years for you,
Kate. I would have waited the whole of my
life."

He believed it. He believed that the love
of the moment was the great love of his life.
He had forgotten Elizabeth. Katharine was

his love; he had waited years for her; he had been faithful to her; he had never thought of marriage with another; lands and possessions meant nothing to him. Thus thought Thomas Seymour during summer weeks at Sudley Castle.

They discussed their plans as they lay on the grass away from their servants and attendants—like a pair of country lovers, he said, simple people without a care in the world.

He talked to her of his plans. "We will get the jewels from my brother and his wife. We'll not allow them to treat us so."

"I would we could rest here for ever and never go back to court."

"Aye, that would be a great joy to me." But even as he said that, he could not help looking ahead to the time when he hoped to be in his elder brother's place. "That woman rules my brother," he went on. "She has persuaded him in this matter of the jewels."

"And I have said that I am happier now, without the jewels, than I ever was, wearing them."

"You are the dearest creature in the world, and I love you, Kate. You are right. What do we want with jewels . . . with rank . . . with ambition? What do we want but this?"

Then he kissed her and they lay on the grass, marveling that all this joy had come to them.

But he could not stop talking of his plans.

"The King will be thinking of marrying soon," he said. "I cannot contemplate a happier union for him than with the Lady Jane Grey."

"Indeed no. I had always meant her to have him. She is the dearest of girls— learned, kindly and of gentle birth. She will wear the crown with grace."

"And she loves us . . . even as doth the King. But my brother and his wife have a plan of marrying their daughter to the King."

"To little Jane Seymour! No, Thomas, that would not do. It must be Jane Grey for him."

"So think I!"

"But why should we meddle . . . ?"

"Dearest, there is our place at court to think of. The more power my brother builds for himself, the more he will rule us. He will be taking our houses and land ere long, to lay side by side with the royal jewelery."

"I do not want to concern myself with our places at court now. I am happy here. . . . I would like to stay here forever . . . forget everything but this."

He smiled, tenderly sighing with her; but he was not the man to throw aside ambition because he had achieved a happy marriage.

"When we talk of these children," she said, "I long for the children we may have."

"I also, sweetheart."

"And then I am afraid, Thomas. I have never had a child. I hope I may bear you one."

He bent over her and kissed her.

"Kate, I too wish for children—sons and daughters. But I would not have you thinking of them if thinking makes you sad."

She said: "I used to listen to the tolling of the bell. 'Sons. Sons,' it seemed to say to me, warning me, reminding me that if I did not give the King a son, it would toll for my death. I prayed for a child then—a royal Prince. Oh, Thomas, I used to think that if I did not have a son I should die as Anne Boleyn died."

"I know," he soothed her. "But that is over; that is done. That is why, much as I desire our child, I would not have you brooding on it. We have each other, Kate. If we have a child, that will be good. If we do not . . . we have each other."

She took his hand and kissed it; and as they walked home, the church bells sounded a merry peal.

It was September, a few days after Elizabeth's fourteenth birthday.

Lord and Lady Sudley had moved to Hanworth, and Elizabeth went with them. All through the summer days, after the newly married pair had returned from Sudley Castle, Elizabeth was becoming more and more aware of the Admiral's watching eyes.

She was a young lady now, she believed. Fourteen seemed grown-up, old enough for a girl to have a husband, if she were a Princess.

She fancied the Admiral thought so too. He had been very bold of late. It was a situation filled with danger; she was living in the household of a man and his wife, and was slightly in love with the man, and he . . . how much in love was he with her?

She did wish that the third person concerned was not her dear stepmother; and she wished too that the Queen was not so openly doting. Yet, thought Elizabeth, if it were not I who caught those stray glances of his, might it not be another? It would be disastrous if the wicked Admiral turned those bold glances of his on someone who did not know how to receive them in the right spirit!

She put on a gown of black velvet, and told Kat Ashley that she was going into the gardens to join the Admiral and her step-mother.

Kat Ashley protested at the dress. "My darling lady, it is too old for you. Black at your age!"

"I am grown up, Kat. Do you not realize that I am fourteen?"

"So you are, sweetheart, but you are but a girl in growth."

"Do you not think the black suits my hair?"

"It does," Kat admitted.

"Then it is time I began to look my age."

Kat put her arms about her and kissed her. "Oh, my lady, I don't want you to be grown up."

"Why not?"

"Because I am afraid. I am afraid of when you grow up."

"Dearest Kat, why should you be afraid?"

"Afraid for you, sweet. Now they say: 'Oh, she is just a child . . .' And they think of you as a child . . . of no importance."

"But I am of importance, Mistress Ashley. I do not wish to be thought of no importance."

"It is safer so . . . until . . ."

"Until, Kat?"

"You know what I mean."

"Kneel and kiss my hand, then."

She took the bracelet from her arm and put the circlet on her head.

"My lady! My lady!" cried Kat in dismay.

"There are just the two of us, so what matters it? And, Kat, you are not to gossip of it."

"No, my lady."

Elizabeth took Kat's ear and pinched it hard. "You gossip too much with Master Parry."

"Oh, my ear! It hurts. Stop, you wild cat. Stop . . . Your . . . Your Majesty!"

They began to laugh, and the bracelet fell to the floor.

"A bad sign!" said Elizabeth, growing pale.

"Nonsense!" cried Kat, sprawling on the floor to recover the bracelet. "Here, let me put it on your wrist . . . where it belongs. Bless you, my love. God preserve you."

"Kat, you foolish woman! You're crying."

"I love you, darling, and that's the truth. So much that I am sometimes afraid."

"I know what you're afraid of. You think of her of whom we never speak. Kat . . . I want to talk of her now . . . and then, afterward . . . never again. Am I like her?"

"No."

"She was beautiful, was she not?"

"She had more than beauty."

"That did not save her. All that charm and all that beauty . . . it did not save her from the sword."

"She was wild and full of levity," said Kat, "and many men loved her. The King was among them. They say he never loved any as he loved her. But that did not save her."

"She was raised to be a Queen . . . raised quickly, and quickly put down. But I would be Queen in my own right. *I* am a King's daughter. Remember that."

"I remember it, my lady."

"And if I will wear a black velvet dress, then I will wear a black velvet dress."

"Yes, my lady, but that does not mean I shall say I like it."

"Why do you not like it, Kat?" Her tone was wheedling.

"It makes you look too old."

"Too old for what?"

Kat Ashley shook a finger at the Princess. "Take care, my lady. You know what I mean. When I see the glances he gives you, I tremble."

"Oh, Kat . . . so do I! But have no fear. I am not so charming as she was . . . and although I have some levity, it is not as great as hers. Many men will love me, Kat, but none shall ever betray me."

And with that she went sedately out of the room and down into the gardens.

There she found the Admiral and her stepmother walking under the trees.

The Admiral bowed ironically as he watched her approach. Katharine smiled, giving no sign that Elizabeth, as far as she was concerned, made an unwelcome third.

How can she remain in ignorance of those glances? wondered Elizabeth. She looked haughtily at the man, to show him that she did not approve of such looks . . . when his wife was present.

"Why," said Thomas, with mock dignity, "it is the Lady Elizabeth. And how think you she looks this day, Kate?"

"Very well and very charming," said Katharine.

"I think not," said Thomas. "I like not her gown."

Elizabeth answered pertly: "Indeed, and do you not? I did not know it was the duty of a stepfather to approve his daughter's gowns."

Thomas raised his eyebrows. "The responsibility of a father toward his daughter through marriage is great; and the more so when she is a Princess, and a Princess who dares parade her charms in a black velvet gown."

"I care not that you do not like my gown," said Elizabeth, turning away. "My mother does, and that is enough for me."

But as she turned, Thomas had caught her. He seized her by the shoulders and pulled her roughly round to face him.

"How dare you?" cried Elizabeth, flushing hotly. "How dare you treat me thus!"

Katharine's innocent laughter rang out.

"He teases you, my dear. Thomas, you

should not tease her so. It is too much teasing, now that she grows up."

"But, my love, she needs to be teased out of her haughtiness. What do you think of this black gown, Kate? 'Twere as though she mourns someone. Does she mourn someone? Do you know, Kate?"

"Nay, she wears black because it becomes her. And it does, Thomas. You must admit it does."

"I admit nothing. She mourns someone. Some secret lover, is it? Why, the girl blushes."

"I do not! I do not!" cried Elizabeth.

"Let her go, dearest," said Katharine. "I believe she is really angry."

"Then she must learn that she must not be angry with her stepfather, who is a very loving stepfather. The wicked child hides secrets from us. Who is this lover whom you mourn? Come, Princess. Confess."

Elizabeth twisted from his grasp, but, as she did so, her gown was torn, exposing her shoulders. She knew that he had deliberately torn it.

"She hath a tolerably white skin," said Thomas. "Hath she not? Methinks it is a pity to hide such sweetness under this ugly black cloth."

"You have torn it," cried Elizabeth, "and you will have to pay the cost of a new one."

"You see how avaricious she is!" He caught her skirt as she would have run away.

Katharine began to laugh. "Oh, Thomas, you must not be so childish. You play such games. Are you really a man or just a boy?"

"Do not heed him," said Elizabeth. "He must amuse himself. It is naught to me that he doth not like my gown. It is naught to me that he hath torn it, since he must provide me with a new one."

"Undutiful!" cried Thomas, lifting her skirts. "Oh, most undutiful!"

They were both tugging at her skirt, and the stitches gave way.

"Would you then tear the clothes from my back?" she demanded. "Here . . . in the gardens?"

"I would," he said.

Her eyes were shining; her mouth was laughing. She could not help it if she loved to play thus with him. It was so safe, with Katharine standing by; it was safe and yet so dangerous. This was the part of courtship which was most enjoyable.

Katharine was quick to see her amusement. Is she completely blind? wondered Elizabeth. Did she not know this man she had married?

He had turned to her now. "Kate," he said, "help me . . . help me tame this wild cat. We'll teach her to parade our gardens in black cloth."

"Thomas . . . Thomas . . . have a care," laughed Katharine.

"Whose side are you on?" demanded Elizabeth. "His or mine?"

"On mine, of course!" cried Thomas. "Hold her, Kate. Hold her, I say. Take her arms and stop her fighting, and I will show you what we will do with her."

Katharine obediently ran behind Elizabeth and put her arms about her.

"No," said Elizabeth.

And "Yes," said the Admiral.

He had taken the jeweled dagger from his belt and, his eyes gleaming with desire for her, he slashed at her skirt with the dagger; he put his hand in the neck of her bodice and ripped it down the front, so that she stood there in her silken petticoats, flushed and laughing, and loving him, exulting in the feelings she could arouse in him.

"Thomas!" cried the Queen. "What have you done?"

He had his hand on Elizabeth's bare shoulder.

"I have taught our daughter a lesson, I hope."

"She should not stand here thus. It is most improper."

"Aye!" he said. "Most improper. But she must not come parading herself in her black gown, looking like a grown-up Princess. She must not blush when we question her as to her secret lover."

"Elizabeth, run in quickly," laughed the Queen. "I pray none sees you."

Elizabeth wrenched herself free. She heard their laughter behind her.

The Admiral put his arm about his wife.

"Dearest," said Katharine, "how I long for a child! And if I am an even more fortunate woman than I count myself already, how that child will love you! Why is it that you, who are so bold, so much a master of men, a great sailor and statesman, know so well how to amuse children?"

"And is the Princess such a child?"

"Indeed yes. Did you not see how she enjoyed your game?"

"She did, did she not," said the Admiral somberly; and he tried to forget the passion Elizabeth aroused in him, in his tenderness for Katharine.

Kat Ashley asked if she might have a word in private with the Admiral.

"My lord," she said, when they were alone, "I trust you will forgive my impertinence, if impertinence it is."

"I would hear it first," said Thomas.

"The Lady Elizabeth came in from the gardens this day—her dress cut away from her, her skin bruised by rough handling."

"And you, Mistress Ashley, witnessed our play from one of the windows?"

"You know that?"

"I know Mistress Ashley," he said wryly.

"It is my duty to look after my young lady."

"That is so."

"My lord, I beg of you to forgive me, but if any but myself had seen what happened in the gardens this day . . ."

"Well, Mistress Ashley, what then?"

"They . . . they might think it unseemly for

a Princess so to behave and . . . and for a gentleman such as yourself. . . ."

"Bah, Mistress Ashley, there was nothing in it. It was but play."

"That I know, my lord, but others have thought differently."

"Rest happy, Mistress Ashley; there is no harm done."

"I trust not, my lord."

"Your Princess is well able to look after herself, were that necessary. The Queen joined in the play, remember."

"I know, my lord. But a dress . . . to be cut off a young lady in such a manner!"

"Never fear. She insists that I pay for another dress. You see, your Princess knows well how to guard her interests."

The strange thing was, mused Kat Ashley afterward, that when you were with him, you believed all he said. He became the benign stepfather, anxious to make a happy home.

But what should be done? wondered Kat.

He must be right. All was well, because it was true that the Queen, his wife, was present.

->-<-

The Marquis of Dorset called at Seymour Place in response to an invitation from the Lord High Admiral.

Dorset was the father of Lady Jane Grey, and he guessed that he had been invited to discuss her future, for he had been warned of this by Sir John Harrington, a friend and servant of the Admiral.

Dorset was warmly received, and Thomas made a point of dismissing all servants before he began to speak.

"My Lord Dorset," he said, "you have some inkling of why I have asked you to call?"

"I understand it concerns my elder daughter."

"The Lady Jane is a charming girl—accomplished, beautiful, and of your noble House. We agree on that matter, and I doubt not that we could agree on others."

Dorset was not displeased. He was himself a member of a great house, but none but a fool like Surrey would refuse a chance of linking himself with one of the Seymour brothers. It was said that young Thomas was biding his time. He was the King's favorite, and the King would not be a minor for ever. He had already married the Dowager Queen. The Princess Elizabeth was being brought up in his household. Obviously Thomas Seymour, Lord Sudley, was already a power in the land, and was going to be of even greater importance.

Dorset was flattered.

"How so, my Lord Sudley?" he asked.

"The affairs of this country need to be closely watched, Dorset; and it is for such as you and myself to do the watching. It is ever so, when a boy King is on the throne. They are already disputing one with another in the Council."

Dorset was becoming excited.

"I should like you to know," went on Thomas, "that I am your friend. And as a token of friendship I should like the wardship of your daughter."

"Why so?"

"The Queen loves her, as you know. We have often spoken of her future, and we should like to have her under our care so that she might be brought up in a royal manner, and that we might have the means of matching her."

Dorset's eyes glistened with excitement. "You have a match in mind, Sudley?"

"I have, sir."

"And the future husband of my daughter would be . . . ?"

"Cannot you guess? They love each other already. I doubt not they have made up their young minds to it."

"You mean . . . the *King*?"

"I do, my lord."

Dorset smiled.

"She is worthy of the match," went on Thomas. "I know of none more worthy."

"I have heard that the Lord Protector would match his own daughter with the King."

"His ambition . . . and his wife's, drive him hard. My lord Dorset, you might wonder that I work against my brother. But I would work first for what I believe to be right for this realm. The King has said to me—for as you know, he is my friend and I am his best-loved uncle—he has said to me that he will not have Jane Seymour, and that it is Jane Grey whom he loves."

"You could further this match?"

"If I had the wardship of the Lady Jane, if the Queen could direct her studies. . . . Marry, I doubt not that you will one day see her wearing the crown."

"My Lord Sudley, I could not refuse an offer which would bring so much good to my daughter."

The bargain was struck, and Dorset's hopes ran high. Thomas Seymour, Lord Sudley, was his friend, and he was pleased with himself. So was Thomas who saw there would be little difficulty in bringing about this match. He was determined that he was not going to let his brother usurp the power he had with the King, by marrying him to young Jane Seymour.

Nay! The King should remain the pet of his dearest Uncle Thomas; he should continue to adore his stepmother; and the King's bride should be a girl who was guided by Lord and Lady Sudley, and one who would love them and help them to keep in power.

So Lady Jane Grey came to live under the roof of the Admiral and the Dowager Queen.

That year passed quickly for Katharine. It seemed to her that her happiness had made wings which it set to the days.

Summer, autumn—and then the winter was upon them.

She went occasionally to court and spent hours in the company of the King. He had changed a little since his accession; he was growing firmer, and the Tudor in him was becoming apparent; there were occasions when he reminded Katharine of his father.

The little boy, whose mother had died when he was born, and who had known only stepmothers, and most of them briefly, had looked to the last of these for affection, and Katharine would always be his beloved mother. He had not looked in vain to her, and if he adored Uncle Thomas and was stimulated by his sister Elizabeth and loved little Jane Grey, he idolized his stepmother.

He wrote lovingly to her when they were apart and, if he was particularly pleased with some Latin verses he had written, it was his stepmother's opinion for which he was most eager.

Katharine knew that the Duchess of Somerset was her greatest enemy, but she was too happy to worry very much about her enemies.

And when Christmas was past and Katharine was sure that that for which she had scarcely dared hope was to come to pass, she believed herself to be the happiest of women.

Thomas was delighted.

"It will be a boy," he said.

Her face clouded, for those words brought back such terrible memories.

But Thomas understood, and he was all tenderness at once.

"But if it should be a girl," he assured her, "then we shall doubtless discover that a daughter of my Lord and Lady Sudley is worth the son of any other pair."

"Thomas, you are the dearest person in the whole world."

He laughed his great booming laughter. "By God's precious soul, I believe I must be, for you are a wise woman, Kate, and you say it."

She took his hand and kissed it fervently. "I can never thank you enough for all you have given me. You snatched me from the dark pit of despair, of horror, and you set me here in the sunshine."

"Speak not of those terrible days. The past is done with, Kate. Think of the future."

She said: "I shall tell Elizabeth first. She will expect to be told. Why, she is like a daughter to us."

He was silent then; he went to the window and stood there, looking out over the gardens of Seymour Place.

Katharine went to his side and slipped her arm through his. "Of what are you thinking?" she asked.

He was silent for a while, then he turned to her and swept her into his arms. "I love thee, Kate. I love thee . . . thee only," he said.

The Duchess of Somerset found at this time that she also was going to have a child. She was delighted.

"I should be delivered a few weeks before your brother's wife," she told her husband. "It is strange, is it not, that we should both be in this condition at this time. I would not care to be in her place. This will be her first child . . . and she is not young."

"It may well be dangerous at her age to have a first child," said the Protector.

"Mayhap your brother has thought of that," said the Duchess slyly.

Somerset looked askance at his wife. She was always bitter against Thomas, but since her pregnancy her venom seemed to have increased; she delighted in making the wildest accusations against Thomas and his wife.

"Why do you say that?" he asked.

"If she died in childbirth, he would be left free for higher game."

"You mean . . . the Princess Elizabeth? The Council would never allow him to marry her."

"I was not aware that he asked the Council's consent to his marriage with the Queen."

"The Queen was not as important to the Council as the Princess would be."

"It was disgraceful. Why, had she got with child a little earlier, some might have thought it was the King's."

"But she did not, Anne; and no one can suspect this child of being fathered by any but Thomas."

"He plans to destroy you, Edward. You see how he plots with Dorset. He will do everything to thwart your plan of marrying our Jane to the King."

"Yes, that he has already done, and the King grows obstinate. He grows up; he declares he will not have our daughter."

"So Thomas plans to bring forth Dorset's girl, and meanwhile he and the Queen are bringing her up in the way they wish her to go! Very clever! They will have both the young Queen and the King doing all they ask of them. Edward will obey his dearest Uncle Thomas . . . as will Jane Grey. We shall see that the most important people in this realm will be my Lord High Admiral and his Dowager Queen."

"I believe he has done this deliberately to frustrate us."

"Of course he has."

"It is a sad thing when brothers cannot work together."

"But you are the elder, Edward; and he, because he has a way of charming women and children, believes he should have your place. He thinks that the manners of Master Admiral are of greater importance to this realm than the cleverness of you, my darling."

"Dearest Anne, calm yourself. It is bad for you to become excited."

"I am not excited, my love. I only know that I shall not stand by and see Lord Thomas play his tricks on us. The King shall have our Jane, and Jane Grey is to marry our boy. As for Master Thomas, if he becomes too dangerous . . ."

"Yes?" said the Protector.

"I doubt not that you, my lord, will find

some way of making him . . . less dangerous."

Her eyes were wild, and her husband was
at great pains to soothe her. Such excitement he knew to be bad for her condition.

But while he soothed her, he told himself
that there was a good deal in what she was
saying. Thomas *was* working against his
brother, and that was something which no
wise man, if he were Protector of the realm,
could allow.

Early morning sunshine coming through the
window of Elizabeth's bedchamber in
Chelsea Palace, shone on the Princess who
lay in her bed.

She was startled. She had been awak-
ened from her sleep by the sound of the
opening of her door. She would have leaped
out of bed and run to her women in the adjoining chamber, but she saw that she was
too late. She heard the low laughter and,
pulling the bedclothes up to her chin, she
waited with an apprehension which was
tinged with delight.

The bed curtains parted and there, as
Elizabeth had known there would be, was
Thomas Seymour, clad only in nightgown

and slippers. He was smiling down challengingly at Elizabeth.

"How . . . how dare you, my lord!" she demanded. "How dare you come thus into my bedchamber!"

He drew the curtains farther apart and continued to smile at her.

"Come, Elizabeth, you know you expect me to pay this morning call. An I did not, you would be most offended."

"It is customary, my lord, to put on conventional garb before calling on a lady."

"What are conventions . . . between friends?" His eyes looked saucily into hers.

She said haughtily: "Pray go, my lord. My women will hear you. Yester-morning they were shocked because I had to run to them for protection against you."

"And this morning," he said, "I was determined to catch you before you could. And, my lady, am I right in believing that you were determined to be caught?"

"I will not endure your insolence."

"What cannot be prevented must be endured." He came closer to the bed. "May I not look in to bid my stepdaughter good morning?"

"Nay, you may not!" But she knew the

sternness of her words did not tally with the merriment in her voice.

"Your eyes invite, Elizabeth," he said; and his tone was no longer one he might use to tease a child.

"My lord . . ."

"My lady . . ."

He was kneeling by the bed, and Elizabeth laughed uneasily. He caught her suddenly and kissed her heartily on the check and sought her mouth. Elizabeth made a pretense of struggling, and this only served to encourage him.

The door opened suddenly and her stepmother came in.

"Thomas!" ejaculated Katharine.

Elizabeth dared not look at her; she knew that her face was hot with shame; she felt guilty and wicked.

Imperturbably Thomas said: "What a wild-cat is this daughter of yours, my love! Refuses to be kissed good morning by her old father. I declare she was ready to leave the mark of her nails on my face."

Katharine laughed—the easy, pleasant laugh which Elizabeth knew so well.

"Elizabeth, my dear, my lord but meant to give you good morning."

Elizabeth raised her eyes to her step-mother's face, and she decided to be wise.

"That I know well," she answered, "but I would be accorded more respect. It is not the first time he has come in, clad thus . . . in nightgown and slippers and drawn the curtains of my bed to laugh at me."

"It is wrong of you both," said Katharine, smiling lovingly from one to the other. "Tom, you behave like a boy of sixteen."

"But hark to the child, my love. She talks of her dignity. What dignity hath a chit of thirteen years?"

"I would have you know, my lord, that I am nigh on fifteen years old."

He bowed over her, his eyes sparkling mischievously. "I beg your pardon, Madam. You are, of course, of a great age and . . ."

"Tom, pray do not tease her so," pleaded Katharine.

"God's precious soul, but I *will* tease her!" He seized the bedclothes and pulled at them, while Elizabeth screamed and clung to them.

"Help me, Kate! Help me!" cried Thomas. "We'll show this chit that she is but our daughter. We will teach her to give herself airs."

Thomas pulled and Katharine helped him. In a few minutes the bed was stripped bare, and Elizabeth lay uncovered except for her nightdress. All three were romping in childish fashion; Katharine artlessly, the other two with a secret purpose behind their looks and actions.

"She is very ticklish, I vow," said Thomas, and they tried to tickle her. Elizabeth wriggled. Thomas held her firmly and bade Katharine tickle her until she should beg forgiveness for her haughtiness.

Kat Ashley came in to see what the noise was about, and so the game was broken up.

"It is time you were up, Elizabeth," said Katharine with mock severity; and she and Thomas went out, laughing together.

As for Elizabeth, she lay back in bed, smiling at Kat Ashley, who was preparing to scold her for her unseemly behavior.

"My Lord Admiral," said Kat Ashley, "may I speak to you?"

"What, again?" said the Admiral.

"My lord, I must tell you that there is gossip about the Lady Elizabeth and . . ."

"And whom?"

"And yourself."

"This grows interesting. What tittle-tattle have you heard?"

"That you and the Princess are more fond of each other than is seemly."

"Have you then, indeed! And how many bastards are we two said to have brought into the world? Tell me that."

Kat Ashley flushed. "My lord, there is talk that the Princess has given birth to a child."

"Who told these lies? They shall lose their heads for this."

"It is not known. I had it from a gossip who had it from another gossip who had heard it in the streets."

The Admiral laughed.

"There will always be such talk, Kat. I'll warrant our little King has fathered many a bastard, if you can believe what you hear in the streets."

"My lord, it is not good that the Lady Elizabeth should be evilly spoken of."

"Next time then, catch the slanderers and bring them to me."

"And you, my lord . . . dare I ask that you will be a little more . . . restrained . . . in your manner to the Princess?"

"I? Indeed I will not. By God's precious

soul, I will tell my brother, the Protector, how I have been slandered. I will not curb my fun. No, I will not; for, Mistress Ashley, I mean no evil; nor does the Princess."

And he strode away, leaving poor Kat Ashley disconsolate and wondering whither this romping would lead, and dreading that the Dowager Queen might eventually understand its real meaning. Then, she was sure, much trouble would await her reckless little Princess.

The rumors came to the ears of the Duchess of Somerset.

She was great with the child she was expecting in August. June was hot and it was difficult to move about, so she contented herself with making plans for the future of her family.

She was growing more afraid of her husband's brother. How she hated him, he who had charmed the King and advanced himself by marrying the Queen.

She sent for one of her serving women to come and sit beside her; she had trained this woman to keep her eyes open when in contact with the servants of her brother-in-law's household. She was wondering whether, if it were proved that immorality was going on in that household, it would be possible to remove little Jane Grey from the care of the Sudleys and have her brought up by the Somersets.

What she had heard so far was promising.

"What heard you this morning, Joan?" she asked her woman.

"My lady, they say that the Princess and the Admiral are acting shamefully . . . more so than usual. He goes to her bedroom, and sometimes she runs to her women, pretending she is afraid of him, and . . . sometimes she does not."

"It disgusts me," said the Duchess with delight.

"Yestermorn he tore off her bedclothes and she lay there without them, my lady."

"I can scarcely believe it."

"The Queen was there. It was a game between the three of them."

When the woman had left her, the Duchess thought a great deal about the rompings which went on in the Admiral's household. Was he wishing that he had not married Katharine Parr? It was clear that he had hopes of the Princess. Suppose

Katharine were to die, which she might well
do, bearing a child at her age, and suppose
the Admiral wished to marry the Princess.
Suppose he asked the King's consent. The
King would refuse his beloved uncle nothing
that he asked.

Her husband, the Duke, was too occupied with his parliaments and his matters of
state, thought the worried Duchess, to realize what was happening. But matters of
state were often decided in bedchambers. It
had been so with the last King. There was
no doubt that the Admiral would try for the
Princess . . . if Katharine Parr were to die.

She would give Joan further instructions.
The woman must become even more
friendly with the servants in the Admiral's
household. Nothing that happened there
must fail to reach the ears of the Duchess of
Somerset.

Both Elizabeth and Thomas felt that this
strange, exciting and most piquant situation
could not continue as it was. It must change
in some way.

Katharine, who was now heavy with her
child, moved about ponderously and some
days kept to her bed. The glances between

the Princess and the Admiral had become
smoldering; each was waiting for the moment when change would come.

It happened on a hot summer's day when
they found themselves alone in one of the
smaller rooms of Chelsea Palace.

As Thomas stood watching her, a deep
seriousness had replaced his banter. They
were no longer merely stepfather and
daughter; they were man and woman, and
neither of them could pretend it was otherwise.

Elizabeth was a little frightened. She had
never sought a climax. She wished to go on
being pursued; she wanted to remain
provocative but uncaught.

She said uneasily, as she saw him shut
the door and come toward her: "There are
rumors about us two."

"Rumors," he said lightly. "What rumors?"

"They are whispering about us . . . here . . .
at court . . . in the streets. They are saying
that you and I are as we should not be . . .
and that you come to my bedchamber."

"What! By morning and in the presence of
the Queen!"

"You must desist . . . or it will be necessary for me to leave your household."

He caught her and held her fast. "I will not desist. I mean no evil."

"If you will not desist, I must leave here."

"You shall not go."

"My lord . . ." she began weakly.

But he interrupted passionately: "Elizabeth, why did you say me nay?"

She was alarmed, and she sought to hold him off. "You loved me not," she said shrilly. "If you did, why did you go straightway to the Queen on my refusal? Did you not turn over in your mind whether or not you could hope even for little Jane Grey? Did you ask my cofferer the extent of my possessions?"

"You know I love you," was his only answer, "and you only."

"I thought I was to you but a wayward child."

"You lie, Elizabeth. You know full well what you are to me."

"And all the rompings and teasings?"

"Were just that I might be near you . . . touch you . . . put my lips close to yours."

She felt weak—no longer Elizabeth the Princess with her eyes on the throne, but Elizabeth in love.

She put her arms about his neck, and they kissed fervently, passionately.

Katharine had quietly opened the door and found them thus. She stood, incredulously listening to the words of love.

Suddenly they were aware of her.

Katharine, awkward in her pregnancy, her hands hanging at her sides, her eyes bewildered, stood there trying to understand this sudden disintegration of her happy existence.

Thomas was abashed; but already he was planning what he would say to her.

As for Elizabeth, even in that moment of fear and humiliation, she knew that this discovery had saved her from herself and the Admiral.

The Queen paced her apartments. She seemed almost demented. She wept, and there was nothing Thomas could say to soothe her.

She despised herself, marveled at her folly; she, who had known the agony of life with a callous murderer, had allowed herself to be deceived by a lighthearted philanderer.

"Sweetheart," declared Thomas, exerting all his charm, all that plausibility which had never yet failed him, " 'twas nothing. 'Twas but a moment of madness."

But she would not listen. She looked at him sadly and remembered so many occasions when the truth had been there for her to see. She had held the Princess while he had cut her dress; she had helped him pull off the bedclothes; she had laughed, simply, foolishly . . . like a child, while those two had deceived her. And that was what they did when she was present; she had now discovered something of what they did when she was not with them.

It was too much to be borne.

Once, when she had lived near to death, she had passionately longed for life; now that she had tasted the perfect life—which had been quite false—she longed for death.

Her feelings for her husband were in a turmoil. Poignant love and bitter hatred alternated.

She did not hear his words, those glib explanations which rose to his lips so easily. She knew that some of the rumors at least were true; he had wished to marry Elizabeth and, failing the Princess, the Queen had suited his ambitions.

She begged him to leave her, and he, seeming eager to please her in all things, obeyed her wishes.

Calmness was what she needed, indifference. She must think of the child she would have; yet even such thoughts were tinged with bitterness, for so often had she pictured them all together—herself, her husband and the child. That false man, that philanderer, had always dominated any pictures she had made of the future.

When she had married the lords Borough and Latimer, she had not expected an ecstatic life; but those lords had not deceived her. When she had married the King, she had known that her life would be filled with dangers; and she had not been deceived in that. But now, that marriage which was to have brought glorious fulfillment to her life, which was to have made everything that had gone before worth while since it was to have led to perfection, was proved to be utterly false, a fabrication, a fantasy which did not exist outside her own imagination.

She must be calm. She would be calm.

Katharine sent for the Princess.

Elizabeth came, shamefaced, expecting abuse. But the Queen smiled at her, not coldly, but, as it seemed, with indifference.

I cannot blame a child, Katharine was

thinking. He is more than twenty years older than she is, and the fault lies with him.

She looked at the girl—this girl who stood near the throne—and she marveled at the folly of her husband. If he had seduced the Princess and there had been tangible consequences of that seduction, he would almost certainly have lost his head. He had known that, and yet he had not hesitated to run risks. Was the attraction so strong? Was the temptation irresistible?

Katharine said: "In view of what has happened, I have no alternative but to send you away."

"Yes," said Elizabeth.

"I would prefer you to leave as soon as possible."

Elizabeth bowed her head.

"How soon can you be ready to go?"

"In a few days' time."

"Then let it be done. I shall not expect to see you or any of your household by the end of the week."

"It shall be done," said Elizabeth.

"That is all. You may leave me now." Katharine turned her head to look out of the window.

Elizabeth bowed and went toward the door, but there she paused.

"Your Grace," she murmured. "Mother . . ."

There was an appealing note in her voice that once would have affected Katharine deeply.

Now she deliberated: Is she wondering what effect all this has had, and will have, since the King loves me as his mother? Perhaps she is going to ask me to say nothing of this to His Majesty. She need not trouble, for I doubt not that the King has heard what the whole court has heard, and that even the people in the streets are laughing at the simplicity of Katharine Parr.

She continued to stare out of the window until she heard the door quietly shut, and knew that Elizabeth had gone.

Little Jane Grey came to her as she stood there, and Katharine was glad that she had this girl with her. She put her hand on the curly head, and suddenly the tears began to fall down her cheeks.

Jane looked at her with great pity.

"Your Majesty . . ." she began, and she too started to cry.

The child's tears sobered Katharine.

"Jane, Jane, what is this? Why do you weep?"

"I weep to see Your Majesty so sad."

"Then I must stem my tears, for I cannot bear to see yours. It is folly to cry, Jane. What good did tears ever do? We should be brave and strong, ready to face anything that is coming to us. Come, dry your eyes. I command it."

And she held the girl against her while Jane began to cry wildly.

"Jane dearest," said Katharine, "we are going to Sudley Castle. We shall stay there until my child is born. I have a desire to be a long way from the court . . . to live very quietly for a while. You shall be my constant companion . . . always with me, my little comforter. How will you like that, Jane?"

Jane put her arms about Katharine's neck, and kissing the tear-stained cheeks Katharine found some small comfort.

On a hot August day the Duchess of Somerset gave birth to a beautiful baby boy.

She was delighted. It seemed to her significant that she and the woman whom she hated more than any other should be having a child in almost the same month, for Katharine Parr's child was due very soon.

She embraced her boy while she visualized a great future for him; but she would feel more sure of the greatness of that future if her husband did not possess such an ambitious brother.

Joan had brought her interesting news: Katharine and her household had left for Sudley Castle, where she intended to stay until after the birth of her child. The move in itself was not so strange. To what more beautiful spot than that castle could a woman retire to await the birth of her child? The strangeness was not in the going, but in the manner of going.

"My lady," Joan had said, "there has been great trouble in the Queen's household. It concerns the Admiral and the Princess Elizabeth."

"That surprises me not," said the Duchess. "The wonder is that the stupid woman did not discover, long ere this, what the rest of her household seemed to know so well. Did you hear how she took the discovery?"

"Most bitterly, my lady. Her servants said that she became hysterical, as she did be-

fore . . . when the King was her husband
and so many thought he would have her put
away from him."

The Duchess smiled and suckled her
baby.

Later she talked to her husband.

"I shall never be happy while your brother
lives," she declared.

"Would you wish his *death* then?"

"As I would the death of all who stood to
harm you, my lord."

"And the Queen?" he asked.

"The Queen is a foolish woman. I fear her
influence, but not herself. They say she is a
bitter woman who cares not whether she
lives or dies. Oh, my lord, a woman in her
state and of her age . . . who has never before had a child . . ."

"Yes, my love?"

The Duchess shrugged her shoulders. "I
do not know. But it would not greatly surprise me if she did not survive the ordeal
before her."

"That is what you hope."

"I like her not. But it is your brother whom
I fear."

"My dear wife," said the Duke, "even if we

proved a case against him, the King would put up a fight for his beloved uncle."

"The King! He is but a feeble boy."

"Feeble in body, but not so in mind. He puts on dignity with each day. If he is but a boy, he is a Tudor; and you know well the strength of his father."

She was silent for a while, then she said: "If the Queen were to die, and it could be shown that the Admiral had helped to bring about her death, the King might not feel so kindly toward his favorite uncle."

"Thomas bring about her death! Nay! He is a philanderer, but he would not murder his wife."

"She is sad, I hear. She cares not whether she lives or dies. This is due to her husband's treatment of her."

The Protector bent over his wife to look at his newborn son.

He smiled at the Duchess, and their eyes were alight with a kindred ambition.

In her lying-in chamber at the Castle of Sudley, Katharine lay, her body torn in agony. But no bodily agony could compare with the distress of her mind.

All through those pain-dazed hours she

was aware of the cloud about her; she was aware that the happy life, the thought of which had sustained her through all her miseries, was nothing more than a myth and an illusion.

Thomas, waiting for the birth of his child, paced back and forth from room to room.

"No news yet? No news?" he demanded. "By God's precious soul, how long . . . how long?"

Some of those who loved the Queen longed to tell her of his distress, but they knew that she would have no faith in it. She no longer believed in him; all his protestations had failed to move her. He had lied to her; he had deceived her; and she would never trust him again.

It was on the last day of August, when the heat was stifling, that Katharine's daughter was born.

"A girl!" The words spread through the Castle.

It was a disappointment; everyone had confidently hoped for a boy. The astrologers had prophesied that there would be a son for the Admiral. He had believed that prophecy; he had gone about boasting of the son he would have, a finer, stronger, more handsome boy than the one just born to his brother's wife.

And now . . . a girl!

But Thomas would not show his disappointment. Full of remorse for the hurts he had inflicted on Katharine, he longed to assure her of his love and devotion.

Elizabeth was far away at Hatfield now, and he would think only of Katharine, his beloved wife. He would make her understand that it was possible for a man such as himself to be fond of more than one woman at a time. And what, he asked himself, was his lighthearted desire for Elizabeth compared with the deep-rooted tenderness he felt for his wife?

He went to her chamber; he kissed her tenderly, and most solicitously he inquired regarding her health. He took the child in his arms and paced the apartment with her.

"Why, bless us, Kate, I'd rather this girl than all the boys in Christendom."

But the magic failed to work now; the charm was useless. It was like a pretty tinkling toy, and she had grown out of her desire for such.

She watched him with solemn, brooding eyes.

He knelt by the bed: "Get well, Kate. Get well, sweetheart. There is no joy for me in this life if thou sharest it not with me."

And she watched him coldly, with disbelieving eyes.

A strangeness had come to her since the birth of her child. There was a fever upon her, and she who had so passionately longed for the child, seemed now to have forgotten its existence.

She lay listless, staring about her with eyes that seemed to see nothing, to have no interest in anyone or anything.

In vain her women tried to rouse her from this terrible lethargy.

"Your Majesty, look at the beautiful little girl. See, she has your eyes. That much is obvious already."

But she did not answer. She lay there, staring before her as though it were another woman's child they held out to her. Little Jane Grey came to her bedside, but she did not seem to know Jane.

"What ails her?" asked the little girl.

"By my faith," said one of the women, "I fear she will die of her melancholy."

The doctors came, but they could not

rouse her. They could do nothing to disperse her fever.

A few days after the birth of the child, Thomas came into the bedchamber, his brow wrinkled, all jauntiness gone.

"Sweetheart," he said, "how fares it with thee now?"

She did not answer him.

"Kate . . . my dearest Kate, it is Thomas. Look at me, my love. Smile at me. Tell me you love me."

She turned her head from him.

She spoke suddenly, but not to Thomas. "Lady Tyrwhit," she cried out, "is that you?"

Lady Tyrwhit, who had been in attendance since the birth of the child, came to the bedside. She knelt and took the Queen's burning hand in hers.

"Lady Tyrwhit, I fear such things within me that I do not think I shall leave this bed."

Thomas knelt and took her other hand. She turned her head to look at him, but she did not seem to recognize him.

"Lady Tyrwhit," she continued, "I am not well-handled. Those about me care not for me. Oh, I am most unhappy, Lady Tyrwhit, because those I have loved, love me not.

They mock me. They laugh at my love. May-hap they laugh now at my grief. They wait for my death that they may be with others. The more good I do to them, the less good they would do to me."

"Sweetheart, sweetheart!" cried Thomas. "I would do you no harm."

She spoke to him then. "I do not think you speak the truth, my lord."

"Kate . . . Kate . . . have you forgotten how we have loved?"

"No, my lord, but you have given me some very shrewd taunts. My Lady Tyrwhit, I do not think I shall live. I do not wish to live."

The Admiral turned appealingly to Lady Tyrwhit. "How can I comfort her? How can I assure her of my devotion?"

Lady Tyrwhit was sorry for him, even while she remembered that his conduct with the Lady Elizabeth had brought his wife to this pass.

"I shall lie on the bed beside her," he said. "I will pacify her. I will bring back her peace of mind. I will assure her . . ."

"Nay," said Katharine. "It is over now. I shall die. There is no need for me to live longer."

"What of the love you have for me?" he cried. "What of our child?"

But she looked bewildered, as though she did not know of what child he spoke.

"I will lie beside you, sweetheart," he said.

"No," she said fearfully. "No!"

"She must not be disturbed so," said Lady Tyrwhit.

Thomas stood back, helpless, filled with wretchedness and remorse.

Katharine closed her eyes.

"Leave her to sleep," said Lady Tyrwhit. "That will restore her peace of mind better than aught else."

And Katharine lay, listening to the voices about her. She seemed to hear whispering voices everywhere. She seemed to see the flushed face of the youthful Princess and her husband's eyes gleaming as they looked at the girl.

She thought she heard voices which told her that the rumors were true. He had wanted Elizabeth; Elizabeth was the greater prize; but he had accepted the Queen . . . temporarily.

Temporarily he had accepted the Queen. And later . . . he would take Elizabeth.

The voices went on and on in her imagination.

She no longer wished to live. She believed herself to be unloved and unwanted; and the tragedy was that, no matter what might happen in the future, no matter what assurances were made, she would never believe them. She could never believe in anything again.

She had set up an idol and worshipped it; she saw now that it had feet of clay.

There was darkness near to her; it beckoned, offering peace.

"Come," it seemed to say. "It is what you need. It is what you wish for yourself. It is what *he* wishes for you."

And she felt that she was drifting forward into that peace.

On a sunny September day the gentlemen and esquires of the Queen's household carried the leaden chest, in which lay Katharine Parr, into the little chapel attached to the Castle of Sudley.

The walls of the chapel were hung with black cloth, and on them, to remind the assembly that this lady had been a Queen, were not only the arms of the Seymours, but also those of King Henry the Eighth whose sixth wife she had been.

After the birth of her daughter she had died, having, some said, no wish to live. Others went further and said that she had been hastened to her death.

Lady Jane Grey, one of the Queen's chief mourners, listened to the service conducted by the Queen's cofferer and recalled what she knew of the life of this lady whom she had loved; she remembered those alarming days when she had been the King's wife, and the strange good chance which had led Nan to the courtyard when Wriothesley had dropped the all-important paper; and it seemed to Jane that God preserved some men and women from disaster whilst He guided the footsteps of others toward it, so that it seemed that each had a destiny to fulfill here on Earth.

What of herself? she wondered fleetingly; and in the stifling atmosphere of the chapel she shivered. Her father was ambitious, and there were plans being made to encircle her head with a crown. How could she, a young girl, know what fate awaited her?

Dear Queen Katharine! she thought. I shall

never see her again. Never hear her gentle voice . . . never see her sweet smile . . .

Now they were carrying the coffin out of the chapel. Soon they would bury it, and it would be goodbye . . . goodbye for ever to Queen Katharine Parr.

The rumors were spreading all over the land. How did Katharine Parr meet her death? There were unpleasant stories which came from those intimate with the Queen's household and who knew of her husband's light behavior toward a royal Princess who had lived under his roof.

Why did the Queen die?

The Princess Elizabeth would be an excellent match for the ambitious Admiral.

The stories grew in wildness. Some said that a midwife had told a tale of being led blindfold to a quiet house that she might deliver a baby. She knew the mother must be a person of high degree, though she could not say more of who she was, except that she was young, fair and imperious. She might well have been a Princess.

The Duchess of Somerset listened to these stories. They amused her; more, they delighted her. But the story she liked best was that which insisted that the Lord High Admiral had decided to rid himself of his wife by poison, and that this was the explanation of her sudden death.

For, as she said to her husband, although the King would be loath to sign the death warrant of his beloved uncle whom he idealized, if he could be convinced that his idol had poisoned the beloved stepmother, he might be more ready to put pen to that necessary document.

It was easy to spread such rumors. They ran through the capital, through the provinces, through the countryside, like fire that is unchecked.

Katharine Parr, the sixth wife of Henry the Eighth, is dead. She married a fourth husband. Was that wise? The Admiral was such an ambitious man. And what part had the Princess Elizabeth played in this affair?

So men and women stopped to talk in the streets of this matter.

"Queen Katharine Parr is dead. Her husband killed her . . . for the sake of the Princess Elizabeth. He waited until the child was born . . . then he poisoned her."

He poisoned her! That became the simple cry which emanated from all the rumors.

The words held a menace, and the shadow of the ax deepened over the heads of those who had lived close to the King's sixth wife.

THE END

THE SIXTH
WIFE

JEAN PLAIDY

A READER'S GUIDE

About the Book

Katharine Parr married young to an older gentleman. Again in her second marriage, the caring Katharine nursed an elderly husband. Now in her thirties and a rich widow, Katharine longs to marry again—this time for love. The handsome and exciting Thomas Seymour promises Katharine a life of romance and happiness, and she eagerly accepts. King Henry VIII, meanwhile, is lonely after "putting away" his fifth wife, and begins to look for another. It is Katharine Parr who catches his eye—and is thrown into a life of danger and intrigue as the sixth wife of the fickle and ruthless Henry VIII.

Katharine's skills as a nurse serve her well with the ailing king, who relies on her to make him comfortable. But as the years pass, no sons are born, and no amount of nursing can distract the restless king from the knowledge that the time to produce more heirs is growing short. Amid religious strife in the court and the country, Katharine's Protestantism makes her vulnerable to powerful nobles who would remove her from the throne, standing ready to provide the king with grounds to arrest the queen. Katharine and her companions live in constant fear of the king's displeasure, which they know could lead quickly to execution. As Henry's health worsens, they dare to hope that the queen will once again be a widow, and once again be free.

Katharine Parr's story is one of forbearance and fear, of hope and heartbreak. When at last the queen is free to reunite with Thomas, she can finally let down her guard and begin the life she has longed for. But Katharine, who has survived constant threat of arrest at court, is finally undone by the man who has vowed to protect her.

Questions for Discussion

1. Katharine urged her second husband, Lord Latimer, to downplay his religious convictions in order to avoid the king's punishment. How far does she follow her own advice to keep dangerous opinions quiet from the court? Does she become bolder as her years with Henry pass? Why?

2. Katharine and her sister Anne agree that the wedding ring around Katharine's finger is akin to a noose around her neck. Does this overstate the case? Does Katharine also derive benefits from the throne? Based on Katharine's experience, is marriage to Henry a survivable state—or was it luck that saved her in the end?

3. In describing Henry's style of leadership, Plaidy says that Henry threatens the nobility and courts the commoners. The reader experiences Henry's reign through the eyes of the court. How do you imagine a commoner would view Henry VIII?

4. When Katharine asks the king for favors, Henry is pleased to be able to grant

her that which he himself quietly wants, allowing him to feel at once benevolent and relieved. Do you think Katharine is aware of this dynamic? Does she orchestrate this dialogue to any degree, or is she sincerely appealing for favors on her own behalf?

5. Do Mary, Elizabeth, and Edward—bound by their relationship to the king but by little else—consider themselves a family? How would you describe their life in the palace? Having seen Henry's queens come and go, why do you think the royal children allow themselves to become so attached to Katharine Parr?

6. Discuss Katharine's friendship with Jane Grey. Why is the queen so fond of the young girl? Is Katharine a good role model for Jane? If Jane were to become Edward's queen, what lessons from Katharine would help her in her role? Are there any ways in which Katharine's example would be detrimental to the pair?

7. Dr. London's plot to forge documents implicating Katharine as a heretic is foiled when Katharine takes a hand in her own

fate, sending a message to those who would destroy her that this queen will not easily be put away. Does this bold and intelligent image ring true throughout Katharine's reign as queen consort?

8. The author often takes us inside Henry's head to witness the suspicions, longings, and justifications that lead him to act so unpredictably. Does this narrative device work to make him more sympathetic as a character, or more dangerous? Do his feelings about conscience and fraternity with God sound like insanity, or are they understandable as the musings of a man accustomed to great power?

9. Elizabeth has many of the characteristics that made her father a strong and respected ruler. Does she also have qualities that could lead her to repeat Henry's cruelty? What do you see as weaknesses?

10. Anne Askew is in many ways a dangerous friend for Katharine to have. Why does Katharine risk so much to help her? Does Katharine relate to her friend's religious zeal, or is she just trying to help a

friend in need? Is she in any way responsible for Anne's fate?

11. Henry VIII is described as a man of many moods and a fierce will. Henry himself repeatedly declares, "A king is still a man." Amid his many personas—sensualist, sovereign, diplomat, conqueror, husband, patient, father—can you identify one "real" Henry? How would he describe himself? What might Henry the man have been like if he were not king?

12. After reading Wriothesley's warrant for her arrest, Katharine despairs until Thomas Seymour urges her to fight for her life. Why does she not fight before this? Does she realize her advantage in having found the lost scroll, or could she have made more of the opportunity?

13. What does Thomas find so alluring about Elizabeth? How big a part of the appeal is her place in line for the throne? Without her political stature, would Thomas have risked so much to seduce her? How do Katharine and Elizabeth compare in his eyes?

14. Why does Surrey deliberately provoke the king with his words and actions? Is he motivated by the same kind of reckless delirium that Katharine sometimes feels—or is something else driving him? Does he harbor a real desire to take power from Henry, or does he court danger out of restlessness?

15. By her fourth marriage, Katharine is an experienced wife—but naïve in the ways of romance. Why does she not see hints of Thomas' indiscretions earlier? Is she foolish to trust him? If she had known about his proposal to Elizabeth, do you think she would have married Thomas? How could she have saved herself?

About the Author

Jean Plaidy is the pen name of the late English author E. A. Hibbert, who also wrote under the names Philippa Carr and Victoria Holt.

Born in London in 1906, Hibbert began writing in 1947 and eventually published over 200 novels under her three pseudonyms. The Jean Plaidy books—about 90 in all—are works of historical fiction about the famous and infamous women of English and European history, from medieval times to the Victorian era. Many were bestsellers in the United States and abroad, although they are currently out of print. At the time of Hibbert's death in 1993, the Jean Plaidy novels had sold over 14 million copies worldwide.